LIVES IN EXILE

LIVES IN EXILE

Evelyn Auerbach

authorHOUSE®

AuthorHouse™
1663 Liberty Drive
Bloomington, IN 47403
www.authorhouse.com
Phone: 1-800-839-8640

© 2009 Evelyn Auerbach. All rights reserved.

No part of this book may be reproduced, stored in a retrieval system, or transmitted by any means without the written permission of the author.

First published by AuthorHouse   12/7/2009

ISBN: 978-1-4490-4304-9 (e)
ISBN: 978-1-4490-4303-2 (sc)

Library of Congress Control Number: 2009911406

Printed in the United States of America
Bloomington, Indiana

This book is printed on acid-free paper.

Dedication

To my family, who always believed in me, my husband Martin and my children, Joshua and Ruth; and to my grandson Morris.

Acknowledgements

I could not have completed this book without the friendship and editorial guidance of Tom Glenn, who read and edited many drafts of this book, and whose support in the final stretch made all the difference. In addition to Tom, the other members of my writing group, Mary Eccles, Ellen Kwatnoski, Lynn Stearns, and Roger Stearns, provided years of faithful support. I became a writer because of the time we spent together. I am also indebted to my nephew, David Greenhill, for his ingenious design ideas, and to his wife, Liz Greenhill, for editorial assistance with the final manuscript.

Foreword

This novel was inspired by a series of events that befell a real family. The characters of Jack Marks and Randall Marks are based loosely on a real father and son whose story was told to Evelyn Auerbach many years ago. Drawing on real events and real places (Washington, Helena, and Regina), Evelyn filled in the details of the lives and deaths of members of the Marks family from her imagination and created a history for Yetta Marks who captured Evelyn's fancy and took over the story. Evelyn's intent was not to convey real history. She wrote to answer the question, "How might these events have come to pass?" Her overwhelming concern was to show the human heart in its quest for fulfillment.

I learned all this over the years Evelyn and I worked together in a critique group. I watched the Marks family story take shape, cried over the estrangement of Jack and Randall, grieved with Yetta at the hurt the family suffered, and bridled at the final challenge—a threat to the fortunes both Jack and Randall aquired, ironically brought on because neither man bowed to the demands of traditional society. I was greatly flattered when Evelyn asked me, Liz Greenhill, and Mary Eccles to do a final edit and proof of the text. Now that our work is finished, Evelyn's book is now ready for you, the reader. May you enjoy it as much as we did.

—Tom Glenn

Chapter One

Elizabeth City, North Carolina

July 1966

The setting sun cast a dull yellow light like a shroud over Larry Wright's double-wide. Late afternoon haze filtered the sunshine. Because of the pall, Yetta Marks couldn't make out the exact color of the siding as they drove down the short tree-lined lane. Elmer Smith, the attorney for Yetta's deceased nephew, parked near the gate in the chain link fence that enclosed the yard. He opened the car door for Yetta and then held the gate. They followed the flagstone path to a wooden porch. The unstained floor was warped, the railings split. The fenced yard was cluttered with children's toys—tricycles, balls of all sizes, and jump ropes. No flowers or shrubs.

Yetta knocked and peered through the screen door into the house. All she could see was a small blank wall. She was too proper to press her nose against the screen to see further. She heard children yelling and the soothing voice of a woman over the noise of a television. She would've guessed pork chops had been fried for supper.

Larry Wright appeared at the door, his sandy colored hair tousled. He wore a T-shirt and shorts and held a beer bottle in his right hand. He squinted at the visitors and then shielded his eyes from the sun. He didn't appear surprised to see them. After Yetta introduced Mr. Smith, Larry pushed open the screen door, stepped outside, and shut the door behind him. He kicked brown pine needles off the porch. "My wife watches kids during the day for a little extra money." He fidgeted with the bottle.

Yetta said, "After you and I opened my nephew's safe and found it empty, I searched Randall's house. I couldn't find his will, the deed to his house, his cash, or coin collection." Yetta motioned toward Elmer Smith. "Mr. Smith was Randall's attorney. He and I think you know something about the missing items."

Larry looked at the floor. "I . . . "

Yetta didn't want to hear any half-assed explanation. "Don't bother denying anything. This is the only deal I'll offer. Return the missing papers to Mr. Smith's office by ten tomorrow and no questions will be asked. We won't worry about the coin collection or the cash. The only things I'm interested in are the will and the deed. Do you understand?" She enunciated the last question carefully.

"Yes, ma'am," Larry said.

Out of the corner of her eye, she saw a surprised expression on Mr. Smith's face. Yetta knew she unnerved a lot of people, especially southerners, who, seeing her bifocals and grey pin curls, expected a sweet grandmotherly-type instead of a sixty-four-year-old feisty broad. Years ago, she'd overheard one of her employees call her that behind her back and took it as a compliment. She liked thinking of herself as tough, although she didn't feel so spunky since Randall died and she'd come to North Carolina to settle his affairs. "If we don't get the papers back, we'll have no choice but to bring in the police."

Larry looked startled.

"Ten a.m. tomorrow," Yetta repeated.

"Yes, ma'am."

Mr. Smith handed Larry his business card. "I'm on Main Street in Elizabeth City. You should be able to find me with no trouble."

"Yes, sir." Larry hung his head again.

As they walked back down the path toward their car, the flying insects parted like the Red Sea for Moses. Yetta wondered how much blood the mosquitoes had sucked from her. "I gave at the office," she muttered as she rubbed her arms. A mockingbird's song came from high in a pine tree.

At ten o'clock the next morning Yetta waited in Elmer Smith's office. Elmer fit Yetta's image of a southern gentleman: brown hair neatly parted and combed, wearing a light tan suit with a bow tie. She guessed, if she turned around, a straw Panama hat would be perched on a coat rack in the corner and, next to it, an umbrella stand with several walking canes.

At ten-thirty, when Larry had not appeared, Mr. Smith called the Wright house. Yetta listened in on the conference table extension as Larry's wife answered the phone.

"Were you the ones here last night?" she asked.

Mr. Smith said they were.

"He seemed right upset and took off soon after you left. I ain't seen him since, and I'm real worried. Wait a minute. Some sheriff's cars driving up right now. Oh, Lordy. Oh, Lordy."

The line went dead.

Yetta looked over at Mr. Smith.

"We'd better call the sheriff," he said,

Yetta listened in again.

Elmer Smith said, "Hey, Jer, a client and I've been waiting for a guy named Larry Wright from over in Winfall. When I called his wife, she said a couple of your cars were coming up to the house. What's going on?"

"Hope you didn't need him for nothin' important. A citizen out hiking spotted his body at Stevenson Point. We found his car parked half a mile away on the side of the road with six empty beer bottles on the front seat and the gas gauge on empty. The guy apparently strolled out to the point, stuck his revolver in his mouth, and blew his head off."

Yetta gasped.

"You all right there, Elmer?" the Sheriff said.

"I'm fine. Just a shock." Mr. Smith put his finger to his lips and shook his head at Yetta.

"Blood was splattered all over. We were picking up pieces of scalp and hair from over nine feet away. Gun to the head ain't usually as messy as this one. He'd put that damn gun at some God damn weird angle that just tore up his eye and the socket. When he pulled the trigger, he must've been laying down with his chin pointed straight toward them pearly gates. That's the only way I can figure it, cause his brains just burst out the top of his head. Don't know how the funeral home will get him fixed presentable."

Yetta covered her mouth. It took all her will power and lots of swallowing to keep the bile down.

Mr. Smith pulled his handkerchief out of his breast pocket and wiped his chin. "You sure this was Larry Wright from Winfall?"

"That's who the car was registered to and that was the name on the driver's license we found in the wallet in the pants pocket."

"Did he leave a note?" said Elmer.

"Who was this guy to you?"

"He was my client's foreman."

"He left a note all neat and tidy on the dashboard. Said he was sorry. It was addressed to Peggy, his wife."

"You didn't find any legal papers in his car, did you?"

"Nope. Car was empty except for the bottles, a box of bullets, and the note."

"Thanks, Jer."

Mr. Smith pushed the intercom button and asked his secretary to bring in two glasses of ice water.

Yetta sagged in her chair. The secretary handed her a glass. Yetta gulped half the water, trying to get rid of the vile taste in her mouth. "Oh my God, what have I done?"

"You haven't done anything. Wright did it all himself."

She clasped her hands together to keep them from shaking. "Was the will and other things worth a man's life?"

"Apparently Wright thought so. You have nothing to reproach yourself about. You offered him a very generous deal. More generous than the prosecutor would have."

She grimaced.

"It was his decision. He could've come in here, fessed up, and thrown himself on your mercy. I venture he'd already destroyed the papers, probably soon after he took 'em. All he wanted was Mr. Marks' cash and coin collection. When he was found out, he chose the coward's way."

"And his wife and children will pay the consequences." She shook her head.

"If Larry's wife doesn't know where the papers are, which I'm sure she doesn't . . . " He waved his hand in the air. "Without a will, things will be more complicated."

Yetta was jolted back into considering her own situation. "What do you mean?"

"The Court will require us to give all of Randall's relatives an opportunity to make a claim for a share of the estate. Then the judge will divide everything according to how many claimants there are and their relationship to Randall." Mr. Smith pointed toward the file cabinets that ran along one wall of his office. "I have a copy of his will and know he intended to leave everything to you. We can enter the copy as evidence of Randall's intentions, but it probably won't make much difference without the actual signed and witnessed will."

"Randall's only relatives are my brother, and me, and his first cousins."

"If the others renounce any claim to the estate, then everything can go to you, as Randall wanted."

"I'm sure they'd do that, but I'd like to make one more try to find the will. I'll wait a few days and then go speak to Mrs. Wright. In the meantime, I better get out to Randall's office and see who I can get to run his business."

It was one o'clock when Yetta arrived at Elizabeth City Sand and Gravel. The workers were standing around the office trailer. They'd already heard Larry Wright was dead.

Yetta recognized several of them from the day before when she'd come to get the will. She had arrived at the trailer around three that afternoon but didn't want to open the safe with all the workers around. She didn't want them to see the cash and the coin collection she assumed were inside, so she spent the time going through Randall's desk and filing cabinets. The only picture on his desk was of the two of them at a family wedding. She couldn't remember whose. He was in a tuxedo and she in her champagne-colored lace gown. Memories of happy times washed over her, but she had to push them away. If she let herself go, she could have a good cry. This wasn't the time or place. In her search, she'd found receipts for payment on his life insurance policy and mortgage, but she needed his will, the actual insurance policy, and his birth certificate.

Randall had said he left his entire estate to her the day he told her about the safe and Larry. He'd even given her a list of everything in it. The list was in her purse. He told her he'd given his foreman the combination so in Randall's absence Larry could get to the emergency cash.

Larry had acted strangely from the moment she called, introduced herself, and said she was coming to straighten out Randall's affairs. He'd even questioned the exact nature of her relationship to Randall.

Yetta had been stunned when Larry finally pulled open the safe door and said, "It's empty."

"It can't be." Yetta bent to look in.

Larry stood. "Sorry, ma'am. Mr. Marks must've cleaned it out before he went to Canada."

Yetta couldn't believe Randall would remove his will without telling her. Maybe he'd taken it home to look over before going to Saskatchewan. Maybe he'd been thinking about changing it. But his lawyer hadn't mentioned anything of the sort when she'd called to tell him Randall had died.

"I'll have to look around his house. It's probably somewhere in his desk at home," she'd said more to herself than Larry. She needed that will. She ran one hand over the back of her neck. "Where could his coin collection be?"

Larry looked at her warily, then shrugged his muscled shoulders. "He probably sold it. I ain't heard him talk about them coins in a long time."

"This is very strange."

She could kick herself. Why hadn't she just asked Larry for the combination and opened the safe herself as soon as she arrived in Elizabeth City? In fact, why hadn't she insisted on getting the combination from Randall years ago? He would've given it to her. If she had it, she wouldn't have had to deal with Larry at all. She just never thought she'd need it because she never expected to outlive him.

She missed Randall more than she could've imagined. It was three weeks since she received the call from the Mounties informing her Randall had died in Regina, Saskatchewan, where he'd gone to settle his father's estate. It had been a long and busy three weeks and she felt numb. First, she traveled to Canada to bury Randall next to his father, her brother, who died a year earlier. She'd had to select a casket and head stone. Then she gathered Randall's belongings from the motel and paid his bill. Thank goodness the motel manager had packed everything in his suitcase. She'd have had a hard time doing it herself. Her feelings were so raw then—grief and even anger at Randall for having been so stupid as to get himself drunk and die. After Regina, she went home to Richmond, Virginia, before heading south.

Now back in the Elizabeth City Sand and Gravel yard for the second time in her life, Yetta asked Johnny, who'd been assisting Larry since Randall's death, to take over running the business. He was apprehensive, but she told him to do his best until they could find a buyer. She told the men they would close the day of Larry Wright's funeral, but they might as well get to work until then. Many of the men shook their heads and ambled away toward the equipment. A few stood talking in groups of two or three, then moved off to their jobs.

She stayed and worked in the trailer, organizing things. Three grey metal desks took up much of the floor space. Boxes of sand and gravel samples filled a corner. Five-drawer file cabinets lined one of the short walls with the grey safe at the end, next to the desk that had been her nephew's. With the air-conditioned breeze circulating through the trailer, she couldn't smell the clammy, salty air on the other side of the window.

She and the secretary, Susie, went through all the papers on Randall's and Larry's desks. They sorted out the orders waiting to be filled from those that had been shipped, gave the unfilled orders to the new foreman, and billed the completed and unpaid invoices. Yetta warned Susie to leave the safe door wide open since no one had a copy of the combination.

They went together to the funeral home to offer condolences to the Wright family. Yetta was glad Larry's casket was closed during the viewing. Despite Elmer Smith's reassurances, she felt guilty enough about what happened without having to look at his face. The sheriff's graphic description of Larry's injuries popped into her mind every time she glanced at the casket. With Larry's body six feet away, Yetta struggled to say, "I'm sorry for your loss," without choking up. Susie was able to say the proper, nice things about Larry, which the family took as coming from them both.

"I wish Mr. Marks was here," Larry's wife said. "He was such a fine man."

Tears welled up in Yetta's eyes.

Three days after the services she called Peggy Wright and arranged to visit that afternoon.

When Yetta arrived, Mrs. Wright shooed the children into the yard and motioned Yetta to a seat on the sofa. "Would you like a glass of lemonade?"

Yetta smiled. "That would be lovely."

It was another hot, humid day. The smell of freshly baked chocolate chip cookies filled the house. A picture of Jesus on the cross hung on the wall over the TV. A photograph of Larry with his wife and two children sat on the end table. The living room and dining area were one big open space separated from the kitchen by a half wall. A narrow hall must have led to the bedrooms.

Peggy Wright brought the lemonade and a plate of cookies. She sat in a rocking chair. "I expected you to have blue eyes like Mr. Marks and talk the same funny way."

Yetta blushed. "He got his eyes from his mother's side. My side are all brown. He talked like they do in Canada because that's where he grew up—in western Canada, in a town called Regina. I grew up in Washington, D.C." She smiled, remembering when Randall, at the age of nineteen, first came to live with her and her parents in Washington and got annoyed at people who imitated him. She took a sip of the lemonade. "I'm so sorry about your husband. Is there anything you need?"

Mrs. Wright slid the plate of cookies in front of Yetta. "We're quite well situated. Mr. Marks gave Larry a big bonus before he left for Canada. I've enough to get by. Somehow, the Lord provides."

The Lord provided, Yetta thought, with Randall's cash and coin collection. Peggy Wright didn't seem to know about the empty safe or Yetta's ultimatum.

Mrs. Wright stretched to look out the front door. "Conrad, stay in the shade. Don't run round. Hear?" Then to Yetta, "I've decided to go on with my son's surgery since Larry got those people in Asheville to give us the money. Thank the Lord. I wouldn't know how to return the money, anyways."

"Surgery?"

"I thought you knew. Conrad has an ingy hernia. No, wait. It's called a gooney hernia. No, that ain't right. I got it written down somewheres." Mrs. Wright went into the kitchen. She came back with a piece of paper which she handed to Yetta.

"Inguinal hernia," Yetta said. " I think that's how you say it."

"Those doctors talk so fast, it's hard to keep up. Anyways, he needs an operation right away for that hernia thing cause his insides ain't right. Larry went to Asheville couple of weeks ago to meet with some organization helps out people like us and came back with enough cash to pay the doctor and the hospital bill. If Mr. Marks had been here, I knowed he would've given us the money. But he was gone already."

Awch un vei. This was the man Randall trusted. "Did your husband say anything to you about holding some papers for my nephew or having to keep some papers in a safe place?"

"No. You missing some papers?"

Yetta put her glass down on a coaster. "Yes. Some important papers that belonged to my nephew. He might have asked your husband to keep them for him."

"Oh, Lord, I can't think of anything."

"Could you look around?"

"Be glad to. Do it this evening. Mr. Marks was always good to us."

Yetta called Peggy Wright the next morning—no will or deed had been found. She made an appointment to see Elmer Smith the next day.

After Yetta was seated, Mr. Smith said, "I've asked the court to name us as co-executors and co-trustees of Randall's estate. They'll require a North Carolina resident to be one of the executors, and I took it upon myself. If you have someone else in mind, let me know and we can change it."

"I wouldn't know anyone qualified."

"Also, I was approached with an offer for the business. I think we ought to consider it. We'd have to ask the court's permission to sell. I'm sure the court will agree because the judge knows the value of a business declines as time goes by without an owner. The proceeds would remain in the estate until final disposition."

"How much and who's it from?"

"The offer's from George Jensen, a competitor, and he's guaranteed to keep on all of Randall's employees. He's offered $75,000 up front and another $25,000 to be paid out over two years."

"At what interest rate?"

"Six percent."

At last some good news—a buyer. Yetta was thrilled, but she didn't want to let on. Somehow, this all seemed too easy. "Do you know this Jensen? Is his credit solid?"

"We're both Rotarians, and he has a very successful business. In fact, he was a friend of Randall's. You know, a friendly competitor."

Yetta wondered who George Jensen was better friends with—Randall or Elmer Smith. Sometimes, she thought, you had to be wary of southern gentlemen. "I'd like to see the offer before I agree to anything."

"I'll call George back this afternoon and let him know we'll be petitioning the court." He smiled. "After we're named as executors, we can have the rest of Randall's assets appraised and begin liquidating."

Yetta noticed how he'd said George, not Mr. Jensen, and resented the pressure Elmer was putting on her. She knew as well as he did the predicament she was in. She couldn't stay indefinitely in North Carolina and run the business, so she needed to sell, and soon.

"Do you think we might advertise for another offer?" she said. "See if we can get a little competition going and maybe a better price."

"This isn't a big city. Not too much going on here in the way of buying and selling businesses. George Jensen is our best bet. I don't know anyone else who knows how to run a sand and gravel operation and has the cash to put up."

Yetta nodded. Without any other acquaintances in Elizabeth City, she had no idea how she'd go about finding a buyer on her own. When she sold her own business, her lawyer had said that one year's gross sales would be a fair price. She had remembered seeing a Profit and Loss Statement in Randall's desk. Now she couldn't wait to get back there and look it over.

"Randall went to Saskatchewan to settle my brother's estate," Yetta said. "Randall had signed off on everything before he died, but nothing had actually been distributed. So we'll have to get an accounting of my brother's estate from the lawyer, Bill O'Brien, in Regina."

"I'll do that. I have his phone number."

Yetta drove straight from there to the trailer. She found the file she was looking for in the bottom drawer of Randall's desk. In it were the P-and-L's for the last ten years. Each year the gross sales and net profit had risen slightly. Amazingly enough the gross receipts for the last year had been one $108,049.56. Yetta was tempted to call the accountant and ask if either Elmer Smith or George Jensen had inquired about Randall's business. What was the point—the price was fair and she had no other good options. She'd just agree to accept the deal and hope it didn't take too long to close.

Yetta knew if she'd didn't stay in North Carolina and run Elizabeth City Sand and Gravel, there might be nothing left to sell. She missed the challenge of running a business since she'd sold her restaurant and bar several years before. She thought it might be fun to work again for a few weeks, keep her mind off things. Anyway, it would be impossible for Susie and the acting foreman to keep things going by themselves and there was nothing pressing for her to do in Richmond.

While Yetta stayed in Elizabeth City, she and Susie had dinner together every Friday night. Susie had a story to tell about everyone and everything. Yetta discovered Susie was forty and had been married and divorced, with no children. Although Susie never admitted to the infatuation, Yetta could sense the strong feelings Susie had for Randall by the way she talked about him. Yetta couldn't guess what attracted a young, good-looking girl like Susie to Randall, but Yetta never had been very savvy when it came to attractions.

After Yetta had been there a month, Mr. Smith called and asked her to come to his office the next morning.

"Good news," he said. "The court appointed us and approved the sale of the business, so we can go ahead and set a transfer date."

Yetta thought about the Jewish holidays coming shortly. "How soon?"

"Two weeks."

"Wonderful."

"Judge Butler wants a copy of Randall's birth certificate. He also ruled that because Randall died without a will we have to notify all of Randall's relatives and give them an opportunity to make a claim for a share of the estate."

Yetta fingered the pendant that hung from a chain around her neck. His tone of voice unsettled her. Her heart beat faster. "Who, exactly, does that include?"

"Since Randall never married or had any children, we'll have to notify all his mother's people and all of your people."

"His mother's people?" Yetta heard her voice go up an octave. "But they never had anything to do with him. The only relative of his mother's he ever knew was a cousin, and he hadn't seen her since shortly after his mother's funeral when he was six."

Elmer folded his hands in his lap and rocked slightly in his chair. "Sadly, the quality of relationships doesn't count when someone dies intestate. I asked the lawyer in Regina to mail me Randall's birth certificate. As to the notices, the judge ordered us to place one in the newspaper here in Elizabeth City, as is customary, one in a paper in Regina, since that is where Randall was born, and one in Washington, D.C., where your family lives."

"This is absurd." Yetta waved the air as if brushing away a fly. "Those people completely disowned his mother when she had Randall. They cast her out and never had anything to do with my brother, Jack, or with Randall. To have to notify them and give them a share of his estate is completely ludicrous."

I sympathize, Miss Marks. Truly, I do." He opened a file. "But we have no choice." He handed her the paper. "I've written this notice and, if you approve, I'll have the newspapers in each city run it for the three weeks the judge requires."

She could do without Mr. Smith's condescension, thank you very much. Who did he think he was talking to—some ignorant North Carolina fool? Yetta read the statement. *Notice is hereby given of the death of Randall Marks on July 4, 1966. Because Mr. Marks died without a will, anybody having an interest in or claim on his estate is hereby notified to contact the executors, Elmer Smith and Yetta Marks at 500 Main Street, Elizabeth City, North Carolina 27909, USA, before March 15, 1967.*

She sat forward in her chair as she handed Mr. Smith the notice. "It's ironic." She shook her head. "The ad searching for the people who shunned my brother and Randall will be placed in the newspaper my brother owned."

Elmer placed the notice back in the folder. "The other piece of bad news is that your brother's entire estate has been secured by the judge."

Yetta put her hand to her neck. "What does that mean?"

"Even though Randall signed all the papers before he died, none of the assets can be distributed. So, you will not be receiving the fifty thousand dollar specific bequest your brother made to you until Randall's estate has been settled."

"Can the judge do that?" She heard her voice rising again. She felt like screaming. She wondered if her eyes looked as wild as she felt. She had a mind to march down to that damn courthouse and personally give Judge Butler a good idea of what she thought of his decisions.

"Judges have wide latitude. You could appeal, but the estate will probably be settled before it would be heard."

She thought Mr. Smith was talking extra slowly. Did he think she was going over the edge?

"How long until Randall's estate is settled?"

"I wouldn't worry, Miss Marks. People rarely respond. The mother's relatives will probably not even see the announcement. At the end of the six months, your brother and nieces and nephews will renounce their share, and you'll receive everything just as Randall wanted. You're probably worrying over nothing."

From your mouth to God's ears, she thought. And then, silently, she said directly to Jack and Randall, wherever they were, "This is what you left to *mutshe* me in *mein alte yawren.*" She pondered *mutshe*. What a great word, it expressed exactly what she felt—mushed up, tormented, tortured, and suddenly old.

Chapter Two

Making Claims

1966

Yetta stayed in North Carolina two more weeks, until George Jensen took over. The last time she left the office, workmen came over to shake her hand and say good-bye. Their kind words about Randall made the leave-taking easier.

Back in Richmond, she had just enough time to straighten out her clothes and pay her bills before heading to Washington, D.C. to spend Rosh Hashanah and Yom Kippur with the whole Marks family. In previous years, she'd arrived in Washington two weeks before the holidays for shopping and visiting. This year there was no time, and she wasn't in the mood anyway. Whatever she already owned would have to do.

Her niece, Dot, and her husband, Howard, met her train at Union Station and drove her to their house. The next day Dot and she stood side by side at the sink. While Yetta used a sharp knife to pluck stray feathers from three kosher chickens, Dot trimmed the fat from the breasts and thighs and washed all the pieces.

In Yetta's opinion, Dot had made the right choice of harvest gold for her kitchen appliances over that ugly avocado green which had been the alternative. The kitchen's large picture windows extended along the back wall of the house. Yetta thought the roll-up shades Dot used were perfect because during the day the room was filled with light, and at night the room felt cozy and secure. Today the sun was so bright they hardly needed the artificial light from the fluorescent fixture.

Dot said, "What I can't figure is why that foreman took everything from the safe. Why didn't he just take the money and leave the papers?"

Yetta shrugged. "Susie, Randall's secretary, told me Larry had a gambling problem—played cards quite a bit and apparently lost a lot, too. Said he was always looking for a game after work. If he couldn't find one, he tried to organize one. Apparently, he used the storage shed at the quarry for games. I don't know if Randall knew about it or not." Yetta swept her hair off her face with the back of her hand. "Who knows if he needed the money to pay off his gambling debts, for his son's surgery, or something else? When no family showed up right away, I guess Larry concluded no one was coming, and he probably thought it would be better to take everything rather than just the cash and coins. Make it look like Randall cleaned out the safe before he left. That's the only thing that makes sense to me. I bet Randall never told him I knew about the safe or its contents."

They put the chickens in two big soup pots and poured in enough water to cover the pieces. Dot took the onions, celery, and carrots from the refrigerator. Yetta peeled the onions while Dot trimmed and cleaned an entire bunch of celery.

"It's hard to imagine," Dot said," that Randall never mentioned you to . . . what's his name?"

"Larry Wright. Who knows? They're both gone so we can't ask."

"Do you think his wife knew about the gambling?" Dot paused for a few seconds. "I bet she did and isn't letting on. You don't feel responsible for Larry's death, do you?"

Yetta calmed her churning thoughts by taking in the tranquil view of trees and shrubs that protected the privacy of Dot's backyard. She shrugged. "In my head, I know I'm not. Larry probably didn't like the idea of going to jail."

"You did what you thought best. He had a lot of other problems going on besides taking things from the safe."

"That's what I keep telling myself." Yetta contemplated an onion. She was tired of trying to solve the riddle of Larry Wright and wondered why all her conversations centered on money and not on Randall's being gone. "Not having the will is screwing things up. These court rulings . . . I can't believe what's going on. It's like Jack and Randall's lives were for nothing, that all their rights died with them." She pushed the onion skins into the garbage disposal. "Everything they ever had has been seized by the court. It's as if they never existed."

"It's outrageous they're holding your fifty thousand dollars. What right does the judge have to do that?"

Yetta took a deep breath. "It's hard to know what's really going on. *Goyim*, and southern *goyim*, at that. I could fight, but I'd have to spend a lot of money on a lawyer. I'm going to get the money eventually, so it's probably not worth it. Even your brother, Art, said that when I talked to him." Yetta rinsed her hands in cold water and dried them with a paper towel. "Mr. Smith thinks in the end everything will be split between Uncle Sammy and me since we're Randall's closest relatives with part of the assets going to you and your first cousins.

"But that's not what Randall wanted."

"The lawyer said I could get everything, as Randall wanted, if all of you renounce any claims on the estate."

"Of course, we'll renounce. The money was supposed to be yours. I'm sure the others will agree. I think everything happens for a reason even if we can't discern it at the time."

Steam was escaping from the soup pots. Yetta lifted the lids, one after the other, and used a wooden spoon to scoop out the scum accumulating on the boiling water. As she finished, Dot added the whole onions and celery stalks and put the covers back on, leaving a little crack for steam. Back at the sink, Dot peeled carrots and Yetta cut them into chunks.

Yetta held the knife in the air. "I'd like to believe there's a reason all of this happened. But I can't figure it out. If Randall had just agreed to be circumcised and married that Maggie all of this trouble could have been avoided." Yetta shook her head. She looked across the backyard and up at the clouds and resumed her chopping. "I've been thinking . . . all of you should claim a part of the estate because I have enough to take care of myself. If I got the whole thing, I'd end up leaving it to you anyway. You might as well have it now."

"I don't know. I'd feel guilty getting part of the money Randall wanted you to have. I think you'd better talk to Uncle Sammy. I know my brothers and I will do whatever you think is best."

Yetta sniffed the air. "Smells like chicken soup to me. Time to put in the carrots." After they added the carrots and salt, Yetta leaned her hip against the counter. "I'll talk to Uncle Sammy at dinner tomorrow night."

Dot turned to look at her. "I want to tell you something I've never told anyone but Howard. I know my father's watching over me. Sometimes I feel his presence so strongly, I hear his voice in my ear. It's as if he died so he could be my guardian angel. I know he's guiding me through life. Maybe Randall is your angel."

Yetta put her hands on Dot's arms. "Sometimes when I look at your beautiful Jonathan, I see Abe, the look in his eyes and the way he holds his body, and I think Abe is with us." She hugged Dot. "You're a very special person and I know your father is very proud of you. When I was at Randall's house I found the cuff links *Zeyde* gave Randall on his thirteenth birthday. Do you remember how *Zeyde* and *Bubbe* had a tradition of giving each of their sons and grandsons a pair of gold cufflinks for their Bar Mitzvah which *Bubbe* continued even after *Zeyde* was gone?"

"I was jealous because I had to wait until I was sixteen to get my diamond pendant."

"Randall never had a Bar Mitzvah but *Zeyde* gave him a pair anyway. I want to give them to Jonathan at his Bar Mitzvah." Yetta turned back toward the windows. She wished she could feel the presence of Randall and Jack and didn't have all this trouble about their money. Why was everything about Jack and Randall so complicated? "What should we make next?"

"The honey cakes, then the baked apples."

"Sweets for a sweet year. Let's hope the year 5741 will be sweet and we don't hear from Bessie Swartz's family."

"Who's Bessie Swartz?"

"Randall's mother."

"I never even knew her first name."

While Yetta sifted the flour, Dot got out the salt, baking powder, baking soda, cinnamon, nutmeg, ginger, honey, and sugar.

The first night of Rosh Hashanah the family rented a hall in a community center and held a potluck dinner. Yetta missed the feeling of the holiday dinners when her parents were alive and they ate in her mother's dining room. The metal folding chairs and rectangular collapsible tables in a room with lots of noise echoing off the cinder block walls wasn't the warm family atmosphere. On the other hand, it was the only way the large extended family could be all in the same place.

Dot and Yetta brought enough chicken soup and matzah balls for fifty. Sammy's wife, Bertha, always brought the brisket. Her brother Abe's widow, Tessie, was famous for her apple and raisin kugel. Others contributed gefilte fish, homemade horseradish, vegetables, apple cake, and tszimmes.

Lives in Exile

At dinner Yetta sat next to Sammy. When she felt the time was right, they left the table together and huddled in a corner. She explained what had happened in Elizabeth City.

He said, "It must've been hard on you having to deal with everything in Regina by yourself . . . then this mess in Elizabeth City. It seems to always come down to money, doesn't it? How will the estate be split?"

At least her brother understood how she felt. "You and I will split half the estate and the other half will be divided among the six first cousins. Bessie's brisket is exceptionally good this year, really tender and tasty."

"I'll be sure to tell her. But we all know Randall wanted you to have the whole shooting match."

"I could get everything if you and all of the children renounced your portions of the estate. But I was thinking the children should demand their part since I would leave it to them anyway."

Sammy studied the floor. "I know Bertha will go along with me on this. Randall and Jack wanted you to have their money. I'd feel funny taking what should be yours so I'd be happy to give my portion to you or the kids, whatever you decide. Are you sure you want to share with the children?"

"If I inherit from Randall and then leave it to the kids, it'll be taxed double. This way half the money will be taxed only once."

"Then, I'll renounce my share. You'll get half and the cousins will split the other half? I'll give my children the skinny when I have dinner with them tomorrow night and you can talk to Dot, Marty, and Art at your dinner."

"I'll have a good chance to talk to them since Tessie and Reuben will be having dinner with his children this year. Thank goodness. I hate when Reuben tries to put in his two cents about things that have nothing to do with him."

Dot's father, Abe, died in 1940, when the three children were young. His widow, Tessie, married Reuben Brodsky in 1960. Tessie and Reuben alternated years between eating with Tessie's children and Reuben's. The honey cake and baked apples Dot and Yetta made were for dinner the second night.

All the nieces and nephews agreed to Yetta's plan. Two days after she got home to Richmond, she called Elmer Smith to get the information for the family. He promised that in the next few days he would send her instructions in writing to pass on to the heirs. He told her he hadn't gotten any response to the notice.

Evelyn Auerbach

She wasn't surprised when she heard Elmer's voice over the telephone on a Thursday morning, five weeks later. She expected him to tell her he had received the assertions from her nieces and nephews and the repudiation of her brother.

He said, "There's been a major development. We've received a communication from a group of Randall's mother's relatives."

"What?" Her heart burned.

"It's too complicated to talk about over the phone. Can you come down to Elizabeth City? Perhaps on Sunday, so we could meet Monday morning."

"Whenever you say."

"I think you should plan on staying for most of the week."

Her respiration rate increased. "Can't you tell me about it?"

"Let's wait till Monday."

As soon as she hung up, she started pacing. Then she circled her bedroom. She frowned at the photograph of Randall and Jack on her dresser. *Gemutshet* was what she felt. Finally, she went into her den. To get a grip on her emotions, she made a list of things she needed to do. First, call Susie to ask her to get the maid to clean Randall's house. Second, check her medications to make sure she had enough high blood pressure pills. Third, call Sammy and Dot, so they would know where she was. Then she called the Greyhound Bus Company and got the schedule for Sunday.

On Sunday evening, when she stepped off the bus, she was surprised to see Susie. At forty, Susie still had the legs to wear a miniskirt with fishnet stockings. Her straight blond hair was cut to just touch her shoulders with bangs that skimmed the top of her eyebrows. Men turned to look at her as she pranced through the bus station in her high heels. Susie kept Yetta's thoughts occupied with gossip from ECSG and distracted from the meeting the next morning.

This time, when Yetta walked into Randall's three-bedroom rambler, it wasn't quite as depressing. She'd gotten used to his being gone. She decided she should survey his belongings and choose what to take home and what to get rid of. She put her suitcases in the guest bedroom.

There weren't too many places to inspect as the house had just enough room and furniture for one bachelor. The Scandinavian furnishings were all lines and angles with few drawers or cabinets. The house didn't even smell the same, no more stale cigarette aroma. The maid had done a thorough job with lemon-scented furniture polish. Randall didn't occupy this place anymore.

First, she went into Randall's study which was done in browns and oranges. On the desk were three pictures. She picked up a dual frame. One side held a picture of her with Randall taken in 1940 on the day they'd opened the West Side Bar and Grill in Richmond. She smiled at the memory. That had been one of the happiest times in her life. How they'd laughed that day and toasted each other. She grinned when she looked at herself—young and thin with her dark brown hair in the same curly style she wore today. Randall was so tall that he had to stoop to get his face near hers even with the additional three-inches her high heels added to her four-feet-four.

He had to stoop even further in the other photo which was of Randall with her parents. They looked like midgets next to him. It must've been taken at the Bar Mitzvah of one of his cousins because Randall was wearing a suit. He looked to be about sixteen and hadn't even grown to his full six-foot-two. He had a kid's picture-smirk on his face. Her mother and father were smiling so broadly and proudly. She rubbed her finger over their faces as she put the photographs back on the desk. It was at times like this she missed them most. They loved Randall so much and he loved his *Bubbe* and *Zeyde*.

The other frame held a snapshot of Randall with his father, Jack. Randall was wearing his Canadian army uniform and had a patch over his left eye. She'd gotten so used to the small scars on his face, she'd almost forgotten about his injury. Jack had the eyes of someone who used to smile but didn't anymore. She wondered when he had stopped and shook her head. So much time wasted in useless feuds. Now they were both gone. She glanced at the pictures again—all of far away places and from long ago.

In the two desk drawers all she found, other than pens and pencils, was a box of stationery, a personal address book, and an AT&T Directory. She wouldn't take any of those things home with her, so she picked up the photographs and walked into Randall's bedroom.

Randall's queen size bed was covered with a gold quilted bedspread, which matched the shag carpeting. She opened the orange and gold drapes. The Mediterranean-style furniture was a medium brown wood. Yetta remembered helping pick the furniture and fabrics about ten years ago. She remembered saying something to Randall about being surprised he wanted to decorate his home with coordinated fabrics and new furniture. He said something about not having to live like a bachelor just because he was one.

Yetta put the two picture frames in the middle of the bed. On one night table was a princess-style telephone. On the other was the Marks family photograph taken in 1908, just before Jack left home. This must've been Jack's copy. The whole family had been together many times since then, but Yetta couldn't think of another time they'd taken a picture. Yetta remembered how her mother insisted on having this picture taken, how her father had objected and then given in as he always did. Of the six of them, two parents and four children, only she and her brother, Sammy, were left. She put the picture on the bed. One of her nieces or nephews might like to have it.

She opened every drawer in the armoire. Nothing but neatly arranged clothing. She was sure Randall's cleaning girl was responsible. Although she felt like an intruder rummaging around in his things, Yetta lifted each pile of clothing to make sure nothing was hidden underneath. She'd have to talk to Susie about getting the cleaning woman to pack up all his clothes so they could donate them to the Salvation Army or somewhere.

In the bottom drawer she found a hat box wrapped with pink ribbon tied in a bow. She sat on the bed and untied the ribbon. Now she remembered when she last handled this box—some forty years earlier she'd placed Randall's mother's treasures in it. She recognized the silver and mother-of-pearl comb, brush, and mirror set. Tears came to her eyes. She put her hand to her chest. She remembered packing the box when she'd gone to Regina to help after Bessie died. She picked up a lavender-colored glass perfume bottle, squeezed the atomizer, and sniffed the air, but smelled nothing. She tried to recollect the scent but couldn't imagine what perfume it had been. Next she found an ornate silver picture frame around a photograph of stiffly posed people. It looked to be about the same vintage as the Marks family photograph. Yetta assumed this was Bessie Swartz's family. She counted five girls plus the mother and father—pursed lips, cold eyes, not one kind or tender face among them.

She guessed Jack must have given the box to Randall and tried to imagine how Randall must have felt when Jack told him all these things belonged to his mother—the relics of a parent he barely remembered. She was sure he handled each item and tried to conjure an image of the woman who'd given birth to him. It was strange Randall never mentioned it. But that was Randall—he kept most of his feelings to himself.

Who could still be alive in Bessie's family? One or more of the sisters could be making a claim. Plus, there could be any number of cousins.

What if the judge split Randall's estate in half? That would still be about one million dollars for each side.

Maybe she should change her decision about dividing the estate with her nieces and nephews. On the other hand, because they were in this together, she had allies. If she didn't share, she'd be fighting the Swartz family by herself. She was determined that those cruel and bigoted people who'd spurned her brother and ignored her nephew weren't going to get any of Jack or Randall's money. Why wouldn't Mr. Smith tell her the problem over the phone? There must be more. She had to put all of it out of her mind.

In the bottom of the box she found her brother's obituary.

Funeral for Jacob Marks Held Today

> Funeral services for Jacob Marks, 73, of 2129 Jennifer St., were conducted this afternoon in Beth Jacob Synagogue with burial in Regina Cemetery.
>
> Mr. Marks is survived by a son, Randall of Elizabeth City, N.C., and a sister, Yetta of Richmond, Va.
>
> He was predeceased by his wife, Bessie Swartz.
>
> Marks arrived in Regina in 1911 and worked for the *Leader Post*, where he ran the press, distributed newspapers, and sold advertising. In 1921 he purchased the newspaper.
>
> Shortly after his arrival here, he became the city's first dog catcher. In the 1920s he began farming in the White City district where he raised grain and cattle.
>
> He retired in 1962.

Yetta hadn't cried for weeks, but all of a sudden she couldn't stop. The tears ran down her cheeks even as she tried to brush them away. She hurried to her bedroom and grabbed a tissue from the box. She sat on the bed and worked to gather her feelings back inside by sighing deeply and concentrating on relaxing her stomach. This wasn't the time to lose control. She went back to Randall's room and returned everything to the hat box. After carefully tying the fraying ribbon, she put it on the bed with the other treasures. From a whole lifetime this was all there was to show for it—a few pictures and an old box with treasures from another life. She didn't know if she wanted this box with its contents or not, but somehow she couldn't leave it with the other things to be given away.

On Monday at nine o'clock, Yetta sat in Elmer Smith's client chair. Mr. Smith placed his folded hands on his desk. "I might as well get to the bad news right off. We've had claims from two of Bessie Swartz's sisters and ten nieces and nephews."

Yetta squeezed the arms of the chair. "Twelve relatives?"

"Apparently, Randall's death made lots of news in Regina. Some of these claimants live there. So they were already alerted. One of the nephews is a lawyer. He read the legal notices and spotted ours."

"Is this nephew representing the group?"

"Yes, with the help of a lawyer from Charlotte. But I haven't gotten to the truly bad news. They are claiming the whole estate. They say that Jack Marks and Bessie Swartz were never married and there is no legal evidence Randall was Jack's son. Therefore, they claim they are Randall's only surviving relatives."

Yetta fingered her pendant. "Oh, my God. That's absurd. Everyone knew he was Jack's son. He looked just like him."

"I'm sorry to have to tell you this, but, that is not legal evidence. I got out the birth certificate and there is no name listed under 'Father.' In fact, your nephew's name is recorded as Randall Swartz."

"I can't believe this is happening. Even though his parents never married, Randall always used 'Marks' as his last name. He always lived with his father. It was Jack who raised him."

"I'm sure that's all true. But it doesn't count in a legal sense."

"It doesn't count?"

"I have some other bad news."

She put her hand on her somersaulting stomach. "What now?"

"Since I'm one of the executors and trustees of the estate, I have to remain neutral. I can't represent you or your family. You're going to have to find your own lawyer, assuming you want to fight them."

She could feel her cheeks tighten. "You're darn right I want to fight them—those gold-diggers aren't going to get their hands on my brother's or Randall's money. It's not right."

"That's how I thought you would feel, so I've made up a list of lawyers I think are competent in the area of estates and trusts." He handed her the sheet. "You'll notice none are in Elizabeth City. I'm afraid you're going to have to go to Williamston or Greenville or even Raleigh to find the right representation."

Yetta went back to Randall's house. She sat at the kitchen table and spread out the paper from Elmer Smith. She read the names several times.

There were four. She didn't know where to begin, so she decided to call her niece's husband, Art, the lawyer in the family. She had to get his office phone number from information. When he came on the line, he said, "Aunt Yetta, are you all right? What's wrong?"

"Nothing's wrong."

"Nothing's wrong? Why are you calling me at my office in the middle of the day?"

"I'm okay, but it's worse than I even imagined. They're claiming the whole estate because they say there is no legal proof Randall is Jack's son and, therefore, they are his sole heirs."

"Absurd."

"That's what I said. I can't believe this is happening."

"Aren't you and Mr. Smith going to fight them?"

"That's the other upsetting part. *Ihn mihtn derihnen* Mr. Smith says he can't represent us, he has to remain neutral. Maybe it's for the best because I'm not sure I trust him all that much. He's given me a list of four lawyers he recommends between here and Raleigh and I don't know where to begin."

"Give me the names. I'll check into them. I'll call you back later this afternoon. Hang tight for a while."

Hang tight. What did that mean? If she'd been younger, she would've handled this herself. Why, now that she was sixty-four, did she feel the need to call on others? Maybe she wasn't as feisty as she liked to think. Then she reminded herself that they were all in this together because they all had claims on the estate and that was what she wanted. She needed to occupy herself, so she took out an Elmore Leonard novel and tried to concentrate on reading.

Late that afternoon Art called back. "I couldn't find out anything about the lawyers in Williamston or Greenville—towns are too small. I called a matrimonial lawyer I know in Raleigh and he said that both people in Raleigh were good. He personally liked Newton Yardley better than the other, so that's who I called. But he was too busy so he referred us to his partner, Isaac—Ike—Stein. I spoke to him already and explained what I knew. He's expecting your call. I think you'll like him."

"I'll call him right away."

"I think we should fight this, but you talk to Mr. Stein. Truthfully, I'm pleased we found a member of the tribe to represent us."

Yetta made the call and started to explain the situation to Ike Stein.

He interrupted her. "Is it possible for you to come to Raleigh so we can discuss this in person? How about Thursday?"

"I suppose so. I could take a Greyhound."

"I'm going to need a copy of the whole file . . . "

Thursday morning Yetta found Ike Stein's office which was across from the courthouse on the fifth floor of a five-story building. His firm, Yardley, Dunner and Mordecai, occupied the entire floor. The reception area was furnished with plush carpeting, leather chairs and sofa, brass lamps, and polished wooden end tables.

As Ike ushered her into his office, Yetta confronted a portrait of a distinguished-looking gentleman hanging over the desk.

"My father," Ike said. "He owned a department store which he inherited from my grandfather. I'm the third generation of Steins in Raleigh. My brother still runs the business."

Yetta blushed. "Myself, I'm from the first generation born in America."

Mr. Stein motioned her to a Queen Anne chair upholstered in a green. He sat behind his desk.

She said, "My parents moved to Washington, D.C., in 1892. We were first in the grocery business which grew into a restaurant provision business."

"My family first settled in Charleston and then found their way up here. This desk was my father's. It's the one in the picture." Mr. Stein smiled. "It's a pleasure to meet you and to help your family through this difficult situation."

Yetta handed Ike Stein the complete file. While he scanned it, she examined the room. First, she compared the features of the current Mr. Stein with the portrait. He appeared to be about the same age as his father. They both had a full head of grey hair, a prominent nose, a firm chin, and bright hazel eyes. She liked the way the present Mr. Stein had looked at her, and his firm handshake made her want to trust him. His manner inspired confidence, but she decided to reserve judgment until she heard what he had to say.

Several family photos sat on the credenza behind his desk. She could see a couple of groups that looked like children and grandchildren. Over the fireplace hung a painting of a ship in the distance with a landing party in a smaller boat being greeted by Indians in the foreground. Bookshelves on the opposite wall held leather bound, very legal-looking volumes. In front of the bookshelves was a conference table that could seat eight people. Yetta heard Ike close the file.

He said, "It seems that the main problem you have is legally proving your nephew was the son of your brother. No hope of finding the will?"

"I don't know how much Art told you . . ."

"He told me your nephew's foreman went into the safe and cleaned it out, took all the valuables and the papers, too, which is a felony."

"I'm sure the foreman destroyed all the papers. That was probably why he committed suicide. He couldn't produce them and knew I would report the theft to the police." She shrugged. "How can we prove Randall was Jack's son—legally, I mean?"

"The first thing we have to find out is if your brother ever adopted Randall. I'll have to be in touch with your brother's attorney in Saskatchewan and have him do a search of the records of the province."

"I think Jack would have told me if he had done such a thing."

"You never know, Miss Marks. People do, and don't do, all sorts of things for reasons we can never comprehend."

"Truer words were never spoken."

He laughed.

Yetta bit her lip. "If he didn't legally adopt Randall, are there other ways we can prove parenthood?"

"There are things like blood types and other declarations that may have been made."

"Even if we prove parenthood, will the Swartz family still get some of the estate?"

"That's a hard question to answer since so much is up to the discretion of the judge. But we can certainly document that your brother intended his estate to go to his family, and your nephew had the same intention. I can't promise anything, but I have some confidence things will turn in our favor." He smiled. "I can do some preliminary investigation. After talking to your brother's lawyer, I should be able to give you a better idea."

Yetta had never spoken to a Jew with a North Carolina accent before. It amused her. "What would your fees be?"

"I don't charge for get-acquainted visits like today. For my preliminary investigation I would charge you seventy-five dollars an hour. If you decide to go ahead and dispute the Swartz family claims, I would require a ten thousand-dollar retainer. As I said, I charge seventy-five dollars per hour for my time, fifty dollars an hour for associates' time, and twenty dollars an hour for secretarial time. I would let you know when the retainer is used up, if it is, and then you would give us another retainer based on our estimate of the amount of time required to complete our work."

"I need to talk this over with the rest of my family since they are involved."

"Absolutely."

"Go ahead with the preliminary investigation. That would give us a better idea of what you think you can accomplish."

"Let me propose this. I'll call the lawyer in Canada this morning and see what he can tell me. I know you're here from out-of-town, so why don't you come back tomorrow afternoon, say around three? That would give him a chance to get back to me with any information."

When Yetta returned to her hotel, she called Art. To fill her afternoon, the hotel clerk suggested she take a taxi over to Mordecai Historic Park. After touring the plantation houses of the Lane and Mordecai families, the home in which Andrew Johnson was born, and the Saint Mark's Chapel, she ate dinner for the second night in The Brownestone dining room. On Friday morning, she went over to the Greyhound terminal and after consulting the schedule bought a ticket to Richmond for Saturday morning. She spent the rest of the morning in the North Carolina Museum of Art and then had a late lunch in a restaurant near Mr. Stein's office.

At three in the afternoon, she was seated in the Queen Anne chair. This time she noticed the plush brown carpeting and the matching drapes with beige sheers covering the windows of his corner office.

Ike said, "I have good news. Although it appears your brother didn't adopt your nephew, Randall did legally change his name to Marks about five years ago. In addition, your brother specifically referred to Randall as 'his son' in his will."

"Will this satisfy the court?"

"It should. The Canadian lawyer is sending me copies of your brother's will, as well as copies of the documents filed with the court in Saskatchewan when Randall changed his name. I'll know more when I see them for myself."

"That's good."

"I've called your nephew, Art, and told him what I've found so far."

"I guess the next step is for me to talk with my nieces and nephews and decide if we want to proceed."

Yetta, Dot, and Art decided the whole family should get together on the Saturday afternoon after Thanksgiving at Dot and Howard's. Yetta was relieved when Art said he would like to do the talking. The thought of having to recount the whole mess out loud filled her with dread.

Dot brought in platters of pastry and fruit which she arranged on her dining room table. The large coffee pot was set up in the kitchen. When the family arrived, everyone stood around munching on the goodies and drinking coffee until Art asked them to take seats in the living room. He stood in the archway between the living room and dining room. Yetta sat in a chair to his right and Dot sat next to her.

Yetta thought Art the handsomest of her three nephews. It wasn't just his good looks, but his easy, confident manner. He had her father's kinky hair with her mother's full lips and high cheekbones. His nose must have come from his mother's side. Yetta amused herself looking from one face to another noting how the family's attributes got mixed and matched in each generation and joined with characteristics from the marriage partners. Dot looked exactly like Tessie. She didn't have any Marks traits at all.

Art told the whole story from Randall's death to the current time. He gave a dramatic account using his hands and body to emphasize his points. Yetta imagined he was very convincing in the courtroom. Everyone appeared engrossed. Even though she had lived it, his retelling moved her. Tears were on Dot's cheeks. Yetta reached out and held her hand.

At the end, Art read a letter from Ike Stein concerning the next steps to be taken and the projected costs. The ten thousand dollar retainer would cover the completion of the investigation, the filing fees, and the actual trial in state court.

Art's suggestion, which he had discussed with Yetta in advance, was that each cousin put up one thousand dollars and Yetta pay the balance of four thousand. At first Yetta argued that she should put up half the money since she was going to inherit half the estate, but Art felt it was easier to deal in round numbers. When you divided the extra thousand six ways, it actually didn't amount to much.

Howard said, "If we successfully challenge the Swartz family, we'll each get at least eighty-three thousand dollars and maybe double that if the Swartz family is disinherited. Not a bad investment."

Dot crossed her arms and frowned.

"It's more like a return on our family's investment in Randall," one of the cousins said. "It was our fathers and Aunt Yetta who set Randall up in business in the first place."

"I'd like to think," Dot said, "that we're doing this because this is what Uncle Jack and Randall wanted. We should do this to carry out their wishes and honor their memories. I loved both of them and would like to remember all the good times we had together."

Sammy nodded. "This Swartz family dropped the ball by disinheriting Bessie when she got together with Jack and then punted when Randall was born. We've got to carry the ball over the goal line for Jack and Randall and not let that family be rewarded for their prejudices and mean ways."

Before they left, everyone agreed to mail Yetta a check. She wondered how many of them had been moved by greed and how many by wanting to do the right thing.

In the middle of December, Yetta was back in Raleigh, in Ike Stein's office. He sat next to her at the conference table so they could more easily review the files together. Yetta read copies of the papers legally changing Randall's name to Marks, her brother's will, and hospital records which showed they had the same blood type. Unfortunately, even though Ike had gotten copies of Bessie Swartz's birth and death certificates, he could find no records of her blood type.

Ike leaned back in his chair. "I'm wondering if there is other evidence we could present?"

Yetta half-turned so she could look at him. "What kind of evidence are you talking about?"

"Why didn't your brother marry Randall's mother? Maybe if I knew the story, I could discern some important facts not readily apparent to you."

"That's a real long story."

He put his hand on her arm. "I'll tell you what then. Since it's almost five o'clock, why don't you let me take you to dinner and you can tell me over dessert."

Yetta glanced at his left hand and noted he wore no wedding ring. But, with men of their generation, one still couldn't be sure and there were all those pictures on his credenza. "Won't your wife object to changing plans at the last minute like this?"

"My wife? Oh, no, I'm a widower."

"I'm sorry."

"*Ohev shalom.* May she rest in peace. She's been gone almost five years. So, what do you say to dinner? And, please call me Ike."

"I say fine to dinner, if you'll call me Yetta."

"Agreed. I'm sure you've had enough of the Brownestone. Why don't I pick you up, say about six-thirty?"

After they were seated in a corner booth of a French restaurant and cocktails had arrived, Yetta said, "Tell me about your children, Ike."

He smiled, played with his fork for a few seconds, and then looked up at her. "I have a son who's a lawyer for the Justice Department in Washington, D.C. He's married to a nice girl and they have two children. My daughter is married to a fabric manufacturer. They do quite well. She lives in Greensboro and has two girls."

Yetta detected red and gold flecks in his hazel eyes. When he talked about his family, his eyes took on a green glow. She smiled. Sometimes, like now, she was sorry she never had children. She'd been counting on Randall to look after her in her old age. *Nechtihger tawg*, what was she going to do? "How far is it to Greensboro?"

"It's about an hour and a half so I get to see them quite often. How about your family?"

Yetta told him about her brothers and her nieces and nephews. "I came close to getting married once many years ago, but things didn't work out." She didn't know why she said that. She felt disconnected from her real life here in this restaurant with this man—maybe it was the waitress with the French accent, the ivy growing around the columns, and the frilly curtains in the windows.

Ike stirred his coffee.

Fortunately he didn't ask any questions. But the silence was awkward, so she said, "My brother, Jack, was a great storyteller. He always had a new *meiseh* to tell when he came to visit. The children used to sit on the floor all around him and beg him to tell a story. We never knew whether they were true or not." She laughed.

"It's good to hear you laugh," Ike said. "All our conversations have been so serious."

"Jack could always make me laugh. He had a joke for every occasion."

"You were close?"

"He left home when I was six. We were as close as a six-year-old sister and a fifteen-year-old brother could be." Her voice turned wistful. "I didn't see him again for sixteen years. By that time I was twenty-two and Randall was six." She sighed remembering the main purpose of their dinner. "I never met Bessie Swartz or any of her relatives. All I know is what my mother told me and what Jack and Randall revealed later."

"Tell me everything you know," Ike said.

Chapter Three

Jack's Journey Begins

Washington, D.C.

1908

The group of Jewish boys sprinted around the corner, behind the Catholic Church, and down the alley. Chased by a gang of Irish kids, they stopped at the end of the alley and huddled together.

Jack, the fastest, had led them there on purpose. He knew from experience the downhill end of an alley was the best place to make a stand. For one thing, gravel and small stones collect in the troughs where alleys meet streets. For another, the enemy is confined to a long narrow space. Opponents have to come at you head-on, like a charging bull—no flanking maneuvers, no way to attack from the rear.

Jack and the others picked up stones and stuffed their pockets, then picked up another handful and hurled them at the enemy. The Irish halted in the middle of the alley and chucked the missiles back.

"Kike."
"Mick."
"Jew boys."
"Mackerel Snappers."
"Christ killer."
"Potato Eaters."
"Go to hell."

Advantage went to the Jews. The Irish tried to advance, but lacking a ready supply of projectiles and having been out maneuvered, they slowly backed up until they reached the far end of the alley, gave up, and left.

The Jewish kids slapped each other on the back. Jack rubbed the spot on his arm where he'd been hit and looked around. No one was bleeding. They all were panting. With each heavy breath, vapor emerged from their mouths and noses. The cold damp spring day smelled of rebirth and renewal, but the boys didn't notice. They didn't dawdle in case the Irish crowd had only retreated and was about to regroup and charge again.

Fifteen-year-old Jack raced home through back alleys that paralleled every street in southwest Washington, D.C. He charged through the front door of the grocery store on 4½ Street, his face flushed from anger and the cold. Before he could slam the door shut, dead leaves swirled in behind him.

"*Bubele*," his mother said, "you got here just in time. I have an appointment with Yetta's teacher, and I don't want to be late. Yetta's over to Sarah's house. Papa went to get a chicken koshered for Mrs. Weiss. You'll have to mind the store." She pulled her gloves on as she spoke. "I'll be back soon as I can,"

With that, Esther was gone.

Jack had wanted to tell someone what happened, but his mother obviously couldn't stop to listen. Anyway, she would've been angry because they'd fought back. She'd have said he should've run home, like a coward, not gotten into a battle with those bullies. His father wouldn't have understood, either. Jack thought his father didn't know how to fight back, that he would've stood there and taken the beating like he did when angry customers hurled insults at him. His father didn't believe the best way to defend yourself was to attack first.

Frustrated, Jack banged his hand on the counter and paced in circles, then stepped through the door that separated the store from the house. He left it open so he could hear if a customer came in. He hung up his coat and then washed his hands and face in cold water at the kitchen sink. That helped to calm him. The bruise on his arm hurt only when he pushed on it. He was tired of the fighting and the name calling that went on all year but escalated around Easter. His mother told him about the pogroms in the Ukraine. His parents thought in America their lives were a lot better because they didn't have to hide in cellars. To Jack it didn't seem all that much different.

From the ice box he took the bottle of milk and holding the top down with the palm of his hand, he shook it to mix the cream. He snatched a clean glass off the drain board, filled it, drank that glass down, and poured another. On his way back into the store, he filched a couple of lemon cookies from the jar. As he passed the newspaper rack, he saw a picture of the American Thomas car. The photograph took up almost the whole page above the fold of *The Evening Star*. He put the glass on the counter and went back for a copy. The car was being loaded on the steamer *Santa Clara* for the trip to Valdez.

Jack sat on a stool behind the counter and read the article which recounted the enormous lead of Montague Roberts and his American Thomas in the twenty thousand-mile New York-to-Paris race.

Jack imagined himself, instead of Montague Roberts, standing on the dock dressed in a long touring coat with his cap set off to the side of his head and a rakish smile on his face, just like in the photo taken in Times Square at the beginning of the race, which had been in the newspaper in the middle of February.

Jack wondered where his father was. He must've gotten into a complex Talmudic discussion with the rabbi, not just any old debate.

What Jack wouldn't give to be free and on the move like those drivers. He wished he could've been Montague's navigator. He envisioned himself leaning over a map, plotting the route across the countryside.

Jack flipped the paper over and read the headline about preparations for the Easter egg roll at the White House. He hated this time around Passover and Easter—so much more fighting among the ethnic groups. "I've got to get out of here," he said to everyone and no one. He dreamed of getting on a train and traveling across the country.

When his mother returned, she gave Jack a smile of great satisfaction. "I got an excellent report on Yetta. Your working with her on her spelling words made a big difference." Her smile dimmed. "*Bubele*, is something wrong?"

Jack was still sitting behind the counter reading the comics. "Today a bunch of Irish chased poor Max Goldberg. If he hadn't run into a group of us walking home, they would have beat him up. It's coming up to Easter, and we're going to have to travel in groups again to protect ourselves." He slammed his hand against the counter. "I'm fed up with this place."

She put her hand over his. Her tone was soothing. "*Boychik, boychik, mein zeen*. Your brothers and sister need you. With all of us working, soon we'll move to Northwest and expand the business. Things'll be better there."

He put his hands together as if in prayer. "Please, Mama, I want to go somewhere else—away from Washington. I want your blessing. I won't wait much longer. The *goyim* wait for us 'kikes' and chase us down the block. You don't want me to fight them. So what can I do?" He wasn't going to let her persuade him to stay as she had in the past. He put his most determined look on his face.

Esther clasped his hands between her warm palms. "Where would you go?" She shook her head. "Things were much worse in the old country, but we survived. Life will be better in the new neighborhood. You'll see."

"Always you bring up Podolyia. That doesn't help." He rapped his chest. "I want to go to Montana, to that city, Helena, to Aunt Golda and Uncle Wolf's. There must be more in the world than this store. I don't want to spend my life inside, always counting the change. I've got enough money saved."

Jack had talked of going west since he was thirteen. Esther had been able to postpone his leaving with the force of her personality for more than two years.

She caressed his cheek. "*Bubele*, you should finish high school. Without an education you can't do anything in this world. What do you want to be when you're grown up?"

"I want to travel to Texas and Alaska and Paris and see different things every day. I don't want to be stuck looking at the same four walls all the time."

Esther's hand came down to her side. "What will Papa and I do without you?"

"You have Sammy and Abey and Yetta. They don't mind working in the store. They like it in Washington. I'm going . . . one way or another."

She held her hands in front of her, palms up and shrugged. "Okay, okay, all right, Jackie. I'll speak to your *tate* and we'll see."

"Please, Mama. Soon."

When all the children left for school the next morning, Esther went into the store to speak to Moishe. He was dressed in his store uniform. A white, starched apron hung from his shoulders to his knees. Beneath it, he wore a white shirt and conservative tie. His compact, brushlike mustache completed his formal appearance. He believed a dignified image gave him protection from the prejudices of some of his customers.

Lives in Exile

"*Oy vei ihz mihr*, Moishe," said Esther. "What are we going to do about Jackie?"

"What can we do? If he wants to go, he will go. So we might as well give him our blessing. Let him *gei gezoonter heit*. We should feel lucky he wants to go to your sister Golda." He put his hands on her shoulders. "We let him keep the money he earned peddling papers. So what could we expect, after all?" He put his hand under her chin. "Don't worry, Esther. He'll come back. When we left Podolyia, we said good-bye, probably forever. Who knows if we'll see our parents before the Messiah comes? At least Jackie'll be on the same side of the big ocean and we know we'll see him again."

She sighed and wiped her tears with her sleeve.

After school, it was Jack's turn to work in the store, a square room with a wooden floor covered in sawdust. His first chore was to sweep. He watched the dust swirl in the light that filtered through the dirty windows and wondered if the dried dirt of Montana swirled the same way. He chuckled remembering how, as a little boy, he used to chase after the dust particles that glistened in the sunlight. His mother had called it angel dust. Did his aunt and uncle in Helena have a wooden floor in their store and did they cover it with sawdust? As Jack spread fresh particles of wood around the wooden block where his father cut meat, the smell of recently cut timber tinged the air. Was the aroma the same in forests or did the scent only come after the trees had been chopped up? A scale hung over the chopping block. Under it sat the bucket for the bones, fat, and trimmed meat. A rendering company collected the contents several times a week. Inevitably drops of blood, pieces of bone, and stray globs of fat sprinkled the floor. The sawdust neutralized the stink and soaked up the messy splatters.

Next, Jack stocked the shelves, making pyramids of cans while, in his mind, vistas of distant peaks loomed above flat plains.

"Jackie," his father called to him, "watch what you are doing. Make sure the labels face forward and are lined up straight."

Next, his father asked him to clean the glass doors of the ice box. Inside, hanging on sharp hooks, were the sides of beef, lamb, and pork. Even though the family kept strictly kosher, they lived in a mixed neighborhood and had to supply their customers with pork. The milk crates, egg cases, and wooden tubs of butter and cheese were stored on the floor. When he and Abey were little, they loved to hide in there on hot summer days, squatting down to make themselves as small as possible, hands over their mouths, giggling, until their mother came looking for them and chased them out. Today, Jack studied at the sides of beef. He wondered how big a cow could be and if a whole cow smelled the way chops and rumps did.

The entire afternoon, his father said nothing to him about going to Montana, gave no hint any discussion with Mama had even taken place. When he went into the kitchen for dinner, his mother sat with him at the table while he ate a large plate of stuffed cabbage with fresh rye bread. Jack said, "*Nu*, Mama, did you speak to Papa?"

"Speak to Papa? Of course, your papa and I talked. We want you to finish this school term. Then you can go to this Montana, if you can stay with Aunt Golda and Uncle Wolf. I'll write to them and ask. I'm sure they can use help in their store."

Jack couldn't believe they had finally given in. He'd thought he'd have to run away. Instead, several days later, he ran to the post office with his mother's letter to his aunt and uncle. He watched as the postman stamped the letter and dropped it in the mailbag. All he could do now was wait.

The return letter arrived three weeks later, on the third day of Passover. His aunt wrote they would be thrilled to have him and included directions on how to get from the Helena train station to Barr's Dry Goods. That afternoon, when he was alone in the bedroom, Jack climbed on the chair and pulled out his cigar box from under the pile of outgrown clothes on the very top shelf. The cigar box was safe there because his mother always asked him to climb up to get down the outgrown clothes for the younger boys to try on. Jack had placed one rubber band across the cigar box so it covered the "I" in Muriel and held the latch in place. Another band crossed the length of the box on top of the first one. That was his security system. He examined the rubber bands. They were exactly as he had left them. He read the letter one more time and put it on top of his French postcards and his money. After he closed the lid, he slid the rubber bands back on and returned the box to its hiding place. As often as he could, he retrieved his treasured letter and read it. After a week, he had the directions memorized and recited them to himself as he drifted off to sleep.

* * * * * * * *

Yetta liked talking to Jack because he always answered her questions— not like her other brothers who laughed at her, or her mother who told her she would understand when she got older, or her father who was too busy or too tired. Every night after dinner she worked with Jack on memorizing her addition and subtraction facts or her spelling words. They sat at the card table in the living room because the wooden top was smooth and easy to write on. When she got her assignment done, as a reward for her hard work, Jack read a chapter to her from a book she picked out.

One night about a month before he left, she looked up at him, eyes wide and said, "Why are you leaving? I want you to stay."

"I'm going to a place where cowboys live, where there are lots of horses and cows like in the story books. There's so much land in Montana you don't have to see a neighbor, if you don't want to."

She couldn't imagine living without her mother and father and brothers around her. "Won't you be lonely?"

"You can go into town and see other people whenever you want. There's lots of blue sky and mountains and trees. Besides, I won't be living out in the wilderness. I'll be living above Aunt Golda and Uncle Wolf's store, like here."

How lonely she'd be when he left. "I don't want you to go," she said.

"I won't forget you. You'll still be my favorite sister."

"I'm your only sister."

"But you're still my favorite."

She giggled.

* * * * * * * *

On Sunday, six weeks before Jack was to leave, the family took a picnic basket down to the Arsenal at the end of 4½ Street. The boys spread the blanket as Esther and Yetta unpacked the roasted chicken, sliced tomatoes and cucumbers, cold string beans, and rolls. While they were eating, Esther said, "Since Jackie will leave soon, I would like us to have a family portrait made by Mr. Zweig at his studio. We can do it in two weeks. That will give Jackie time to have a new suit fitted."

"Oh, Mama," they all whined in unison.

"I don't want any arguments. I've made all the arrangements."

"Esther, this is an expensive idea," said Moishe. "Maybe we should think this over,"

"I've thought it over very carefully. Jackie needs a new suit to take with him anyway. I want this portrait taken. It may be the last time we are together for a while." Tears formed in her eyes.

"All right." Moishe looked over at Jack and the other children. "Let's not spoil this glorious afternoon. Look at the sun, the trees. Smell the air. Has there ever been a more wonderful day? Who has a joke to tell?"

June 20th dawned bright and sunny and not too humid. Tomorrow Jack would be leaving. He'd volunteered to help his father in the store that morning so he finished his oatmeal in six spoonfuls and gulped down the large glass of milk. First, his father told him to restock the bushel baskets that stood in the center of the room. Jack had to go into the cellar, haul up crates of vegetables and fruits, and dump them into the baskets. He sneezed every time he entered the cellar because of the stench of damp earth in the cramped, low-ceilinged area. Since it was summer, he had to lug lots of crates—string beans, pea pods, spinach, kale, carrots, cabbage, sweet potatoes, apples, pears, melons, peaches, plums, bananas, and grapes. His father liked the baskets to be overflowing.

Then he had to bring up the twenty-pound tin container of lard. On that trip he carried a stick to knock down the spider webs in the back corner of the cellar where the lard was stored.

When he'd finished, Moishe said, "Jackie, take yourself a piece of fruit."

Jack picked a soft purple plum, leaned against the basket, and polished it with his thumbs.

His father took it from him and wiped it with the corner of his apron. "You know you're going to be a young man traveling by yourself, so don't believe everything people tell you. Lots of people are out there looking for opportunities to cheat and swindle. It's one thing to have a friendly conversation, to discuss the weather. But never let anyone know how much money you have or where you keep it. Some people may want to play card games or gamble with you. You must keep away from them."

"I know these things, Papa. I've been around."

"You've only been around Southwest Washington, *mein zeen*. There is much more to the world."

Just then Mrs. O'Neill came in to buy vegetables for her dinner.

After she left, Moishe began again. "Jackie, I worry about you and I want you to be safe. Is this so bad?"

"No, Papa."

"Your mama's going to miss you. Write her often. If you decide what you are looking for is here in Washington, we will be glad to have you back. Don't forget that. *Vershtate?*" Understand, his expression asked. Moishe took a ten-dollar bill from his apron pocket and pushed it into Jack's hand. "Don't tell Mama."

"Thanks, Papa." Jack wanted to hug his father but didn't.

That afternoon Jack pulled the shoe boxes where he kept his toys from under his bed. He put his collection of bottle caps on Sammy's bed, his box of toys soldiers on Abe's bed, and a doll he had bought for Yetta on her bed.

His mother came upstairs with the clothes she had washed that morning, already dry from the sun. "*Bubele*, put some of your money in each pocket and in different places in your bags. The best thing to do is to pin most of your money inside your clothes. That's how we traveled from Podolyia." With that she produced two large safety pins. "Give me some of your money and your traveling suit. I'll do it for you."

He counted out the money for the ticket and for the meals he would eat and added a little bit more, just in case. Then he handed the rest to his mother.

When he turned his back, she added a ten-dollar bill and pinned some of the bills to the inside of the trouser pocket lining and the rest to the inside of his breast pocket. Then she went downstairs to finish cooking supper.

He climbed up into the closet to get his cigar box. Before he opened the box, he listened at the doorway for his mother. He could hear her rattling pots in the kitchen. He took out his French postcards and looked quickly through them before he put them back in the box. He took the letter from his aunt and put it in one of his traveling suit's pockets. He replaced the rubber bands around the box. After he put a layer of socks and underwear in the bottom of the suitcase, he placed the cigar box in the middle. On top of that he packed his new suit, his freshly ironed shirts and handkerchiefs, his work clothes, and two copies of the family portrait.

His mother had five copies made—one for herself, one to mail to her mother and father, one to mail to Moishe's parents, one for Jack to keep with him, and one to send with Jack to her sister. He removed the photo from its protective cardboard cover. His mother had carefully penned "The Marks Family, 1908" on the back.

He studied the picture. He'd inherited his mother's straight hair and thick soft lips along with his father's large broad nose. Sammy was the opposite, with his father's kinky hair and thin lips but with his mother's thin straight nose. The brothers were the same height. Jack had his father's wiry build and narrow shoulders. Sammy, on the other hand, had broad shoulders and a barrel chest. They were both almost as tall as their father, but he couldn't tell from the photograph because his father was seated with Yetta on his lap.

His mother, a buxom woman, looked beautiful, seated next to his father in her favorite black taffeta dress, with a high lace collar and pleated and ruffled bodice. Her long brown hair was rolled up over a black taffeta ribbon which tied at the top of her head in a bow.

Yetta wore an identical dress in pale blue, although in the photo it looked white. Her hair was parted on one side. A bow held her brown curls off her face on the other side. Both Esther and Yetta wore high button shoes with cloth uppers.

What was missing from the photograph was his mother's engaging smile and dancing eyes. The photographer had made them all stare straight ahead with a serious look so they could sit absolutely still while the camera worked.

Abe stood between his brothers in his first pair of long pants. The two older brothers and their father wore suits with high lapels. The linen shirts were starched and pressed especially for the occasion. All four of the males sported four-in-hand ties that took forever to get just right.

Jack put the photograph back in the cover. He was excited about meeting the aunt he'd heard so much about. Aunt Golda and his mother looked so much alike in his parents' wedding photograph. He wondered how much alike they actually were. He'd find out in only three days.

The next morning, when Jack tramped downstairs and into the store with his suitcases, he found the whole family waiting. "I guess it's time." He shook hands with his brother, Sammy, and they smiled at each other. His father clapped him on the shoulder.

"Thanks for everything, Papa," Jack said. "I'll write soon."

"*Gei gezoont und kumn gezoont.*" Go in good health and return in good health. His father's voice cracked.

Jack managed a weak smile and turned to the door. His father and brothers stayed behind to mind the store so his mother and sister could go with him to the train station. The three of them tramped to the platform in the middle of 4½ Street and waited for the trolley. As it pulled away, the three in the store and the three on the trolley waved.

Jack, Esther, and Yetta got off the trolley on Massachusetts Avenue right in front of the train station. He stood at its entrance and read the inscription out loud:

> HE THAT WOULD BRING HOME THE
> WEALTH OF THE INDIES MUST CARRY
> THE WEALTH OF THE INDIES WITH HIM
> SO IT IS IN TRAVELING—A MAN
> MUST CARRY KNOWLEDGE WITH HIM
> IF HE WOULD BRING HOME KNOWLEDGE

Jack didn't know about the Indies part, but he sure hoped to come home wealthy. He knew exactly what he was doing—looking for adventure. He guessed whenever he returned home he'd have a lot more knowledge. He shrugged, continued into the enormous waiting room, and headed straight for the ticket master's window, the family in tow. He counted out his money and plunked it down on the marble sill. "A ticket to Helena, Montana, please, sir."

The ticket master thumbed through the stubs and said, "First you take the train to Chicago. In Chicago you change trains to the Great Northern's Empire Builder to St. Paul. In St. Paul, you catch the Northern Pacific for Helena. The train for Chicago leaves from track eleven. Boarding will start in twenty minutes. Have a safe journey, young man."

Jack knew all that but was polite and waited for the man to finish. "Thank you very much, sir." Several weeks before he'd taken the trolley to the station and gotten a copy of *The Official Guide of the Railways, 1908*. He'd studied it very carefully.

They sat on the rosewood benches to wait for the announcer to call the train. The stone walls, stone floor, and high ceilings kept the waiting room cool even in June. A colored woman was going from bench to bench rubbing the wood with a rag she dampened with a reddish fluid from a bottle. The fragrant polish scented the air.

"Don't forget to use the paper cups I gave you to drink the water," Esther said. "I hear the scooper on the train is used by everyone without a cleaning in between. I gave you enough food to last to Chicago. You'll have to buy food after that. Look for clean places. Always watch your bags. There're thieves everywhere."

"I will, Mama. Don't worry. I'll write you as soon as I get to Aunt Golda's. Maybe one day you'll come out to Montana to visit."

"We'll see. We'll see." Forcing a small smile through her tightly pressed lips, she caressed his face with the back of her fingers and straightened his hair.

"Ladies and Gentlemen," called the announcer, "the Chicago Limited is now boarding on track eleven. All aboard, please."

Jack's heart pounded. His knees felt weak. He wondered if he could stand. He looked at his mother. "I guess this is it."

Her eyes filled with tears. She rummaged in her purse and pulled out her handkerchief. "Okay, let's go." She dabbed at her eyes, stood, and took Yetta's hand.

They followed Jack through the concourse out onto the platform for track eleven. He planned to travel in one of the front cars. When he first caught sight of the engine, he was surprised—it was huge. The wheels alone looked higher than his head. He strained to get a good view of the brass bell atop the middle of the engine. Even from several cars back he could feel the waves of heat wash over him. He hugged his mother, told Yetta he would see her soon, and kissed her on the check. He bounded up the steps of the second car, found an unoccupied bench, hauled his bags onto the overhead rack, and waved to his family through the open window.

Pretty soon the call "All aboard" echoed from one conductor to the next. Jack stuck his head out the window and watched as each conductor picked up his stool and pulled himself onto the train. The engineer rang the bell and the train lurched forward. Jack waved and smiled and laughed.

They waved back.

Esther blotted her tears. "Safe journey," she called.

When he couldn't see them anymore, Jack sat on the bench. "Wow." He'd actually gone and done it. He'd left his family and was on his own. He smiled broadly and looked around at his fellow travelers. None appeared as happy as he felt. A few were reading their newspapers, a few looked out the window, a few chatted with the persons sitting next to them—but none was as elated as he. He was floating and could float the whole way to Montana.

* * * * * * *

Yetta eyes filled with tears at the memory. "Mama and I rode back to the store in silence." She pulled her handkerchief from her purse and dried her eyes.

Ike put his hand over hers.

"Many years later," Yetta said, "Mama told me that at that moment when the train disappeared from view, she thought back to the last time she'd seen Podolyia. She'd been perched on the front seat of a wagon seated next to Papa, waving good-bye to her mother. Each of them waved until they could no longer see the other. She described those amazing twin emotions of emptiness and excitement she felt when she left home. She had a knot in the pit of her stomach. Her heart pounded. She wanted to jump down and run back to hug her mother one more time and at the same time she felt that if she spread her arms she could have soared above the clouds all the way to America." Yetta looked at her hand under Ike's. "I'm sorry I never thought to ask Jack what he felt as he lurched away from us."

Chapter Four

Helena, Montana

1908

That first morning on the train, Jack was so excited he didn't know what to look at first—the scenery or his traveling companions. The conductor came by, took his ticket, punched holes in it, and pushed the stub into a slit in the rail over his head.

Across the aisle, with his back to the window, a man had three upside down cups and a thin board on his lap. "Hey who wants to take a chance? Who has a quick eye? Tupps is my name, cups is my game. Find the ball and win a nickel." Jack guessed he was from Baltimore from the flat way he pronounced his vowels. With a pale face and a very pointed chin, he looked to be in his early twenties. Under his straw boater, his blond hair was slicked straight back. The yellow and white seersucker suit jacket was buttoned although he slouched against the window. When a few people turned around, he put a small ball under one cup and then moved all the cups around the board. Tupps kept up a constant patter encouraging the men who hung over the seat backs or stood in the aisle to take a chance and place a bet.

Jack, fascinated, watched from across the car, peering around bodies. Finally he stood on his seat, clinging to the overhead rack. The air at that height was thick with cigarette smoke which stung his eyes and made him cough. After a few seconds he adjusted to the stink and the atmosphere and was able to get the view he'd hoped for. He knew there must be some trick involved but he couldn't figure it out. The bettors were almost always wrong, but every once in a while someone won, which kept everyone interested and wagering. After a half-hour Jack was sure he could pick the right cup almost every time. It seemed that wherever Tupps' right hand stopped, that's where the ball was.

Suddenly, the huckster's lookout called "coming," and everyone took a seat and picked up a newspaper or gazed out the window until the conductor passed through the car. Then play began again.

After they left the Frederick, Maryland, station the gambler called, "Hey you, young man. You got good eyes. You wanta bet your eyes are faster than my hands?"

At first Jack didn't realize Tupps was talking to him. When he saw everyone looking at him, Jack pointed to himself and said, "Me?"

"Yeah, you. You've been watching this whole time. Bet a nickel, win a nickel."

The other passengers drew back, making space for Jack. Jack didn't know what to do. His father's words echoed in his head. *"Some people may want to play card games or gamble with you. You must keep away from them."* Everyone was staring at him, waiting for him to accept or decline. He'd been watching this guy for what seemed like hours, so he was pretty sure he could win.

He moved across the aisle, pulled a nickel from his pocket, and placed it on the board as he'd seen the others do. Tupps moved the cups around and around. His right hand ended on the center cup. Jack was sure the ball was there. He pointed to it and the man raised the cup. Thrilled to see the ball, Jack said, "Let it ride." The crowd cheered. Jack's smile was as wide as the train car was long. Tupps pulled a nickel from his pouch and placed it on the table with a flourish. Jack's heart pounded. It was his first time gambling for real money—not the penny-ante stuff he'd played with his friends. This time Tupps' right hand ended on the left cup, but the ball wasn't there. The showman raised the center cup to show everyone where the ball really was.

Tupps scooped up both nickels. "Sorry, son, wanta try to win back your nickel?"

Jack felt that if he'd gotten it right once, he could do it again. He took another nickel out and tried again. His fingers itched, so he rubbed them on his pants. This time Tupps' hands flew around the board so fast Jack had a hard time keeping his eye on the cup. He decided to go with his instincts. He picked the center cup, but this time the ball was under the right cup.

Lives in Exile

"This time I'll give you double, if you can pick the right one."

Jack thought for a moment. He wanted a chance to win back the ten cents he'd lost, so he placed another nickel on the board. He felt sweat accumulating in his armpits. Again he picked the wrong cup. He started to move back to his seat.

Tupps placed a hand on his arm. "I'll give you another chance and move the cups slowly this time."

All around him the men patted his back and called out encouragement, so he tried again. After he'd lost fifty cents—enough for lunch and dinner that day and he hadn't even been on the train three hours, he shuffled back to his seat and sat looking out the window while other suckers took his place. *"I know these things, Papa. I've been around."* He'd found out how little he knew. He'd done exactly what his father had warned him against and lost his food money in the bargain. He stared out the window but saw nothing.

Tupps finally left the train in Pittsburgh. Some of the bettors and observers took up playing pinochle, others took naps.

Jack tried to figure out how he was going to buy all his meals with the money he had left in his pocket. He was afraid to take out the money his mother had pinned in his clothes, afraid his pocket might be picked. After calculating and recalculating, he figured he'd just spend less at each meal. He chuckled to himself. He could make it. The train arrived in Cleveland and then skirted Lake Erie. Things weren't so bad. He was on his way to Toledo and then Chicago.

In the evening, when he couldn't see out the window, he started reading Conrad's *The Secret Agent*, the book his English teacher had given him when he went in to say good-bye. He'd never read a whole novel through from start to finish, just for fun. As the days went by, he discovered he genuinely liked it. He couldn't wait to find out how the story ended, and when it was over wished he'd had another book. Playing solitaire, on his traveling bag, occupied him when he was tired of everything else. He kept away from the other passengers now—like his father had warned him.

The roast beef sandwich he bought in Saint Paul was the most flavorless food he'd ever put in his mouth. It wasn't the first time he'd sampled *trayf*. More than once he'd smuggled forbidden cookies from the store and eaten them behind the school. At the lunch counter in an F. W. Woolworth's Five-and-Dime he once shared a pork hot dog with a friend. He chose the roast beef because it was the cheapest non-cheese sandwich the vendor had. He was sick of the cheese he'd been eating to save money since he'd finished the food his mother sent with him. With the waxed paper wrapping he scraped off the gobs of mayonnaise lathered on the meat. The kaiser roll tasted like cardboard, and the roast beef was rubbery. The thrill of being able to eat whatever he wanted faded. To make things even more miserable, a fly buzzed around his head. He finally swatted at the damned annoyance until it flew out the window.

With his hands clenched around the handles of his possessions, he slept fitfully. Weird nightmares kept waking him. In one, a robber held up the train. Just as the ringleader pointed his gun at Jack and pulled the trigger, Jack woke up. Then he dreamed the train broke down in the wild and he had to hike through streams and over mountains until he fell off a cliff and woke up with a jolt in the middle of falling. He couldn't imagine why he had these strange fantasies, maybe it was the constant motion and the non-kosher food.

When the conductor called out, "Helena . . . next stop Helena . . . all for Helena," Jack sprang from his seat and yanked his suitcases from the racks. He wrested open the door at the end of the car, stepped into the vestibule, and stood behind the conductor who was leaning out the opened upper half of the outside door. The smell of burnt coal mixed with fresh pine swept over him. Every other time the train stopped Jack had been sitting, so he hadn't realized the full force of a train braking to a halt. This time, the sudden jolt almost knocked him over, so he positioned his bags between his legs. Another jerk threw him against the wall. With his right hand he grabbed a metal bar to steady himself. When one of the suitcases started to slide across on the metal floor, he stretched out his leg and pulled it back, then squeezed the bags with his calves. Even though he'd been able to keep his balance, he felt his hat flying off his head. With his free hand, he flattened the top of his cap. After all these days, he thought he had learned how to "ride the rails." The conductor said, "Brace yourself." Jack barely had time to react before the train slowed suddenly, screeching to a halt.

The conductor jumped off and reached back into the train for the wooden stairs. Jack stepped down onto the platform and marched toward the street.

He traversed the small station which was nothing like the cavernous Saint Paul or Washington stations in either size or crowds. Here a dozen or so people moved through the aisles between the half-dozen wooden benches. The ceiling was low, and the single rectangular room dimly lit. Outside the station, he set his bags on the wooden sidewalk and put his

Lives in Exile

hands on his hips. Most of the surroundings looked like home—cobblestone streets, trolley cars, and stores with names painted on the windows. The only brick building was the station; everything else was wood.

But it did smell different out west. Cleaner, drier, more crisp—like the narrator always said in the serials he read in the newspaper. And, like the descriptions in the paper, the towering peaks rose behind everything like large teeth on one of his father's bone saws. They reached into the heavens looking more like a picture than anything real. Even in June the summits had patches of gleaming snow that reflected the sunlight and turned the sky into the clearest pale blue. From the train window, he'd watched the mountains grow from little bumps in the distance to huge rock and pine-covered behemoths. But he couldn't appreciate the enormity of them until he stood on the motionless earth at their feet.

He tried to imprint his first view of Helena so he'd be able to recall it whenever he wanted. He thought he might burst or maybe dance a *kzatske*.

As he picked up his bags, he recited Aunt Golda's directions one more time. "Cross Station Street and walk up the street which dead ends right in front of you. That is Main Street. Walk uphill to the third intersection which will be Bridge Street. Barr's Dry Goods is on the corner."

The right side of Main looked more intriguing, so he crossed over. The sign on the corner building said "Station Street Saloon." Swinging doors filled the entrance. Jack stood on his toes and peeked in. He was surprised to see a sawdust-covered floor. He couldn't conceive of its purpose in a saloon. Inside, a man was singing "In the Shade of the Old Apple Tree" in a splendid tenor voice. The scent of beer and cigarette smoke floated through the door. He'd read about Carrie Nation smashing up bars back East, but in Helena, Budweiser was still king. He strode uphill, passing a wooden Indian standing guard outside Levy's Cigar Store. A pharmacy across the street had familiar globes hanging in the window filled with blue and red liquids.

The young women he passed averted their eyes, but all the men and older women nodded or smiled. Men wore cowboy hats and boots with high heels like those he'd seen in pictures. He wondered how much the boots cost. He'd like to get a pair. He pictured himself in one of those big hats with the wide brim.

He stopped to look in the window of a millinery store, at the hats decorated with artificial fruit and bird feathers. One reminded him of his mother's favorite that she wore to shul on the High Holidays. His mother, what was she doing right now? Making supper, he figured. A saleslady swished a feather duster across the shelves and then covered all the hats with a sheet. Jack realized it must be close to closing time.

As he approached the third intersection, Bridge Street, he spotted Barr's Dry Goods. It would've been hard to miss with the big black letters across the picture window. On display were bolts of fabric and pairs of boots stacked on shoe boxes.

His mother had been going to send a telegram saying he was on his way so he hoped he was expected. He straightened his tie, brushed his hair back, and walked in. Behind the counter stood a woman who could have been his mother.

Jack said, "Hello."

Aunt Golda shrieked, "*Oy vei, oy vei*. Wolf, it's got to be Jackie!"

She ran around the counter, hugged and squeezed him and kissed him on the cheek. "I can't believe it. You're here."

"Give the boy a chance," a male voice called from behind him. When Aunt Golda finally released him, he turned around and shook hands with Uncle Wolf. Even though his mother had told him Uncle Wolf had red hair, he was startled by his kinky orange-red mop and full rabbi's beard. Jack had been expecting the dark brown-red hair like most Jewish people he knew, not the orange-red of his Irish neighbors. Wolf wore wire rimmed glasses which were perched far down the wide bridge of his nose.

Golda put her hands on her hips and surveyed him. "Wolf, he's got Esther's hair and lips, don't you think? But, Jackie, you look an awful lot like Moishe. Please Wolf, let's close the store. It's only fifteen minutes early."

Wolf stroked his beard. "Okay. You go ahead upstairs while I finish up."

Jack hadn't said one word beyond hello. Neither of them appeared to notice. Golda went behind the counter. "Follow me." Jack was surprised to find a playpen tucked back there. Golda picked up the baby. "This is Louis." She smiled and nuzzled the baby's check. Jack followed her into the stock room where two little girls played on the floor. Golda said, "Let's go upstairs, *maidellas*. Rose, you carry the crayons and paper. I'll introduce you to your cousin when we get up there. Scoot." She guided the smallest girl toward the steps by placing her palm on the child's back. On the climb up the steps, Golda applied a helpful hand to her rear end.

When the five-person parade arrived in the living room of the upstairs apartment, they all turned to face Jack. "Rose and Frieda, this is your big cousin, Jackie."

Four round eyes looked up at him. Two mouths hung open.

Golda laughed. She had his mother's broad smile and dancing eyes. "Let me show you around. This is the living room and dining room . . ." She waved her hand toward the back of the apartment, ". . . and that's the kitchen." She ambled into a hallway off the living room which went toward Main Street and he followed. The first room was Aunt Golda's and Uncle Wolf's bedroom. Jack would share the middle room with Louis. The last bedroom with windows facing both Main and Bridge belonged to the two girls.

"Why don't you put your things away while I get the dinner ready? If you want to wash up, come in the kitchen."

He sat on the bed and looked around. It was quite small—barely large enough for his bed, the crib, the chifforobe, and the table stacked with diapers. A window right over his bed looked out on Bridge Street.

He took his clothes out of his suitcases and laid out some clean clothes to change into. The rest he placed in the drawers in the chifforobe. Then he took off his suit. When he unpinned the money and counted it out, he had more than he thought. He smiled when he realized his mother must have added ten dollars when she attached the money to his clothes. How he wished he'd had the ten dollars in his pocket for food. On the other hand, if he'd known, he might have gambled more away.

After he unpacked, he asked Aunt Golda if he could help her.

"Not tonight," she said. "Tonight you are the guest of honor. Tomorrow is soon enough to start working. I happened to make your mother's favorite dinner tonight."

He'd known from the minute he stepped into the kitchen they were having stuffed cabbage from the delicious aroma of cabbage, tomatoes, and beef. "I love it." His stomach was growling. "I should write a letter to Mama and Papa to let them know I arrived. Can I do it now, while you're getting dinner ready?" He longed to ask when dinner was being served, but thought that would be rude.

During dinner and until the children went to bed, they pestered Jack for details of his train trip. He told them about the scenery, the book he read, and the gambler, leaving out his own misadventure. Aunt Golda wanted to know about his parents, his brothers, and sister. No detail was too insignificant for her curiosity.

As he drifted off to sleep, Jack remembered the newspaper story about one of his heroes, Teddy Roosevelt, riding into Helena behind a team of horses while campaigning for President. Jack wondered if Roosevelt had ridden down Bridge Street.

On his first Friday night, the whole family planned to go to Temple Emanu-El for services. At dinner that night Wolf said, "It's not going to be what you're used to. It's not even what I like. But it's the best we got here. The rabbi's a real modern thinker. But 80 percent of the Jews can live with him and his ways, so he stays."

Golda said, "Now Wolf, don't give Jack such a negative impression. The rabbi and rebbetzen are nice people. A lot of people think he has a lot of *saichel* because he adjusts for the problems of living in Montana."

"What kind of Temple is it?" Jack said.

Wolf waved his hand in the air as if swatting a fly. "Reform."

Jack didn't relish the thought of going to shul but he didn't want to do anything that might offend or upset his aunt and uncle.

The service wasn't too unpleasant—it was short and in English. The best part of the evening was the *Oneg Shabbat*. Cakes and cookies were displayed on a cloth-covered rectangular table in the social hall. At one end of the table two women sat and poured coffee and tea from two silver urns. At the other end was a large silver punch bowl. Jack ladled himself a glass of punch. Most people stood around in small groups talking. While he was munching a brownie and surveying the crowd, his aunt appeared accompanied by someone close to his own age.

Looking at the stranger she said, "This is Max Zimmerman from one of the finest families in Helena. Max, this is my nephew Jack."

Max was taller than Jack with dark brown hair and eyes. He was dressed in an expensive-looking seersucker suit styled like the ones Jack had seen in clothing store ads. Max had a thin straight nose and wore his thick hair brushed straight back from his forehead.

From the way Max smiled at his aunt and then rolled his eyes when he turned toward him, Jack knew they were going to be good friends. Jack grinned and held out his hand.

Outwardly Jack and Max had little in common. Max's father not only owned a clothing store but had an investment in one of the quartz gold mining companies, and he'd helped raise the money to build Temple Emanu-El. Max dressed in the best fabrics and the newest styles. He was two years older than Jack and had an air of cool confidence. By contrast, Jack felt his place in society as the son of a poor immigrant.

Lives in Exile

On their first evening together, Max and Jack had been taking a stroll around Helena when they passed a man lighting the street lamps and hollering about what movies were playing, what stores were having sales, and the general news of the day. Max called him over. "This is Sean Donovan, our 'spieler.' This here's Jack Marks. He's the Barr's, of Barr's Dry Goods, nephew. I'm giving him a tour of Helena."

"Pleased to meet you, young Jack," Sean Donovan said. "Have you been down to The Line yet?" Sean slapped his arm, "I know young Max will take you there right soon."

When Sean was a block away, Jack said, "He looked familiar."

"Maybe you saw him in the saloon," Max said. "When he finishes his rounds, he ends up in the saloon singing for beer. Got a pretty good tenor voice."

"What's 'The Line'?"

They walked downhill west of the railroad station. They came to the end of a street lit with so many red lights the cobblestones and the wooden buildings had a red cast to them. Several men sauntered up and down the road nodding to the windows.

"What's this?" Jack said.

Max said, "'The Line.' All the whores with madams live in these houses." He looked around and pointed. "At the end of the street are the shacks were the old ones live. I never bother with them. Don't you have a street like this where you come from?"

"Not that I know of."

"What kind of girl do you like?" Max started strolling down the street.

Jack followed, embarrassed and intrigued by the half-naked women sitting and standing in the windows. "I like all kinds."

Max tipped his hat to one of them.

The girl leaned forward and gave them a good view of her cleavage.

"That one has bosoms like watermelons," Max said, "and she doesn't like being tickled. For myself I find brunettes with small bosoms are the most passionate. There's a girl a few doors down on the left likes to ride you like a horse. What sort do you favor?"

Jack took another look at the one with bosoms like watermelons. She pulled down her top and gave them a full view. "I favor them all," he said.

Max chuckled and waved. "Do you prefer blondes or brunettes, large bosoms or small?"

Jack mentally ran through his French postcard collection. They all aroused him. He said, "I like them all."

Max turned to look at Jack. "You're a virgin." He paused as if reassessing Jack. "That's right. You're only fifteen. I'd forgotten you're two years younger than me. My father made an arrangement for me for my fifteenth birthday present."

"Birthdays weren't celebrated where I lived."

"My father picked one who was my age and hadn't been at it too long, so her body and her face were still attractive. Her breasts were shaped like grapes. Tasted like them, too. She was thrilled to be my first. She's gone now. Ran off with some miner, I heard."

Jack flushed. The idea of his own father arranging a date with a prostitute for him as a birthday present was unimaginable. When he'd met Mr. Zimmerman, he seemed like a regular father.

"I guess I'll have to pick someone for you," Max said. "I'll treat."

Jack's felt his stomach do a flip. He'd always fantasized his first time, but this was happening too quickly. What could he say? "It's a little late tonight. My aunt is expecting me home soon."

"You're right. Your first time shouldn't be on a whim. It should be planned."

Jack spent the next four nights in anxious anticipation. Finally, on the appointed night, he waited in front of the store for Max, who said, "After extensive research I have made my choice. She's young, beautiful, and very skillful. You can thank me afterwards."

He accompanied Jack to a brick house with a fat pink cupid over the door and introduced him to Liza. She took his hand in hers and pulled him along after her up the stairs and into her room. The air was perfumed with roses. The first thing that caught Jack's eye in the candle-lit room was the bare bed with a dark wooden headboard and footboard. There was no blanket or top sheet, only two pillows. In the corner stood a washstand with a bowl, pitcher, a few towels. A sofa and two occasional chairs covered in red horsehair were grouped near the piano at the opposite end of the room. In between was a fireplace on one wall and a dresser on the other. A vase of flowers sat on the piano and another on the mantel.

The evening began with Liza playing the piano and singing "Frankie and Johnnie" in a very sensual, low, throaty voice. Jack felt like he was in the middle of one of the romance serials he used to scoff at. He couldn't take his eyes off Liza, and her voice blocked out all thought. Afterwards she stood and allowed first her robe and then her gown to fall off her shoulders.

Her skin was so pale and translucent, Jack thought he could see through it. At first he was afraid to touch her for fear he would puncture her shell. She soon took over and guided his hands to her breast. Her curly golden hair hung down to her waist. When she tossed it around her shoulders, the ringlets veiled her large pointed breasts. He liked the way her hair tickled his shoulders when she bent over him in bed. Max had even arranged for a bottle of champagne and cake, which Liza served him on a china plate when they finished.

Emerging onto the street, he felt as if the world had been changed forever. Nothing would ever be the same—the stars sparkled, the moon gleamed, the red lights dazzled. He was a man.

Jack couldn't get enough of Liza. He returned as often as he could. But she was expensive—the majority of girls charged fifty cents, Liza, a dollar. Max tried to get him to go with other girls, but Jack would have none of it.

Chapter Five

Helena, Montana

1909 - 1911

On Saturday evening, October 23rd, 1909, a year-and-a-half later, Jack and Max sat on the bench in front of Wolf and Golda's store.

"Let's go to the movies tonight," Jack said. " The spieler called that *The Count of Monte Cristo* is playing at the Rialto. I'm in the mood for an action picture."

Max loved to tease. "I'd rather see if Liza is busy tonight." She was still Jack's favorite. "There's always action down there."

"I don't want to spend the buck. I'd rather go to Station Street, if it's not going to be the movies. We can have a beer and listen to old Sean Donovan sing. I'm kind of broke tonight."

"What're you saving your money for?" Max asked.

"I'm thinking of taking a trip back to Washington to see my family next summer. It'll be two years since I left."

He had only the money his aunt and uncle could pay him. No prosperous future was, as yet, in the offing.

When they stepped into the Station Street Saloon, Sean Donovan was finishing "Old Black Joe." He stood next to the piano with a group of five or six men around him. As he held the last note, someone handed him a beer and suggested, "The Girl I Left Behind." The piano player started the introduction, and Sean, after a long guzzle, sang again. The more Sean drank the fuller his voice became. Jack estimated he'd already had five beers. Pretty soon he'd be crying through all the songs.

Toward the back of the saloon, the dealer in a poker game dealt cards to a group sitting at the large, round wooden table. One of the players took aim and sent a stream of spit into the brass spittoon. Most of the patrons leaned against the brass rail at the bar, drank beer, and chatted with their neighbors.

Jack and Max sauntered up to the bar, each placed a foot on the bottom rail. Jack shouted, "Two beers, Joe," and held up two fingers to the bartender. When Joe approached with the beers, they each plunked down a nickel. Jack turned his back to the bar to blow the foam onto the sawdust floor.

The Station Street Saloon hadn't changed since he'd come to town. Whatever the color of the walls originally, they were now dark from the grime of cigarette smoke. At any time of day, the establishment smelled sour of stale beer. On his first visit to the saloon, Jack had found the purpose for the sawdust—to keep the floor dry. When he tried to blow the foam, as was the local custom, it dribbled down the side of the glass. Max had roared. Now Jack could blow with the best of them.

He watched the film gleam in the dull light until it was absorbed into the sawdust, then he surveyed the others standing near him while he waited for the alcohol warmth to spread from his belly. The Saturday night regulars were there, nearly all bachelors and miners. In the mirror over the bar Jack saw a stranger standing next to him. He turned to get a good look. The man was a few years older than Jack with long blond hair, dressed in corduroy pants and heavy shoes.

"New in town?" Jack asked.

"Yeah. Trappin' over in Minnesota when the big fire broke out last summer. Ran for my life. Heard the fires were spreadin' north so headed west. Ended up here."

Max leaned forward and looked around Jack at the stranger. "Heard those lightning fires were real bad."

"Terrible smell of smoke. Sky like night all the time."

"What you been doing since?" Jack asked.

"Workin' my way west. Thought to try a hand at some minin' for a while over at Virginia City. But money's run out, and this is far as I got."

"There are a couple of quartz gold mines around here," Max said. "Bet you could get a job."

Lives in Exile

The stranger took a swallow of his beer and said, "Don't fancy workin' for a company much. Rather be on my own. But since it's October and I ain't got no money, been thinkin' that's what I should do."

"I'm Jack Marks, and this is Max Zimmerman."

"Tom Baker. Glad to meet you."

"I hear they're looking for miners over at Helena Mining," Jack said.

Tom pointed toward an empty table. "You boys like to sit over there, play a game of pinochle, and talk a while? Gettin' tired of standin' here talkin' to myself."

"How do you play three-handed pinochle?" Max asked.

"Same as four-handed. Played all the time with Pa and my brother." Tom asked the bartender for a deck, ordered a fresh round for them. They took their glasses and sat at a square wooden table. Tom shuffled five times and then dealt three cards at a time to each of them until they had fifteen cards each. After each round of dealing, he put a card in the "kitty." Tom won the bidding, took the kitty, and announced hearts as the trump. Tom and Max each ponied up a nickel for the set.

Max asked Tom, "How long were you in Minnesota?"

"Born on a farm there. Ma died when I was a baby. Pa worked me and my older brother hard. Just decided to take off when I was thirteen. My brother didn't want to go. He felt kinda sorry for Pa."

"What'd you do?" Max said,

"Worked different places, mainly sweepin' and shelvin', cleanin' up saloons. One day hooked up with a trapper. Taught me everythin' I needed to know. Worked with him couple years. Liked the life. At eighteen, started trappin' on my own." Tom shrugged. "Where're you from, Jack?"

"Washington, D.C. Have two brothers and a sister plus my parents back there."

Tom won the first hand and started dealing the second. Max ordered a pitcher of beer.

When they'd finished the bidding, Tom asked Jack, "What'd you do back there?"

"My parents own a grocery store. Us kids took turns working after school, all day Saturday, and half-day Sundays—doing the chores, you know."

"Why'd you leave?"

By this time the beer had swelled through Jack's blood and made his body feel released, including his tongue. Jack told him about the school he went to and how everybody was divided up into groups according to their ethnic background. "Of course, there were no coloreds in my school. They went to their own school, but they used to fight like everybody else in their own gangs on the playgrounds and in the alleys."

"Some of the people helped me most were coloreds," Tom said.

"There was no mixing in Washington—in schools, bars, or anywhere. You had to stick with your own and be ready to defend yourself all the time."

"So, you two Jewish?"

Jack hadn't meant to tell this stranger he was Jewish. Back in Washington when he'd been asked a question like that, it was usually followed by an obscenity, which led to a brawl. The beer was loosening the muscles that held the anger in its place. He tried to keep the anger clenched inside to no avail. The urge to stand up and call out this stranger was too strong. He threw his cards down on the table and started to rise.

Max put a hand on his arm. "What of it?"

Tom stayed seated and put up his hands in a calming gesture. "Nothin', nothin' really. Just never met any Jews before that I know of. Don't mean nothin' to me."

Jack studied Tom's bloodshot eyes and even in his inebriated state could detect no animosity there. Jack settled back down.

Tom held out his hand.

Jack clasped it. His heart slowed to a normal beat again and his belly flopped back into its place.

Max gathered up the cards. "I think it's my turn to deal." He passed out the cards. "A man came by to see my grandmother when she was organizing a dinner to raise money to build the new opera house. He said he wanted to be placed at 'a table on the floor,' meaning near the dance floor. But my grandmother's English wasn't so good and she misunderstood." Max imitated his grandmother's accent, "'I'll be glad to see that all four legs of your table touch the floor.'"

Max and Tom laughed.

"Bet your grandmother understood and was pullin' the man's leg," Tom said,

"I think you're right."

Tom held up the pitcher as a signal to the bartender. "I'll buy this round."

Jack picked up his cards. "Let's bid."

After the bidding was over and the melds made, Max said, "Have you heard the one about the man whose family was so poor he had to quit school and work to help support his younger brothers and sisters? He never learned to read. So, when he married and started doing business, he signed his checks, 'XX.' He soon prospered and was a very rich man. One day he got a call from his banker, 'Mr. Smith, I need to ask you about this check we have here. We aren't sure you signed it. All these years, you've been signing your checks, 'XX,' this one is signed with three Xs.' Mr. Smith said, 'Since I've become so wealthy, my wife thinks I ought to have a middle name.'"

Even Jack chuckled at that one. "Sorry I got so upset."

Tom swatted him on the shoulder. "Let's forget it."

After they said good-night to Tom and started walking uphill toward Barr's Dry Goods, Max said, "What the hell was that all about?"

"What?"

"You were ready to slug him cause he asked if we were Jewish."

"Guess I haven't rid myself of all the old stuff from Washington. I though he was about to call us kikes or worse."

"I thought you knew things are different here. I can only think of one time when someone called me a name because I was Jewish."

"He's not from around here, but you're right. I shouldn't beat the pistol."

People did mix here. Jack guessed that was because nobody had lived in Helena very long. It wasn't like Washington where a new immigrant group was always replacing an old one which caused conflicts between those who hadn't made enough to move on and the new ambitious ones.

On Monday morning Tom got a job at the mining company, and the three young men started spending all their free time together. Tom lived the life Jack had been dreaming of—all on his own, taking care of himself, responsible to no one, going wherever life took him. Jack envied him his courage.

He realized he was closer to being on his own, but Golda had been going to Temple more Friday nights, and kept suggesting various girls to Jack. She'd even started hinting it was time he started keeping company with some nice Jewish girl and thinking about settling down. Getting involved with a girl was the last thing he wanted. He'd scrupulously avoided entanglements. He never danced with anyone more than twice at any social, and he never walked any girl home. Golda had suggested there might be room for him in the business. Jack doubted that. There couldn't be enough profit to share with another family and, anyway, that's not what Jack wanted. That's why he'd left Washington.

When Jack told Max about his aunt's nudging, Max said, "You think you got it bad. My mother invited the rabbi over for Rosh Hashanah dinner so I could meet his daughter."

Jack chuckled.

"Rachel's nice enough," Max said, "but if my mother thinks I want to marry into a rabbi's family, she's got another thought coming. It's bad enough I have to show up at Temple on the holidays. I couldn't stand having to sit there every Friday night."

From the beginning, Jack and Max set out to show their new friend all there was to do and see in Helena. Sometimes, the trio went to see the latest play at the Palace, but they preferred the movies at the Rialto or the Empress. They liked to sit in the balcony and boo when the villain captured the heroine, imprisoned her in a shack and placed a keg of dynamite with a burning fuse near her chair. They cheered when the hero rushed in, stamped out the fuse, clasped the heroine to his chest, and finally chased the villain out of town.

Tom especially liked the plays where the villain made the woman pregnant and then refused to help her. The hero always beat up the villain in the last act of those dramas. Jack couldn't figure out what about those stories appealed to Tom. He liked them least.

One night a couple of months later while Golda cleaned up in the kitchen after dinner and the children played with their toys, Wolf and Jack sat at the table. Wolf massaged his beard, "Most people in Helena are pretty tolerant of the behavior of the young men because there aren't too many young women around. But you and young Zimmerman and this miner fellow are developing quite a reputation. People are talking. Max Zimmerman won't have any trouble since his father is a big *macher*. But you don't have that advantage." Wolf lit his cigar.

Jack squirmed in his seat. "We're just having a good time. We're not bothering anybody."

Wolf blew a ring of smoke above his head. "As far as I know, Aunt Golda hasn't heard the gossip. But I'm sure some well-meaning *yente* is bound to tell. Then she'll feel she has to write your mother. I don't think you want that. You're a good worker, Jack. I like having you in the store, and it has made life easier for Aunt Golda, but you've got to think about your future and our reputation."

Jack shrugged. What did his uncle want? The sales were always higher when Jack was in the store. "I don't want to cause any trouble. I just want to have a good time. Sitting around reading books and talking evenings makes me restless."

"It's hard for me to understand, Jack. When I was your age, in the old country, we always worried about having enough food to eat and what new rules the *goyim* were going to think up next. Life was a struggle every day. It is so much better here in America."

The old country, the old country . . . how many times had Jack heard the same thing from his mother? "I appreciate everything you and Aunt Golda have done for me." Inside, Jack seethed, the nerve of Wolf, threatening him like that.

Over the next week Jack calculated how much money he'd need to leave Helena. He didn't know where he wanted to go, but he needed money for a train ticket and a hotel room and meals before he got a new job. Then he'd need money to rent a room once he got the job. His aunt and uncle knew he was saving for a trip to Washington which he could use as his excuse. Then he'd leave for somewhere else. The only person he'd tell would be Max.

The problem was he was having a hard time saving since Tom had come to town. If he told Max his plan, maybe Max would help by not suggesting such expensive evenings.

Then one night Tom said, "How 'bout takin' an apartment together? Tired of livin' in the boardin' house. Figure that with three sharin', wouldn't cost no more. What do you say?"

Jack looked at Max.

Max shrugged.

In his mind Jack assessed how this would affect his plans to leave town. On the one hand paying rent meant he wouldn't be able to save as much. On the other hand he'd be able to get away from Wolf and Golda's sooner. Maybe he wouldn't need to leave Helena. "I sure would like to, but I'd have to ask my aunt and uncle for more pay since they give me room and board."

"Point out how much they'd be savin' on feedin' you," Tom chuckled. "Can't be fun sharin' a room with a three-year-old."

"You got that right," Jack said. "Max, think you could swing it?"

"My mother's idea," Max chortled, "is that I live at home until I get married. Right now she has her eye on Sarah, the pharmacist's daughter. But I'll talk to my father. He thinks I should 'sow my oats.' I'm sure he'll understand and give me a raise."

"Great," said Tom. "Let's look tomorrow after work."

They found a furnished apartment to rent. The landlord was willing to put in a bunk bed and a single bed in the bedroom.

Jack chose to approach Wolf rather than Golda because he calculated he had a better chance of getting Wolf to agree. He waited until they were alone in the store and he'd made a good sale, hoping that would put Wolf in a generous mood. As Jack told him about the plan and the apartment, Wolf appeared to like the idea because he smiled and nodded his head, but when Jack ended his monologue with a request for a pay raise, Wolf frowned. Wolf stroked his beard for a few moments and then offered an extra dollar every week. In advance, Jack had figured the minimum he needed for rent and food was a dollar. He'd been hoping for a buck and a quarter but decided not to press his luck, so he shook hands with Wolf.

That night Jack told Golda about the apartment while he was drying the dishes. She sighed and looked as if she was going to cry. She said, "I knew the time was going to come when you'd want to be out on your own, but I hoped it would've been when you were getting married instead of moving in with friends."

Jack shrugged.

Soon Jack and Tom were going to The Line by themselves. Max, with strong nudging from his mother, took up with Sarah and spent several evenings a week keeping company with her. Jack visited Liza as often as he could afford her. She frequently played the piano for him, singing her favorite, "Turkey in the Straw." Her deep, throaty voice still appealed to him. When she sang, it seemed they were the only two people in the world. Even after two years, her breasts and translucent skin tantalized him. Liza giggled when she rubbed her nose and lips against his chest. The hair on Jack's head was straight but the black hair on his chest was tightly curled and it tickled. He loved to pull his hands through her curly golden hair. His passion rose when her breasts skimmed across his chest.

One night, in October 1910, when he could hear rain rattling the tin roof, Liza finished a song and came over to where he was sitting propped up in bed. She touched him gently, rubbing his neck first, then brushing his ear and neck with her lips. He could hear the sound of trees straining in the wind. He felt warm and comfortable. When she pressed against him, he could feel the softness of her legs and belly. She slid beneath him and their rhythms merged. He lost consciousness of his own body. Later, he awoke with her naked body pressed against his. Asleep, she looked so innocent and appealing. Jack wanted to be a hero, like in the movies, rescuing Liza from her life of prostitution. He moved his leg, and she opened her eyes.

Impulsively he said, "Let's get an apartment together. I'll take care of you and you'll take care of me. What do you say?"

She looked at him as if he were crazy, pulled the sheets out from under her, and sat up. She brushed him off with a wave of her hand and swung her legs over the side of the bed, turning her alluring back toward him. "Don't be silly. Do you think I'd want to clean your house, wash your laundry, and cook your meals? What would I get out of it?"

He sidled over to her, flung his arms around her, squeezed tightly, and whispered into her rose-scented hair. "You wouldn't have strange men putting their hands on you, and I'd take care of you."

She put her chin on her chest. "Are you some rich man who can afford to buy me as many pretty dresses as I want from Zimmerman's? Like I buy for myself now?" She pulled his arms from around her. "No. I'd have to scrimp and save just to buy one pretty dress. That's not the life I want."

In truth, Jack could have made persuasive arguments about love, commitment, and a family. But when he thought of what his family in Helena and Washington would say, the would-be-hero remained silent. He shook his head, gathered his clothes, got dressed, and left. He'd have to be content with the visits as he could afford.

* * * * * * *

On April 22, 1911, the young men decided to treat themselves to a festive dinner to celebrate the approaching spring. Dressed in their best suits, they presented themselves at the Helena Hotel dining room. The maitre d' ushered them into a private room, to a table set with a white cloth, silverware, cloth napkins, a glass of toothpicks, a bottle of ketchup, and another of Worcestershire sauce. It smelled of laundry detergent and bleach, mixed with the scent of freshly-picked wild lilacs. They chose wild chicken, which the waiter informed them the owner shot that very afternoon. Max suggested champagne.

After they toasted the warm weather to come, Tom said, "Been thinkin' of going north this summer to Canada to trap. Enjoyable livin' with you boys this last year-and-a-half, but I want to be my own boss and on my own schedule. Trappin's a hard life but you got nobody tellin' you what to do. How 'bout you boys comin' with me? Could teach you how to track and set traps."

Max leaned forward. "I've decided to ask Sarah to marry me after the dance next Saturday night. I might as well take the plunge. If she accepts, I won't be going."

"Wow." Jack sat back in his chair. "That's a big step. Are you sure?"

"I think she's the one for me. My father wants to make me a partner and change the store name to Zimmerman and Son. He thinks we can increase business if he goes on a buying trip to New York this summer. If things go well, we might even expand." He put his arms on the table and played with his fork. "There's a small house not too far out of town he's willing to help me buy. I guess everything is pretty much settled if Sarah is willing. I'm planning on talking to her father Saturday afternoon."

"That leaves me kind of high and dry." Jack recovered enough to offer a toast to Max, the groom, on his good fortune.

"Tom, I want you to be in Helena for my wedding. Jack, I'm counting on you to be my best man."

"That's a great honor, Max."

Tom punched Jack's arm. "So . . . comin' with me?"

"What're your plans? I thought trapping was done in winter."

"A fella at the mine said there's good trappin' north of this town called Regina in Saskatchewan. Plannin' on goin' up there at the end of May to check out the area and get my traps fixed up before settin' out for the season. There's lots work to be done before you start haulin' in the furs."

Jack drew lines on the tablecloth with his fingers. "I don't think I'm interested in trapping. But I'll travel as far as this Regina with you. I'd like to see what this country up north is all about."

"You'll be back to be my best man, right?" asked Max.

"Tell me where and when and I'll be here," Jack said more boldly, now that he'd made a decision.

When he told his aunt and uncle the next night at dinner Aunt Golda said, "I don't know, Jackie. I've heard things are wild up north in those Canadian towns. And what are we going to do without you? You've learned all the stock and you know what the customers want even when they don't."

"You'll find someone even better, I'm sure," Jack said,

"A young man has to find his own way," Uncle Wolf said. "Your mind seems to have been somewhere else lately. You've been late many mornings and anxious to leave each evening."

Jack caught the perturbed look Aunt Golda gave to Uncle Wolf. Even after Jack announced he was leaving, his uncle couldn't resist making a nasty remark. He was glad to be moving on.

Tom and Jack spent many evenings planning their trip. Tom suggested they pool their savings and buy things they could resell in Regina at a profit. "People up north are always anxious for pretty things."

To begin with, they needed to buy a wagon and mules. They'd be able to take turns driving, since Jack had learned all about wagons and mules on sales trips he and Wolf made several times a year to remote mining camps. With whatever they had left, he suggested they buy jewelry and small household items.

Tom asked Jack to find out which trails to follow and how to get to Regina. Jack estimated the trip would take two weeks. First, they would travel north, following the river to Great Falls, Montana, and from there further north to Medicine Hat in Alberta. Then they would head straight east to Regina.

On May 21, 1911, Jack hugged his aunt and Max, kissed his cousins, shook hands with his uncle, and climbed in the wagon next to Tom. He wore the high heeled boots that had been a gift from Golda and Wolf his first Chanukah in Helena, Levi jeans, a denim shirt, and his brand-new black Stetson. He was no longer that easterner who had gotten off the train three years ago. His future shone as brightly as the sun which burned high in the sky. He saw no clouds in the heavens or on his horizon.

Chapter Six

Saskatchewan

1911-1915

Jack and Tom shared the job of driving the wagon. The roads followed streams and ancient trails across mountain gaps and wide valleys, through evergreen forests carpeted with layers of pine needles.

In the evenings, Jack worked on setting up the camp while Tom went off to shoot a rabbit, a blue grouse, or even a wild turkey. Tom rarely needed a second shot. When Jack heard a blast, he knew dinner was on the way. While they ate Tom explained how to recognize signs and signals of animals. Jack tried to remember every word.

Freer than he'd ever been in his life, Jack relished every moment of the journey. In his blanket roll with a travel bag for a pillow, he contemplated the stars, wondering how long they'd been hanging up there and how far away they were. He didn't know if the birds' chirping or the pink glow of dawn woke him, but he loved to lie in his bedroll, shiver in the chill, and watch the mist rise off the meadows and burn away with the sun.

On the fifth day of the trip Tom let Jack creep along behind him during the hunt. Jack marveled how in one motion Tom could cock the hammer, raise the gun, sight along the barrel, and pull the trigger. That evening, walking back to their camp with the dead rabbit, Tom said, "How'd you'd like to learn to shoot?"

Thinking it would be easy, Jack said, "I'd like it fine."

After dinner Tom picked up the shotgun and said, "This here's a basic side-by-side double barrel. First thing, when anybody hands you a gun, break it open and make sure it's not loaded. That's a rule. If'n they don't, you know they're amateur. Here."

Jack took the gun and imitated Tom as he pantomimed working the hinge at the back of the barrel.

Tom took the gun back. "These here shells are six shot. 'Bout the right size for rabbit, turkey, small game. Inside is the powder, a cap, and the pellets. You put shells in there." He pointed to the opening. "Don't load now." He closed the gun. "Pellets spread out in a pattern." Tom made a spreading out motion with his fingers and hands. "Too far away and you'll miss. Best distance is 'bout as far as that." He pointed to a tree fifteen yards away.

He showed Jack how to cock the hammers, raise the gun, place the butt plate against the front of his shoulder, his cheek along the stock, and put his finger on one trigger and then the other. After practicing a few times Jack got the hang of where his hands should be, but he had such a hard time closing one eye and sighting along the barrel, Tom finally decided he would have to learn to sight with both eyes open.

Tom said, "Main thing is you got to anticipate where the rabbit's going and aim slightly ahead of it. They move as fast as sinners running from the devil. If'n you sight on where they's at, by time pellets get there, damn thing's moved on."

Jack practiced all evening—cock, raise, shoulder, cheek, pull. Cock, raise, shoulder, cheek, pull. Finally his arms were so tired he had to quit.

That night Jack took out his mother's last letter from the cigar box. When Tom saw the box, he said, "Can I look at your French postcards?"

Jack laughed. "Sure, anytime." Jack was glad to have something special he could share with Tom. Jack unfolded the letter and read it by the light of the campfire while Tom made appreciative whistles and coos.

> Running from place to place will not help you find yourself. What you need to find is inside you. It is with you wherever you are. Measure yourself against others—those you admire and those you do not. Examine the choices you have made when life has brought you to a fork. Then you will know who you are and where your place is. Your family is waiting for you and hoping you will find your way back to us.

Somehow being out in the open made these things easier to think about. "I'm not running from place to place," he whispered. "I've only gone from Washington to Helena. I stayed for three years, for God's sake." When he thought of all the places Tom had been, he concluded

Lives in Exile

positively he hadn't been running around. So far he felt he'd made all the right choices. "I'm definitely not ready to go back. There's so much more to do and see."

The next evening Tom handed Jack the shotgun with a stern look. Jack broke it open to make sure it wasn't loaded. Then Tom handed him several shells to put in his pockets. Tom loaded his pockets too. With Tom pointing out signs along the way, they walked to an open bushy area. He instructed Jack to load the shells. They continued across the meadow, until they saw a rabbit hopping in the high grass. Jack did as he'd practiced. When he pulled the trigger, the kick knocked him back against a tree as if he'd been slugged hard on the shoulder by a three-hundred-pound brute. He rotated his shoulder and rubbed the area he was sure would be black and blue.

Tom said, "First thing, you yanked the trigger instead of pulled. Second, you didn't have the butt tight to your shoulder. Now you got a bruise." Tom kicked the dirt. "Made all the beginners' mistakes. My fault. Should've practiced shootin' at trees. Practice after dinner." Tom held out his hand for the gun.

Jack handed it to him and watched him break it open and reload the empty barrel.

Tom clapped Jack on his good shoulder. "Don't be looking so sad. It'll take a while 'fore you going be good 'nough to hit a rabbit."

"I know—Rome wasn't built in a day."

"Now you sound like Max."

In the evening, moths and flies flocked to their campfire. Both men kept a fly swatter next to him as they sat and talked. After they killed a bug, they swept it up on the flap of the swatter and dumped it in the flame and watched it spark like a shooting star. Tom told Jack the bugs in June were nothing compared to the bugs of July. To protect yourself you had to cover every inch of your body and even then some of the more ferocious ones bit you through the cloth. Jack wasn't looking forward to that experience.

He wondered about his life in Regina. He tried to figure out what he could do if he wasn't going to work in a store. He knew he was a good salesman. Maybe he'd keep the wagon after they sold the load of things they were carting to Regina. He could take special orders and travel to a larger town to fill those orders—become a traveling salesman of sorts.

The next evening they camped near a stream and fished for dinner. After they ate, Tom set up targets. Each time Jack anticipated the kick and jerked back. Tom stood right behind him and made him stay with it until he learned to squeeze the trigger and didn't flinch. Jack liked the satisfied feeling he had when he blew the bark off the trees.

Tom reminded him rabbits didn't stand still like trees. Jack spent several minutes swinging the gun in an arc as if he were chasing a rabbit.

Over the next few days Jack came close to hitting a rabbit. A few days later, a rabbit stopped and stood absolutely still next to a clump of grass. He bagged it.

Tom laughed. "You're one lucky son-of-a-gun, getting a rabbit to sit still and wait for you to kill it."

Nothing Tom said could take away the thrill. That dinner was one of the best he'd ever eaten.

"You get one on the run," Tom said, "and I'll pay for your first dinner in Regina."

Jack vowed that before the trip was over he'd do that.

The last night they camped out on the plain east of Moose Jaw next to a stream. When Jack spotted a rabbit, he cocked, raised, shouldered, sighted, and pulled the trigger. This time based on skill and experience, not luck, he killed a rabbit on the run. He whooped it up so hard, if his family could've seen him, they would've thought he turned into a *chasid* or a wild Indian.

Tom danced around the rabbit with him. "First night in Regina, dinner's on me. Didn't forget."

That night he sifted through the cigar box and found an article Yetta had cut out of the newspaper and sent him soon after he arrived in Helena.

> July 26. The German automobile Protos became the first to reach Paris in the grueling race from New York, but there was little reason to break out the schnapps. The Germans were penalized days for infractions along the way, thus assuring the American Thomas car of carrying off the top honors.
>
> The Protos motored into the French capital last night on a final run from Vladivostok. However, the Protos had been delayed in Idaho by repairs and thus was shipped by railroad from Pocatello to Seattle in order to sail with the Thomas car to Siberia. The Americans, meanwhile, had tried to go by way of Alaska but snow conditions forced a change in the route.
>
> The automobile race committee decided not to disqualify the Germans for the railroad trip but rather penalized them 15 days on the final leg to Paris. And the Thomas car received a 15-day allowance for its fruitless journey to Alaska and back.

The German driver, Lt. Koeppen, on leave from the Kaiser's army, concluded, "I wish the roads in America were as nice as the people. Altogether, the trip has been a great success."

Jack remembered that day in March when he'd come home after the brawl in the alley and read the article about Montague Roberts and the cars being loaded on the steamer—the day his mother agreed to talk to his father about going to Helena. He remembered how angry and frustrated he'd been then. Not now. Now he was sitting in the middle of the wilderness, living his dream. He felt like crowing. Even though he wasn't dressed in the touring coat and cap he'd wished for in Washington, his boots, Levis, and Stetson were excellent substitutes.

He wondered what his friends were doing—if Max Cohen was working in his father's tailor shop or if he'd gone to law school, if Sol Golden had married Hilda Wolpe. He'd ask his mother in his next letter. He knew what his brothers and sister were doing. They were working in the new, bigger store on Connecticut Avenue, Northwest. He shuddered. That could have been his fate, instead of hunting, fishing, and roaming the west.

Lying in his bedroll, he thought about the boy he'd been, who'd lived in Washington and worked in the grocery store, dreaming to be on his own. He didn't recognize that person anymore. He didn't know exactly who he was, but he could ride, fish, shoot, cook, care for animals. No one he knew in Washington could do those things. He could go anywhere and take care of himself—maybe not as well as Tom, but good enough. Life had brought him to a fork, and he'd chosen the right direction. He wasn't ready to go back home—not by a long shot.

Regina, the capital of Saskatchewan, popped up in the middle of the flat golden prairie. At the edge of town they passed the headquarters of the Royal Canadian Mountain Police. Sitting on a corral fence were several Mounties in red uniforms who gave them the once over. Jack and Tom saluted.

They rode slowly through town on streets of compacted dirt. The buildings were one-story and wooden. Glancing from side to side they glimpsed a post office, school, blacksmith shop, churches, several general and dry goods stores, and astonishingly, a newspaper office. In Regina they didn't have to rely on old Sean Donovan to cry out the news of the day. In the middle of town, at the intersection of Main and Capital Streets, was the masonry Capitol building, three stories high, taking up a whole block.

They drove all the way down Main Street then turned around and went back to City Hall. Tom suggested they ask the constable where they might find lodging. The officer directed them to Mrs. James, a ruddy-cheeked, gray-haired widow-lady with a ready smile.

Her whitewashed wooden house was four blocks off Main Street. She rented three bedrooms on the second floor and took in laundry. She showed them a clean, fairly large one with a four-poster bed, dresser, desk, rocking chair, and a mirror over the dresser. The walls were papered in a vine pattern with a light green background. The curtains were white. A floral still-life decorated the wall over the bed. The purple chenille bedspread matched the roses in the painting. Jack opened a dresser drawer. He smelled the sachet of dried flower petals before he spotted the packet in the back corner. He didn't want his underwear to be perfumed. He must have made a face because Mrs. James chuckled.

Her own bedroom was on the first floor along with the parlor and the dining room. Jack glanced around her parlor painted dark red and filled with curvy-backed furniture and heavy red drapes. On each end table sat a small metal lamp with a multicolored glass shade. Mrs. James proudly exhibited the photographs on her mantle in ornate wooden frames. One was of her deceased husband and the others of her two sons and their families, living in other parts of Canada. An upright piano took up most of the wall opposite the fireplace.

All the meals were served in the dining room furnished with a large oak table, matching chairs, and side board. The walls and drapes were a dark green. In the center of the table was a bowl of apples. In the kitchen, Mrs. James introduced them to her helper, Colleen, a young Irish immigrant whose family lived on a farm not too far outside of town.

When they'd finished the tour, Mrs. James said, "Well, lads, I have only the one room available right now. You're welcome to it for one dollar a week each."

"My friend will be leaving in a few weeks," Jack said. "What's the price for one?"

"Buck fifty including breakfast and supper."

"Maybe you'd like to swap the first week for something we have in our wagon," Tom said.

They showed her their wares. She picked a large soup pot and a strainer.

"These'll do just fine."

Jack opened the boxes of jewelry and made a show of picking out a large silver brooch which Mrs. James could wear in the center of her blouse along the collar line over her ample bosom. He held it up to her face. "Oh, Mrs. James, the brooch makes your beautiful blue eyes shine."

She laughed heartily, fluttered her eyelids. "You're a fibber." She traded the brooch for the second week.

Tom chortled. "Do ya' know of others who might want to buy household supplies or jewelry?"

"I'll help you draw up a route of farms you might try."

Tom paid for Jack's dinner, as promised, in a restaurant on Main Street. They spent the next two weeks traveling around the countryside selling their goods. On several afternoons, when they arrived back at the boarding house, someone was waiting who'd heard about them and had come to see what they had to sell. One evening Mrs. James invited several of her friends over to see the jewelry. Pretty soon they'd met a large portion of the population. Jack flattered the ladies and showed respect to the men.

In the end, they sold the mules and wagon. Jack didn't know what he was going to do. After the past two weeks, he knew that making a living by selling goods from the wagon was not for him. He should've known that after the trips to the mining camps with his uncle, but on the trip north he'd gotten carried away with romantic notions of what such a life could be like. Having to load and unload merchandise which had to be paid for in advance, plus the cost of care and feed for the mules, made the chance of profit very small. The reality of the slow pace of lonely travel from place to distant place didn't appeal to him.

While Tom spent a couple of days getting his traps ready, Jack looked for a job. He asked the Constable if he needed an assistant. The response was negative. He saw a couple "Wanted - Sales Clerk" signs in windows but resisted inquiring about them. One was in a dry goods store and one in a pharmacy. He saw those jobs as dead-ends. He considered going further north with Tom.

At breakfast the next morning, Jack asked Mrs. James. "Any ideas about where I could look for a job?"

She tapped her fingers on the table. "Just yesterday I was talking to Mrs. Johnson. You remember . . . she's the lady you sold the gold watch to . . . for her husband. He's the owner of the newspaper. I think you ought to go over to his office and see if he could use you."

He went right over to the newspaper and introduced himself.

Mr. Johnson said, "Are you the Jack Marks I've been hearing so much about?"

"Only if you've been hearing good things. I'm looking for work. Mrs. James suggested I try here."

Mr. Johnson chuckled. "That Mrs. James. She's quite a lady." Mr. Johnson motioned Jack to a chair next to his desk. "I need an assistant. You might fit the bill." He leaned forward. "What I need is someone to travel around the area selling advertising and distributing the papers. The pay is three dollars a week. I'll supply the horse and pay for its feed and board. If you don't have your own saddle, I can furnish one."

"How many advertisers do you have right now?"

Mr. Johnson pulled out a piece of paper from his top left drawer and handed him a list. "I'm hoping to double this over the next year."

Jack looked over the list. He was familiar with most of the businesses from his trips with Tom. "Where would I have to travel?"

Mr. Johnson opened the drawer again, pulled out a larger sheet of yellowing paper folded several times, and spread the map over his desk. With his finger, Mr. Johnson traced several routes for Jack to follow. "You'd sell and distribute from Thursday to Saturday and then again on Monday and Tuesday. We print on Wednesdays. I'd need your help running the presses and folding the papers. What do you think?"

"I promised a friend in Montana I'd be the best man at his wedding in October. So I'd need a few weeks off to make the trip."

"We can work that out. Anything else?"

Jack didn't know what questions to ask because he'd never known anybody with a job like this. The pay would certainly cover his expenses. "I'll take it." He wanted to shout "whoopee." This was the chance he'd been hoping for—a job that didn't mean working in a store.

July 4th, the day Tom left, was Jack's first day at work. When Tom was ready to go, he sat on his horse with all his paraphernalia draped around him and said, "Looks like you got yourself settled. I'll be back in time to go with you to Max's wedding. Take care."

Jack felt peculiar all day because he was alone in a strange place. Every July 4th he could remember he'd gone to watch a parade and listen to speeches by politicians. The evening ended with a picnic and fireworks. But this July 4th was like any other business day in Regina. It was a creepy feeling. He never imagined he'd feel this way.

Even though it was Tuesday, Mr. Johnson thought he ought to hang around the office and learn the things he would need to know to sell advertising, like ad sizes and prices. On Wednesday he helped with the printing. Thursday he started off on his route.

He worked hard all summer to prove himself to Mr. Johnson. Every week, one of the ten Jewish families in Regina invited him for dinner. He was always happy to go for some familiar food, but he carefully avoided entanglements with any of the eligible women. Most evenings he worked at the newspaper or had a beer with the "boys" at the saloon and played a hand or two of cards. Occasionally he patronized one of the prostitutes who doubled as waitresses at the saloon. He went to the vaudeville whenever a troupe came through town. At night he read from a novel for a half-hour before he went to sleep. On his sales trips and when he was invited out to dinner, he always carried a book to trade.

By the middle of September, when he hadn't seen or heard from Tom, he began to plan his trip to Max's October 22nd wedding. His best choice was to take the train west to Vancouver, another one south to Seattle, and a third east to Helena. The alternative of heading east through Saint Paul would take even longer. When Tom hadn't shown up by October 15th, he left a note and set off.

On this journey Jack brought several books including O. Henry's *The Four Million*. He was glad he'd brought a book of short stories since the scenery captured so much of his attention. At first the train crossed rolling prairies, then raging rivers, and finally sparkling ice fields high in the mountains, before entering vast forests of evergreens on the other side of the Rockies. In Manitoba, when the train stopped to take on water, a moose with a five-point rack moseyed up to the window. He and Jack studied each other for three minutes before the moose moved on.

Early one evening when he glanced up from his reading, he was startled to see a grizzly bear tearing apart the trash bin next to the water tower. When the bear finally ambled away, the train men left the cars to do their work. At night the northern lights put on a display more spectacular than any fireworks.

He wished he'd had time to explore the cities of Vancouver and Seattle. Instead he spent his time waiting for the next train. The closer and closer he got to Helena the more he thought of Liza. At night, he stared out the window and imagined her image reflected back at him.

When he got to the sidewalk in front of the station in Helena, he put his bags down and surveyed the town as he had on his arrival three years ago—the Station Street Saloon was still on the corner with its swinging doors. When he looked up the hill, he glimpsed the blue and red globes of Sarah's father's pharmacy window. He took the same hike up Main Street. As usual, the Levy Cigar Store wooden Indian waited to salute him. When he got to Barr's Dry Goods and walked in, he got the same greeting from his aunt. "*Oy vei, oy vei.* Wolf, it's Jackie." She was as glad to see him as she had been the first time. But this time the three children came running from the back room, calling his name and jumping up and down until it was their turn for a hug. His uncle even smiled when they shook hands. His aunt made stuffed cabbage for dinner. The sofa in the parlor was his bed now since Louis was using Jack's old one.

He and Max spent that first night at the Station Street Saloon. As usual, old Sean Donovan was singing for free beer. It was like old times between him and Max.

Jack told Max about the note he'd left. "I have a feeling Tom'll show up just in time for the ceremony."

"That would be exactly like him," Max said. "I wish I could've put you up at my parents' house. But with all the relatives coming . . ."

"I'll be all right."

"I bet you're itching to get down to The Line."

Jack shrugged. "It might be nice to see Liza and the other girls."

Max punched him lightly on the shoulder and laughed. "Liar, liar, pants on fire. You're sitting there trying to figure a way to ditch me and run on down there."

Jack's face turned red. "Okay, but I wasn't thinking about how to get rid of you, just how to get down there."

"I'll go with you."

"What would Sarah say?"

"What she doesn't know won't hurt her."

They stopped in front of the brick house to gaze at the fat pink cupid over the door. It was early so Liza was still in the parlor with the rest of the girls. In May, when they'd parted, she'd sobbed. Now she said, "Oh, it's you."

He'd been expecting her to run into his arms and kiss him passionately. The tone of her voice told him everything he needed to know about how she felt. The disappointment must have shown on his face because she strode over to him and put her arm through his. "Don't worry, honey. We'll have a good time tonight." She smiled.

He allowed her to lead him over to her madam who held out her hand. He withdrew his wallet from his breast pocket and handed her a dollar.

As they started up the stairs, he turned around to look for Max who was talking to two girls. Max waved.

When they got to Liza's room, she sat him down in one of her occasional chairs and sauntered over to the piano. "What was that song you liked so much?"

"Turkey in The Straw," he said lamely.

While she sang, he tried to recall why he believed she cared for him. She'd always acted so excited to see him. She listened to all his complaints about his uncle and always sympathized. She declared him handsome and great in bed. Had that all been an act? Was money all there was to it?

He tried to remember why he thought he'd cared for her. He listened to her singing—what a stupid song. And her voice—what was it he liked about her voice? He couldn't remember. Had he been such a fool to think he'd been important in her life?

When she finished her song, she sashayed toward him. On the way across the room she undid the tie on her robe and let the robe fall off her shoulders. Through her filmy white gown he could see her nipples. He remembered all the things he liked to do to her nipples. She bent over to move his legs apart and gave him a good view of her breasts while she ran her hand up his body from his crotch to his lips. Then she straddled his lap, undid his tie, unbuttoned his collar and shirt. For a few minutes she stroked his bare chest while she kissed him and nibbled on his ear. She took his hand and placed it on her breast. She stood up and holding his hand in place led him to the bed.

Before he left he assured her he'd be back. He knew, in fact, he'd be back several times because, despite his disappointment, she was still the best. As he walked to his aunt and uncle's he wondered what would've happened if she'd agreed to marry him. Nothing good, he judged. He'd been damn lucky.

The next day Max took him to see the house he and Sarah would share after the wedding. "So, how's good old Liza?"

"The same."

"Those Canadian girls must be really something."

"Let's drop the subject, okay?"

They went to the tailor to get Jack fitted for the suit and top hat he'd wear as best man. That night he had dinner at Sarah's house with her family. She and Max appeared very happy together. Jack wondered if he would ever find anyone to share his life.

He visited Liza that night without Max. He didn't know why but he wanted to impress her with how well he had done for himself. Maybe she'd regret turning him down a couple of years ago. He told her about his position as Assistant Editor in charge of advertising and how he owned three suits now. To dazzle her he left her an extra dollar on her dresser.

The wedding was held a few days later at Sarah's house under a *chuppah* held by Max's first cousins who'd come from San Francisco. Everyone shouted *mazel tov* when Max smashed the glass on his first try. The reception was in the dining room of the Helena Hotel.

Everyone asked Jack what he was doing in Regina. He was proud to tell them, although he must have said it fifty times. He looked prosperous in his new suit. Jack even overheard his uncle bragging about how well Jack was doing in Regina. Under the watchful eyes of their mothers, several of the single women openly flirted with him but he pretended not to notice. The next evening Sarah and Max took the train to San Francisco for their honeymoon. Jack was part of a large group gathered at the train station for the big send off. They sang *"Chusan, Challah, Mazel Tov"* and showered the bride and groom with rice.

After dinner he told his aunt he was going for a walk and, of course, ended up at the house with the pink cupid. The madam said, "Liza's been waiting for you up in her room. She's turned down everyone else tonight." She held out her hand.

He gave her a dollar.

She held out her hand again. "I said she's turned down everyone else tonight."

He realized he'd made a mistake being so generous the last time and thought about calling her bluff, but this was his last night so he put another dollar in her hand and started up the steps. In truth, he would have been very disappointed if Liza'd been busy. Then it hit him. What's this all about—giving up a sure payday on the chance I might show up? He stopped in front of her door and thought about pivoting and going back down the stairs, but then he'd have to face the madam and ask for his two bucks back. He wanted Liza and he was sure he could handle whatever it was she'd cooked up. He knocked.

"Come in," Liza called out. When he opened the door, she stood across the room with her hand on the fireplace mantle. She said, "Hi, sweetie. I've been waiting for you."

All of a sudden he was "sweetie."

She usually greeted him in her robe, but tonight she had on a long sheer red gown slit down the front almost to her waist and up the sides to the middle of her thighs. Her body appeared to throb as she walked toward him. She wore matching satin slippers and had her hair pulled back with a red ribbon. She put her arms around him and squeezed, pressing against his torso. She kissed him passionately.

He couldn't help himself. His body took over and responded.

"Let's get you more comfortable." She urged his coat off his shoulders.

He unbuttoned his pants.

When they finished, Jack was exhausted. He lay back and closed his eyes. He felt good. He felt calm. When her weight lifted off the bed, he opened his eyes and watched her parade across the room. Every few steps she turned and looked back at him. She wore nothing but her high-heeled satin slippers. From the piano top she lifted a plate of apples and several napkins.

She carried these as if they were an offering back to the bed and sat facing Jack with her legs extended to her side, high heels still on. She expertly peeled the apple and fed it to Jack one small piece at a time occasionally wiping his mouth with the napkin. Then she sauntered across the room again. This time she came back with a tray holding a decanter of brandy and two glasses. Jack pulled himself up. He liked this royal treatment. She set the tray on the bed and poured a glass for each of them. She handed one to Jack displaying her body to him. He enjoyed the show.

"A year or so ago," she said, " you made me a very attractive offer which I foolishly refused. Do you recall?"

He sniffed and then sipped the brandy. "What offer was that?"

She held the glass to her lips and looked over its edge at Jack. "You proposed marriage to me." She pouted. "Don't you remember?"

"I do." So this is it, he thought.

She sipped, taking her time. "If the offer's still good, I'd like to take you up on it."

Why was she interested now? What had changed? Where was the heroine in distress he wanted to rescue? Where was the woman he thought he needed to protect? If he turned her down flat, the evening would be over. "You know I'm living in Saskatchewan now."

She shifted her body toward him.

"I don't have a place of my own," he said. "I'm renting in a boarding house."

"You think it might work out?" She put her glass down on the night stand, took his glass and placed it next to hers, then snuggled up next to him.

"I hadn't thought about it recently." His voice was raspy.

She moved her body into position, poised over him. He grabbed her hips and pulled them toward him as he pushed up.

"We'll need a couple of rooms—one for my kid," she said.

Kid, kid? What was she talking about? He focused his mind on the coupling of their bodies and pushed himself into her as he came.

He fell back onto the bed, his eyes closed, breathing hard. She rolled off him and caressed his chest. He pushed her hand away. He needed to collect himself. He needed to get out of there.

After a few seconds, Liza said, "What do you say? You'll get a place for the two of us and my kid?"

"You have a kid?" He sat up and put his feet over the edge of the bed. While waiting for her answer, he held his breath.

"She's six years old."

He could breathe again, the child wasn't his. He walked over to the wash basin and cleaned himself off with the rag. "I don't think it'll work out, Liza. I've made promises to a woman I've met and I don't see how I could take you back with me to Regina."

Liza stood and put her hands on her hips. "You never mentioned another woman."

"I didn't see the need to. I paid you for your time."

Her face bloomed a bright red, and she turned her back.

He quickly put on his clothes, buttoning as he hurried toward the door. He put his hand on the door knob and turned to look at her. She still had her back to him—the back he'd once found so alluring. "Good-bye. Hope to see you when I'm in town again."

She didn't respond. He walked out. He wondered how she'd end up, how she'd leave this cupid-topped house. Would she still be young and pretty going off with a man, or would she become an old used-up whore in one of the shacks? He'd put his money on young and pretty.

Jack left the next day on the afternoon train. His aunt and cousins saw him off. He was glad to be on his way back to his new life in Regina.

When he came through the front door of the boarding house, he found a letter from Tom on the hall table. Tom had miscalculated the days and by the time he arrived in Regina it was too late to travel to Helena, so he'd already returned to his traps.

Over the next few years, Tom usually showed up in Regina at the beginning and end of the trapping season. The fur business was good and he had quite a stake. In the fall of 1914, when Jack walked into the restaurant where he was to meet Tom for dinner, he found Tom already there. The old shotgun was leaning against the table next to his seat.

After they sat, Tom pointed to the shotgun, "This is the gun you learned to shoot with. Been usin' it all these years, but finally decided to get myself a new one."

Jack smiled and put his hand over the barrel.

"Thought you might like to have it for your own," Tom said,

Jack's thoughts wandered to that night when he shot his first rabbit on the run. Mr. Johnson had given him a pistol to carry on his trips, but he'd love to have the shotgun. He smiled. "What do you want for it?"

"Now you've insulted me." He grinned to show he was kidding. "It's for a gift."

"A gift?"

"A kind of remembrance of the good time we had together all those years ago. You don't have to check—it's not loaded."

By 1915, Jack was living in Mrs. James' larger back bedroom which had a sofa, and an easy chair. He got letters from Max twice a year at Rosh Hashanah and Passover. Max and Sarah had produced two children in four years. Zimmerman & Sons was now a chain of three stores in three cities. Although Jack had a few friends, none had grown as close as Max or Tom.

As he traveled around selling advertising, he heard interesting stories. Mr. Johnson suggested he write them up for the paper and eventually gave Jack his own column. That year he'd written several articles about stray dogs in town and attacks on farm animals by roving packs. One evening, after scaring off a dog terrorizing a young girl, he concluded the town needed a dog catcher. He decided to make this proposal at the town meeting the next week. He wondered if he could stand up in front of the whole town and talk. It was one thing to sell an ad to one shop owner or shoes to an individual but quite another to persuade the whole town to adopt his idea. What if they thought his suggestion was stupid? He chose to approach it as if he was selling an ad to a reluctant customer, to explain his idea clearly, and be committed to his concept.

Evelyn Auerbach

When the mayor called on him, Jack rose with trembling knees and said, "I propose the town hire a dog catcher."

The mayor said, "Come to the podium to speak."

He hoped his knees wouldn't buckle as he strode the fifteen steps to the front. "When I travel around the area, I run into packs of dogs who have been abandoned or chased off and left to fend for themselves. They often find their way into town creating all kinds of trouble and nuisances. They get into garbage cans spreading the trash all over the streets. They chase house pets and bark at the children. Last week I had to rescue the Palmer girl who was cornered by a pack of wild dogs."

He paused for dramatic effect.

"The town needs a dog catcher to protect its citizens." When he sat, his palms were wet and his heart thumped, but he'd said it all. When his ears stopped buzzing, he was amazed to hear a general murmur of approval.

After a debate, in which many others took up his cause, the assembled residents voted to make this an elected part-time position that would pay five dollars per month.

The next morning Mr. Johnson said, "I'm proud of you, Jack. You were very persuasive at the meeting. I hope you're planning to run for the job. You'll be a shoo-in. I'll write an editorial in your favor."

Jack ran unopposed and at the age of twenty-two was one of the best known and most popular citizens of Regina. He got up early every morning and strolled through town looking for strays, shotgun in hand. He developed traps and devices for capturing dogs and maneuvering them into the pens he'd built. He kept the strays for a while until he could find a home for them. If he didn't place them within a reasonable amount of time, he took them to a spot a mile outside of town, shot them, and then burned their bodies.

One evening, after he'd been dog catcher for six months, he looked through the box in which he kept the letters from his family. He came across the letter from his mother. Well, Mama, he thought, I have found my place. I don't have to wander anymore. This is what I was looking for—respect and acceptance.

Chapter Seven

Boarders

1916 - 1917

One night in the summer of 1916, Jack walked into the dining room and Mrs. James said, "This is Miss Bessie Swartz from Saskatoon, my cousin's daughter, who's come to teach school."

Miss Swartz smiled cautiously at Jack. Her luscious lips were full, her sad eyes blue, the heart-shaped face framed by reddish-brown curls. His heart faltered.

"Hello." Her voice was soft and warm.

Jack wanted to sound intelligent, like a newspaper professional, and say: *We certainly are glad you arrived. Miss Tolson can't teach the sixty children expected this term. I'm sure she'll be glad to split the group into two. Have you had experience?* Instead he took his chair which was next to hers and said, "Did you arrive on this afternoon's train?"

She nodded yes and did not utter a word the whole meal. The conversation among the rest of the diners turned to events in Regina. Several times he glanced at her and thought she'd been looking at him, too.

After dessert she said, "Excuse me," and immediately went upstairs to her room.

Jack looked at Mrs. James with raised eyebrows, his head cocked to the side. In return, she glared straight at him with tightly pursed lips. He concluded no amount of charm was going to pry any information out of her. He'd bide his time.

In bed that night, as he composed the story he would write for the paper to announce the arrival of the new school teacher, he heard a mewing like the sound of a baby animal crying for its mother. He got up and looked out the window at the beautiful full moon. Nothing out there. Should he get dressed and go search for the wounded or distressed animal? Since he was Regina's first and only dog catcher, he wasn't sure of his responsibility in this situation. He peered through the window again. He couldn't see anything, even in the shadows. The whimpering stopped. Maybe the mother cat had returned. Grateful, Jack returned to bed.

The next morning he said, "Mrs. James did you hear strange noises in the night—like a kitten crying?"

"No."

"I wonder if Miss Swartz did?"

He didn't get the chance to ask because she didn't come down before he left to make his morning rounds.

After his dog catcher duties, he stopped by Miss Tolson's house, the School Board president's store, and the Lutheran Church parsonage to gather information for his article. The information he gleaned was meager. He had to go with what he had.

NEW TEACHER ARRIVES

On Tuesday, August 20, 1916, Miss Bessie Swartz arrived in Regina to begin her duties as elementary school teacher at the Regina Public School. Miss Emma Tolson will continue to teach the upper grades. Miss Swartz, a Saskatoon native, most recently taught in the Sunday school of the Saskatoon Lutheran Church.

Even though news of the war in Europe dominated the front page, Jack found a space below the fold for the announcement.

At dinner that night, he said to Miss Swartz, "I hope you'll be pleased with the article I wrote about your arrival."

Miss Swartz looked at her plate. Jack was puzzled. Later he caught her glancing at him. He was struck again by her vulnerable beauty.

That night he heard the whimpering noises again. He got out of bed and scanned the area. *What the hell was going on here?* He concluded he had to investigate. As he tiptoed past Miss Swartz's room, shotgun at his side, he realized the sound was coming from behind her door. Holding his breath, he stood listening to her weeping for several minutes. Should he do something, or, should he pretend he hadn't heard? He was tempted to fling open her door and take her in his arms and comfort her as his movie heroes always did when the heroine was in trouble. Real life was more complicated. He crept back to his room.

The next few nights, when he heard her sobs, he imagined scenarios that would lead a woman of Miss Swartz's loveliness to leave her home, come to Regina, and cry in her bed every night. First he surmised a fiancé must have run off with another woman and left her humiliated and betrayed. In another scenario her father had been accused of a terrible crime and, though innocent, sent to prison. In his imagining he went to Saskatoon and uncovered the real perpetrator and then married Miss Swartz.

In his nightly fantasies, he rescued her from her sadness. He imagined their kiss after he told her everything would be all right. He imagined making love to her, passionately and fervently, as he did with Liza. He dreamed of caressing the soft skin on her face, her breasts, her hips. Some nights, he could almost feel her body against his. He could see her radiant smile and how her gorgeous blue eyes would shine after they made love. When his craving for her became too distracting, he spent fifty cents on the whore at the saloon.

At dinner, he had to force himself not to gawk. When he was alone with Mrs. James, he tried to casually ask questions about Miss Swartz, but he didn't find out very much. Mrs. James put herself between him and Miss Swartz as much as possible. Over the weeks Bessie's nighttime crying diminished and eventually stopped.

She spent the evenings in the parlor with Jack and the other borders, a couple who rented the front bedroom. Each member of the group took turns reading to the others from novels. When Bessie took her turn she read in a soft, melodious voice with wonderful inflection and dramatic affect. Jack sat mesmerized.

In the afternoons, when Jack returned from work, he often heard Miss Swartz practicing the piano. One evening, after several months, the parlor group persuaded her to play for them. She giggled when they applauded and then quickly covered her mouth with her delicate hand, stood, and curtsied to her audience. This was the first time Jack had heard her laugh.

Sundays, Jack timed his morning stroll so he would pass the Lutheran church as services concluded. He hoped to offer himself as her escort home, but, she was always occupied with one or two of the neighbors or the ever-watchful Mrs. James. So he tipped his hat, smiled, and kept walking.

Jack tried not to look at her with the longing he felt. Was he in love with her? Was this what love felt like?

From conversations he accumulated details of her life which he fit into the life story he'd created in his imagination. If they were at dinner or in the parlor and he turned around suddenly and found her looking at him, she would blush. At those times he would conclude she was interested in him, too. Other times her eyes passed right over him. Then he thought she merely observed him as a fixture in her universe and he doubted she was aware of his interest. Jack was bewildered and fascinated.

One evening in June 1917, as he walked down the street he saw Mrs. James out in the yard. She appeared to be waiting for him.

"As you know the boarders moved out of the front bedroom," she began abruptly. "I thought this would be a good opportunity to visit my son, William, in Vancouver, for a few weeks. I want to trust you, Jack Marks, to behave like a gentleman. You and my cousin, Bessie, will be here all alone." She held up her hand to stop Jack as he tried to interrupt. "I am not blind, Mr. Marks. This is Hilda James you're dealing with. I see the looks you send her way."

Mrs. James wagged her finger at him. "Her reputation must be unstained if she is to continue to teach school here in Regina. I'd hoped Colleen could spend the night but she must go home to help her mother with her ailing father. She will continue to make the meals and clean the house. Can I depend on you, Mr. Marks?"

"Of course you can, Mrs. James. I will be the soul of propriety." It occurred to him it was summer and the school year over. He wondered why Miss Swartz wasn't going to visit her family in Saskatoon. At least she hadn't mentioned going and obviously Mrs. James wasn't expecting her to go, either, but he decided not to ask.

Tuesday, after Mrs. James boarded the train, Jack and Bessie had their first dinner alone. Jack couldn't think of a thing to say. His throat was dry so he kept drinking water. This was his chance. He finally had her alone—or almost alone. He told himself he'd better pull himself together or she would think he was an idiot. To make conversation, he told Bessie about the years in Helena and his friend, Tom. She listened intently and laughed at his funny stories. With each laugh, he relaxed a little more.

After dinner, he sat at the table in the parlor writing a letter to his mother while Bessie played the piano and Colleen cleaned up in the kitchen. After Colleen left, they worked on a jigsaw puzzle together. Bessie's floral perfume permeated the air around him. When Bessie excused herself,

Lives in Exile

Jack sat in the parlor with his book, but he couldn't see the words. In his mind, he replayed the entire evening, considering the meaning and nuance of every word. What did it mean that she brushed her hair back when he told about selling the ad to the barbershop, or she fluttered her eyelashes when he mentioned how much he liked his new Ford, or she turned to look out the window when he told her about how hot and humid it was in Washington at this time of year?

The next evening, Wednesday, Jack suggested they go for a drive in his automobile. He promised to have her back before dark. The automobile actually belonged to the *Leader Post*. Mr. Johnson had bought it for him earlier that year and let him keep it at home and use it whenever he wanted. As they set out, Bessie was nervous. She explained she'd only been in an automobile a few times. To help her calm down, Jack sang some of his favorite tunes. Soon Bessie laughed and sang "Good Old Summertime" along with him in a voice every bit as loud as his. They launched into a raucous "Give My Regards to Broadway." He felt as though his heart might burst. It's rare to meet a woman as bold as Bessie. As they drove along through the ranches and wheat fields, he told her about his family.

Finally, Bessie talked about herself. All of her grandparents came from Germany. They settled on farms near Winnipeg. When her parents married, they decided to try their luck further west and ended up near Saskatoon. She came from an all female pride of five sisters, no brothers.

Jack, as promised, returned well before dark and parked the car where it was very visible. If any of the neighbors had seen them leave together, he wanted them to know they were back.

Thursday, Jack came home late from work. Bessie had eaten and gone to her room. Colleen left a plate of food for him in the ice box. That night Jack heard Bessie crying for the first time in months. He stood outside Bessie's door for many long minutes. Several times he raised his hand to knock but each time dropped it to his side. Eventually, she stopped. He wondered what had caused her to begin crying again.

At dinner, on Friday, Jack's curiosity was so strong, he lied, "I received a letter from my mother today. Have you any mail from home?" He thought that might be the cause of her distress.

She said, "No."

To keep up the lie and perhaps coax her into more conversation, he said, "My parents moved their store and started a new business. My younger brother is keeping company with a nice young woman. My mother thinks they might get married soon."

"That's nice."

When that didn't work, Jack chose to take another tack. "You're looking a bit tired. Are you feeling well, Miss Swartz?"

"I feel fine. I didn't sleep well last night. Thank you for your concern."

"I know a beautiful place out in the country," Jack said, "where the river takes a wide turn and the ground is covered with wild flowers. Would you like to drive there with me? It's beautiful in the early evening."

She hesitated. "I'd like that."

In the car, Jack sang but he couldn't get her to join in. When he stopped the car, Bessie jumped out without waiting to be helped. She walked purposefully along the river bank. Jack hurried after her. Suddenly, she stopped, let out a short wail, and started to cry, holding her head in her hands.

Jack wondered if she had gone mad. He didn't know what to do. Finally, he lightly touched her shoulder, "Miss Swartz, Bessie."

"Oh, dear. Oh, dear."

"Bessie, please, can I help you. Please, Bessie."

"I just couldn't hold it in any longer. I'm so homesick. The smell of the flowers and grass reminded me of home." She waved her hands in the air. "Nobody can help me." She collapsed on the ground, propped her elbows on her knees, and held her head in her hands.

Jack sat beside her, twisting his straw hat in his hands. *What should I do? What should I say?* He handed her his handkerchief and then sat silently and waited.

"I'm so embarrassed." She looked at him with swollen red eyes.

"It's all right, Miss Swartz, Bessie, I . . . What's this all about?"

"I can't talk about it. If anyone should find out, I'm sure I would lose my job and the affection of my cousin, Mrs. James. Then I would have no place to go. As homesick as I am, I can't go home again. Ever."

With that her tears flowed again, running steadily down her cheeks. Jack put one arm around her, took the handkerchief from her hand and wiped the tears away. "Really, Miss Swartz, I've heard you crying in your room at night and never said a word to anyone. You can trust me."

Her eyes grew very large. She put her hand over her mouth. She hurriedly gathered her skirt, stood, and started toward the car.

He ran after her, took her by the arm, and swung her around. "I am your friend. I can't imagine you've done anything so terrible it would change that."

"Mr. Marks, you don't know. You just don't know." She tried to turn away from him, but he held on. They stood face to face, their eyes locked. Jack willed her to speak. Finally she sat on the ground and Jack sat next to her.

She said, "I was working as a clerk in a tobacco store in Saskatoon. A boy named Johnny, whom I went to school with, started coming in regularly. He always stopped by just before closing. Several times he asked me if he could walk me home. I was thrilled. He was so handsome and so well-liked by everyone, except my parents. His family worked as hired hands. My father told me I could not let him walk me home anymore. I was heartbroken." Her eyes squeezed shut. "I told Johnny the next time he asked me. He said he would go part-way and my parents would never know. I loved being with him. Several months later he said he was going to leave town. He wanted to try his luck in Seattle and begged me to go with him."

She gulped and lowered her eyes. "I did. I ran away with him. We lived together in Seattle. We told everyone we were married and got jobs as clerks in stores. For almost a year we were very happy although I missed my family. I wrote letter after letter but they never wrote back. Then he lost his job. Thank goodness I had hidden some of the money I earned and never told him about it."

She contemplated the scenery for a few moments. "He couldn't find another job. He started drinking and gambling and staying out all night. Eventually one night he didn't come back. I looked and looked for him. I went to the police station. There was no trace of him. I finally decided to go home, to Saskatoon. The money I'd hidden was just enough to buy a train ticket back. When I got home, my parents would hardly speak to me. People stared at me on the street. I didn't know what to do. I spent most of my time lying in bed. It was such a struggle to get out."

She wrapped her arms around her body. "I felt so sad. Everything was too much effort. I wanted to sleep all the time. My married sister, without telling anybody, wrote to our cousin, Mrs. James, about me. She left out the part about Seattle. She told her a young man I was very fond of had left and I was very sad. She asked if Mrs. James would let me come stay with her. Mrs. James wrote back about the teaching position and suggested I apply. My sister applied for me, again without telling me. When I got the position, my sister told me what she had done. My parents were very pleased and packed me up and sent me here. They told me to be very careful because I could not come back."

She looked away. "I've been so lonely and miserable. Yesterday was one year since Johnny abandoned me. I don't know how he could have done this to me. I thought he loved me."

He caressed her cheek with the backs of his fingers wiping away her tears. "It'll be all right."

She turned and looked at him.

He smiled. "You don't have to cry anymore." Suddenly, he noticed how far down the sun had gone. "We better get back or it will be dark."

The whole way back she averted her eyes. He couldn't think of anything casual to say that wouldn't sound stupid and was afraid of upsetting her.

In his room that night, Jack lay down in bed, got up and paced a bit, sat on the sofa, sat in the easy chair, lay down in bed for a while, and on and on for most of the night. He'd finally learned the real story of Bessie Swartz. He knew her father hadn't been an axe murderer or embezzler. Those kinds of things only happened in the movies. Running away to Seattle without being married, however, was shocking. He thought she'd been brave and daring to leave home with this man. He admired her courage and understood she was a woman who didn't live by conventional rules.

In the morning he sat at the breakfast table, watching the stairs, waiting for her to come down. Colleen asked, "Everything okay, sir?"

"Yes." He'd better be careful, or he'd give everything away. He had to get out of there. Colleen probably reported whatever gossip she knew to everyone she met.

That evening at dinner, Bessie and Jack's conversation was strained. Jack rolled his eyes and pointed toward the kitchen. He hoped Bessie understood the signal meant they had to be careful in front of Colleen. She nodded as if she did.

After dinner they sat in the parlor and took turns reading aloud *Chicago Poems* by Carl Sandburg. Jack hardly heard the words, his ears focused on the kitchen. When Colleen said good night and the door latch clicked, Jack looked at Bessie. Her face flushed. Jack reached for her, to comfort her. To Jack's surprise, Bessie jumped, as if startled, and ran up the steps to her bedroom.

Jack sat stunned. During the day he had planned an evening of intimate conversation and, perhaps, some hand holding. In his mind, he had gone over what he would say, how she would respond. He wanted to talk about his plans for the future, about his feelings for her. He hoped this might lead to a kiss or even something more passionate but he was willing to be patient and bide his time. Bessie was in a fragile state. He planned to be discreet and sensitive. Instead, he sat there alone. All the carefully thought-out phrases and sentences lost. He hoped she would return, that she had gone to her room to compose herself. Five minutes, ten minutes, fifteen minutes passed. The clock on the mantel tick, tick, ticked. He gave up and went upstairs. Light shone though her transom. He put his ear to her door. At least she wasn't crying.

In his room, he removed his jacket, tie and collar. He couldn't stand not knowing what she was thinking, so he stepped into the hall and knocked on her door. "Bessie, are you all right?"

He felt her presence on the other side. He thought she was hesitating, deciding whether to let him in. Without realizing it, he held his breath. After a few moments, she opened the door. Her long, reddish-brown hair hung down her back shining in the flickering light. Her sleeveless nightgown hung from her shoulders, draped over her uncorseted breasts. He stood there, looking from the top of her head down to her bare feet and back again. Slowly, she lifted her eyes to meet his.

"I love you." He took her in his arms and kissed her tenderly at first and then deeply, passionately. She responded with equal fervor and intensity. He guided her toward the bed. They made love tenderly. Afterwards she put her head on his shoulder. She stroked his face and the tight curls of the hair on his chest. He loved the feel of her warm body curled around his. Finally, they slept for a while. When they awoke, Jack reluctantly returned to his room. They couldn't afford to take a chance on Colleen discovering them.

On Sunday morning, when Bessie left for morning services, she begged Jack not to meet her in the church yard. She felt it was best they not be seen in public together. She'd been invited for Sunday dinner by a couple from church, anyway.

Jack felt lost the whole day. In the afternoon he found himself in Bessie's bedroom, the room that had once been his. He played with the hairs in her brush. He opened her chifforobe and fingered the fabric of her dresses. The perfume of her toilet water washed over him. He guessed the photo next to her bed was a picture of her parents and sisters. He wondered if she had a picture of that damn Johnny hidden somewhere. The temptation to open her bureau pulled at him. He resisted.

When Bessie returned, she found him working on the puzzle. As they sat together, Jack said what he had planned to say to her the night before.

She interrupted him when he got to the part about his plans for their future together. "I'm very fond of you. In fact, I probably love you, too. But I'm not ready to make a decision about the future. Can't we just go on for a while?"

"Of course we can, if that's what you want." Jack was startled. He assumed Bessie, after her experience with Johnny, would want a commitment, especially after their night together. They did not speak for a while. She kept confounding him.

"Would you like to go upstairs?" he finally said.

She blushed and nodded.

This time he led her to his room. First, she helped him remove his clothes and then she allowed him to undress her. They slept in his room with the curtain open so the rising sun would wake them and Bessie could return to her room before Colleen arrived. Jack had never slept the whole night with a woman in his bed. After that night, he knew he didn't want to sleep alone again. He'd have to find a way to make this work.

They spent the next six weeks with each other. He refused all the usual invitations for dinner. "I have to work late" or "I'm working on a story" soon was replaced with "The press broke down and I have to help the pressman" or "The owner of the dry goods store in Harper asked me to come see him this evening about an ad." Each evening they waited for the door latch to click behind Colleen and her footsteps to fade away. Most nights they left the lights burning in the parlor for passers-by to see as they crept up the stairs and fumbled to find each other in their darkened bedrooms. Occasionally they would turn off the lights in the parlor and turn on all the lamps in both bedrooms. They stayed away from the windows so as not to create shadows. Every three or four nights Jack would try to talk to Bessie about the future. But she shushed him and kissed him passionately. Not since Liza had he known someone who enjoyed lovemaking so much and didn't seem to be interested in marriage. In Colleen's presence, they were formal with each other. He felt confident they had successfully protected themselves from detection.

Then a letter arrived from Mrs. James. She expected to return on August 15th, which was two weeks away. Jack felt trepidation. Throughout dinner he thought about what he could say to persuade Bessie to marry him. That night as soon as the door shut behind Colleen, Jack pulled his chair close to Bessie and said, almost in a whisper, "Please, Bessie, you must listen to me now. I can support both of us very well. I make a good salary from both my jobs. I've been saving a part of my income every week and have a considerable savings account at the bank. I know we can't get married in Canada because of our religious differences, but we can take a trip to Helena and get married by the Justice of the Peace there. I want to buy a home and have a family of our own. I never thought I wanted any of those things until I met you. They were always somewhere way in the future, if ever. Now, I don't want to be apart from you."

Bessie studied the floor. He had expected an immediate yes from her. He thought she wanted him as much as he wanted her.

"Why won't you look at me?" he said. "Is it because I'm Jewish that you haven't wanted to talk about a future together?"

There, he blurted it out. The thought he had been trying to push away, which nagged at him from the back of his brain. One day, when he allowed these thoughts to run rampant, he even considered the enormous cost of converting to Bessie's religion. It frightened him. But today, thinking she might reject him, he impulsively concluded he would do whatever it took to be with her the rest of his life.

She looked up at him. "Dear Jack. That's not it. Canada's laws against intermarriage are ridiculous. You are the kindest, most considerate person I've ever known. For a long time I've felt God abandoned me. I've only been going to church because of my position. It's one of the requirements of the job. No." She looked down at the floor again. "I don't know how to say this. I'm so frightened you'll reject me like my family did. I . . ."

He took her hand and squeezed it in both of his to give her encouragement. "There is nothing you could say that would make me stop loving you."

"I'm pregnant." Bessie looked into his eyes.

Jack couldn't believe what he heard. He kept shaking his head as if to force the thought into his consciousness. *Pregnant, pregnant, pregnant.* He kept repeating it to himself. Finally he looked her full in the face and smiled. "Pregnant?" he said out loud.

"Yes. I think so," Bessie said hesitantly. "You aren't thinking this baby could belong to someone else, are you?"

Jack answered firmly and carefully, "Absolutely not. I'm just surprised. I had never considered this possibility. That was foolish, I see now."

"I was thinking maybe we could go away together."

"Go away? Why can't we elope to the United States, get married, and come back here? I have good prospects here. I've talked to Mr. Johnson about eventually buying the newspaper from him. Regina is growing rapidly into a city and I think there's real potential for the newspaper. I have enough money saved to buy a house for us. People respect me here. After all, they've elected me dog catcher several times."

"Yes. But how will they feel when they find out what we've been doing?" asked Bessie. Her face turned bright red.

"There has to be a way to work this out."

"Jack, we don't have much time. Cousin Hilda is returning in two weeks."

"Then I'll start looking for a house for us. It will take a few weeks to work things out. I should be able to conclude a purchase in a month. We'll make plans to be married then." Jack got down on one knee. "Will you marry me, Bessie Swartz?"

"This is all happening so fast. I don't know what to do or say. Please forgive me, Jack. I do want to be with you. But I don't want to live in town. I'm going to have to give up my teaching position. I don't want to be around town to see the looks and hear the snickers, especially now I'm pregnant. It was bad enough being the object of gossip when I returned to Saskatoon from Seattle."

"That's okay." Jack shifted tactics like the excellent salesman he was. He sat back in his chair. "I always wanted to own a ranch. I think the Smiths are considering selling out. I'm sure I could swing the purchase of their place. Do you want to set a date so I can write to my friend Max and arrange to be married in Helena?"

"In Helena? Let's talk about getting married another time. I can't make any more decisions tonight." Bessie's tone was agitated. "You find the ranch for us and then we'll decide. Right now, all I can think about is what we are going to tell Cousin Hilda."

"Let's worry about Mrs. James tomorrow. We've made a pretty big decision tonight." And he kissed her on her lips and then covered her face with kisses. He moved to her ears and then down her neck. He unbuttoned her blouse, planting a kiss above every button.

At first she was stiff, but eventually she rubbed the back of his head and his shoulders.

He could feel her yielding to his fondling. "Let's go upstairs."

When they had finished making love, he caressed her belly. "A baby," he said. *My baby growing in Bessie.*

First thing the next morning Jack spoke to the president of the bank and arranged to purchase the ranch.

Between periods of tears and comforting they debated what they would tell Mrs. James. Bessie insisted they not tell anybody about the baby. Jack, who could usually talk anybody into anything, tried to persuade Bessie to set a wedding date, but Bessie would not even consider it. All Bessie wanted was to get to the ranch. Over the weeks she smiled less and less and she even stopped laughing at his attempts at humor. By the end of the second week she barely responded to his questions. In all the movies and plays he had ever seen and in all the novels he had ever read, when the woman became pregnant, the hero was the man who came to her rescue and married her. But Bessie wouldn't let him be her hero.

Here he was, madly in love with Bessie, begging her to marry him and she kept refusing. Maybe when he got her to the ranch, she'd relax. He rebuked himself for being such a cad, never even considering the possibility she would get pregnant. How could he have been so stupid? He decided he would stand by her and the baby no matter what happened.

During the last few days before Mrs. James came home, Bessie hardly left her room. Jack ate dinner by himself. After dinner, he sat in the parlor. In his mind he urged, pushed, and hurried Colleen out the door so he could go upstairs to Bessie. When he entered her darkened room, he always spoke in low soft tones. When she answered him, he would lie down next to her and hold her. She wouldn't let him turn on the lights. When he asked why she stayed in her room all day, she said it was morning sickness. Only she had it all day. He wasn't sure that was the truth. But he didn't know what else to think. He told how much he loved her and waited for her to say she loved him, but she never did which left him disappointed and frustrated.

"When I get her to the ranch, when I get her to the ranch . . ." he repeated over and over in his mind. He was sure things would be better then.

At their second dinner Mrs. James said, "I've been home two nights now and Bessie hasn't come down for dinner. Do you know what's the matter?"

He said, "I don't know what is going on with Miss Swartz. She may not be feeling well. We haven't eaten dinner together for several days now."

"I don't like the tired look in her eyes. You're looking kind of peaked yourself."

"I'm fine."

"Humph," said Mrs. James.

"Has she had the doctor in?" asked Mrs. James.

He trembled inside. "I wouldn't know, Mrs. James. But I would like to talk to you about another matter. The opportunity to purchase the Smith ranch has presented itself and I bought the property. I'll be moving out in the next few weeks, probably around the first of September."

"I'll be sorry to see you go after all these years, Mr. Marks. When did you say you would be leaving?"

"By the first of September," said Jack. He had a hard time looking her in the face.

For the next couple of weeks Jack tried to give Bessie reassuring looks and whenever possible touch her hand or her arm. Once or twice he turned her door knob late at night, but she had locked the door. Desperately, he whispered, "Bessie, Bessie." He listened for the sound of her bare feet on the wood floor. But heard nothing. He dared not call her name any louder or knock for fear of disturbing Mrs. James.

On the many nights when Bessie didn't come down for dinner, Mrs. James had Colleen take her a tray. "Poor dear," Mrs. James said to Jack, "you should have written to me about her illness. I wish she'd let me get the doctor."

Frustrated, Jack took to writing long letters to Bessie which he slipped under her door. He would stand there, listening, hoping to see a light come on. But he never detected movement or light, and he received no replies.

On Friday, August 30th, 1917, Jack purchased the Smith ranch.

Finally, on Saturday morning, Jack found a note under his door. It simply said, "Pick me up Sunday at three o'clock. Come to the back door." It was signed "Bessie."

As he packed his belongings in the automobile, he looked toward Bessie's window, hoping to catch a glimpse of her. But she didn't appear. Finally, he could dawdle no longer, so he drove the ten miles to their new home.

That Sunday, as he approached the back door he heard Mrs. James say, "Why're you waiting here?"

Before he could knock, Bessie said, "You have been so kind to me, Cousin Hilda, I don't know how I will be able to repay you. I told the school board president and Miss Tolson I won't be able to teach this term. The Pastor's wife agreed to substitute for me. Jack Marks is picking me up any minute and I will be leaving with him." Bessie hardly paused for breath.

Jack didn't know what to do. Obviously, they hadn't seen him. Should he knock? Should he call out?

Before he could decide, Mrs. James said, "I'm going to have a few words to say to Jack Marks when he arrives, you can be sure of that. What kind of gentleman is he? He promised to behave properly. What has happened here? I demand to know."

Jack called hello through the door. Bessie opened the door and stood there in her hat and gloves.

"Just the man I wanted to see," Mrs. James said.

Bessie said, "I'm as much to blame as Jack for anything that happened."

"You two running off together? How are you two going to be married? You know the law."

"Cousin Hilda," said Bessie, "we don't have time to talk right now. We have to get going. Jack, my bags are upstairs. Please help me with them."

Bessie pulled Jack past the glaring Mrs. James.

Chapter Eight

Births

1918 - 1924

A long sweeping driveway led from the road to the one-story ranch house. Jack stopped just after the curve, where the view was best. He insisted they get out of the car. Standing next to Bessie, he put one arm around her and pointed with his other hand. "The picture window on the left is in the living room. The windows on the right are our bedroom's."

"Where's the front door?"

"You can't see it from here. It's around the side of the living room. When you walk in there is a beautiful stone fireplace on the right. To the left is the dining room and further left is the kitchen which has an outside door so you can bring your groceries right in. I bought the furniture from the Smiths, too."

"Where's the baby's room?"

"It's behind our bedroom. Between the living room and our bedroom is a hallway which goes to the bathroom and the back bedroom."

While Jack carried in her suitcases, Bessie, in her hat and gloves, sat in the rocking chair near the picture window and sighed.

Randall Aaron Marks was born on April 1, 1918. Bessie played with him, fed him, taught him sounds, words, colors. When she was in one of her good moods, no one was allowed near the baby but her. When she was in one of her sad moods, she barely noticed Randall or anyone else. Then she'd lie in her bed or sit in her rocker and cry for hours on end. Sometimes Jack would take her by the chin and turn her head toward him. He tried to make her look at him, but her eyes remained focused in another place and time.

He yearned for her to share in his business successes, but Bessie had no interest. When Jack acquired the *Leader Post* from Charles Johnson in 1921, he bought her a diamond pendant. She said a simple "thank you" and put the necklace away in a drawer. To Jack's mind, she barely recognized his existence, even when she was in an agreeable state.

His evenings were spent reading novels, smoking cigars, and drinking one tumbler of scotch after another. He insisted she sit with him, so she did—in the chair near the fireplace knitting, if her disposition was content, or gazing into the fire if she was in one of her sad periods. Gone was the woman who had relished making love. Gone were the sweet caresses and warm cuddling.

Before Randall's birth, Jack hired an Indian woman to tend to Bessie and the new baby. Shining Star was *Métis,* a blend of French and Indian. When Bessie sat in her rocker near the window and cried all day, Shining Star comforted her and cared for Randall. Every evening, no matter what happened during the day, Shining Star had dinner ready for Jack, Bessie, and Randall.

When Randall was five, Bessie became pregnant again. Jack viewed it as being as close to an immaculate conception as one could get. Bessie only let him touch her four or five times a year when she was in one of her untroubled periods. The pregnancy did not go well. Bessie spent most of the time in bed, her eyes fixed on the ceiling.

On April 19, 1924, Jack was awakened by Bessie's moaning. He called her name but she didn't answer. He shook her and got no response. He screamed for Shining Star.

Shining Star came running, gathering her bathrobe around her.

"Call the doctor."

Shining Star ran for the phone in the living room. Within a few seconds she was back. "No phone. Couldn't get the operator."

Jack, with Randall sitting beside him, drove at top speed into town to the doctor's office. Randall asked Jack questions but Jack only heard his voice, not the words. "It'll be all right," was his reply each time. On the return trip, the doctor sat in the front seat so Jack controlled his urge to barrel down the road. When he brought the car to a stop in front of the house, the doctor had his hands on the dashboard, bracing himself.

Lives in Exile

Randall was lying across the backseat. From outside they could hear Bessie's screams.

In the bedroom they found Shining Star trying to hold cold compresses to Bessie's blood-red face. The doctor pulled out his stethoscope and listened to Bessie's heart. He pursed his lips, looked over at Jack, and shook his head. "Why don't you take the boy for a walk? It'll be a while here."

Jack felt helpless. "If you think that's best . . ." He looked over at Shining Star.

She nodded and gave him a weak smile. He squeezed her hand.

Jack and his son strolled down the driveway toward the road. "Is Mama going to be all right?"

"I'm sure she'll be fine. That's what mamas do. They have to push the baby out so they make noises. But then, when the baby comes, everything is okay."

Randall thought for a few seconds and then shrugged. He looked back toward the house. Jack did, too.

When they got to the main road, they sat on the log bench Jack had installed several years earlier so Shining Star would have a place to sit while she waited for her relatives to pick her up. To keep Randall occupied, Jack identified the make and model of each car that passed and described some of its features. When Randall could identify the car on his own, he got to put a pebble in a pile on the bench. Jack promised to exchange the pebbles for pieces of candy. Each time Randall added to the mound, he let out a yelp.

After a while Randall asked for a drink, so they started back. Jack put Randall on his back and galloped. Randall giggled.

Jack sat Randall at the kitchen table with a glass of water and went to check on Bessie. When he entered the bedroom, the doctor was leaning over Bessie with his stethoscope on her abdomen. He looked up at Jack and frowned. "Can't hear the baby's heartbeat. Isn't a good sign."

Jack froze. "What do you mean?"

"Everything could be fine or the baby could be in trouble."

"What're you going to do?"

"Not much at this point. We have to wait for nature to take its course. In a while I should be able to pull the baby out with the forceps."

"Sit with her," Shining Star said. "I'll make lunch for Randall."

Jack sat in a kitchen chair next to the bed. The doctor sat in the rocking chair at the window.

The bedroom was the same as the day he'd brought her to this house—the same dark mahogany double dresser and headboard. The two night tables with their matching brass lamps and green shades were still on either side of the bed. She never even changed the chintz curtains and matching bedspread with the roses in a vine pattern. Mrs. Smith had used the same fabric on the pads of the rocking chair. The only things Jack had added were the rose-colored scatter rugs on either side and at the foot of the bed. He'd painted the walls a medium green in the two days he had before he'd gone to get Bessie.

Each time a contraction came, Jack and the doctor held Bessie in a sitting position and urged her to push. When the contraction was over, Jack caressed her forehead with the cool cloth. She moaned the whole time and looked at Jack with frantic eyes, her body in constant motion. When Shining Star came back, she brought another kitchen chair. She told Jack she'd put Randall down for a nap so both Jack and Shining Star sat vigil next to Bessie.

After a half hour the doctor said, "We can't wait any longer. Each of you take one of her legs and pull it back as far as you can."

With the forceps the doctor pulled the baby out. "It's a boy."

Jack grinned. "Harold Marx."

The doctor hit the baby on its buttocks. Jack waited. The doctor held the newborn upside down and rapped the bottoms of its feet. The infant never made a sound. The doctor laid the baby on the bed. The sight of the blue child with the misshapen head caused Jack to cry out. Shining Star grasped his hand. He looked at her. Tears rolled down her cheeks. Jack reached out to touch the baby's motionless chest. Shining Star clutched a tiny fist. When Jack looked up, the doctor was standing nearby holding a white blanket. With a tilt of his head, Jack signaled Shining Star and they stepped back. After wrapping the baby in the blanket, the doctor put the bundle on the rocking chair. Bessie seemed to know what happened because she had turned her face away. Jack sat and held her hand. Following the delivery of the afterbirth, the doctor gave Bessie a shot to help her sleep.

Jack, at Shining Star's urging, left the doctor and Shining Star to clean up the bedroom. He went into the living room and poured himself a stiff scotch and then stepped onto the front porch where he sat in a rocker. Not long afterwards, he heard the doctor's voice from the living room. As Jack went through the front door, the doctor put the phone down. "I called my wife to come and get me. I'll take the baby to the funeral home, if you like."

Jack's mouth dropped open. He hadn't even thought about what happened next. "Thank you."

"I'll go clean up—" He gestured toward his bloody white coat and gloved hand.

Jack nodded and went back into the bedroom to sit with Bessie. In a little while he heard a car pull up. The doctor came into the room and closed his medical bag. Jack stood and reached for the baby. He carried the bundle to the doctor's car.

"I'll be back after dinner to check on Mrs. Marks," the doctor said.

Jack watched the doctor's car until it disappeared down the road.

When he went back in the house, Shining Star was standing in the kitchen doorway with Randall. She said, "Sit with Mrs. Marks. I'll make dinner. Go get your coloring book, Randall. You can work at the kitchen table."

After Randall dashed to his room, Jack ran his hand through his hair. "What are we going to tell him?"

"I'll tell him the Indian legend about the great hunter who lives in the sky and chose the baby to be his helper and carry his arrows. So when Randall looks up at the stars, he'll be able to pick out the hunter and see his brother trailing along behind. Tonight I'll show him the star that's his baby brother."

"Are you making that up?"

"That's the legend. Go sit with Mrs. Marks now."

Jack gave Shining Star a hug. He'd never hugged her before, but felt the need for the comfort of another human. At first Shining Star kept her arms to her sides, but after a few seconds she responded.

When Jack returned to the bedroom, he found Bessie asleep, breathing evenly, her face colorless. He turned the rocker back toward the window. He thought about all that had happened that day—Bessie's screams, her writhing body, her blood-red face as she tried to push the baby out. And then, the fearful sight of the baby—all blue, never making a sound. Dead before the doctor pulled him out, after hours and hours of worthless labor. Jack put his head in his hands and wept.

Over the next two days, Bessie seemed to sink away, her face paler and paler. Not even hugs and kisses from Randall nor his pleas could draw her back to them. The doctor gave Jack no hope. Bessie's body pulled in on itself, her knees drawing closer and closer to her chest. Finally, too weak to breathe, her lungs rattled as she squeezed out her last breath.

On April 23, Jack found himself in the cemetery of the Lutheran Church. His feet sank into the soft earth as he walked toward the hole with the mound of earth next to it. The ground in cemeteries always seemed damp to Jack, damp with all the tears that had been shed there. He scanned the head stones. Soon there would be one for Bessie. *Eighteen ninety-six - nineteen twenty-four* would be carved into her stone. Bessie Swartz Marks was the name he'd have them use for Randall's sake. Underneath would be etched *Harold Marks, infant.*

Jack glanced behind him. Randall stood several feet back clutching Shining Star's hand. He looked so frightened, his eyes wary. Jack wanted to give him a reassuring smile, but he couldn't manage to move the corners of his mouth. Randall leaned into Shining Star; she squeezed his hand. In her silent way, she'd taken care of all of them since the day Jack brought her home from her village.

Hilda James was there, although they'd hardly spoken since the day he snatched Bessie from her boarding house, almost seven years ago. The only other person who attended was the Lutheran minister who said the appropriate prayers and left.

So, there Jack stood, in the middle of the church cemetery, gazing down at the plain pine box that would hold Bessie and the infant together for eternity. Traditions deeply ingrained compelled him, despite his disbelief, to chant the Kaddish, the Jewish prayer of mourning, "*Yitgadal, veyitkadash, shmei raba . . .*" He fell into the rhythm of the words and the familiar tones. He closed his eyes and swayed back and forth like the old men he used to make fun of in synagogue. "Ashes to ashes, dust to dust. *Ohev shalom*, may you rest in peace, dear Bessie and tiny Harold. Amen."

Jack opened his eyes. To complete his obligation, he had to cover the coffin with dirt, but he couldn't move. His heart was crushed with anguish. When he bent to pick up the spade, the muscles in his back and thighs twisted like the cords in a hangman's noose. But this was his responsibility, as a Jew, to cover the coffin. He put his foot on the spade's back edge and pushed it into the mound of dirt. He shoveled the soil over the coffin. The clods, heavy with moisture from the spring melt, clumped as they hit the wood. The sounds bruised his heart like hammer blows. The grave diggers started toward him ready to finish the job. He waved them back and took off his jacket. He needed to do this himself. Another shovel full, more shocks to his heart. Tears flowed down his cheeks. Sweat dripped from under his arms and ran down his back but he shoveled until the grave

Lives in Exile

overflowed. He saw Bessie's beautiful, soft face before him, the face that had mesmerized him. The fragrance of her floral perfume surrounded him. He looked at the three people with him and shivered in the late afternoon chill of a waning sun. Weariness overcame him. "Let's go home." He walked away without looking back and, as soon as he was in the house, ran water over his hands, as traditional Jews do.

He sat at the table, his Muriel cigar stuck between the first two fingers of his left hand, a double scotch in his right. Hilda James helped Shining Star in the kitchen. Randall played on the floor with his toy soldiers. Bessie's death wasn't real to Jack until he'd filled her grave. It surprised him, this need to invoke the traditions of his past. "Why?" he asked himself. No answer came; he'd had to do it. He felt buried, too. The burdens of his business, his obligations to his child now without a mother, and the responsibilities of a household pressed on him like the weight of the earth on the coffin.

He turned to Randall and wondered whom he looked like. Odd he'd never thought about it before. He had Bessie's thin, straight nose and her full lips and beautiful blue eyes that captured Jack's heart the first time he saw her. His broad shoulders and narrow chest must have come from Jack's side—they were so much like his father's.

"Poppa, Poppa," called Randall, "this one's the Kaiser."

Jack half-expected Bessie to waddle out of the bedroom, like she had those last few weeks. Shuffling, her swollen feet encased in slippers, her pregnant belly shifting from side to side, her hands splayed across the back of her hips, asking Randall to be quiet.

At dinner, Jack said to Mrs. James, "Please write your cousins, Bessie's parents and sisters, about her death. She hadn't heard from them these last seven years. I don't want to have anything to do with them now."

Before Mrs. James could reply, a car honked as it came up the drive. Jack went to the doorway, his hand shaded his eyes from the last rays of sun that spread across the flat prairies. The Western Union boy handed him a telegram.

> DEAR SON STOP SENDING YETTA STOP WILL ARRIVE ST PAUL TRAIN TUESDAY STOP LOVE MOTHER STOP

Jack had sent his own telegram to his family when Bessie died and he longed for one of his mother's comforting letters in return. But it would be several days, maybe a week or more, before he heard from her. Even though it had been fifteen years since he had seen his family, his mother knew when he needed comfort, encouragement, or prodding. She had not approved of his arrangement with Bessie. Besides everything else, Bessie was a *shiksa*. But after letters back and forth filled with questions and explanations, she accepted their relationship and was always anxious for news and pictures of her grandson. It surprised him that his mother would send Yetta by herself until he realized Yetta was twenty-one. Standing in the doorway with the telegram in his hand, memories of her leapt into his mind. He smiled to himself. His thoughts were interrupted by Randall's insistent calling.

"Poppa, Poppa, what does the telegram say?"

"It says your Aunt Yetta is coming from Washington, D.C., for a visit. She'll be here next Tuesday."

"Where will she sleep, Poppa? There're no extra beds."

"It's a shame the new bedroom isn't finished. I guess we'll have to figure that out."

Where *could* Yetta sleep? The house had only two bedrooms—Jack and Bessie's and Randall's, shared with Shining Star. Jack had contracted for a new bedroom to be built on the back of the house. He was enlarging Randall's bedroom, too. Work had begun several weeks before the baby was born, but he had told the men to take the day off when Bessie was in labor and then had postponed the work even longer. Now he didn't know what he was going to do with the half-finished room.

While Shining Star gave Randall his bath and got him ready for bed, Jack and Hilda James sat in the living room, both absorbed in their own thoughts. Jack blew smoke from his cigar as he surveyed the living room. This room always pleased Jack. He loved the big picture window, so unusual in this part of the country. He loved the blue damask fabric in the curtains and covering the sofa on the long wall opposite the fireplace.

Jack took a sip of his scotch. Mrs. Smith had good taste. The striped fabric on his favorite easy chair and ottoman perfectly matched the blue and the gold that covered the pads on the rocking chair. Placing the easy chair next to the fireplace with its back to the front door made the grouping cozy. Having the rocking chair between the fireplace and the window meant he could turn it to face whichever direction he fancied. For the first time, he noticed all the fabrics were worn and dirty. *I'll have to replace them shortly.* He hoped Mrs. James would leave as soon as Randall came in to say goodnight. He wanted to be alone.

Mrs. James leaned forward. "Jack, there are some things I should tell you. The first is I'm trying to sell the boarding house. As soon as I do, I'm moving to Vancouver to live with my son."

"Sounds like a fine idea." Jack stubbed out the cigar.

She sat back on the sofa and folded her arms across her chest. "The second is something Bessie's mother wrote me many years ago. I'm sure you don't know about it, and I think you deserve to know the truth. In fact, one day while you were at work, I came out here to confront Bessie. She became hysterical, violent really."

"Bessie?"

"She attacked me with her fists."

"I can't believe it." He wondered what malicious lies he was about to hear.

"Shining Star witnessed the whole thing. Bessie actually threatened to harm me, if I told you or anyone else. She ordered me to stay away from her, you, and the ranch."

Jack was astounded. "I can't imagine her reacting that way to anything. She was usually so passive."

"I told her what her mother had written me." She paused. "I don't know how to say this except straight out and hope I'm doing the right thing. You have a son and I think you have a right to know. Bessie had eloped to Seattle with a young man she knew from high school. Apparently, her husband abandoned her and she had to come back to Saskatoon. She stayed there only a few weeks before they shipped her off to me."

"Why are you—"

"She never divorced the young man."

Jack's heart pounded. He fell back into the chair. *Oh, my God, my God.*

Mrs. James half stood. "Jack, are you all right?"

He blinked continuously as he tried to focus on a response. "Sorry. . . Didn't mean to. . . So shocking. Take a while to adjust to this. . ." His voice drifted off.

Shining Star brought Randall into the room. Mrs. James smiled, "Come here, you handsome young man, give Cousin Hilda a kiss goodnight."

"Goodnight, Cousin Hilda. Goodnight, Poppa." Randall put his arms around his father's neck. "It'll be okay, Poppa. Shining Star said she's going to take good care of us."

Jack managed to give Randall a feeble smile and patted his back. "Goodnight, Randall. Sleep tight."

After Randall left the room, Mrs. James said, "I hope I did the right thing in telling you this now."

"It certainly explains things I found difficult to. . . I loved Bessie."

"I know you must have. I better be on my way. It's getting pretty late. I'll let you know before I leave for good."

Alone, Jack sat by the fireplace, the embers still glowing, the lamp next to him lit, his eyes closed. Tears ran. He felt a hand on his shoulder. "Bessie," he almost said. Then he remembered it couldn't be. His eyes jerked open.

"It's all right, Mr. Marks," Shining Star said. "Everything will be all right."

Jack took his handkerchief out of his back pocket and wiped his cheeks. "You knew everything Mrs. James told me. Didn't you?"

Shining Star sat on the sofa and they watched each other. He'd never really looked at her before.

Finally, she said, "I don't know exactly what Mrs. James told you. But if you mean, about the fight they had, yes, I knew about it."

"You knew what got Bessie so upset, don't you? You knew about her being married to somebody else." Jack choked on his words.

She answered very quietly. "I knew."

Jack banged his hand down on the arm of the chair. "Why didn't you tell me?"

"Mrs. Marks threatened to fire me if I told you or even mentioned it to her again. I didn't want to leave you, or Randall, or Mrs. Marks. You needed me so much."

"We did."

They sat in silence.

"Goodnight, Mr. Marks." Shining Star rose and left the room.

Jack turned out the light and headed to his room. In bed, he sat up trying to read, but couldn't concentrate. He closed the book and studied at the empty place and undented pillow next to him. Thoughts rushed through his head. *Did I ever really know her? Even though we hardly talked, I feel this big hole in the center of my gut. Hardly talked, hah, we hardly touched. What happened? What happened to that bold and daring girl I knew at Mrs. James' boarding house? Did I really love her?*

He put his book on the night table and turned out the light.

Did I ever love her? Hard to remember seven years ago before there was a ranch, before there was a Randall. I loved the person I thought she was. Her coy smile and sparkling eyes. When she looked at me, I thought we were the only two people in the world. I so desperately wanted to be her hero, like in the movies. I wanted to live out the great adventure I saw on the stage and screen. I guess I imagined her to be the person I needed her to be. What did I know? What a young fool I was.

He swung his legs over the edge of the bed and slipped his feet into his slippers. He padded over to the rocking chair, pulled the curtain back and sat, wrapping himself in the afghan, as Bessie had done every day for that whole first year.

Here she sat. I wonder what she saw out there besides the mountains and the sky. Obviously her life was nothing like she planned, if she ever planned anything. I don't even know what she wanted out of life. Thank goodness for Shining Star. The day I found her was my luckiest. I wonder how she was ever able to coax Bessie out of this room. Randall was probably the one who did it. Bessie did love Randall. Shining Star will have to stay overnight with her relatives while Yetta's here. I hope Yetta won't mind sharing the room with a six-year-old and sleeping in Shining Star's bed.

He left his room pulling the afghan around him against the cold night air. Once in the easy chair near the fireplace, he put his feet up on the ottoman. A shaft of white moonlight came through the slit in the curtains and brightened the hearth stones. He dozed. When he woke, he walked to the picture window and pulled back the damask curtains. Red streaks of dawn shot from the horizon. He sighed, ambled to the fireplace, and placed both hands on the mantle. The logs were burnt out.

Why didn't I press her about marrying me? Maybe then she would have told me the truth. What did she always say when I brought it up? "It wouldn't change anything so why bother." I should have insisted on talking about it. What was our life all about anyway?

Jack felt a hand on his. He wasn't shocked to find Shining Star standing next to him. How beautiful she was in the early morning light. The combination of French and Indian created a compelling mixture in Shining Star's face. The narrow European shape with the slit-like eyelids of the Native American, European nose and mouth, and a skin color only slightly darker than his, were beguiling. Here was the women who'd brought him comfort and caring for so many years. He put his arms around her and pulled her to him. She took his hand and led him to his bed.

When he woke up, he was at peace. He reached for her, but the bed was empty, as empty as when he first tried to sleep last night. The sheets were smoothed and the pillow flat. He wondered if making love to Shining Star had been another one of his fantasies. But he felt so satisfied, so fulfilled, it couldn't have been a dream.

He found her in the kitchen preparing the morning meal. She acted as if nothing had happened. Breakfast finished, Jack patted Randall on the head and went to his office.

After dinner, he sat in his easy chair with his usual scotch and Muriel cigar and read the *San Francisco Examiner*. Shining Star did not return to the living room after she put Randall to bed. When Jack's eyes drooped, he went to his room. A few minutes later, he heard his door open and shut. Shining Star crawled into bed next to him. He put his arms around her. "I've been waiting for you."

On Tuesday, he ate lunch at the ranch. Randall jabbered away about all sorts of things, excited about the arrival of this aunt he had never seen. Jack kept his eyes focused on Shining Star, her golden body with short, sturdy limbs. His thoughts were jumbled and confused. He felt like a man who had come down out of the mountains onto the plains—a parched hermit, who suddenly realized he had missed too much in his solitude and yearned to fill the emptiness. Still, he wasn't sure sex with Shining Star was the answer. It had been five nights like he hadn't known in years. She knew him, knew what he needed, what he wanted. During the barren years he had often been tempted to visit a whore house and spend an hour or so with one of the girls. But his commitment to Bessie and their child was too strong. So he had endured. Now he didn't know if he could go back to that lonely mountain. But he had no choice. Yetta was about to arrive.

"How will we know Aunt Yetta when she gets off the train?" asked Randall.

"Go get my family picture off the dresser."

Randall skipped off to find it.

When he returned and handed Jack the picture, Jack said, "This picture was taken just before I left home. I was fifteen. This is me. This is Bubbe. And this is Aunt Yetta sitting on my father's, your Zeyde's lap. She was six years old when we took this picture, just like you."

"You look funny, so skinny, Poppa."

They arrived in town in plenty of time to meet the train, so they parked near the station and wandered. They ended up at the Royal Canadian Mounted Police Training Center. From the edge of the corral, they watched the riders put the horses through their paces. Every time a horse jumped over a barricade, Randall clapped his hands and whooped. Jack laughed.

"That's what I want to be when I grow up, Poppa, a Royal Canadian Mounted Policeman."

A train whistle sounded. Jack looked at his watch. "The train's almost here. We've got to run, Randall."

Jack held his straw hat in one hand and with the other dragged Randall east on Eleventh Avenue, across Wascana Creek, and then south on York to the station. They arrived, both huffing and puffing, as Yetta stepped off the train. Her eyes danced back and forth between the two of them and she smiled, a laughing smile, like his mother's. He would've known her anywhere. She'd changed very little. Now she was more mature, a carbon copy of his mother and Aunt Golda with her thick lips, shiny brown hair, and those big brown eyes. He took her in his arms feeling the comforting embrace of his whole family in hers.

"I don't usually let men breathe heavily in my ear," Yetta said laughing.

Jack, still panting, laughed and picked up Randall. "Give your Aunt Yetta a kiss."

"Aunt Yetta, why are you crying?" asked Randall.

"Because you are so handsome, and I've missed seeing you so much, my *boychik*."

"What's a *boychik*?" Randall asked.

Jack answered, "A *boychik* is a young man."

Yetta raised her eyebrows and glowered at Jack. "We're going to have to do something about his education."

"I'm going to go to school after the summer," Randall said.

"I'm not talking about that kind of school," said Yetta. "Let's send Bubbe a telegram to tell her I'm here so she can stop worrying."

Chapter Nine

Yetta

1966

Ike Stein put his fork down on the dessert plate and pushed it aside. "How did you talk your mother into letting you go?"

Yetta sipped the last of her coffee. "It was her idea. Sammy and Abe were married and my mother still did all the office work for the store and the provision business. I worked the cash register and watched over the help. Mama felt it would be easier to send me than to leave me with all her responsibilities." Yetta looked around the restaurant. "Do you realize we're the only ones here?"

"Maybe we should take pity on the owners and leave. I could take you to your hotel and we could sit in the lobby so you could finish the story."

"It's getting late and there's a lot more. I'm only up to 1924."

"I tell you what. Have lunch with me tomorrow. I'll take off the whole afternoon. Maybe we could ride over to Durham or something. Then I'll have my girl make dinner for the two of us."

She wasn't sure she knew him well enough to have dinner with him at his house, alone or even with the maid. She'd only met him five weeks ago. Hell, women were burning their bras all over the country. It was almost 1967. She could have dinner with a man at his house.

The next day they drove over to Durham, near the Duke campus, and ate in an old house that had been converted into a restaurant. The original dining and living rooms were decorated like a café with wooden tables and red-checkered curtains. The same material covered the seat cushions. Ike said that in the summer they served on the front porch, too.

Yetta sniffed. "They bake their own bread."

After they ordered, Ike asked, "How was your first train trip to Regina? What year was that?"

"1924 and uneventful. My mother got me a sleeping compartment. She even tipped the porter to bring my meals. When I changed trains, I tipped the next porter. The hardest part was finding something I wanted to eat on the menu."

Ike appeared disappointed. "Weren't you bored?"

"I was mainly scared. My mother and father had filled me with stories about all the bad things that could happen. What worried me the most, though, was what my parents wanted me to do—convince Jack to come back to Washington. Obviously I wasn't successful since he stayed in Regina until he died."

"Did you recognize your Jack after all those years?"

"Immediately. Jack and Randall must have been running for the train because when I saw them their faces were flushed. Jack looked like he used to when he ran in from school, red cheeked and hair all mussed." She laughed. "Randall was so adorable. I started to cry." She shook her head. "What shocked me was to discover he didn't know even the most basic Yiddish words."

* * * * * * * *

That night Yetta helped Shining Star give Randall a bath and get him ready for bed. "It'll be great fun to share a room with you," Yetta told him. "Would you like me to tell you a story before you go to sleep?"

"My mama used to tell me stories. Why did she have to die, Aunt Yetta?"

"Your mama would come back if she could. I know she was very sad to have to leave you. You're such a wonderful, handsome boy." Yetta caressed his cheek. "I know a great story to tell you about a long time ago when God brought a great flood to cover the earth. Would you like that?"

Yetta stayed with Randall while Jack took Shining Star to her sister's house. She had a cup of hot tea waiting when he returned. He hadn't had tea in the evening for years.

"Jack, can we talk?"

"Of course, can we not talk? It's just the two of us."

"Are you planning on Randall being a *yiddisha mensch* or a *goy*? Not that the *goyim* will give him a chance to choose."

Jack gulped a mouthful of hot tea. "Why do you ask?"

"I gave him a bath tonight."

"Oh, you mean because he's not circumcised. Bessie wouldn't permit it. Anyway, according to Jewish law, he isn't Jewish because Bessie wasn't and she wouldn't let him be converted."

"As if that will make any difference to the gentiles."

"*Mein sheine shvester*. I know Mama sent you out here to talk me into coming back to Washington. We might as well straighten that out right now. I'm not sure what I'm going to do about many things. But this I know—I'm not leaving Regina."

"Such a speech." She threw her hands in the air. "Finish your tea before it gets cold. I'm going to bed now. It's been a long day. *Aguten nacht*."

The next night Yetta told Randall the story of Abraham and his acceptance of the covenant with God. A cup of hot tea waited again for Jack when he returned from delivering Shining Star to her sister's.

After he finished his tea, Jack lit a cigar. "I can't believe how easily I've fallen back into the pattern of answering questions with questions. I've worked so hard to break those habits. In Montana, I studied the way non-Jews talked and imitated them as best I could. I haven't spoken in Yiddish since Helena and yet it came back effortlessly."

"Maybe you haven't left your old self as far behind as you thought."

They fell silent.

The next night Yetta asked, "What was Bessie like?"

"That's a hard one," Jack said. "I probably should be drinking something stronger than a *glezele tei*."

Yetta laughed. "But at least your tea's in a cup and not in a *yahrtzeit* glass."

He told her the story Hilda James had told him the evening after he'd buried Bessie. "Why, after Bessie told me so much—about running away to Seattle, being abandoned, and then returning to Saskatoon in shame, why didn't she add that one last thing—about marrying that damn Johnny? She must have been so lonely and afraid that when I offered to take care of her, she grabbed on. She must have been terrified the whole seven years that if she told me the whole truth I would've left her."

"How could you? You loved her, and you had Randall. If she'd told you from the beginning, things would've been very different. Maybe she wouldn't have been so depressed. Maybe she would've been happier."

"I don't know. Maybe I was so desperate to be her rescuer and hero I didn't see what I didn't want to see."

This became their pattern: Yetta put Randall in bed and told him a biblical story while Jack drove Shining Star to her sister's. When he returned, a cup of hot tea waited and they talked.

Yetta loved the intimate talks with Jack. He told her all the most minute details of his life except for one—his relationship with Shining Star.

Yetta saw the way he touched Shining Star's arm and smiled at her when he came home from the newspaper. She noticed the way their heads bent together as soon as they got in the car. She also caught the shy grin that came over his face when Yetta told him he ought to continue building the addition so Shining Star could have her own room. Yetta suspected they were lovers, but couldn't bring herself to ask.

Every week Yetta received a letter from her mother asking about her progress in persuading Jack to move to Washington. As the summer went on, the inquiries became more urgent, and, finally, at the beginning of August, when Yetta had been in Regina for three months, her mother wrote she was to come home before Rosh Hashanah—with Jack. That left Yetta with a dilemma. Should she return to Washington or stay in Regina to raise Randall?

When Yetta went to her bed in the room she shared with Randall, she always smoothed his covers and caressed his face. She worried about who was going to raise this boy and love him. She knew this wasn't what her mother intended, but this was the situation as she perceived it. So the decision was hers, stay or go?

She spent many hours contemplating what her life would be like, what her prospects would be if she stayed. It would be so different from in her life in Washington—living in a rural community surrounded by *goyim*, only twenty Jewish families, not many her age, male or female. Would she stay in Jack's house and raise Randall? Then what? She'd be isolated and alone except for Jack. If she went to work, where could she work? She'd be surrounded by strangers for whom she'd be an oddity. In Washington she had the rest of her family, her Jewish life, and her friends. Jack liked it here, even thrived on that kind of life, but she didn't know if she could.

Shining Star was the reason Yetta was able to leave. She saw how much Shining Star loved Randall and how much he loved her. She knew she would be leaving him in good hands. On the night they decided on her departure date, she said, "Won't you consider moving back to Washington?"

"I can't. Please understand. I'm successful here. I think the time may be right to turn this ranch into a real one, with cattle and grain. Even more important, Regina is my life. I like it here. People respect me. I am a *gantzer knakr*. I have influence as the owner of the newspaper. Can you appreciate what that means to me?"

She worked hard to restrain her tears. "After all we've shared this summer I can, but I don't want to lose this closeness we've built. I want to see my nephew, and I want him to get to know his Bubbe and Zeyde. You shouldn't deprive him of that." She couldn't bring herself to tell Jack she had thought about staying. She wondered how he would've reacted. Would he have told her about Shining Star?

"How about next June I bring Randall to Washington for several weeks? If things go well, I could leave him until the end of the summer and then come back and get him."

Maybe that would be an acceptable alternative.

Two weeks before she was to leave, Jack asked her to help pack Bessie's belongings. All her clothes were still in the closet and dresser. Yetta and Shining Star bundled up the clothes while Randall played in the room. Yetta thought it was a good idea for Randall to watch so he would know what was happening and not have to wonder about it.

When they finished the bureau, Yetta put a small box on the bed and called Randall over. "Would you help me put some special things in this box? Bring me your mother's comb, brush, and mirror set from the dresser."

Randall put down his toy truck and did as Yetta asked.

"These must have been very special to your mother. They're made with silver and mother-of-pearl. See?"

"Mama used to brush her hair a lot when she sat in the rocking chair."

Yetta wanted to cry. Poor Randall. "Now put them in this box."

Randall did.

"See that perfume bottle on the dresser? Bring it here."

When Randall brought the lavender-colored glass bottle, Yetta squeezed the atomizer under his nose. He said, "That's what my mother always smelled like."

"That was her perfume."

"Now get that the picture." When Randall brought it, Yetta said, "This must be your mother's family." She put it in the box.

Evelyn Auerbach

Yetta glanced around the room. "I guess that's it. I have some nice pink ribbon to close the box with. Will you help me tie the bow?" Randall held his finger on top of the knot. "When your poppa comes home, we'll have him put this box in the attic, and when you grow up you can have your mother's special things to remember her by."

* * * * * * *

After lunch, Ike suggested they walk around the campus. The sun was shining and the air was warm for December. The only inhabitants were the bare trees and bushes with dull-looking leaves. All the students had deserted for the Christmas vacation, but the stone buildings covered in ivy and the college greens provided a beautiful environment to stroll and talk.

Ike said, "Your brother obviously did very well in Regina."

"The newspaper was profitable and the ranch thrived. He bought cattle, hired a foreman, and built a barn and a bunk house for the ranch hands. He went on to buy a potash mine."

"What did your mother say when you came home without Jack and Randall?"

"I played up how well Jack was doing and how respected he was in Regina. And then true to his word, Jack brought Randall to visit for the summer."

"Your parents must have liked that."

"Randall spent every summer with us until he went into the Canadian army. He was very close to my parents."

"You never married?"

"I'd gotten to be very independent that summer in Regina, and then I took over more and more responsibilities in the business in Washington. Every time I got close to being serious with someone, he always wanted me to become a housewife and let him be in charge. I kept waiting for the right man who would like my independence. He never came along. I wonder sometimes if I made a mistake."

"If you were happy and satisfied, then I say you did just fine."

"The best part of my life was Randall. He was my surrogate son."

They headed back to the car. As Ike took her hand to help her into the car, he kissed her cheek. She said, "Oh, my."

He blushed. "I hope I didn't offend you. You're a wonderful person and I wanted to show you how wonderful I think you are." He squeezed her hand.

Yetta nodded and got into the car.

Before Ike pulled out into the street he turned to her and said, "I think we're going to be great friends."

Yetta blushed.

"How did Randall come to live in Elizabeth City?" He put the car into drive.

Chapter Ten

Randall's Story

Washington, D.C.

1937-1938

Randall would remember Tuesday, August 23rd, 1938, as the happiest day of his whole life. He asked Maggie Goldberg to marry him and she said yes.

That evening began, as usual, with dinner in his grandmother's kitchen. The table fan hummed as the blades attempted to stir the air. All sources of heat had been eliminated—the overhead lights were off, the oven unlit. The three of them—Randall, Aunt Yetta, and Bubbe—sat at the white wooden table with the matching chairs, Randall in his undershirt, Yetta in her office clothes but without her stockings, shoes, and jewelry, and Bubbe in a loose-fitting house dress. With her handkerchief, Bubbe wiped the beads of sweat from over her eyes and lip. They ate salmon croquettes with applesauce, corn on the cob, and a salad. Roasting anything would have made the kitchen unbearable. No one wanted a heavy meal anyway.

During dessert, Aunt Yetta said to Randall, "Uncle Sammy, Uncle Abe, and I have been talking about your proposition."

Manny Ancel, Randall's best friend and the son of the owner of The Ukrainian Inn Restaurant, had told Randall the restaurant was for sale. Randall suggested to his aunt and uncles that they buy the restaurant which was one of the Marks Company's best customers.

Aunt Yetta swallowed a spoonful of Bubbe's famous chocolate pudding. "Your idea is good. The numbers you've worked out look right to us. The profit you figured appears reasonable because we'd be buying all the provisions and the liquor wholesale through our own business, as you pointed out. Do you know why Adolph Ancel wants to sell? We thought Manny was all set to take over."

Randall savored the cold creamy pudding sliding down his throat. "Manny's going to marry Becky and go into her father's hardware business. The hours are more regular."

"I didn't know."

"Don't say anything until you hear official-like."

"Sammy and Abe and I think you're right. We ought to snap it up, not just for the restaurant, but because it's got the banquet room, too. You know how we run the Marks Company. 'All for one and one for all' just like The Three Musketeers. And there're three of us, too." She pointed the spoon at him. "We thought we'd up your salary, and when the restaurant/party business really gets going and makes the profit you project, we'll make you an equal partner. What do you think?"

"Great." Randall hugged and kissed his aunt and then his grandmother. He settled back in his chair. "How did you get Uncle Sammy and Uncle Abe to come around? They acted so set against the idea when I suggested it."

"Abe needed to be convinced you could run the business. I pointed out to him how well you've done this past year. How our customers really like you and how you've increased our sales. He had to agree you're good with people and have good business sense." She swallowed another spoonful of pudding. "Then I pointed out to Sammy how much more money we could make. Sammy went over the figures and couldn't find anything wrong with them, so he had to give in. Abe has already called Cousin Harry to write up a contract. We think you should go with Abe to present it to the Ancels since this is going to be your baby."

"You're the best, Aunt Yetta. I guess there's something I should tell you. I've been thinking of buying a ring for Maggie. I thought I'd give it to her on the anniversary of our first date, in a couple of weeks, just before Rosh Hashanah."

"Wonderful, *bubele*," Bubbe said in her yiddish accent. She glanced over at Yetta with raised eyebrows. "Maggie seems right for you. Have you talked?"

"We've talked about what I want for the future and what she wants, but we've never actually said the words *marriage* or *wedding*. Don't you think she'd say yes?"

"Why shouldn't she say yes?" Bubbe said. "Anyone can see how crazy she is for you."

"I want to call Maggie right now, okay?"

"I can see you've got *spielkes*. *Gai*, scoot." Bubbe shooed Randall toward the hall and the phone. When Randall left the room, Bubbe sighed and said, "What're we going to do? Didn't Jackie tell him?"

Yetta pulled her blouse out of her skirt and then tugged her slip away from her body. "I don't think he did. At least neither one of them said anything to me. I think we have to wait. Maybe it won't matter to Maggie."

"*Bubele*, they're an orthodox family. How could it not matter?" She put her hand to her cheek. "What're we going to do?"

Yetta put her face in front of the fan for a few seconds and pulled out her blouse to let the air go down. "I think Jack's hoping it'll cause a big problem and Randall will go back to Canada." She paused. "It would mortify Randall if we tried to discuss this with him. This is a father's responsibility."

Bubbe wiped her forehead with her napkin. "Maybe we should get Abe or Sammy to speak to him."

Yetta shook her head. "I don't know. That would cause a lot of talk in the family. Then it's sure to get out."

In the front hall, Randall sat at the telephone table and dialed Maggie's number. After finding out that Maggie's parents were out, he decided to go over and tell her the news in person.

When he got to Maggie's street, he jammed the car against the curb and bounded up her walk. She appeared at the screen door as he reached out to knock. Randall took her in his arms and kissed her right there, in the doorway. He didn't care who saw them.

Maggie caressed one of his hands with both of hers and drew him toward the kitchen. "What's this all about? Not that I'm complaining."

Randall smiled. He loved looking at her. He especially liked walking behind her. He thought she strutted like a model with those hips swinging from side to side, although he'd never actually seen a model. Tonight she reminded him of pistachio ice cream, his favorite flavor. She had on lime pedal pushers and a matching sleeveless blouse. Even her shoes were lime green. With Maggie everything always matched—her gloves, her handbag, her shoes. Her shiny brown hair was arranged in tight rolls around her face. She had a way of patting her hair and pursing her lips, Mae West like, when she was pleased with herself.

Maggie pushed him into a chair and sat down across from him, still holding his hand. He told her about the restaurant and the arrangement with his aunt and uncles. "This means we can talk about a future together, if you want." He thought his chest must be expanding a foot with every heartbeat. It almost hurt.

"I want. Oh, Randall, I want." Maggie sounded like she was going to cry but she had the biggest smile he'd ever seen.

Randall thought Maggie had the most beautiful white teeth. "Then you'll marry me?"

"Yes." She whispered.

Randall spoke fast. "It can't be right away. I have to save up money for a car, a house, furniture. So we'll have to wait, and I won't be able to spend so much on our dates. I hope that's okay. I love you very much."

"I love you, too." She patted her hair and pursed her lips. "All my friends will be so jealous. You're the most handsome guy around with your blue eyes and the most exotic, with your funny way of saying 'o's'."

He leaned over and kissed her. She put her head on his shoulder, and he held her.

Randall said, "Don't say anything to your parents yet. I want to do this the right way and ask your father's permission. You don't think he'll say no?"

She sat up. "Why should he say no? If he does, I'll kill him and then we'll run away together."

Randall laughed. "When should I ask him?"

"He's usually in the best mood on Sunday afternoons. . . I know . . . I'll ask my mother to have you over for dinner. You should tell them all about the new business. Afterward, suggest going for a walk and ask him while you're out. Does that sound good to you?"

"If you think it's the best plan . . . "

"I have some money saved," she said. "We could use it for the furniture."

"No, keep that for an emergency. And I don't want you to work after we're married."

She looked down at the table. "You want to make babies right away?"

Lives in Exile

He tried to get his head low enough so he could look her in the eyes. "I hadn't thought about that. But we could practice right now, if you want."

She looked up. "Randall Marks, I know it may be fashionable in some circles but not in mine. I want our wedding night to be special and mean something. You understand?"

"I understand. I just thought maybe. . ."

"Well, get those thoughts out of your head."

* * * * * * * **

Randall had arrived in Washington, D.C., one year earlier, in August 1937. He immediately started working for the Marks Company. A few days later, while making restaurant deliveries, he met Manny Ancel, a friendly sort, who suggested they meet later that evening at the pool hall at Georgia and Missouri Avenues.

Manny racked the balls. "You got a girl?"

Randall chalked the cue. "No."

"Tell you what. My girl, Becky, has a friend named Maggie. On Saturday night why don't the four of us go to the movie at the Fox and get some ice cream afterwards?"

"Sounds good."

"I'll set it up and let you know when you make the delivery on Thursday." Manny swigged his beer. "You're pretty good at this here pool."

Randall sipped his beer. "There wasn't much else to do where I grew up."

"Where was that, anyway?"

"Regina, Saskatchewan."

"And just where is that?"

Randall chuckled. "Western Canada, on the prairie."

"That's why you talk so funny." Manny racked the balls again. "What do your folks do out there?"

Randall didn't think he talked funny. He thought all these people in Washington sounded funny with their you'alls and their UMbrellas. "My father's the publisher of the newspaper. He owns a couple of other businesses, too. My mother died when I was six."

"May she rest in peace. How come you didn't stay out there?"

"It's kind of a long story. You know this Maggie?"

"Yeah, sure." Manny paused to light his cigarette. "Nice girl, stacked. Her parents own the kosher butcher on Georgia Avenue. She's a bookkeeper at one of them fancy dress stores on F Street. Dresses real nice. Want a smoke?"

"No, thanks. Gave it up after the army."

Manny stood his cue straight up and looked at Randall, his eyes opened wide. "You were in the army?"

"Canadian. Trained for the signal corps. Got out last year."

"Some of my buddies are meeting down at the Hot Shoppe. You wanta go?"

"Yeah, sure."

One Saturday night, a few months later, when Randall and Maggie were sitting in Aunt Yetta's car a few blocks from Maggie's house, she said, "I loved 'Camille'." She rolled her eyes. "It was so romantic. Didn't you love Greta Garbo?"

"Yeah. It was great." There were only a dozen other movies he'd have rather seen.

"You'd have rather seen 'A Day at the Races', wouldn't you?"

Randall grinned. She seemed to know what he was thinking.

"You're sweet." She reached across the front seat and took his hand. "I'm glad you suggested parking here so we could talk."

He looked directly in her eyes. He loved staring into her dark brown eyes. The first time he saw her he knew he wanted to know her. Now that he knew her, he knew he loved her.

Maggie, like most of the girls, loved his full lips and bright blue eyes. He had the most engaging smile, friendly—the way he opened his lips and showed his teeth. Despite the scar than ran up his left temple and across his forehead, most people would have said he was handsome. As it was, the scar was hardly noticeable. The doctor had been skillful and left only a thin line. She reached up and touched his scar. "How did that happen?"

"The army sent me for signal training down in Moose Jaw. One day we were out on maneuvers. I was with my buddy, Arthur, poor bastard. Sorry, Maggie."

"That's okay."

"Anyway, Arthur took out the long distance signal gun. He held it up with his right hand, like you're supposed to, and pulled the trigger. Instead of the flare going up, it exploded inside the barrel. He lost some fingers, his right eye, and I don't know what else. I was a couple feet away. I think a big piece of the barrel must've hit me in the eye. Other smaller pieces cut my face and this whole side of my body." He showed her a scar which ran across his palm.

She caressed it.

"I was in the hospital for a few months. They sewed up my face and hand but my eye was a mess." He touched his eyebrow. "For a while they thought they might have to take it out."

"Oh, God. You can't tell by looking at you." She squinted at his eye. "It looks normal."

"They were able to save it. But I lost most of the sight. I can just see shadows. At first, I had terrible pounding headaches. I had to be where it was quiet and dark. When the pain went away, it took me a while to adjust. I'd lost my depth perception. About six months after the explosion, they discharged me and sent me home. I had nightmares about the accident for a while." He touched his forehead. "Now only the scar is left."

"Why did you join in the first place?"

He looked at the scar on his palm. "My dad and I weren't getting along. This was in '35 after graduation. He wanted me to work for him but I wanted to get out on my own. We were having huge arguments, more like battles, followed by long silences. So I enlisted."

"Why didn't you stay in Regina after?"

"My father still treated me like a kid, watched every little thing. Besides I wanted to get away from the small town where you see the same people every day and everybody knows your business. You have no idea how free I feel here. I know I ended up working for my family but it's not the same as working for your father, at least my father. I thought I'd start out here and then see what happens. But I'm beginning to really like it."

She leaned over to kiss his eye and her breast pressed into his hand. She didn't pull back. He kissed her.

"I'm crazy about you," he said when they drew apart.

"I'm crazy about you, too."

Randall wasn't sure how far to go with Maggie. If she had been one of the high school girls he had dated in Regina, he would have been trying to get his hands inside her clothes by now. If she'd been one of the girls he and his army buddies dated during training at Moose Jaw, they would have gone to bed on the second or third date. But she was a Jewish girl from Washington, from a good family. He didn't know the rules and didn't know whom to ask. This kind of information you just absorb when you grow up in a place. He wouldn't dare discuss Maggie with any of the guys he'd met because that could give a girl a bad reputation. So he waited and tried to figure out her signals. But it was hard to know when to stop when they were making out and his blood felt hot.

The next Saturday night they went with Manny and Becky and two other couples to a club that played swing. Randall didn't think he danced very well though Maggie complimented him. She danced the fast dances like they were the only two people in the place. He loved the way her breasts bounced. He sometimes caught himself imagining her in bed. During the slow dances, she pressed up against him. At the table she sat so close to him her hair tickled his face. She smelled like gardenias.

On the way home, he parked the car away from the street lamp a few blocks from her house. He took her hands, pulled her toward him and kissed her. He felt her tongue on his lips. In a frenzy, he kissed her cheeks, forehead, ears, neck. As he kissed down the V-neck of her blouse, he drew his hands under her arms and then caressed her breasts. She leaned back and moaned.

"I need to breathe," she said as she took both his hands in hers.

"Breathing is good," he said.

She laughed her easy laugh. She resisted when he tried to pull her back toward him.

Maybe he had gone too far. He stroked her hand while he tried to think of something to say that wouldn't sound like a line.

Maggie said, "What're your plans for the future?"

Then he knew for sure she really liked him. "I haven't figured that all out. Aunt Yetta, besides lending me her car every Saturday night, wants to show me how to run the family business. Mostly, I guess, I want people to like me and I want, you know, a regular life. I'd like to be my own boss, have a cute secretary, but not too cute. I see myself sitting in a nice office with a big wooden desk with two picture frames on it, one my wife and the other my children. The secretary's desk would be right outside my door. There would be Venetian blinds and drapes on the window and a big potted plant in the corner. The secretary would sit in the chair across from my desk taking dictation." He paused for a moment and touched his scar. "It would be great if my father and I could get along—you know, go to a ball game or go fishing together and swap stories. It would be nice if I could ask his advice when I had a problem like when I was a kid. Aunt Yetta says I'm a good businessman." He shrugged his shoulders. "My father's great with people. I didn't think I was, but, I guess like father, like son, as they say."

She patted her curls. "So you're staying in Washington and not going back to Regina?"

"Definitely yes."

Maggie moved closer. "I'm glad."

Randall said as he pulled her into his embrace. "I'm glad you're glad."

In June, Jack came for his annual two-week summer visit. During dinner that first night, Bubbe said, "So, did you know our Randall is keeping company with a young woman?"

"Yes, Mama, Randall wrote me about her."

"She's coming for Shabbos dinner. Right, Randall?"

"Right, Bubbe."

"Wait till you meet her, Jackie. She's a *sheine maidel* and she makes our Randall very happy."

Randall could feel the heat rising from his toes. He wanted Maggie with him right now. He always felt more sure of himself when she was with him.

After dinner, as Randall was walking toward the phone in the back room to call Maggie, he heard Aunt Yetta say, "She's an orthodox girl. You need to talk to him, Jackie. You're his father."

Randall called out, "Poppa, Maggie said to tell you she's looking forward to meeting you tomorrow night."

Randall and his father were sharing the twin beds in Aunt Yetta's room. Randall waited for his father to tell him whatever Aunt Yetta wanted them to talk about. But Jack said nothing.

The next night, Friday night, fifteen people sat around the mahogany dining room table—Uncle Sammy and his wife, Uncle Abe and his wife, all six of Randall's first cousins plus Randall, Maggie, Jack, Yetta, and Bubbe. All the talking stopped when Bubbe, with a triangle of lace covering her head, stood next to the server and lit the Shabbos candles. She waved her hands over the flames as if to draw the light toward her and then recited the blessing. Randall's oldest cousin, Martin, stood next to Bubbe. He raised the silver wine goblet toward the group and recited the traditional prayer in Hebrew and in English. At Bubbe's, the Shabbos meal always began with a bowl of chicken soup with a matzah ball. This was followed by brisket, raisin kugel pudding, tszimmes, and salad.

After dinner, the family sat around Jack in the living room. Jack set a bottle of scotch and a glass tumbler on an end table. He poured himself a drink and then pulled out his cigar. He offered the bottle around to his brothers, but no one took it. Bubbe turned on the fan to blow the smoke toward the open window.

"Uncle Jack, tell us how Helena, Montana, got its name," asked one of the younger nephews.

"I told you that story two summers ago."

"But I was two years younger and don't remember," Randall's cousin said.

"Okay." Jack took another swallow. "It was close to a hundred years ago when prospectors found gold in streams way out there in Montana. There weren't any trains way back then. So the prospectors came on horses and in wagons and some of them just walked. They first called Helena 'Last Chance Gulch'. There weren't any stores in the gold fields, so a few smart-thinking people loaded up wagons with goods and clothing and all sorts of things and went to where the miners were."

Jack poured himself another scotch. "Two of those smart-thinking people were cousins of ours named Helen and Isaac Cohen. Only they didn't go to Last Chance Gulch. They went to Virginia City, another boom town, close by. Our cousin, Helen, took care of those miners. She cooked for them and helped them out when they were sick or injured. Now these prospectors moved around a lot, going from gold strike to gold strike. So some of them ended up at Last Chance Gulch. Pretty soon Last Chance Gulch got to be a pretty big and important place. The people who built houses there had a meeting and decided they needed a better name for their town. One of the prospectors who had come from Virginia City suggested they name the city after our cousin, Helen, who had been like an angel to them. When the majority agreed, Last Chance Gulch became Helena."

"Do you believe that, Uncle Jack?"

"I sure do. It was told to me during the time I lived in Helena by my best friend's father who'd been at the meeting himself. Some people try to say it was named after a place in Minnesota but that's only because they don't like the idea of a city being named after a Jewish woman. But that's the truth, I swear."

Jack finished off the second glass of scotch and flicked the ashes from his cigar into the ashtray. He poured himself another drink.

Bubbe said, "*Kinder*, it's time for 'The Shadow'."

The cousins raced through the dining room to the back room and Bubbe's radio.

The voice of Orson Welles boomed. "Who knows what evil lurks in the heart of men? The Shadow knows!"

All the adults turned.

"Turn it down," Uncle Abe called out. When they could hear themselves talk again, Abe said, "So, how're things going up in Regina?"

"Thank God for the newspaper. People still got to advertise even during hard times. The grain business sure went to hell. But it looks like it's coming back."

Abe said, "Thank God for the U.S. Government and its workers who still like to eat and, now, to drink. We survived the depression okay because of them."

Sammy said, "You think Joe Louis will be able to defeat Max Schmeling this time?"

"Don't you ever think of anything but sports?" Abe said. "I hope he flattens that German. Things in Europe are getting worse. You can't keep giving in to people like Hitler." He shook his finger. "Any Jew who stayed after Goering's warning to get out of Germany is crazy. There're rumors they're going to start making Jews carry identity cards. What else are they thinking of?"

Abe's wife patted his arm. "You'll give yourself a stroke and we're having such a nice visit with Jack."

Sammy said, "Did you read about that Yankee, Johnny Vander Meer, pitching his second no-hitter in a row?"

In the car, on the way home, Maggie said to Randall, "Your father's charming. It's hard to imagine why he never remarried."

Randall didn't know what to say. Should he tell her about Shining Star? About the *Métis* Indian woman who raised and loved him, who lived with them since before he was born, whom he loved like a mother and who slept with his father? Would Maggie understand they couldn't get married because of the laws against mixed marriages so they lived together? Randall instinctively knew Shining Star was a forbidden topic in Washington even before he made his first visit. He had never talked about her with Zeyde and they talked about everything else. Aunt Yetta knew Shining Star well from the summer she lived with them. But she never asked about her, either.

"You really like him?" Randall said. He wished he could see her face but with the hard rain, the lightening, and the thunder, he had to concentrate on the road.

"It's funny the way he can keep the cigar in his mouth and talk out of one side. Does he always have a cigar in his mouth?"

Randall laughed. "Yeah. He always does."

"You should give him a chance and try to be friends again. You haven't seen or talked to him for almost a year."

When Randall got home, Bubbe and Aunt Yetta were still cleaning up in the kitchen.

"Where's my father?"

"He was very tired so we sent him up to bed," Aunt Yetta said.

Randall started putting the china up in the cabinets for them.

"Mama, why don't you go to bed, too?" Yetta said. "Randall and I will finish up."

"All right, then. *Aguten nacht.* Sleep tight." She kissed Randall on the cheek and gave a royal wave as she stepped through the kitchen door toward the stairs.

Randall took the platter from Aunt Yetta. "Do you consider our family orthodox?"

Aunt Yetta pointed to the top of the cabinet next to the stove. "We're orthodox in some ways like keeping kosher, but in others we've made accommodations to the American way of doing things."

Randall stretched his whole six foot frame and managed to place the platter on the shelf. "What do you mean?"

Aunt Yetta picked up the rag and started wiping the counter tops. "Bubbe and Zeyde had to keep their store open on Saturdays because that's when most people got paid and bought their groceries. We keep the Marks Company open because restaurants need us to deliver provisions and liquor to them on Saturdays. Otherwise, we wouldn't have many customers. But people like Maggie's family might not consider us orthodox because they're much more observant."

Randall hung up the dish towels on the bar. Was that what Aunt Yetta meant last night? Why would it be necessary for his father to talk to him about that? Aunt Yetta would've been a good mother. He wondered why she never got married. She was smart and good looking. She was lots of fun, not at all like some "old maid" prude. She always got her hair done in the latest style with no gray, either. And she dressed real smart. She had the same twinkling brown eyes and laughing smile as Bubbe.

Late Sunday afternoon, Aunt Yetta suggested the four of them go to the Chinese restaurant for supper. "I hear they have a new chef from China who used to cook in New York."

"Only if you let me treat and we ask Maggie along," Jack said.

The hostess sat them at a round table. Jack sat between Maggie and Bubbe. "When I lived in Helena," Jack said, "there was a whole section of

Chinese. My friends and I used to eat in one of their restaurants. There aren't any Chinese in Regina."

"What was Randall like as a boy?" Maggie asked.

"He was a good looking kid. He had a whole box of toy soldiers which he loved to play with. Did Randall tell you the training center for the Royal Canadian Mounted Police is in Regina?"

Maggie shook her head.

"When he was a kid he said he wanted to grow up to be a Mountie." Randall blushed.

Maggie squeezed Randall's hand under the table.

Randall dropped his father, Aunt Yetta and Bubbe at home first. Then he drove Maggie home.

Maggie said, "Your father's very proud of you."

"You're kidding."

"Didn't you notice the way he looked at you after your grandmother said you were a wonderful grandson?"

"I guess I didn't."

"You haven't really talked. Have you?"

"What can I say?"

"Say? Tell him how happy you are. Tell him how well things are going. It couldn't have been easy raising a boy all by himself."

"We had a housekeeper." I'm a jerk, Randall thought, making Shining Star, a housekeeper.

When he got back, his father was sitting up in his bed, smoking his cigar and reading *The Good Earth*. It always amazed him how much his father liked to read and how much reading he did. It's ironic that a high school dropout, who left home at fifteen, had ended up a newspaper publisher. But as Aunt Yetta often said, life could be strange.

"How're you doing, Poppa?" Randall's ritual greeting when he was a kid.

"Not so bad," which was the required reply. He looked at Randall.

"How's Shining Star?" Randall said.

"She's fine, the same. But I think she's lonely without you. There isn't enough to keep her busy. So she's taken to going to her people during the day. She's glad to get your letters." He put his bookmark between the pages and placed the book on the night stand. "I like that Maggie of yours. I can tell you do, too."

Randall sat on the edge of the bed, untied his shoes and took them off.

"How long you two been going out now?" Jack said.

"Almost a year."

"You got any long term ideas with her?"

As he unbuckled his belt and unzipped his pants, Randall crossed the room toward the closet. With his back to Jack, he said, "How'd you know my mother was the right one for you?"

Jack didn't know what to answer. He'd never discussed Bessie with Randall. Was this the time to tell Randall they had just lived together and pretended they were married? Was this was the time to tell him about the huge mistake he'd made? "That was a long time ago." He puffed on his cigar.

Randall hung up his pants and snatched his pajamas from the hook. "But you must remember."

"Your mother was beautiful. You have some of her features—your nose, your straight hair, your blue eyes. She was everything I dreamed about as a young man. She was very intriguing." Jack paused. He'd gone far enough.

Randall turned around. "But did you want to be with her all the time? Did she make you feel smart and strong? Did you want to make her proud of you?"

"Is that they way you feel about Maggie?"

Randall got into his bed. "Yes."

"Then she's the one for you. But be careful, son. Women aren't always what they seem."

"What do you mean?"

"Just be careful. Women have a way of fooling men." Jack turned off the light.

In the car, on the way to the train station at the end of his stay, Jack said, "I'm glad things are going so well for you here in Washington, son. You're getting good experience. When you're ready, I want you to come back and learn my business so you can take over when I retire."

Oh, God. He's not going to start this again. "You're never going to retire. What would you do with yourself? Anyway I thought you understood I don't want to live in Regina."

"I've built a good business and I don't have anyone else to leave it to. It's your obligation. You owe it to me."

"I want to see how things go with Maggie."

Lives in Exile

"Of course. We'll talk about it another time. Just don't count your chickens before they hatch."

Randall thought of Maggie when he should have been thinking about other things. Once, at lunch time, he told the delivery man to drive down the street where she worked. He hoped he might catch a glimpse of her.

"Man, you got it bad," the Negro driver said.

"I don't know what you mean."

"Driving down the street like this. Don't you have no pride?"

Randall hadn't known a Negro before he came to Washington. Once, when Randall said this to the oldest driver, the man replied, "You mean there ain't no Negroes up there in Canada?"

"Not where I'm from."

"You mean white people do all the housecleaning jobs and street cleaning jobs?"

Randall blushed. "No, those jobs are done by the Indians mostly."

"Are there many Jewish people up there?" asked the driver.

"No, not where I live."

"Then I'm glad I don't live there. You Jewish folks treat us Negroes best. Maybe it comes from having been slaves once yourselves."

Randall didn't know much about that. His father didn't make a big deal about being Jewish. Only his grandparents and Aunt Yetta cared that he considered himself Jewish.

Chapter Eleven

Engagement

1938-1939

Randall felt himself getting warm. He guessed his face was red. Hoping Mr. Goldberg didn't notice, he struggled to repeat the speech he'd practiced and memorized. "Mr. Goldberg, Maggie and I have been going out together for almost a year. She's very special to me." The pain in the center of his chest felt like he'd been hit by a baseball.

"Her mother and I think so, too."

"I don't know if Maggie told you, but I'm twenty-one. I've been in the Canadian army." He pointed toward his scar. "This comes from an injury I got in the army which blinded me in my left eye."

"Maggie told us. A terrible accident."

In one breath Randall said, "I'd like your permission to ask Maggie to marry me. My prospects are good, and I'm a hard worker." He was relieved—he'd gotten it out.

Mr. Goldberg took a deep breath, "We'd be very happy to welcome you into our family—a nice *Yiddisha mensch* from a good family. Besides, if I don't say yes, I'm sure Maggie will have my head." He chuckled.

Randall shook Mr. Goldberg's hand. "Thank you, sir. I'll take good care of her."

Evelyn Auerbach

The rest of the day was a blur of happiness and good feelings. He remembered holding Maggie's hand the whole day and stealing a kiss whenever her parents weren't paying attention.

That evening he knew he had to find the courage to write a letter to his father. This was going to be even harder than asking Mr. Goldberg for permission. For almost an hour, he sat in the back room at his grandfather's desk. A sheet of glass covered the desk top with a green blotter on top. His grandfather's meerschaum pipes stood in a round holder at the back left corner. The faces on the bowls stared at him. He could smell the tobacco. The aroma tickled his nose and reminded him of the wood pile outside his house after a soaking rain.

Many summer evenings he'd sat on his grandfather's knee at this desk while Zeyde studied each pipe. "Which face looks right to you today?" he would ask Randall. After the choice was made, Zeyde stuffed the tobacco down into the bowl and let Randall make the last push with the tamper. When Randall was old enough, he would hold the match to the pipe while Zeyde sucked until the tobacco burned. Randall wished Zeyde was there now to help him figure out how to tell his father he wasn't coming back.

Randall shook his head to clear away the memories so he could concentrate. He weighed every word he wrote.

Washington, D.C.
August 27, 1938

Dear Poppa,

    I have several pieces of very good news. First, Uncle Samy, Uncle Abe, and Aunt Yetta have decided to purchase a restaurant and party room business from one of their customers. They want me to be the manager. They have given me a good raise in salary. When the new business is profitable, they have promised to make mean equal partner in the Marks Company.

    Second, I have asked Maggie Goldberg to marry me. Her father has given his permission. We haven't set a date yet because I need to save some money to set us up properly. Aunt Yetta is helping me shop for the ring which I plan to give to Maggie in twelve days.

> I have thought very carefully about all we talked about when you were here in June. I have considered the wonderful opportunity you offered me in Regina, but I feel my future is here in Washington. I know you will be very disappointed, but I hope you will try to see this from my point of view.
>
> Please send my regards to Shining Star.
>
> Love,
>
> Randall

On the anniversary of their first date, Randall took Maggie to the Shoreham Hotel Terrace for dinner and dancing to the music of Barney Breeskin and The Blue Room Orchestra. He'd asked around and discovered this was the "premier place" for proposals among Maggie's friends. Randall bought a new suit and Maggie wore a new strapless evening dress of pale pink lace with a matching satin bolero jacket. The evening was Randall's big splurge before the saving and scrimping began. The weather that night was typical of Washington in August—hot, humid, and a very little breeze. Gardenia centerpieces perfumed the air. Randall and Maggie stuck to the fox trots which Randall felt he had mastered. At the end of the evening, while the band packed up, they strolled through the garden to the swimming pool. Randall guided her to a chair. He knelt to make the official proposal. When she accepted, he placed the engagement ring with an almost perfect, round, three-quarter karat, blue-white diamond on her left hand. Afterwards they went to Maggie's house where her parents waited. Maggie and her mother hugged and kissed while Mr. Goldberg pumped Randall's hand. It was one of the few times in his life Randall could remember being at the center of so much happiness and excitement. Even though Maggie was the focus of all the commotion, he had generated the happiness and he basked in the warmth of the love that flowed around him.

The next day Randall and Maggie sat close together at her kitchen table on which she had arranged a stack of writing paper, several sharpened pencils and her father's adding machine. The Formica top felt cool even in the hot and humid kitchen.

"How much money do you think we should spend on a house?" Maggie said.

"I think we could get a nice one for about $9,000. So we'd probably need a $1,000 down payment. And a $1,000 for a new car. What do you think it would cost to furnish a house?"

Maggie thought for a minute. "I know a nice bedroom suite runs about $325. It does cost a little more to set up a kosher kitchen, though. So for all the necessities, I bet we could do it for about $1,000. So that means we need to have $11,000, all together."

"No, no. For the house we only need to have a down payment and money for settlement costs. Somewhere between $1,000 and $2,000 total is enough for the house. Plus the other $2,000. We need close to $4,000. Still . . ." Randall put his face in front of the fan which sat revolving and rotating on the corner of the table. "Maybe we could do with a good used car for a start. I bet we could get one for about $700. Oh, and let's not forget our honeymoon."

"So how much do you have in your savings account?"

"One-hundred-fifty dollars. Bubbe said I shouldn't pay her room and board anymore. It's her engagement present. So, I'll have five dollars to save each week. And, if I save my $350 salary increase . . . how long will it take us?"

Maggie, the bookkeeper, pressed the number tabs and pulled the arm of the adding machine. "It will take us from one-and-a-half to two years." She pouted. "I'd hoped we could get married next year, in December. December is such a good month. You don't have to worry too much about snowstorms and Shabbos is over early so we could have a Saturday night wedding."

Randall stroked her arm. "Maybe we can do better. I'm going to work real hard at saving as much money as I can. Why don't we wait until next June? We'll see where we are. Then we'll decide what to do. Okay?"

On Tuesday, October 1st, 1938, Randall turned the key in the lock of The Ukrainian Inn "Deliveries Only" door. Stale air with a scent of pine greeted him. "It smells clean," he said to Bubbe who waited at the bottom of the stairs.

"It shouldn't smell clean?"

He reached in and found the light switch. With his outstretched hand he helped Bubbe up the steps and through the door.

Bubbe squeezed his hand. "A beautiful kitchen."

Randall moved ahead of her into the dining room and turned on all the lights and the ceiling fans. His pounding heart seemed to be racing ahead of his body.

He turned around and held out of his arms as if to say, *here you are*.

Bubbe said, "*Bubele*, I've never seen such a big smile."

"I shouldn't smile?" He mimicked her accent.

They laughed.

He stood in the center and turned around in a slow circle taking in all the details—the dark parquet floors, the gold-on-gold flocked wallpaper, the paintings of mountains and castles.

Bubbe strolled from table to table until she got to the gold sheer curtains in the big picture window. First, she fingered the material and then drew the curtains aside to look out on Thirteenth Street. "It's a good location." She wandered over to the hostess desk and took out a menu. "You're changing the menu?"

"We'll see what the chef says after our meeting."

"How do you get to the party room from inside?"

He swung his arm toward the kitchen and bowed. "This way, madam."

Bubbe pushed the swinging doors into the kitchen but didn't go through immediately. "No squeaks. That's good." In the kitchen she stopped to inspect the burners on the iron stove and opened all the oven doors. She practically stuck her head in, to look in all the corners.

Randall used his key to open the doors marked "Settings," "Linens," and "Pantry." The linen closet smelled of soap and bleach. A vision of Shining Star bending over the ringer tub in the laundry room flashed through his head.

Bubbe walked over. "These aren't closets. These are rooms. Four people could stand in each one."

She followed him up the stairs, through the serving kitchen and into the party room. At the far end was a raised platform for a band. The window was covered in a gold-pleated opaque drape. The floor and wallpaper matched the downstairs except no pictures hung on the walls.

"This is your future, Randall. For you and Maggie. I know you'll make a big success."

"I'm going to try real hard, Bubbe. I want you and Maggie and everyone else to be proud of me." He gave her a kiss. "Thanks for coming down with me, my first day."

"*Bubele*, I wouldn't have missed it for the world. This is why Zeyde and I left the Ukraine forty-five years ago." She pointed her finger at his chest. "So your father, your aunt, your uncles and you could have a better life than in Podolyia."

"I think you were very brave."

"Pfff. We didn't have much choice. What's buzzing?"

"The chef must be at the door."

At the end of the day he picked up Maggie. As soon as he pulled the car to the curb in front of her store, Maggie opened the door and started talking. "How'd it go?"

"I just dropped off the new menu at the office. Chef Bernard and I worked out a great one. Mr. Ancel was right. Chef Bernard's gifted. Tomorrow, his assistant's coming in and they're going to prepare all the items we came up with. The aunts, uncles, and Bubbe are coming at dinner time to taste. Can you come, too?"

"I'd love to."

"On Thursday, I'll price everything out and, if necessary, re-taste any changes. We plan to have the menu printed next week."

"So, you and the chef got along good?"

"Yeah. He liked my ideas."

Maggie asked, "How about the grand re-opening party?"

"The party's on for Sunday, the 23rd."

On October 23rd, the entire Marks family stood by the front door and greeted their friends, business associates, and all the people who had booked parties during the next several months. The tables were set with gold tablecloths and gold napkins. Golden mums in clear glass vases decorated every table. Main courses and side dishes were served in the dining room. Waiters supplied the drinks and seconds of everything.

Upstairs in the party room, a band played while desserts were served. They had set the tables with white tablecloths and napkins and purple mums. It had been Randall's idea to expand the dessert menu and go for the after-theater crowd on Thursday, Friday, and Saturday nights. Randall convinced the "three musketeers" a late dessert could make up a third seating and be very profitable. There weren't many places in Washington open late enough for people looking for a snack after an evening out. Chef Bernard hired a special *sous-chef*. One by one the uncles came over to clap Randall on the shoulder and tell him how great everything looked and tasted. Each one said, "Great idea, this party of yours. Great for business."

Maggie followed Randall around as he greeted each group of people. When they got to Manny and Becky's table, they sat.

"You've got a talent for the restaurant business," Manny said. "I would never have guessed."

Lives in Exile

Randall said, "We're going to make your wedding the most talked about shindig of 1938."

Becky and Manny's wedding was held in December. Randall took his place among the groomsmen but didn't hear a word of the service. His entire attention was focused on Maggie in her powder blue Maid of Honor dress. He jumped when Manny stomped on the glass to smash it. At the reception Randall ran from place to place trying to socialize like a guest and supervise the waiters at the same time. He found time to dance a bit with Maggie and sit with her for a few minutes at a time. He worried she felt abandoned.

On the way home, she said, "Nonsense, I had a wonderful time. I danced with Becky's father and Manny's father and lots of my friends. You forget I've known Becky almost my whole life and Manny for a long time, too. We have all the same friends. I'm the only one who's found a catch from far away."

"But I don't want you finding some local guy and dumping me."

"That'll never happen." She kissed him on the cheek, tickled his neck, and then blew gently into his ear.

"Stop or I'll have an accident."

She giggled. "You really want me to stop?"

"No, but I can't concentrate. Let me find a place to park."

He turned a corner and found a dark spot with no houses nearby. Randall lied. "I got a letter from my father yesterday. He said how pleased he was for us—the restaurant and all. He thinks you're wonderful and I'm a very lucky guy. He's right, of course." He caressed her cheek. "You are the most beautiful girl in the world."

"That's what I wanted to hear. And you are the best kisser in the world."

"And how would you know?" He pretended to be upset.

"I'm not telling."

Pretty soon the car windows fogged completely.

At home, he jumped in the shower. He let the cold water run all over him for as long as he could stand it. *God, I wish I hadn't lied to Maggie about hearing from my father. Now, if I tell her how upset I am about my father ignoring my letter, I'll have to tell her I lied to her. Stupid, stupid, stupid. Why don't we chuck it and get married? I've about halfway paid back the Marks Company for the car loan. If we got married, we could live here or with her parents. Lots of couples do. Maggie'd go for that, I bet. But people who get married before they have the money never seem to get ahead. Pretty soon there's a baby and they're still at their parents' house. No, I want to be on our own. What'm I going to do? Just have to keep concentrating on the goal and hope the sacrifice is worth it.*

The next weekend they talked again about the money they needed to get married. Maggie wanted to count the several hundred dollars in wedding gifts she was convinced they were going to get. Randall refused to consider that as part of the $4,000 they needed. "That would be counting our chickens before they hatch. We'll use the gifts to buy some of the furniture we didn't count as necessities."

But she did convince him to let her add the five dollars a week the restaurant was now paying her for helping out as the weekend hostess.

The restaurant was closed on Mondays and Tuesdays. On those days, Randall picked Maggie up at work. Usually they ate dinner with her parents on Monday and at Bubbe's on Tuesday. "At least we're saving money," they told each other over and over to keep their spirits up.

Just before New Year's Randall found a letter from his father on the "mail table" in the living room. He ran up to his room to open it. It was a card. On the front was embossed "Congratulations to the Bride and Groom." Inside, the printed greeting said, "May all the hopes and plans you two are sharing come true in the wonderful years ahead." All Jack had written was "Have a nice life! Father." A check for twenty-five dollars U.S. fell on the bed. "That's it, no note, no nothing," Randall said out loud. He crushed the check in his fist and lay back on the bed. *Damn him, damn him.* He lay there in his suit for a long time, staring at the ceiling with his hand over his forehead. The phone rang in the hallway.

Aunt Yetta called, "Randall, it's Maggie."

"Tell her I'm already in bed and I'll call her tomorrow, please." He was afraid if he talked to her, he would blurt out the whole story.

Aunt Yetta called again, "She said that would be fine. Are you feeling okay?"

"I'm fine, just tired."

"Good night, then."

Even though Randall could hear the radio playing downstairs, he got up and tiptoed around his room. His bedroom was over the kitchen and he didn't want Aunt Yetta and Bubbe to hear him. He stuffed the card and the crumpled check in his bottom drawer under the pile of sweaters. Back in bed, he realized Shining Star must have had a hard time convincing his father to send even that miserly check. Well, Jack'd have to wait until a mountain grew in Regina to get a thank you note or for the check to be cashed.

On the day Randall left for the army he'd wanted to give his father a hug or at least a handshake. He wore his only suit. He had packed his underwear, socks, one pair of pants and some shirts. He added the photograph of his mother with her family, the one of his father, mother, and himself in the living room of their house in Regina, and the photograph of Bubbe and Zeyde on their twenty-fifth anniversary which his grandmother had given him after Zeyde died.

When he was ready to go, his father sat at the end of the sofa, vigorously puffing his cigar. A bottle of scotch sat on the end table with an empty glass. As he approached, his father turned away. Randall stopped and waited a few seconds but his father didn't turn back. Finally there was nothing to do but leave. As he moved toward the door, his legs felt like rubber. He didn't think he could hold his shoulders up they were so heavy. Shining Star waited for him with her hand on the doorknob. They stood facing each other. She took his hand. Their eyes searched each other's face, saying their good-byes. Shining Star had told him, many years ago, the story of how the *Métis* men had said good-bye silently to their women when the warriors went off with Riel to fight the government during the rebellion. Now he knew how they felt. After a few moments they nodded to each other, he glanced at his father, and stalked out. The recruiting officer waited out front. Randall had wanted to cry as they drove away.

He was older now, and he could hold out, too. This time his father would have to make the first move. He wasn't going to go home from Washington as he had from the army—injured and devastated. He had Maggie and he had a future. He hoped Shining Star could feel him sending his love to her even though they weren't looking in each other's eyes.

On New Year's Eve, Becky, Manny and several of their friends decided to celebrate at The Ukrainian Inn so they could all be together. Randall started drinking before midnight. By 2:00 a.m., when it was time to close, he was plastered. The head waiter, Manny, and Maggie took care of everything while Randall sat at a table and sang.

Manny said to Maggie, "Come on, we'll drive you and Randall home."

"No, thanks. I'll manage."

"But how'll you get him into the house?" Manny asked.

"Don't worry."

They helped Randall into the car.

When Maggie sat in the driver's seat, Randall said, "Maggie, Maggie, Maggie. How's my little Maggie?"

"Embarrassed. That's how. What's going on? I never saw you like this, and don't you dare throw up till you get to a bathroom."

He started picking at the collar of her coat, trying to unbutton it. When he couldn't, he gave up and started rubbing her chest. "Maggie, Maggie, Maggie."

"Quit it. What's the matter with you?" She pushed his hand away. "You're disgusting."

He turned to the window and started singing "You Are My Sunshine."

She managed to get him out of the car and up the front stairs onto the porch, propelling him into one of the green metal chairs. Holding his keys up to the porch light, she moved them around on the ring, trying to figure out which one was for the front door. As she was trying one of the keys in the door, Randall reached under her dress with both his hands and began to massage her thigh.

She stepped out of his reach and left him grabbing for her. "When we get inside, we're going to have a talk about this behavior." When they got to the kitchen, she started making coffee while he flopped into a chair.

He tilted the kitchen chair back against the wall. "Come on little Maggie, show me what you got."

"Shh. You're going to wake up Aunt Yetta and your grandmother."

He stood up unsteadily. "You wanta see what I got?" He held her around the wrist, tugged her toward the front hall, and yanked her up the stairs. "Come on little Maggie, I'll show you what I got." In his room, he pushed her on the bed.

She hitched herself into a sitting position. Tears streamed down her face. She shivered.

Randall turned his back to her. He reached down, opened the bottom drawer of his dresser and pulled out the card and check. He screamed, "There it is. That's all he sent. The fucking bastard." He threw the card and check at her.

Bubbe and Yetta were at the door in their bathrobes.

"What's wrong?" Yetta asked.

With a trembling hand, Maggie reached over the edge of the bed to pick up the card and check that had fallen on the floor. With the other hand she wiped her cheeks. "Randall got a little drunk and wanted to show me something."

Randall cried out, "I wanna talk to Shining Star."

Yetta said to Maggie, "We'll take care of him. Why don't you go on? Everything will be okay."

Maggie turned to Randall. "If you think so. I'll take his car." When she left, she had the card and check with her.

It was early afternoon before he called her. "I'm sorry, sweetheart, for whatever I did. Aunt Yetta said I was loud and obnoxious. I don't remember too much. Did I ruin the evening?"

"Why didn't you tell me the truth?" she said in a quiet voice.

"I've always told you the truth." He tried to remember what he might have said. "Anything I said while I was in that state shouldn't be trusted."

"You were drunk and you gave me the card and check your father sent you. 'Have a nice life! Father.'"

"Oh, God."

"Why didn't you tell me the truth? I could've helped you. Don't you trust me?"

He whispered, "Of course I do. I love you. I was afraid you'd think he was rejecting you when all he was doing was rejecting me."

"We need to talk."

"Come over in about an hour. Bubbe and Aunt Yetta are going to a New Year's Day party."

When the doorbell rang about an hour later, he let her in. He had shaved and combed his hair but he still looked like a dried-up cow chip. They sat on the sofa under the front windows. "I'm sorry," was all he could say. With his eyes he pleaded for forgiveness.

"Who or what is Shining Star?"

Randall put both elbows on his knees. He hunched over and rubbed his temples. "That's kind of complicated."

Maggie put her hand on his shoulder. "I love you. I love you," she said with the emphasis on "you."

"But maybe you won't when you hear some of these things."

"Whatever happened between you and your father is just that. The only thing that matters is what happens between us. I want the complete truth."

"How'd you know about Shining Star?"

"That's one of the things you said last night, 'I want to talk to Shining Star'."

"Shining Star is our housekeeper, but she's much more. When I was a child, I loved to hear her tell the story of how my father found her. He went over to the *Métis* village when he needed someone to take care of my sick mother and the baby who was to come. That was me. *Métis* are people who are part French and part Indian. Shining Star was the first person my father spoke to in the village. She was standing on the corner waiting for her sister to come out of a store. A white man, my father, walked up and asked her if she knew someone who wanted a job. She was cautious. She'd heard many bad stories about white men. But when she looked into his eyes, she saw a wounded bear calling to her. The bear stood on its hind legs and reached out a paw. She heard its plaintive roar, so she left her family and friends and came to live with us. The whole story seemed magical to me, the way Shining Star told it."

"That's touching. But why did you want to talk to her last night?"

"I don't remember too much about my real mother except she was in bed a lot and she used to sit in a rocking chair by the window in her bedroom. I mostly remember her being sad. I had a brother who died when he was born. My father took me in to see my mother before she died, too. I hugged and kissed her and pleaded with her not to leave me. When I was a kid, I thought it was my fault she died. That I wasn't good enough. Oh, God." Randall stood up and stepped over to the fireplace. He put both hands on the mantel and peered at the fake coals in the wrought iron bin.

Maggie followed him and put both her hands on his shoulders and laid her face in the middle of his back.

He turned around and held her. "Shining Star was always there for me in her silent way. It's hard to know what she's thinking from her face. She only speaks when there's something important to say. Anyway, soon after my mother died, she moved into my father's bedroom."

"You mean they slept together?"

"They still do."

"But how could your father . . ."

"I guess he loves her. They can't get married because of the laws in Canada. I think she's beautiful." Randall put his hands on Maggie's cheeks. With his thumbs he traced the outline of her bones. "She has a narrow face like yours." He ran his thumbs across her lips and up the sides of her nose. "A nose and mouth like yours but not as beautiful." He brushed his lips across hers. "Her eyes don't open as wide as yours. Her skin color is golden. She takes good care of us." He hugged Maggie again. "I had plenty of friends at school but I never brought anyone home. The mean ones used to tease me. 'Who's that squaw that's always following you around?' or 'Do you eat buffalo meat every night for dinner?' I couldn't let anyone come to the house because they might realize Shining Star and my father slept in the same room. There would've been hell to pay."

Maggie reached for the arm of the sofa and sat.

Randall crossed his arms and leaned back against the mantel. "The main reason I left Regina was so I could figure things out. My father never taught me about being Jewish. I didn't know who I was. I just knew I didn't want to live my father's life, so I left. I've never met any of my mother's family, so I came here. But I miss Shining Star."

"Do you know anything about your mother's family?"

"My father's never said a word about them. I vaguely remember a cousin, Hilda, I think, from my mother's funeral. I don't remember anyone else. I don't think he's ever met them, either. Shining Star told me my mother came from Saskatoon, north of Regina. That's all I know."

Maggie said, "You haven't said a word about the card and the check."

"Did I really throw them at you?"

"Yes."

"God. I'm sorry. When I drove my father to the train station last June, he started in on me again about coming back to Regina and working for him. I told you about the battles we had before I enlisted. Anyway, I said I wanted to wait and see what happened with you. He seemed to accept that. In August, before I gave you the ring, I wrote him about the restaurant. I didn't get a reply until last week and that's what I got—the card and the check. What a shit!"

"Randall, he's still your father."

"I said shit and that's what he is."

"Have you been drunk like that before?"

"A few times—in high school and in the army. But never like that. I'm so sorry, Maggie."

"Anything else you haven't told me?"

He shook his head. "Still love me? I don't know what I'd do without you."

"I love you. Nothing you told me has changed my mind. We don't have to tell anyone else, not even my parents about . . . Shining Star and your father. Just don't ever lie to me again. You don't think she would come to our wedding, do you?"

He kissed her. "Shining Star would never leave Regina, and I promise not to lie to you again."

"You need to figure out how to get along with your father."

"It'll be fine as long as he stays in Regina and I'm down here."

Randall had never felt so close to anyone as he felt to Maggie.

As June, 1939, approached, Randall's desire for Maggie almost overwhelmed him. He wanted to touch her, hold her, and lie in bed with her. He hated the minutes and hours they were apart. He wanted to share everything that happened and he wanted to know minute by minute what happened to her. The first Sunday in June they sat at her parents' kitchen table again to go over their finances.

"How does it look?" he asked.

"Pretty good. We have more then we thought. I guess not going out to movies and for ice cream can improve the finances. But we're not even close to $4,000 yet. We only have two."

"But I've already paid for the car, remember?"

"That's true."

"Why don't we get married in December? We could buy furniture and rent an apartment for a while. The net profit is good at the restaurant. I've a feeling the "three musketeers" are going to give me a raise in October. We'll just have to keep saving for a house. What do you say?"

"I say yes." She threw her arms around his neck. "I'm going to call Rabbi Shapiro right now and make an appointment for next Sunday so we can get a wedding date on his calendar." When she hung up the telephone, she said, "We're meeting at 10:00 a.m."

Randall picked her up in his arms and carried her up the stairs. "Which room is yours?"

"Are you going to be good?"

"I'm going to be good for six more months, that's all. Which room is yours?"

She pointed to her door.

He laid her down on her single bed and stretched out next to her. He held her close from knees to lips. "The next time we do this we're going to be married and naked."

"I can't wait."

He kissed her gently and caressed her face. "Now I've got a restaurant to open." He left her on the bed.

Lives in Exile

Just before the restaurant closed, Maggie phoned Randall. "My parents and I've been talking. Can you come over here after you close up?"

"Sure. Is there a problem?"

"No problem. We want to talk about the wedding. My mother's nervous because there's only six months until December."

"Only six months. It seems like forever to me."

They talked about bridesmaids and groomsmen and colors and time. Two things were decided. The reception was going to be at The Ukrainian Inn and Randall was going to ask Manny to be his Best Man.

He got home so late Aunt Yetta and Bubbe had already gone to bed. At breakfast he told them about the plans and his appointment with Rabbi Shapiro. Also, the Goldbergs had invited them over for dinner Monday night.

The next Sunday, Randall wore his favorite suit. His stomach was doing flip-flops as he drove over to Maggie's. Even though he was on time, she was standing by the screen door. She was trembling so he held her hand and helped her down the walk. In the car she sat very close to him.

"This is ridiculous," he said. "We're going to get married and there's nothing he can say to change that. Right?"

"Right," she said. "But I still can't stop shaking."

The rabbi's enormous desk took up half the room. Facing the desk were two upholstered chairs for visitors. Bookshelves lined three of the walls. In among the hundreds of volumes were menorahs and spice boxes and pointers. The fourth wall was hung with pictures of old men with long beards, dressed in dark suits, with hats on their heads.

"So you've decided to get married in December," the rabbi said. "That's nice. I know all about Maggie's family since they're members of this congregation. And, Randall, I know your father's family, too. But your mother, was she Jewish?"

"I assume so. I was never told otherwise."

"What was her name?"

"Bessie Swartz."

"Do you say Schwartz or Swartz?"

"It's s-w-a-r-t-z, as far as I know."

"So, when and where were you Bar Mitzvah?"

"I never was Bar Mitzvah. We lived in a place with very few Jews."

"I see. Maybe you'd be interested in some of our adult education classes. We'll talk about that another time. Do you know the name of the Mohel who performed the circumcision? Perhaps there is a certificate?"

"I was never circumcised."

Maggie gasped.

The rabbi sat back in his chair and pressed the fingertips of both hands together.

"Is there a problem?" Randall asked.

The rabbi said, "This is a very delicate situation. Before you can be married, you're going to have to be converted."

"What does that mean?"

"It means you are going to have to study Judaism with me and then be examined by a group of rabbis. In the end you will have to be circumcised. Since you are an adult, this is minor surgery which a doctor will perform under the supervision of a Mohel. I don't see how this can be accomplished in six months time."

"And there's no way you will marry us without the studying . . . and the . . . circumcision."

"That's right. You're not Jewish according to rabbinic law," the rabbi said. "Circumcision is a commandment of God. It's a sign of the covenant between God and the Jews. It's required of all Jewish males." The rabbi paused. "Obviously, you'll need time to think this over."

Randall looked at Maggie. His mind shot back to one Saturday when he was about twelve and he'd gone to shul with his Zeyde and they'd read the Torah portion about the circumcision of male babies. At dinner that night Randall asked why he wasn't circumcised. Zeyde had said, "Don't worry about it. You're Jewish if you think you are. Not too many people want to think they're Jewish these days."

In the car, Randall said, "I . . ."

She wagged her finger at him and glared—her eyes narrowed and burning, her face hardened and scowling. He stopped speaking.

When they got to her house, she didn't wait for him to open the door. She got out herself and stomped up the walk.

He opened his door and stood up. "I'll call you later."

She kept marching.

At the restaurant Randall paced the whole evening. Every once in a while he would stop by the phone but then move on. He needed to talk to someone but had no idea whom to call. Maggie was so mad. He didn't know why she wouldn't talk to him in the car. He knew Jewish men were circumcised and he wasn't, but Zeyde had said he was Jewish and he always thought he was. When he'd asked his father about his religion, his father had said religion was only a balm for the masses and wasn't important to

Lives in Exile

their lives in Regina. He thought about calling Aunt Yetta, but the subject embarrassed him.

Randall met Maggie the next evening in front of her store, as usual. She didn't smile, just got in the car. Her skin was blotchy, her eyes swollen and red. The atmosphere in the car was awful.

"I told my mother we wouldn't be coming for dinner tonight," she said. "My mother called your grandmother and told her we were postponing—that she wasn't feeling well. We need to go somewhere we can talk."

"The Hot Shoppe. It's usually not too busy on Monday nights. We'll ask for a corner booth."

They didn't talk again until after their hamburgers and French fries had been served. He couldn't believe how messy her hair was. She didn't look like herself at all.

Maggie hit her first finger on the table to emphasize her point. "In December you said you'd told me everything important. How come you didn't mention you weren't circumcised?"

"I . . . I . . . I didn't know it was important or I would've told you. My family told me I was Jewish. I always thought I was. Don't be mad, please?" He used his most soothing voice.

"Didn't you know you had to be circumcised to be Jewish?"

"My Zeyde said I was Jewish if I thought I was and I always thought I was. Sweetheart, isn't there some way we can work this out? Maybe some other rabbi won't care." Randall opened the ketchup bottle and poured some on his burger and potatoes.

Maggie's face contorted when she looked at her food. "Randall, every rabbi is going to care. Don't you understand? You're not Jewish." She banged her fist on the table. "No rabbi is going to marry us until you are. You're going to have to convert."

Randall took a sip of his chocolate milk shake. "I've thought about it . . . and that's out. I've always been Jewish and I'm still Jewish. I don't need a circumcision to prove it. We could be married by a judge."

She pushed her plate away. "What do you mean 'that's out'?" Her voice had risen an octave.

Randall responded in a quiet tone. "I mean I'm not going to let somebody cut the tip off my penis to prove a point."

She turned her head. "Don't be so vulgar—especially while we're eating."

Randall put down his burger, took her hand, and waited until she looked at him. "A penis isn't vulgar. It gives pleasure and it's necessary to make babies and I'm not letting anybody cut mine."

"But all Jewish men have a circumcision when they're eight days old and they still make babies." She was pleading.

"Yeah. But that's when they're infants. I'm an adult, in case you hadn't noticed." He regretted his sarcasm when he saw the look that came over her face.

"Can you please take me home?"

When they got to her house, she took off her engagement ring and put it in his hand. "I'm sorry, Randall, but I can't marry you."

"Maggie, please, sweetheart. I love you. Don't do this. Think it over. Is a circumcision that important? I haven't changed."

The tears flowed down her cheeks. She touched his face. "I can't marry you if it's not a Jewish marriage. You think it over. If you change your mind, I'll take the ring back."

He grasped her hand but she pulled away. He watched until she went in the front door and then he put his head on the steering wheel and sobbed. He drove down to the restaurant and let himself in. He called his grandmother, "I'll be home late. Don't wait up." Then he took a bottle of scotch and a glass and sat at a table near the window. He watched the few cars that were on the street and the traffic light on the corner turn from red to green to yellow to red.

"Randall, Randall."

He heard his grandmother's voice. Something was shaking his arm. He lifted his head. "Where am I?"

"You're here, at the restaurant."

"What am I . . . oh." He held his throbbing head with his hand.

Aunt Yetta said, "What's going on? You didn't come home last night. We called Maggie's house. Mrs. Goldberg says your engagement's broken. That's all she would say. What's this all about?"

The tears started as the pain returned. He didn't want to cry but couldn't hold it in.

His grandmother took him in her arms, "*Boychik*, what is it?"

"Did you know I'm not circumcised?" His stomach was doing somersaults.

Aunt Yetta cried, "Oh, God. Of course, we knew. We gave you baths when you were little."

Lives in Exile

"Why didn't you warn me? Why did you let me go to the meeting with the rabbi?" He moaned. "Why wasn't I circumcised as an infant?" He felt like throwing up, but managed to swallow it down.

Aunt Yetta said, "Your mother wouldn't allow it."

"Was my mother Jewish?"

"Didn't your father ever tell you? He was supposed to. We didn't know if he had or not. Damn him. No, she wasn't Jewish."

"So, I'm not really Jewish then."

"If you'd had a Jewish education you'd have known," Aunt Yetta said.

"I guess that's technically right."

"Why didn't Zeyde tell me the truth? Why did he tell me that to be Jewish all I had to do was think I was?"

"He knew we'd never convince your father to allow you to be circumcised, so that was the easy way out. Obviously, it was wrong."

"So, damn it, why didn't you tell me after I became engaged to Maggie?"

"You're the victim of a conspiracy of cowards. Bubbe and I hoped that it wouldn't matter to Maggie. Because she's Jewish, all your children would automatically be Jewish. And, obviously, you were willing to have a kosher home. No one wanted to tell you that you weren't who you thought you were."

"Who am I then?"

Bubbe put both hands on his shoulders and said, "You're Randall Marks, my grandson, and you're Aunt Yetta's nephew and we love you very much."

"But Bubbe, Maggie doesn't."

Chapter Twelve

Defeat

1939

Randall stumbled upstairs and crawled in bed. He grunted every time Bubbe and Yetta came to check on him. They brought him chicken soup for dinner, but he wouldn't sit up. On Wednesday, Yetta called the head waiter and told him Randall had influenza and wouldn't be in for a few days. By Friday afternoon, when he hadn't shaved or showered, Yetta called a family conference for the next morning. On Saturday they all sat around the dining room table with coffee and a piece of apple cake, except for Bubbe who had tea.

Abe moved the spoon around the saucer. "I don't understand why he won't have a circumcision."

"I think it's all tied up with what happened to his eye in the army," Yetta said, "and his feeling that people should accept him for who is. In his mind, he's Jewish."

Bubbe cut a second piece of cake for Sammy. "I'll try to talk to him, and so will Yetta, but we should think about what else to do. He's been in bed since Sunday."

Abe waved off another piece when Bubbe pointed the knife at him. "I think we need to urge him to officially convert. If he wants to stay in Washington, that's what he's going to have to do." He stirred his coffee and sipped. "We have to consider our options. We could call Maggie or her parents and try to talk with them about the situation."

"I'm totally against that," Tessie said. "It would upset Randall even more if we interfered."

Bubbe took a sip of tea. "That would humiliate him. He's a grown man."

Abe said, "We could call Jack and ask him to come right away. After all, Randall's his son."

Yetta shook her head. "That's absolutely out. Randall would be furious. This situation is mostly Jack's fault. I warned him this kind of thing could happen the very first night I spent in Regina after Randall's mother died. Mama and I even asked him to talk to Randall last June. I think Randall's doesn't know who to be angrier at—Jack, Maggie, Bubbe, or me. We have to figure out something that Randall will accept."

"Why didn't you or Mama talk to us about this before?" Sammy said.

Yetta put her hand to her neck. "That was a mistake. I had no idea the rabbi was going to question him so closely. I thought we still had time."

"So taking him up to Regina ourselves is out of the question, too?" Abe said.

They all nodded their heads.

Yetta looked at the others around the table. "Maybe I should call Manny Ancel and see if he'll come over and talk to him. Maybe it would help to talk to someone his own age, and Manny is his best friend."

"That's the best idea so far," Tessie said. "We could also call Dr. Shuman. I hear there's some medicine he could give Randall to make him feel better, you know, not so sad. While he's here, he could talk to Randall about the . . . operation."

"I'm opposed to giving him drugs." Abe said. "That will only prolong the problem."

"You're probably right," Tessie said.

Sammy adjusted his chair so he sat further back from the table. "We could just wait a few more days. Mama said there was some slight improvement today. He took a shower."

Silence.

Abe looked at each one around the dining room table. "Does anyone have any other ideas?" They either shook their heads or waved their hands to show they had nothing to add. "The only idea on which we all agree is to call Manny Ancel. Other than that, I guess we wait. Yetta, do you think we ought to call Jack and, at least, let him know what's going on?"

"Not yet," Sammy said. "Let's wait and see what happens with Manny."

On Sunday morning, Yetta telephoned, "Manny, I was hoping you could come over and cheer Randall up. He's a little blue about what's going on with Maggie."

"Frankly, Miss Marks, I don't know what I could do. Becky's been spending a lot time with Maggie. Maggie's a wreck over this whole thing, you know. Honestly, I think Randall's being a jerk. If he loved her, he'd do this for her."

"I see."

On Sunday, Randall took another shower and ate dinner. On Monday, he ate in the kitchen in his pajamas and robe, although he barely spoke.

On Tuesday, at breakfast, he asked, "I can't understand why my father didn't tell me. Was he being cruel? Did he hope this was going to happen and that I'd come running home again?"

Bubbe started to weep. She reached for Randall's hand and held on.

Yetta took Bubbe's other hand. "Your father doesn't really care about religion. He doesn't think it's important. That's one of the reasons he left Washington—to find a place where he could just be himself and not labeled by his religion. As far as he's concerned he found that place in Regina. He probably thought you would grow up and stay there and it wouldn't make any difference." She looked at Bubbe. "We make you a promise. No more secrets among us."

Randall rubbed his scar. "Okay." He held out the Kleenex box to his grandmother. "Bubbe, do you have any pictures of my mother? I've been trying to remember what she looked like."

Bubbe wiped her eyes. "I seem to remember your father once sent a picture of the three of you together. It's probably up in the attic. Why don't you get dressed and we'll go look? We'll need the ladder from the basement."

In the hallway, Randall opened the ladder, clicked the stabilizing bar in place, scrambled up, and pushed open the ceiling hatch. He climbed into the attic and reached down to help Bubbe.

Brushing his hand away, she grasped the two sides of the ladder and sprinted up the steps. "I've got some *shmates* to dust off the trunk and the boxes." She handed him a rag. "Use this." She looked around. "Do you see any mouse droppings?"

Randall looked around and shook his head.

"Good."

He wiped the chair but couldn't rub off the musty smell. He laid another rag, an old Turkish towel, on the floor and sat on it.

"This is the trunk we brought with us from Podolyia to New York and then to Washington," Bubbe said. "It's been with me since I got married. Open it. Let's see what we can find."

Randall fished out a yellowing piece of paper. "Here's a letter dated June 21, 1892."

"Read it to me."

"It's in Yiddish."

"Dear Moishe and Esther," she translated as she read. "How are you? I can't complain. I was glad to receive word of your successful arrival in New York. Our *landsman*, Abraham Winograd, wrote to tell me of how he found you at the dock and got you situated on Orchard Street. I am sorry I could not be there to greet you. I know it seems strange to be a Marks instead of a Markovitsky. But this is the way of those Immigration Officers-*mamzerim*. You will get used to it like I did."

"Was that really our name, Markovitsky?"

"Yes, that was Zeyde's name when I married him."

"What does '*mamzerim*' mean?"

"How can I explain? I'll just say it. It means 'bastard.'" Bubbe turned bright red.

Randall smiled. "Why did they change our name?"

"Lots of people who came through Ellis Island got their name changed by the Immigration. So many people were waiting to get in, the officers didn't take the time to understand what you were saying. If a name was too hard, they shortened it." She shrugged. "We didn't like Marks at first but then we realized it was much more American than Markovitsky, so we were satisfied."

She continued the letter. "Life in Washington is full of many opportunities for a hard-working person like you, Moishe, especially with a fine helper like Esther. Soon you will have a baby and you need to be thinking about your future. An Irishman down the block wants to sell his house and move to another section of the city. You could get the property very cheap. It would be a fine location for a grocery store. This area needs one. Now people have to walk several blocks. It wouldn't take much money. I'll lend you. You'll pay me back when you can. After all, what is *mishpucha* for and thank God I'm able. Don't worry about not knowing the grocery business. The jobbers give good advice and are eager to extend credit. You could turn the living room into the store and live in the back

Lives in Exile

and upstairs rooms. Your expenses would be very small. The house is on 4½ Street, the major business street in Southwest. This is a very good deal. Don't think about it too long. Your cousin, Max."

She paused. "It's a shame you never met cousin Max. He was a real *mensch*. He helped a lot of our *landsleit* to get settled in America."

"What are '*landsleit*'?"

"*Landsleit* are people who come from the same *shtetl* in Europe. Do you remember what a *shtetl* is?"

Randall shook his head.

"A *shtetl* is a small town or village."

"What did you and Zeyde do when you lived in New York?"

"I worked in a sweat shop, doing piece work, making coats. For a few extra pennies I sewed at night in our room. Zeyde peddled rags from a hand cart all through the Lower East Side." She patted Randall on the shoulder. "We soon learned the streets in the *Goldeneh Medina*, that's what people in Europe called America, the Golden Land, were not paved with gold."

"Gold. Did you really believe the streets were paved with gold?"

"Sure. That's what everybody wrote to their families. Life here, no matter what, was still better than under the Czar, in the Ukraine. At least there were no pogroms."

"A pogrom?"

"*Oy vayes meer, mein kindt.* Gangs of gentiles roamed the *shtetl* beating up Jews who were foolish enough to venture out. Sometimes our Passovers were ruined because of a pogrom. We would hide in the cellar, sometimes for days, while they burned down the wooden homes and businesses." She squeezed Randall's hand.

Randall's mouth hung open. His forehead crinkled. "Why did they do that?"

"Those priests of *Yashke Pundrik* told their people during Easter how the Jews killed Jesus Christ. Of course, it wasn't true. But, they were told we were the 'evil people' and they blamed all their problems on us. One time I remember my papa and one of my brothers had gone into the woods to get some logs for the stove and couldn't come home until the middle of the night. My mother kept food and water in the cellar when it got close to Passover, in case we had to escape down there quickly."

Randall kissed his grandmother's cheek. "I wish my father told me stories like that. He never talks about the past. He only talks about the future and what he wants from me."

Bubbe rubbed his shoulder. "Maybe he didn't like the past and only talks about the future because he wants to make it better for you."

Randall held up a picture with frayed edges. "What's this?"

"Our first store on the corner of 4½ and D Streets. That's me holding Yetta and that's Zeyde, of course. Your father is the tallest and those are your uncles."

"I miss Zeyde."

"Me too, *bubele*. He was a good man. I'm thinking of one of Zeyde's favorite Klezmer tunes. 'Me without you and you without me is like a door knob without a door.' That's how we were."

Randall studied the photograph. Bubbe looked the same, maybe a little smaller. She was still that thin, buxom woman with a laughing smile.

Bubbe said, "We'd better look for that picture you want or we'll be up here the whole day talking and never find it. I think it's in an envelope addressed to us in your father's handwriting." She rummaged through the trunk. "Here it is. This is what you want."

"I lost my copy after I was injured in the army. This was taken in the living room of our house. Mama's sitting in my father's favorite chair. He's standing in front of the fireplace."

Randall carried the picture with him down to Zeyde's desk. He propped it up on the pipe holder. He took out paper and pen and began a letter to Maggie. He started several drafts before he finished one. He was almost done when he sensed someone standing in the doorway. He turned.

"Are you writing to Maggie?" Yetta said. "I hope you don't mind my asking." She sat. "What have you decided?"

Randall twisted to face her. "I can't have that circumcision. It would be mutilating my body. To me, I'm Jewish. A rule which says only men with circumcisions are Jewish? That's silly. I've tried to convince myself to do this for her, but I can't. I would feel disfigured, and I can't feel like that the rest of my life." Randall massaged his scar. "It's not only the operation, the rabbi says I'd have to take classes to learn about being Jewish. That's bunk. You and Bubbe and Zeyde told me all the bible stories over and over again and I went to shul with Zeyde all the time. I know about keeping kosher. What else do I need to know?"

"I'm sure the important thing to Maggie is the circumcision. She probably wouldn't care about the classes and we could find a rabbi who'd marry you."

"Aunt Yetta, I appreciate your concern, but I've made up my mind."

"You have to do what you think is right. If it's not right for Maggie too, then the marriage won't work."

In his letter, Randall included a check for an amount equal to the five dollars a week Maggie had put into his savings account. He hoped he would hear from her but didn't expect to.

On Wednesday, he went back to work. For the next couple of weeks business was slow—the summer months usually were. Randall had the distinct feeling, though, that people whispered about him behind his back. He realized he should have expected that.

On a Tuesday morning in early August, the "three musketeers" asked him to come into the office for a conference. All the fans were going full speed. The air was already hot and humid. Randall didn't think the overnight temperature had gone below eighty.

Abe, who had his shirt collar open, sat at his desk in front of a whirring floor fan. "We've been hearing rumors people are not coming to the restaurant because of the situation between you and Maggie."

Each of the three desks was along its own wall facing the center of the room. Yetta's desk was closest to the door. Randall sat in a chair next to her. "What do you mean?"

Abe continued, "This is a hard thing to say. Apparently, Mr. Goldberg has been telling his friends and customers you shamed his daughter by deceiving her. That you didn't tell her about your circumcision or should I say lack of one. And, therefore, allowed her to think you were Jewish when you aren't."

"How could he do that?"

"It gets worse. Apparently, there's a kind of boycott."

Randall tried to catch his breath. He strode across the wooden floor to the window, leaned against the frame, and glared into space. The morning haze still clung to the street. Finally, he turned and faced the group. "We can't allow my situation to ruin the business. I guess we should hire a manager to run the restaurant for a while, and I'll move back into this office and supervise things from here."

"That's what we thought too," Sammy said. "Just until things die down. I'm glad you had the same idea. You've down a great job of building up the business, and there's no reason to let it go down the drain."

"Maybe I should try and talk to Maggie about this."

"I don't know if that's a good idea," Yetta said. "I've heard she's bitter. It might be better to wait a little longer."

After Randall left the office, Abe walked over to Yetta's desk and placed his arm on the file cabinets that lined the wall behind her. "It's only going to get worse. I think he should go back to Jack. If he stays here much longer, the scandal is going to spread to all of us. Tessie says she thinks people are already whispering about us."

"Who cares?" Yetta said. "People are always whispering. In a few days it'll be someone else's misfortune."

"You're wrong. He's never going to be able to marry a Jewish girl now, so he'll marry a *shiksa* and that'll cause more talk and humiliation."

"We should be thinking about Randall and what he's going through, not ourselves."

Sammy wiped his forehead with his handkerchief. Yetta put her head in her hands.

Several nights later, after three beers, Randall drove to Maggie's house on her parents' bridge night. When she opened the door, her hair wasn't combed and she wore no make up.

"What do you want?" Maggie said.

"Can I come in?"

"No."

"I'm sorry." He stammered. "I didn't mean to deceive you. You have to know that. I always thought I was as Jewish as anybody else. I'm sorry. I would never have hurt you on purpose." He extended his hand toward her. "Please, can I come in so we can talk?"

She leaned back. "No. I got your letter. I don't understand why you won't do this for me."

He rubbed his scar. "It's hard to talk standing on the doorstep."

"This is as far as you're going unless you're willing to become a real Jew."

"We're talking about my manhood here. I already have a scarred face. I can't be mutilated any more."

She put both hands on the door. "Mutilated? I don't understand that."

"Can't you understand? I wouldn't be the same as I've always been. I wouldn't be whole."

"You'd be the same as every other Jewish man." She pushed her hair off her face. "What would people think of me if I married someone who wasn't really Jewish? I'd be ostracized. No one would talk to us."

"So what?" He shrugged. "Who needs them as long as we have each other?"

"That's easy for you to say. You didn't grow up here and really don't belong. My parents don't want me to have anything to do with you. I told them how your father is sleeping with that Indian slut. They think maybe you're sleeping with her, too, since you love her so much. I'm glad I'm rid of you. You and your whole awful family." She started to shut the door.

He blocked it with his hand. His voice was quiet. "How could you betray me like that? I would never have done that to you. Those are things I've never told anyone else in the world. You knew that. How could you?"

"So you don't think you betrayed me?" she screamed.

"If I betrayed you, it wasn't on purpose, it was from ignorance. But you betrayed me deliberately. It doesn't even compare." Randall turned toward the street. He was trembling. It took effort to put one foot down after another. Bitter tasting juices swirled in his mouth. He swallowed again and again.

When he got home, he raced to the basement, got the ladder, climbed up to the attic and got his suitcases. Back in his room he flung open the big one and started throwing things from the drawers into it. After a few minutes of frantic activity, he sat on his bed and allowed his head to fall into his hands. *Why can't Maggie understand? Why is what everyone else thinks so important to her? We could've gone to live somewhere else where no one would have known, if she felt she couldn't stay here. What's so important about Washington? Why can't she accept me for who I am? Who knows if I'd be the same physically after the surgery? Putting your prick in someone else's hands? After the surgery I wouldn't know who I was. A part of me would be gone forever. I'm not the same person I was before I lost my eye and this part of me is even more important.*

"Randall, what are you doing? Why is the ladder in the hallway?" It was Aunt Yetta.

He continued throwing his things in the suitcase. "I'm taking the train to Regina tomorrow. I want to tell that bastard what I think of him. I want to ask him why he did this to me."

"Stop. Please."

He hesitated.

"Come downstairs and talk to Bubbe and me," Yetta said. "If you're going to go, I'll help you pack your things so they won't be ruined. Come downstairs."

They sat in the dining room because it was cooler. Randall smoothed his hair and shook his head. "I made a terrible mistake. I went to see Maggie. I should have listened to you, Aunt Yetta. You were right. It was awful. I trusted her and told her things I've never told anyone else."

"But that's the way it should be when you're getting married," Bubbe said.

"She was the wrong one to trust. She's twisted everything around and made it sound sick. She's told her parents and probably Becky and Manny, too. I'm so humiliated. I've got to get out of Washington."

"Can you tell us what you told her?" Yetta asked.

He put his face in his hands. "God. I'm so embarrassed. How could everything go so wrong? It's all his fault."

"You told her about Shining Star and your father," Yetta said, "how they live together?"

Bubbe gasped.

"I'm sorry, Mama."

Randall said, "How did you know?"

"I didn't know for sure but it's been pretty obvious to me for a long time. Nobody else suspected because they never met Shining Star." She looked at her mother and then back at Randall. "You told Maggie how you feel about Shining Star, too?"

"Yeah, I did." Randall kneaded his scar. "And I told her some other things I've kept inside for a long time. She's very bitter. She used terrible words. She feels betraying me was fair because I betrayed her."

"But you didn't do it on purpose," Bubbe protested.

"That's what I told her, but it's too late. I've got to figure out my life all over again. I thought with Maggie I knew what I wanted and how I was going to get there. Now nothing makes sense. Maybe living in Regina is the right thing for me. There at least I know where I stand."

"Wait until Monday," Yetta said, "and help us straighten out the business. Things might look better by then. If not, it'll give you time to get all your belongings together and pack properly."

"Maybe I should sell the car while I'm still here."

"Don't be hasty. You might decide to come back. If not, I'm sure we can sell it for you."

"I might as well call my father now." He took a bottle of scotch from the breakfront.

Bubbe frowned. "Do you think that's wise?"

"Don't worry, Bubbe. I'm only going to have one drink, and whatever I have to say to my father I'm going to say in person, not over the telephone."

He took the bottle into the kitchen and put some ice into a glass. Then he went to the telephone and dialed the operator. "I'd like to place a long distance station to station call to Regina, Saskatchewan. That's in Canada. The number is Mounty 5900."

Jack answered.

"I'm coming home in a few days," Randall said, "if that's all right with you."

"You've broken up with Maggie?"

"I'd rather not talk about it, but yeah."

"I'm sorry, son. Let me know which train and I'll meet you."

After he hung up, he took his drink to his room and started to put his things back in order. He heard a knock and opened the door.

Yetta said, "How'd it go with your father?"

"It went okay. He didn't even gloat. I don't know what to think."

She sat on his bed. Randall took the chair.

"Give him a chance," Yetta said. "He can't be happy with how things are between you. You're his only child. His flesh and blood."

Randall looked at the toes of his shoes.

"You feel he betrayed you," Yetta went on, "that he tricked you. He loves you and I'm sure he never realized how much this would hurt. Try to forgive him."

Randall looked out the darkened window.

She hugged him. "Bubbe and I are going to miss you so much."

When she was gone, Randall didn't move from the chair. *Why am I going home? Is it because it's a good place to hide out? I want my father to respect me, but I keep coming back to Regina with my tail between my legs. How am I ever going to get his respect this way? Where else can I go? Should I give up and do what he wants? Damn him. This mess is all his fault. He should have warned me. He knew Maggie's family's orthodox. Why did he let this happen?*

On Monday morning Randall woke at five-thirty. He put on his bathrobe and went downstairs. It would be an hour and a half before Bubbe or Aunt Yetta got up. He sat in Zeyde's favorite red velvet chair that now wore its floral summer slipcover. Even four years after Zeyde died, he still felt surrounded by him. Every afternoon, during his summers in Washington, he and Zeyde used to sit in this chair together and Zeyde would read him the comic strips. Randall thought about those wonderful afternoons and the Saturday mornings when he went to synagogue with Zeyde—all the men wrapped in tent-like prayer shawls, shutting out the world and chanting in Hebrew. Sometimes the congregants swayed from side to side, sometimes they rocked back and forth, sometimes they bowed from the waist, and sometimes they rose up on their toes. He endured the three hours of boredom by dreaming of the food served afterwards—the pickled herring with onions in the juice, the gefilte fish balls with purple horseradish, and the best brownies in the world. When Zeyde wasn't looking, he sneaked a swallow or two of the sweet red wine from the small paper cups left on the table after the blessing. The brownies he saved for last. He loved to maneuver the creamy chocolate around in his mouth, savoring the taste before he swallowed. It took him a full three minutes to eat a brownie, one tiny bite at a time. But his favorite part of Saturday was the stroll with Zeyde back and forth to this house, just the two of them. Randall could ask him anything and often did.

"Why do you move up and down when you pray?" Randall asked when he was seven, the first summer he visited.

"So my whole body can pray to God," answered Zeyde.

"Why do you stand on your toes during that one prayer?"

"To imagine I am flying toward God."

"Why do boys and girls kiss?" he asked when he was ten.

"When you kiss someone you really like, it feels good."

"Do you kiss Bubbe?"

"Yes."

"Why did my mother have to die?" he asked when he was thirteen.

"That's a very hard question for which there are no good answers. Some things we have to accept as God's will and this is one of them."

"Do you think there is a heaven?"

"I believe when the Messiah comes we will all be judged by how many of the six hundred thirty-seven *mitzvot*, good deeds, we performed. And there will be a heaven on earth for those who are judged worthy."

"Do you think my mother will be judged worthy?"

"I'm sure she will."

On their last walk together, when he was seventeen, Randall asked, "Why doesn't my father let me make my own decisions? Why does he think he has to tell me what to do?"

"This is because your father loves you and he only wants the best for you." Zeyde stopped walking and cradled Randall's cheek in his palm.

"You have to be patient with him. He doesn't know a high school graduate can have his own ideas. Soon he will realize you're grown up." Zeyde shrugged. "What do you think you want to do?"

"Poppa wants me to work at the newspaper," Randall said as they resumed strolling. "But I don't know. I was thinking of coming here to Washington to get a job with Uncle Sammy and Uncle Abe. I could rent my own place. What do you think, Zeyde?"

"I think you and your father need to work this out together." Zeyde reached up and patted his shoulder.

Randall remembered how white Zeyde looked a few days later when he found him in the living room slumped forward in this chair, the newspaper clasped in his hands. When Randall went into the dining room to set the table for dinner, he saw the top of Zeyde's head with his kinky, grey hair. He thought he'd fallen asleep. He'd stepped toward him calling his name, to wake him up. But Zeyde didn't move. When he got close, the whiteness of his skin and Zeyde's absolute stillness scared him. He reached out his hand tentatively and touched him. He was cool. Then he yelled for Bubbe.

Bubbe called an ambulance. She sent Randall out on the front porch to wait. He wondered if Zeyde had cried out for help to him or Bubbe as they worked in the kitchen preparing the chicken. When he looked in the window, Bubbe was pacing, wringing her handkerchief in her hands. Several times she stopped to touch Zeyde's face. The ambulance man called their doctor and the police.

"A massive stroke," the doctor said when he came to sign the death certificate. "At least he wasn't in any pain."

Randall wished he'd had a chance to say good-bye to his best friend. Aunt Yetta said the same thing when she came home from work and learned Zeyde was dead. The police were still there. They hadn't taken Zeyde away. Aunt Yetta called Mr. Danzansky at the funeral home and two men in black suits and solemn faces came with a stretcher. Randall sat on the stairs with his arms wrapped around his knees while they laid Zeyde out and covered him over. Bubbe groaned and Aunt Yetta whimpered. The hearse was pulling away as his father came sprinting up the steps.

"Why was there a hearse here?" His father was breathless.

Bubbe and Aunt Yetta clung to him and cried. Then his father called the family, and all the uncles, aunts, and cousins gathered at Bubbe's, and they all cried again. Over and over Randall told the story of how he had found Zeyde and what he had looked like. Every person who arrived at the house wanted to know what happened. At sixty-five Zeyde had stood straight with his wiry, muscular build. His smooth skin made him look younger and with the little brush mustache, quite dapper. His compact body gave the impression he could spring into action at any minute. That he should die without warning was shocking to everyone.

Still remembering, Randall ambled through the house. When he arrived two years ago, the house had seemed empty because Zeyde wasn't there. He'd known Zeyde wouldn't be there ever again, sitting in one of the bouncy green metal chairs on the concrete front porch, clapping his hands as they came up the front steps. Knowing didn't make the house less empty. During this stay he'd lost his innocence. He now knew how truly painful life could be. He thought he had known before—his mother's death, his injury, his estrangement from his father. But the pain of this experience with Maggie seared him in a way the others hadn't. He stood in the back yard under the apple tree with the big broad limbs he often climbed as a child. Then he wandered through the kitchen with the porcelain stove and sink where they washed, cleaned, and cooked the apples he'd picked before they took turns at the hand grinder and made the apples into applesauce. He crossed the speckled linoleum kitchen floor into the back room with the wrap-around windows that gave a great view of the backyard and alley which ran along the side and back of the semi-detached house. In the back room he touched Zeyde's meerschaum pipes one more time. He examined the serving dishes and crystal stemware Bubbe kept in the dining room breakfront. In the living room, he ran his fingers over the flower print fabric in the curved wood frame of the sofa he loved. He looked out the front window and then walked into the front hall and up the stairs. He remembered how Bubbe used to get upset with him when, as a kid, he tried to slide down the banister. He loved the two-story house. There was more privacy here than in the one-story home in Regina.

The small back bedroom at the top of the stairs was his. It contained his single bed, a small dresser and a straight-backed chair. Aunt Yetta slept in there when he and his father visited together. Otherwise Aunt Yetta occupied the larger side bedroom, painted a pale blue, with twin beds, mahogany headboards, and matching double dresser. The white, nubby summer bedspreads covered the beds, and white curtains with blue and green flowers hung in the window. When he was young, he and Aunt Yetta used to share the larger room since it was cooler. A glass-paneled door, left open in the summer to allow cross ventilation, separated the porch from her bedroom. In the fall, the porch screens were replaced with glass panels. He guessed one of his uncles would help Bubbe and Aunt Yetta this year since he wouldn't be here to do it.

On the hottest nights he'd slept on the chaise lounge out on the porch. Some of his happiest memories from childhood were of waking up right after dawn while birds chirped and flitted about in the apple tree.

Bubbe's bedroom took up the whole front of the house. It always smelled like Bubbe. When he was little, he sometimes sat on the covered bench at her vanity and sniffed the powder puff in her pale rose-colored china powder box with the white and green flower on the top. That was her smell. He used to open her drawers and sniff so he could smell the fragrance that came from the packets of sachet she kept in every drawer. Now he stood in the upstairs hallway and imagined Bubbe's room, papered in a green floral design with matching green bedspread and curtains, and inhaled her scent.

At the end of every summer, when he left, he knew he'd be back in ten months. This time as he drove away and looked back at the house, he wondered when he'd see Bubbe and Aunt Yetta again.

Chapter Thirteen

Regina

1939-1940

Tuesday afternoon Jack met Randall at the train. On the way to the house he said, "Glad to have you back, son. Wait till you see how good the wheat looks this year. It's beautiful. How's everyone in Washington?"

"Fine." Randall laid his head back on the seat and turned so he could look out the side window. He guessed his father got the picture because he didn't ask any more questions. The wheat *did* look especially beautiful this year. He took several deep breaths. It was good: the smell of earth and growing things.

Randall sat up as they started up the road to the house. The small room which had been Randall's first bedroom was now his father's office. Randall would be sleeping in the addition finished after his mother died, the room that had been his before he moved to Washington.

Shining Star stood at the picture window. As he came in with his luggage, she smiled and nodded, her arms folded across her waist.

He dropped his suitcases, took her by the shoulders, and kissed her on the cheek. She gasped and covered her mouth with her hand.

Jack laughed. "The boy has changed. Never did that before."

Randall stood facing Shining Star with his head down. He felt her hands on his face, pulling him toward her. She planted a kiss on his forehead. She looked him full in the face. "Glad you home," she said in her combination French and Indian accent.

"I'll go put my things in my room."

His bedroom looked exactly the same. He let his eyes wander over every object—bed, bookshelves, plaid bedspread and drapes, wooden desk. When he left, he had been full of anger. The anger was still there, but more than anything he wanted to feel safe. *Is that what I came for, safety? Am I looking for a place to hide?*

Jack called, "Randall, dinner."

At the table Jack said, "Did you talk to any interesting people on the train?"

"Not really."

"Was it hot in Washington this summer?"

"Normal."

Jack tried again. "The price of wheat has been rising."

"That's good."

They ate the rest of the meal in silence. When they were finished, Jack said, "Come sit with me in the living room. Would you like a drink?"

Seated in his usual place, Jack lit one of his Muriel cigars. "I need an advertising salesman."

"I thought I'd look around for a restaurant management job."

"No need to look. You have a job with me. If you want to take a break, you could volunteer at the Harvest Festival. I was talking to Bob Harrison over at the lumber yard about newspaper coverage of the Festival, which is coming up in a couple of weeks. He said he could use some help hauling lumber and building booths, strictly volunteer."

"I'll stop over at the lumber yard tomorrow. After that, I'm going to look around and see what jobs there are." It felt good letting his father know he might be back in Regina but that didn't mean his father had won it all.

Thursday, Randall walked into the Harrison's Lumber Yard office.

The receptionist said, "Hey, aren't you Randy Marks?"

He looked. "You're Linda Radkowski, right? I remember you."

Linda chewed gum like a cow chewing its cud. Her blond hair lay flat against her head in Marcel waves which looked as though they were glued in place. When he got close he could barely smell her perfume, lilac, because of the burning cigarette sitting on the lip of an ashtray filled with dozens of butts.

"You're looking great," he said. "Did you ever marry Stanley Kreig?"

She squinted her blue eyes at him. "What a memory. Naw, almost. Didn't you join the army or something?"

He touched his scar. "Yeah. After I got out, I went east to work with my father's family. Just got back yesterday."

She inhaled the cigarette. "Good to see you again. Bob's out in the yard. He said to tell you to come on out when and if you got here."

Randall started toward the door.

"Hey, Randy," Linda said. "There's a band from Edmonton playing over at The Cue Ball tonight. A bunch of us are meeting there at eight. You want to join us?"

"Sounds good."

At eight that evening Randall sauntered in the door at the restaurant end of The Cue Ball. It was where the high school kids hung out and the adults came to drink and dance. They weren't too strict on who drank what. He blinked his eyes several times to try to adjust to the dimness. Same old place from what he could see through the haze of cigarette smoke—part pool hall, part restaurant, smoke-filled and loud. Around three sides of the room were the booths—the same grey Formica-covered tables with bench seating and in the middle of the room were the same square tables with chairs. Some of the tables at the far end had been removed for a dance floor. A bead curtain separating the eating area from the bar and pool tables had been drawn back. He saw pinball machines in the back. That was new. He heard a voice he recognized as Linda's calling, "Over here, Randy."

The group had pulled one of the square tables over to a booth so everyone could sit together. Linda was wearing a tight-fitting shell top which made her breasts stick out, almost pointed. When she turned around to say something to the group, he caught a glimpse of her round rear end. Her bright red lipstick matched her top. Randall suspected she chewed gum in her sleep. Her mouth appeared to be always in motion. His jaw ached thinking about it. When she smiled, she never showed her teeth. He guessed that was to keep the gum in her mouth.

She put her arm through his and introduced him. "You remember Randy Marks from high school?"

They slid over to make room for Randall. He ordered a beer.

One of the guys said, "Hey, Randy, what you been up to since?"

"I've been here and there. Working in the restaurant business mostly."

"I heard you joined the army."

"I did that for a while, too."

"Sounds like you were back east, picked up an accent."

The band started playing and Linda said, "How 'bout a dance?"

It was good to hear those Canadian o's again. He danced with Linda and the other girls at the table and then shot pool with the guys. He vaguely remembered these boys from high school. They hadn't been in his small circle of friends. Toward the end of the evening the band started playing slow tunes. He and Linda danced the last dance together. As they strolled toward their cars, Linda said, "Some of the gang are going to the movies on Saturday night. Want to join us?"

The movie was a romance—boy gets girl, boy loses girl, boy gets girl back and lives happily ever after. The group went for ice cream afterwards. Randall was physically with them, but he was thinking how Maggie would've loved the movie. He remembered how she rolled her eyes when she talked about the love scenes. He was stuck in the boy loses girl part and questioned whether he'd ever get to the lives-happily-ever-after part. He wondered who Maggie was with. The idea she was letting someone else kiss her disturbed him. He couldn't believe he still felt that way.

Linda rapped his head with her knuckles. "Knock, knock. Is Randy home? Can he come out and play?"

"Sorry."

"You sure were lost in dream land. I hope we aren't boring you too much."

"You aren't boring me at all. Sorry."

As Randall walked Linda to her car, she said, "How 'bout coming for dinner on Wednesday night? I make a great stew. We could play some cards with my parents. They usually go to bed pretty early, though, so we could have some time by ourselves."

"Sounds nice." He looked at the ground and shuffled the dirt around with his foot. "I've just broken up with a girl in Washington. We were engaged for almost a year. Planned to be married in December. Just wanted you to know. If you want to change your mind, I'll understand."

"Nope. Out of sight, out of mind, I always say."

"Wish it were that easy."

Randall wished it were easy to be home again. Sunday morning he spent sitting in his room writing a long letter to Aunt Yetta and Bubbe telling them about his trip and what he had been doing the last few days. He knew they'd be happy he'd gone out with Linda and her friends and was keeping busy with the Festival. In the afternoon he drove to the post office so the letter would go out on Monday's train.

On the way back from town it occurred to him his father had been leaving him alone. That wasn't like him. He usually went straight for what he wanted. He slammed the steering wheel. Did his father know what was going to happen, with his vague hints to be careful of women? Still his father's new attitude was a surprise. For the first time in years he wasn't pressuring Randall into anything. *Maybe he's concluded he'd been taking the wrong approach. Maybe Shining Star's convinced him you can catch more flies with honey than with vinegar. Or maybe he's just waiting for the right time to pounce.*

At lunch, Jack said, "I'd like you to start at the paper on Wednesday."

"I'll let you know." *So he was waiting for the right time.*

"Come on, Randall. That's why you came back here, wasn't it? I thought you'd figured this out. Regina's the best place for you. If you're going to stay you might as well start learning my business. You haven't been around for the last four years and things have changed."

He had to admit that last part was true. Anyway, he hadn't found anything else he wanted to do. He might as well find out what his father's business was all about. "I'll start Wednesday. I won't be home for dinner, though. I've been invited over to Linda Radkowski's, an old friend from high school."

Jack gave Shining Star a look. "Sure."

Jack was puzzled, as he confessed to Shining Star that night in their room. "I've been waiting for Randall to give me a hard time about not being circumcised and ask lots of questions about Bessie. I certainly gave him the chance today."

Shining Star said, "That what you call a chance? He get to it when he ready. The wound too raw."

"What will I tell him when he asks?"

"The truth."

He tapped his cigar on the ashtray. "But what's the truth? There's always more than one truth. My years at the newspaper have taught me that. Even now I don't know the whole story about Bessie. How can I explain?"

Shining Star said, "He old enough. Tell him everything."

Jack ground out his cigar.

Wednesday night was pleasant enough. The dinner was good and the pinochle fun. After her parents had gone to bed, Linda taught him how to play canasta laying all four hands out on the table. Then they played with two hands up and two hands down. Linda suggested they sit on the sofa and talk. Suddenly she was all over him. Her hands were everywhere—in his hair, rubbing his chest. When she started massaging his stomach, he pushed her hands away. "Linda..."

"Shh," she whispered, "you'll wake up my folks. Leave everything to me."

She unbuttoned his shirt and unbuckled his belt, then opened his pants. She took off her blouse and let down the straps to her slip. She unhooked her bra and let it fall into his lap.

He kissed her passionately, massaging her back. Slowly he worked his hands around to her breasts.

She laid back on the sofa. He pushed himself up on his knees over her. Almost immediately after he entered her, he came and then collapsed on her.

After a few minutes, she said, "Why don't I use the bathroom first?"

He raised his body to let her squirm out from under. Then rolled on his back and pulled up his pants. *How could I have let this happen? No protection, either. That's all I need right now. Knock up some girl I don't care about. Can't let this happen again.* He felt her fingers tickling him. He sat up.

She sat down as close as she could.

"Linda..."

"Don't worry, I know you don't love me. You're still pining away for that girl in Washington. I understand. But I got the hots for you and obviously you've got them back."

"Linda..."

"Don't be so serious. Can't we just have some fun together?"

"But, Linda, next time we have to use protection. I don't need any more complications in my life right now."

She stroked his face. "Whatever you say. You are a handsome devil." She kissed him firmly. He felt her tongue inside his mouth.

He put his hand around her back and held her to him. The he pulled away. "Got to go."

"Want to go dancing over in Ely at the Paradee Café Saturday night? You can bring along any kind of protection you like."

"Sounds good. As long as you understand . . . I'll pick you up at eight."

At dinner on Saturday he told Shining Star and his father he was going out. Jack said, "Be careful. Some women can be very devious."

Randall slammed his hand on the table. "Damn you. What does that mean?"

"Randall, watch your tone. That Maggie was a real bitch. Haven't you figured that out yet?"

The several seconds of absolute silence were like the center of a hurricane. And then the fierce wind of words flew. "Watch my tone. That's all you can say. How about, 'I'm sorry.' Or, 'this is why I didn't tell you.' All you can say is 'Watch your tone and that Maggie was a real bitch.'"

He stormed out of the house, jumped in the pick-up truck and drove off leaving a swirl of dust in his wake. His anger subsided a few miles from the house so he slowed down. *Why didn't I tell him what I think of him? Why am I always running away instead of standing up to him? I'm a coward.*

When he pulled up to Linda's house, she ran out to meet him before he could get out of the truck. She got in without waiting for him to open the door. He pulled her toward him and kissed her forcefully.

"Whoa, big boy. What's this all about?"

"Just felt like it."

On the way back from the Paradee Café, they drove out into the prairie. He felt like he was in high school again—having sex in the back of a pick-up. On his way home he had to laugh out loud. These Catholic girls were something even with all that hell and damnation stuff.

Two or three times a week Randall and Linda went out drinking and dancing or to a movie, sometimes with the group and sometimes alone. The evening always ended out in the prairie in the back of the pick-up.

One night Linda said, "Have you thought about what we're going to do when it really gets cold?"

Randall shook his head.

She was sitting close to him in the cab. She whispered in his ear. "Why don't we rent a little house together."

"Do you know what you're saying?"

"I'm saying I'm crazy about you and I know you care about me. You're the best guy around. What do you say?"

"I've never said I love you."

"I know that. But you've said I'm wonderful and things like that."

His voice rose. "Are you suggesting we get married?"

In a low voice she said, "You could do worse, a lot worse, Randy."

Randall thought she might cry. "I know I could," he said, "but I've got a lot of things to work out yet. We've only really known each other, what, seven weeks? I'm not even over my ex-fiancé." He took a deep breath. "At this point I don't even know what I want to do with the rest of my life. Do you?"

"I know I want a husband who will be good to me and treat me right. I'd like to have a couple of kids. Wouldn't you?"

Randall looked across the invisible prairie. "I don't know. I don't know if I want to stay here in Regina or even in Canada. I just don't know."

She put her hand on his shoulder. "Sorry. Didn't mean to push. I'm crazy about you."

He turned his head to look at her. "Can't we keep on the way we are for a while?"

"Sure."

On the way to his house he thought maybe he should let this relationship cool. On the other hand, he hadn't met anyone else. If it weren't for Linda, he would've felt very alone.

In the six weeks since Randall slammed his hand on the dining room table, he and his father had talked only about business and only when necessary. He rarely saw Jack at work since selling advertising required Randall to go to the customer's place of business. At home, Randall and Jack were civil, if distant. Shining Star observed it all in her silent way.

Randall would have liked to talk to her, but he didn't know what to say or where to begin. The problem was between him and his father. Finally, on Thursday night at dinner, Shining Star said to Randall, "Would you like to invite Linda to come to Sunday lunch?"

Randall gawked at his father and then back at Shining Star. "Are you sure?"

Jack said, "If she's important to you, we want to know her."

"Do you still think she's a devious woman?"

"I didn't mean Linda personally. I was just trying to tell you to be cautious."

"You warned me about Maggie in the same way. Why?" He was yelling.

Jack glanced at Shining Star. She nodded at him. He got up from the table, stepped to the bar, and picked up two glasses and the bottle of scotch. "Let's sit in here." Jack crossed to his favorite chair. Shining Star started clearing the table.

Randall followed Jack and sat on the sofa. Jack leaned forward and poured two fingers of scotch into each glass. He handed one over to Randall.

Lives in Exile

Randall made up his mind, whatever his father said he wasn't going to run away this time. He was going to stay and have it out. His throat was so tight from the tension he coughed. When he swallowed the first gulp, his eyes filled with moisture.

Jack pretended not to notice. "My experience with women has not been very good. The first girl I fell in love with was a whore in Helena named Liza. She worked on The Line with all the other prostitutes. In fact she was the first girl I ever . . . was intimate with." Jack pulled out his Muriel and lit it. "Liza was young and good looking. She lived in a brick house with a fat pink cupid over the door and a madam, a great hulk of a woman, who looked over every customer before she let them up with one of her girls. She sized me up pretty well—a kid and not too well heeled. She let me in anyway, because of my friend, Max."

Jack refilled his glass and Randall's, too. He could still visualize Liza with her curly golden hair. He pictured her large breasts and translucent skin. Jack smiled at the recollection. "She often played the piano for me. For some reason, her voice appealed to me. I tried to imagine myself the hero, rescuing Liza from her life of prostitution. This was around 1910."

"You don't have to tell me all this," Randall said.

"If I don't tell you everything you won't understand. I used to go to the movies a lot with Max and my other friend, Tom. We'd sit up in the balcony and boo when the villain captured the heroine and imprisoned her in a shack. He'd place a keg of dynamite with a burning fuse near her chair. We cheered when the hero rushed in—" Jack raised his fist. "—stamped out the fuse, saved the heroine, and then chased the villain out of town. In those days I liked to imagine I was a hero, the one who swooped in and saved the damsel in distress. That's who I wanted to be, anyway."

Jack stood, strolled to the picture window, and looked over the prairie. "One time I tried to talk to Liza about finding an apartment together. She brushed me off." He waved his hand in a gesture of dismissal. In his head he could still hear her voice saying, "Oh, you're being silly."

Jack walked back to his chair and poured himself another glass of scotch. He saw Shining Star walk through to the bedroom.

Randall couldn't believe his father was talking to him like this. Their life together had been one of silences. Randall said, "This Liza doesn't seem too devious. She sounds pretty straight-forward. She was a whore."

"You're right. It was my over-active imagination wanting to believe she loved me and wanted to be rescued."

"Do you know what happened to her?"

"No. I've been back to Helena only twice—once for Max's wedding. When I went the second time, she was gone, no one knew where. That was the time I took you to visit when you were, what, eight or nine, Max told me the whole Line had been torn down."

Randall said, "I know you met my mother at the boarding house where you both lived."

"Your mother was a whole different kettle of fish. I fell in love with her the first moment I saw her."

Randall decided to ask the question he always wanted to know the answer to, "Why didn't you get married?"

"In Canada, by law, Jews and Christians couldn't get married in those years. We could've gone to the U.S., but your mother was never well enough to make the trip, at least that's what she always told me."

"What do you mean?"

"Your mother's cousin owned the boarding house where we lived. Her name was Hilda James. You might remember her. She moved to Vancouver after your mother died. The night we buried your mother, Hilda told me your mother was married to another man. Apparently, she eloped to Seattle with a man named Johnny. After a year he abandoned her. She went back home and her family shipped her off to Mrs. James as soon as possible."

Randall stood up and with his glass of scotch walked over to the rocker. "Are you sure this story was true?"

Jack looked up at him. "It made sense out of a lot of things that puzzled me. Your mother told me most of the story herself. She just left out the part about being married. Anyway, Shining Star later told me your mother confessed the whole sorry tale to her."

Randall sat and rocked for a few seconds and then stopped. "You must've been furious."

"I was for a long time. But now I realize how sad and desperate she must have been. I've forgiven her. She did the best she could."

"Why did you stay here? Why didn't you go back to Washington?"

"As always there're several reasons. There was Shining Star. She would never have fit in with the family. I already owned the newspaper. So I had a good business. People treated me with respect. My being Jewish doesn't appear to be a big deal to anybody. In Washington being Jewish made you very different. There were a lot of things you could and couldn't do. You know the *goyim*. You were there. I like living in a place where you know most of the people and they know you. You'll see—life is easier here."

Randall leaned forward. "Why didn't you tell me not being circumcised was a problem?"

Jack held out the bottle of scotch. "I was wrong. Up until you met Maggie it didn't look like it would matter. I've always wanted you to work with me and eventually take over the businesses that I've worked hard to build. Your chances of meeting and marrying a Jewish girl seemed remote." He poured some liquor into Randall's glass. "First you ran off to the army and then to Washington." He put the bottle down. "I felt betrayed. I'd been working hard all these years so you'd have this great business to take over and you weren't interested." He took a swallow from his glass. "Then you meet this nice orthodox girl in Washington and it looks like you're not coming back, so I didn't tell you what you should have known. It was selfish and very wrong of me."

Randall sighed. Why did people betray each other? Why hadn't his father learned from his own experience? "I'm going to go to bed now. Got to get up early for work."

"Can you forgive me?"

Randall grimaced and didn't answer. He walked to his bedroom. *What does it mean to forgive? Does it mean to forget? I don't think I can forget all that's happened in the last year and my father's part in it. Does it mean to accept what's happen and not be mad about it? If that's it, I'm nowhere near ready, but I'm not as angry as I was.*

"I'm puzzled," Jack said to Shining Star in their room. "I told him all my secrets and he hardly responded. I don't get the kid. He doesn't react when you think he should, and then he blows his stack at the least little thing."

"Give him time. You told him lots of stories. He needs time to think things over."

"I wish I understood him better."

"He's a lot like you."

Chapter Fourteen

Regina To Richmond

1940

Randall arrived home from a date with Linda one night in March, 1940. The living room lights were all on as he came up the drive. It was two in the morning. His internal alarm jangled. He bolted through the front door. "What's going on?"

Shining Star, in the rocker, held two knitting needles suspended with two pieces of sweater trailing.

Jack looked up from his book, removed the cigar from his mouth and placed it in the ashtray. A glass of scotch rested on the end table. "We were waiting for you. I got a call from Washington. Abe died today."

Randall sank onto the sofa. "God."

"Tessie was always telling him to calm down or he'd have a stroke and that's what happened." Jack took a swallow of scotch. "We won't make it in time for the funeral, but I think we should get on the morning train. Yetta's very worried about Mama."

"I'll start packing."

After Randall closed the door to his bedroom, Shining Star said, "You know he not coming back."

Jack stared at her. "What do you mean? Of course, he'll come back. This is where he belongs. This is where is future is."

"He not coming back. He not happy here. He been staying because he don't have other place to go."

"You're wrong. He's coming back. He's happy. He has a good job and that girl, Linda."

"When he tell you he not coming back, let him go. He never be happy here. Just because he doesn't want what you want doesn't mean you made a mistake by living here. Let him find his own way."

Randall had set his alarm for 5:30 a.m. He quietly left the house and drove over to Linda's. The sky was shades of pink and purple. Dew clung to the thin branches of the trees. As hard as he tried to avoid it, he ended up waking her parents. Randall and Linda sat on the sofa and whispered while her mother made coffee. He'd already apologized half a dozen times for waking them.

"You're never coming back," Linda said.

"I'm coming back. Where else would I go?"

"This is the end of us." The tears ran down her cheeks. She pulled a handkerchief from the pocket of her pink terry cloth robe and wiped her eyes.

Randall hugged her and then held her hand. This was the first time he'd seen her without makeup. True, her makeup was always smudged by the time they finished making love. But with her naked face she looked so much younger and prettier.

"You're going to see Maggie. She'll probably want you back."

He put his arm around her shoulders, and she laid her head on his chest.

"Maggie doesn't want me. If she did, she'd know how to get in touch. I'm planning on coming back, but if I don't, I'll send for you."

"You mean it?"

"Yes." Even when he said it, he didn't know why. He didn't love Linda the way he had Maggie. But she looked so pathetic and he knew how much she wanted him. Anyway, he was coming back.

"You promise?"

"On my honor."

As soon as the train started moving, Randall closed his eyes.

Jack pictured his family standing around an open grave.

"What're you thinking about, Poppa?" Randall said.

"I was thinking about all the people I've buried."

"Oh." Randall picked up that morning's edition of the *Leader Post*.

Jack opened his book but his thoughts drifted toward Bessie. He'd been thinking a lot about her in the last six months. Even after sixteen years, he was still trying to figure things out.

They changed trains in Toronto. The connections were excellent, and they were able to immediately board a train for Detroit.

When the train arrived in Detroit, Randall followed the red cap with their luggage to the baggage claim area while Jack went to see if they could book a sleeping compartment on the next train to Washington. After the luggage was checked, Randall met Jack at the station restaurant. While they ate their salads, Randall said, "How old was Uncle Abe when you left Washington?"

"He was eleven. I remember I gave him my toy soldiers. I gave Sammy my bottle cap collection. The three of us shared one room. We were pretty close, as close as three brothers can be. Do you remember your toy soldiers? They're probably in a box in the attic somewhere."

"I remember playing war with them. Look's like there might be another war soon."

"I think you're right. Fortunately, you won't have to fight with that eye of yours."

The waiter brought their main course. Jack conjured a picture of Randall as a six-year-old sitting on the floor playing with his soldiers after they came back from the cemetery.

"Poppa," Randall said. "Why do you think Aunt Yetta never got married?"

"What?" Jack pulled his mind back to the present. "I guess the right person never asked. I know she had a couple of chances."

"That's a shame."

"You've been keeping company with Linda for six months or so now. Any future there?"

"I don't know."

"She seems pretty stuck on you." Jack waved the waiter over. "I think we'd better pay the check and get our luggage. It must be getting close to boarding time now. I sent a telegram to Yetta so she'd know what train we're coming on. I suppose Sammy will pick us up."

Once they got their luggage stowed in their compartment, Jack and Randall went to the club car while the porter made up their beds. They each ordered a scotch and Jack pulled out one of his Muriels.

Randall said, "I keep thinking of Bubbe. Do you know where they are sitting *shiva?*"

"Probably at Abe's house."

"Bubbe looked so old the day we buried Zeyde. The wrinkles in her face seemed so deep. Will Bubbe be wearing one of those ripped ribbons again?"

Tears came to Jack's eyes. He had not thought of all those symbols of mourning before this moment—the covered mirrors, the low stools. "Yes. I guess the rabbi will have one for me, too. I forgot, I shouldn't have shaved this morning. It didn't occur to me."

"I don't think Bubbe will notice. She'll just be glad to see you. So, they'll have services every night at Uncle Abe's like they did for Zeyde."

"I'm sure. That's probably going on right now."

When they returned to their compartment, they got ready for bed. They both lay in their bunks, Randall on the top one, Jack on the bottom, the sheets tucked tightly around them. Jack used the little light next to his head to read. But the smell of fresh, crisp sheets, the rocking of the train, and the rhythmic clacking of the wheels on the tracks made him drowsy quickly. The last image that floated through his mind was of Bessie sitting in the rocking chair by the bedroom window with Randall in her arms.

Two nights after *shiva* was over, Jack and Yetta sat at the kitchen table sharing tea and cake. A nighttime stillness enveloped the house.

"I've met a man," Yetta said.

"That's wonderful. Who is he?"

"Arnold Gross. He's the Seagram's representative. You met him yesterday. He paid a *shiva* call—the balding guy with the Brooklyn accent. Whenever he's in town, several days a month, we go out. He's based in Richmond." Yetta played with her spoon. "He wants me to move down there."

Jack put his hand over hers. "And you want to go?"

"Yes."

"So, when's the wedding?"

"At first, I'll get my own apartment and then we'll see. He says there are good business opportunities in Richmond area. But that leaves the Marks Company and Mama."

Jack smiled. "You must've thought about it."

"With Abe gone, I think we should sell. We've had offers over the years. It shouldn't be too hard. Mama could stay here in the house. She could take in boarders or she could move in with Sammy and Bertha. That's the hard part—Mama."

"Look, she can still take care of herself. What she does is her decision. You do what's best for you. That's what she'd want you to do. Have you told Mama or Sammy yet?"

"I was going to and then Abe had the stroke. I thought I'd wait a few more days."

"What kind of business are you thinking of?"

"Arnold thinks a place like the Ukrainian, but with a bar." She hesitated. "I've asked Randall to go with me and help me set up the business."

Jack's face turned red. He slammed his hand on the table. "What? How could you do that to me?" He clumped to the back door and glowered out the window into the darkness.

"Randall wanted to talk to you, but I persuaded him to let me talk to you first. He's very unhappy in Regina. He doesn't know how to tell you."

With his back to her he said, "You could've fooled me. He's got a good job and he's doing very well at it, by the way. He's been going out with this Linda since the week he got back." He turned his glowering face to her. "What's not to like?"

Yetta looked away. "Regina's a small town. It's very isolated. Almost everything revolves around farming and mining. He likes more tumult, more possibilities. He thought if he pretended to be happy, eventually he would be. Try to understand. He's your son and he's a lot like you." She frowned at him. "But he's not you. He genuinely likes the restaurant business. He likes the *shmoozing*. He likes different things happening every day. Can't you understand?"

"Not really, but I don't have a choice, do I?" He rubbed his eyes.

"Let him go, Jackie. You did the right thing for yourself, living in Regina. It doesn't mean you were wrong if Randall chooses something else for himself."

Randall sat on his bed writing a letter to Linda.

March 14, 1940

Dear Linda,

When I last saw you I honestly believed I would be coming back to Regina. But since I've gotten to Washington, my aunt has offered me the chance to go to Richmond, Virginia, with her and help her start a new business. My aunt's met a man who lives in

Richmond and she wants to move down there. Would you like to come with me?

It looks like my aunt and I will be in Washington for two or three months more to settle things here. Then it will probably take a couple of months to get the business going in Richmond. You could come to Washington soon and work for the Marks Company while we are straightening things out. I'm sure we could find you a room to rent in a house near us. Or, you could wait until we get to Richmond and come directly there. We are planning on opening a restaurant and bar with a party room on the second floor. It would be similar to the restaurant we had here in Washington. I told you about it.

I haven't spoken to my father about this yet. I know he will be very unhappy with my decision. But it's something I've got to do. Please don't say anything to anyone for a while.

Let me know what you think.

Randall pondered how to sign the letter. He finally added "Love, Randy." When he read over the letter, he wondered if he should add some words about how he felt about her. He missed her more than he thought he would. So he added a "P.S. I miss you very much and hope you'll join me."

What he could say to his father? Jack was going to be livid. "I've got to do what I got to do," he said to himself.

On Monday morning, Jack and Bubbe sat at the kitchen table each with a second cup of coffee. Yetta and Randall had gone down to the office to go through Abe's desk.

Bubbe said, "This morning Yetta told me about her plans. I'm anxious to meet this Arnold Gross again, now that I know who he is. I hope this works out for Yetta. I was always so worried about her being alone after I'm gone."

Jack sipped.

"Listen, my son," Bubbe said. "Let Randall *gei gezoonter heit* and with your blessing."

"That's what everyone keeps telling me. I had this vision of us working together for several years and then his taking over the business."

"*Bubele,* you think it was easy putting you on that train for Montana when you were fifteen? He's twenty-two already. Don't make him feel guilty. You wanted to make it on your own, didn't you?"

Jack nodded. "But I was on an adventure to meet cowboys and see mountains and face strange animals."

"You asked for Papa's and my blessing because you needed to be free to find your own way. Do the same for Randall."

"You had three other children. I only have him. I've spent half my life building a business to share with him. He's rejecting me, everything I thought was important, and all I've worked for."

"He's not rejecting you. He wants to find his own way. Have you talked to him about it?"

"I'm waiting for him to bring it up."

"You're being foolish, Jackie. Take what you can have of him and be grateful."

At dinner that night, Yetta said, "I told Sammy about my plans. He said he had a suspicion about Arnold and me."

"What did he say about selling the business?" Jack said.

"He said something about Abe being our quarterback and without a quarterback, you didn't have a team or something like that. The end result is that on his own, he'd been thinking we ought to sell the provision part and the Ukrainian and keep the liquor."

"So, *nu*," Bubbe said, "what's he going to do now?"

"He's going to think it over, but he's pretty sure he wants to keep the liquor business himself. He wants to talk to Bertha about it."

"So, *Bubele*, when are we going to get to meet this Arnold of yours?"

"He should be in Washington next week."

"He'll come to dinner, and we'll get a chance to get acquainted."

The next morning Randall suggested to Jack they go downtown and see the cherry blossoms. He thought being on neutral territory might make things go better. They drove to the Jefferson Memorial so they could stroll around the Tidal Basin. The sun filtered through the haze of falling petals. The water in the pond was so still they could see their reflections. Randall's knees felt weak, and he couldn't keep his hands still. He wondered if his father noticed. Finally, they settled on a park bench.

"Aunt Yetta says she talked to you about her plans and wanting me to go to Richmond with her."

"She did." Jack tried to keep the anger from his voice, hoping he still might persuade Randall he was making a mistake.

"I know you must be disappointed. I tried hard to like it in Regina, and I actually thought I did until I got back here to Washington."

Jack turned to face Randall. "That's a bunch of crap. First, you run away to the army and then to Washington. A girl rejects you so you run back to Regina. Running from one disappointment or problem to the next.

That's your pattern. You think you're going to get my money and not have to work for it. You got another thing coming, buster."

Randall's face turned bright red. "You can keep your damn money."

Jack slapped his face.

Randall thought for just a second of slugging his father. He put a hand on his cheek.

Jack's voice was cold. "I've given you a chance to grow up in a place where no one cares who you are or where you came from. I given you a life free of all the religion and rules I had to deal with when I was young. You're twenty-two. Don't you think you ought to have figured out what you want by now and be grateful for what you've got?"

"What I've figured out is that you're never going to have another chance to hit me." Randall turned around to look at the water. He hoped for an apology.

"I have to pack. I'm leaving tomorrow." Jack turned and started walking toward the car.

Randall stuffed his hands in his pockets and marched behind him. *I'm doing what I have to do and what's right for me. God damn you to hell.*

The next day Sammy drove Jack to the train station. Jack turned to look at him and said, "How did everyone but me know Randall wasn't happy in Regina?"

"Sometimes the trainer is the last to know how the fighter is thinking."

"Sometimes I don't know what you're talking about."

"I mean you were concentrating so hard on trying to get Randall to do what you wanted him to do, you didn't pay any attention to what he wanted. You've got a good kid, Jack. Let him find his own way. Did you know what you wanted when you left home?"

"I didn't. But I was only fifteen. By the time I was twenty-two I had a pretty good idea."

"So. Some people know earlier and some know later. You're the one who's going to have to adjust."

"If I'd been offered the same opportunity in Washington that Randall has in Regina, I'd have never left."

"Are you trying to kid a kidder? You were offered the same possibilities. Look what Papa and Mama started for the rest of us—a business that supports three families in a nice style. You wanted to leave no matter what, so you left. Give the kid a break."

"You're dead wrong. He's paying me back for not telling him about Bessie and the circumcision."

Jack contemplated the steps he had to take to change his will and the ownership of his property so Randall would get next to nothing when the time came.

Two weeks later Randall received a letter from Linda. She wanted to know if he loved her. She said she wasn't going to come if he didn't love her and want to marry her.

Randall sat at Zeyde's desk, thinking. *Do I love her? That's hard. Do I miss her? Definitely. I miss talking to her. I miss her laugh and her body, that wonderful body. Marry her? Spend the rest of my life with her? I don't know. I have to make up my mind or, if I can't, that's an answer, too.*

Randall picked up the pen and wrote, "Dear Linda, I love you and miss you, too." He stood and leaned over the desk to read what he had written. He paced around the room. *That wasn't too hard.* He sat and wrote some more. "I miss talking to you every day. I miss hearing you laugh at my stories. Most of all I miss your naked body next to mine. Will you marry me?" *Wow.* His hand started to shake. He had to put down the pen for a couple of minutes. He wrote, "I thought we'd get married by a judge in Richmond. It's a lot less complicated that way. At this point, it would probably be better if you would meet us there."

He wondered why he had suggested she come to Washington in the first place. That would have made things very difficult for Bubbe—all the gossip.

He wrote, "Aunt Yetta and Uncle Sammy have a buyer for the business. They're negotiating the price and terms. Aunt Yetta thinks we should be in Richmond by the end of April. I thought you should plan on coming in the middle of June. How does that sound to you? Don't write back. I'll call you in a couple of weeks when things are more settled. I want to ask you to marry me and I want to *hear* your answer." He signed the letter, "All my love, Randy."

He decided not to tell anybody about his plans until after he'd talked to her on the phone. No need to get everybody excited until he knew for sure what was going to happen.

It was Sunday, May 15th, at three o'clock, Regina time, the precise time he had written Linda to be by the phone. His palm was so wet the telephone receiver slipped through his hand. He dried his hand on his pant leg, stuck his forefinger in the zero hole, and dialed. As the wheel clicked back to its resting place, minutes passed, or so it seemed. He gave the operator Linda's phone number and told her station-to-station. No need to call person-to-person. Linda should be there, waiting.

"Hello." It was a male voice.

Randall stuttered. "Is Linda there?"

"Linda? Who is this?"

"This is Randy Marks. Mr. Radkowski?"

"Oh, my God. Randy. Didn't you get my wife's letter?"

"No. What's wrong? Where's Linda?"

"My wife wrote you about the car accident."

"Was Linda hurt? Is she okay?"

"I don't know how to tell you this, but Linda's dead. She died instantly. Thank God she didn't suffer."

"I . . ." Randall was numb. He looked at his hand and was surprised to find the receiver was still there.

"I'm sorry you had to find out this way. We found your letters after she was gone."

"I'll . . ." He couldn't think of a thing to say. "I . . ."

Mr. Radkowski was crying. "It's okay. The shock and all. Get in touch again when . . ." he sobbed, " . . . you're ready. Good-bye."

Randall went to his bedroom and sat on the edge of the bed. He put his head in his hands. The questions started racing through his mind. *When was the accident? Where was the accident? Who was in the car?* Then he remembered Mr. Radkowski had said she died immediately. He lay back on his bed and moaned. He wanted to cry but the tears wouldn't come.

Chapter Fifteen

Arnold's Wake

1966

Driving to Ike's house, after their stroll around the Duke campus, Yetta tried to picture his home. It was a little game she liked to play with herself when she met someone new. For Ike, she imagined a spacious colonial with a circular driveway, an abundance of bushes and trees. She suspected he had an elegant but comfortable living room. In the backyard, she saw a flagstone patio with plenty of magnolias and weeping willows.

She was pretty close to right. Ike's house was formally decorated in soft greens, metallic gold, and royal blue. The sheer gold drapes in both the living room and dining room had green damask valances and side panels. In the dining room a chair railing separated the wallpaper of hunting scenes from the lower painted wall. Crown molding circled the ceiling of all the large rooms.

As soon as Yetta walked into the house, she smelled the food. Ike ushered her into the dining room and held her chair as she sat. He poured iced water into their glasses and took the chair at the head. The maid had prepared fried chicken, mashed potatoes, string beans, and a salad. She served them on a table set with an ecru linen cloth, fine china, and sterling flatware. Did Ike eat like this every night? She guessed he did. French doors opened from the dining room onto a patio which met her expectations, except for a swimming pool, which she hadn't foreseen.

After dinner they went into the living room. Yetta settled on the sofa which was upholstered in heavy green-on-green brocade. Ike chose one of the side chairs covered in a green and blue patterned velour. The lamps on the occasional tables had been a Chinese vases. Two matching lamps on either side of the sofa were alabaster Corinthian columns. Ike poured them each a glass of wine from the carafe on the coffee table. "My wife and I learned to enjoy port on a trip we took to Portugal. I hope you like it. It's been so long since I had anyone to the house."

"Have you thought about moving into an apartment?"

"I have, but inertia keeps me rooted. You made a bold move when you left Washington for Richmond. What happened with Arnold Gross?"

"It's an embarrassing episode in my life, one I'd like to forget."

"If you tell me, I'll tell you a humiliating story about myself."

She chuckled. "I can't believe you ever humiliated yourself."

"There's the time I got tipsy at a pool party and fell in the pool fully clothed."

"That's pea-sized compared to my story." Yetta laughed. "If I tell, will you promise me two things?"

"A good lawyer never makes a promise without knowing the *quid pro quo*, but I promise to put whatever you tell me under the category of attorney-client privilege."

"That's one of my requirements. The other is that we'll never speak of it again."

"I promise with one caveat. Since I don't know the story, I'll only speak of it, if necessary, in the course of this case."

"You've got a deal. I'd have to tell you part of it anyway if I wanted to explain the full story of how Randall ended up in Elizabeth City." She considered where to begin. "Randall, Arnold, and I opened the Westside Bar and Grill in June 1940. We painted the walls a deep ruby and hung original oils on the walls. On Friday and Saturday nights we featured dance combos in the downstairs bar area which was more like a cocktail lounge than a neighborhood bar and eventually we became popular with an upscale crowd. Upstairs was a moderately priced restaurant."

* * * * * * * *

During the day, Yetta worked while Arnold and Randall slept. She ordered all the supplies and managed the staff. In the evening, she went home to the two bedroom apartment she shared with Randall and made dinner for him and Arnold. Then, she slept while they worked. Arnold, who had his own studio apartment, oversaw the bar, and Randall, the restaurant. Randall tried to recover from his shock about Linda by focusing on work.

One day, six months after they opened, Yetta settled at her desk, opened a drawer, and pulled out her cash journals. She posted the cash receipts and the checks and, using the adding machine, she footed the columns. When everything balanced, she prepared an Income Statement. Her heart fluttered when she discovered they'd made a profit—their first profitable month. She laughed out loud. Wanting to share her excitement, she put her hand on the telephone to dial Arnold when a notion of a more personal celebration popped into her head. A tingle ran up her spine. Arnold had done so many romantic things like bringing her flowers, cards, little trinkets. She would make this a romantic occasion.

She left the restaurant with the folded papers carefully tucked in her purse and a bottle of Moët under her arm. As she rode an almost empty city bus to his apartment, she imagined his startled look when he opened the door to find her there in the middle of the day. She pictured the suspicious look he'd give her when she'd hand him the bottle of champagne. At first, he would give her his usual kiss and hug. But when he saw the Income Statement, she fantasized how the hugs and kisses would become more exuberant. She fancied the feel of his heavy morning beard and the tickle of his mustache.

This might be the time to set a wedding date, now that they were making a profit. That would make her mother happy. As she walked up the steps to his apartment, she hummed *"Chusan, Challah Mazel Tov,"* Congratulations Bride and Groom, and giggled. She couldn't believe herself, giggling at her age. In front of his door she reached for the knocker but stopped. She remembered the in-case-he-got-locked-out key in her purse. She put the bottle of champagne on the floor and fumbled in her pocketbook. When she found the key, she put it in the lock and turned it slowly with two hands. After the final click, she picked up the bottle, twisted the doorknob, flung open the door and yelled, "Surprise."

The room was shadowy, dimly lit by only the light from the bathroom. Yetta caught a glimpse of a naked woman yanking a sheet up over her head and she thought she heard a squeal. She'd seen a flash of big breasts and blond hair. She blinked several times to try and focus her eyes. Arnold was sitting up in the bed. She hadn't suspected he had so much hair on his chest, what with his bald head.

"What're you doing here?" Arnold said.

It took a few seconds for her brain to register what she was seeing—Arnold and the new waitress in the Murphy bed, dirty dishes on the dinette table, clothes in a heap. Her head was going to burst. Her heart was on the verge of rupture. Then it all sank in and she shrieked, "You *mamzer*, you *shmuck!*"

She raised the champagne bottle while she deliberated bashing in his head. He appeared to know what she had in mind because he shrank under the sheets, holding out his large woolly arms over his head to ward off the blow. She turned and slammed the champagne bottle against the door frame. That felt good, so she pounded it a few more times, hoping it would break. When she turned back, Arnold and his friend were running for the bathroom. Yetta started after them. The woman went through the door. Arnold turned around and with his hands extended toward her cried, "Please, Yetta. It's not what you think. Put the bottle down. We can work . . ."

"You naked *putz!*" She hurled the bottle at him. He shut the door just in time. The Moët crashed into the upper panel. The woman screamed. The bottle had smashed an indentation in the wood, leaving fracture lines and slivers of wood on the floor.

Yetta pounded on the door with her fists. She seized the champagne bottle and bashed a hole in the door. Through it she saw Arnold and the woman cowering in the bathtub. The woman was screaming for help. Yetta spun around and stalked out. As she left, she slammed the door as hard as she could.

By the time she got to the street, tears streamed down her cheeks. She dropped the champagne bottle into a trash can.

She'd never used the words *schmuck* or *putz* before. She pictured the look of horror that would've come over her mother's face, if she'd heard her. That vision started her laughing and crying at the same time. The image of Arnold naked popped into her head. He'd had such fear in his eyes, fear caused by her. That felt good. She didn't know she'd had it in her.

Not wanting to get on the bus with her emotions out of control, she trudged the mile and a half to her apartment.

As soon as she came through the door, Randall said, "What's wrong?"

"Everything," she said and plopped into a kitchen chair.

He followed her into the kitchen. "Can I get you anything?"

"How about a cup of tea?"

They sat at the table while she told him.

Lives in Exile

Randall's eyes went wide. He rubbed his scar. "God, Aunt Yetta. I saw him flirting with the waitresses and the customers, too. Sometimes he'd take people into the office, but I never thought . . ."

A vision of the sofa in the office whipped through Yetta's head. She thought about the times she and Arnold had kissed and touched each other on that sofa and about the times he tried to pull her down next to him.

Randall looked at her with sorrowful eyes. "I never suspected anything was going on . . . I guess I should've. I guess I was absorbed with my own troubles. I never thought Arnold was a . . ."

"A real jerk." Tears filled her eyes. She retreated to her bedroom where she lay on her bed and had a truly good cry. Here she was, an old maid, thirty-eight, who'd finally made a commitment to a man—a genuine loser. She spent the rest of the afternoon looking out the window at the bare trees and the grey sky.

All night she slept fitfully. When she was awake, she relived the whole last year with Arnold over and over, how he captivated her and then deceived her, reducing her to an hysterical maniac. She ended up crying every time. *How could she have been such a fool?*

As the early dawn turned the blackness of the night sky into a reddish glow, she knew she didn't need Arnold, didn't want Arnold, even hated Arnold. She wanted to keep the business and get rid of him. She'd put up all the money so deleting him from their partnership should be no trouble. She'd get a hold of a lawyer that morning because she never wanted to see Arnold again.

The realization hit her like a blow to the gut, what she'd actually been to Arnold—not a fiancée, not a companion for life, but his banker. The pain made her double over. She put her head on her arms and lay on the table for a while, crying softly because she didn't want to wake Randall. When the tears stopped, she walked into the bathroom and washed her face with cold water. That helped, so she snatched her washcloth and ran cold water over it. She pressed the cloth against her eyes. The cold made the swelling subside somewhat. She put the washcloth around the back of her neck. Her body cooled.

Back in the kitchen she found the telephone book and skimmed through the yellow pages for a lawyer. She didn't want to use the man who'd helped them buy the business and wrote up the partnership agreement. He was too buddy-buddy with Arnold. She wanted to find a Jewish lawyer with some *saichel*, some shrewdness and wits. She didn't know how many Jewish lawyers there would be in Richmond, but she just didn't trust gentiles. She found the name "Solomon Cohen" and made an appointment for ten o'clock.

Then she found the name of a locksmith and arranged for him to meet her at the restaurant at nine.

In the end, she had to buy Arnold out. She'd put up all the money for the restaurant and still had to pay him off. Her lawyer had said, "It's your choice. Get rid of him fast and easy or spend several years and lots of money going to court. In the end, it'll end up costing you the same." Just because they'd written that damn partnership agreement. Arnold had said it was for her protection in case something happened to him. Well nothing happened to him, everything happened to her, and guess who the agreement protected?

* * * * * * * *

"It wasn't just his lying and his cheating," Yetta said. "He'd spun me a tale of the golden life we were going to have together. I'd bought it hook, line, and sinker. It was the dashing of my fantasies that truly hurt."

"Life has a funny way of throwing you curve balls," Ike said.

Yetta laughed. "You need to meet my brother Sammy. He's always talking in sports metaphors and half the time we don't know what he means." She put her glass down on a coaster. "Eventually I went out with other men I met at the bar, but I never found anyone I wanted to marry." Yetta was lost in her own thoughts for a few minutes. "Randall was the one I worried about the most. His heart really wasn't in his work after Linda died and the business with Arnold. He used to *schmooz* with people, but the spirit had gone out of him."

"What brought him to Elizabeth City?"

"Sometimes you have to be in the right place at the right time. Randall was working the bar one night about a year later, substituting for the usual bartender, when a man came in with the story of his father-in-law wanting to sell his sand and gravel business. Randall jumped at the chance."

"It seems like he had a natural head for business like his father."

"He sure did. He took the opportunity and made a big success. You have to believe in fate, don't you?"

Ike nodded. "When he left, why did you stay in Richmond and not go home to Washington?"

"I guess I have some of my brother Jack in me. I discovered I liked being on my own, in a city without any relatives looking over my shoulder.

I liked having my own business and being responsible only to myself. To be truthful, I also was embarrassed and felt very foolish."

"You were conned by a person who probably made a good living conning women. You grew up in a family of men who always looked out for you, so you had no experience dealing with a man like him. You shouldn't have blamed yourself."

"That's what Randall said. But I thought I should've been able to see through him. It was his bald head and impish grin that made me trust him."

"I'm glad I have a full head of hair and I'll try not to grin impishly."

Yetta blushed.

"Why do you think Jack was so insistent that Randall come back to Regina?" Ike asked.

"I think that somewhere down deep, he felt guilty about leaving the family and his religion, about wanting to be on his own, isolated from the rest of us." She sighed. "If Randall chose to live the same life, then that would've been an affirmation that he had done the right thing. By choosing to live elsewhere, especially with the rest of the family, and wanting to identify himself as Jewish, I think Jack felt Randall was demonstrating his, Jack's, guilt and bad choices."

"What happened to Randall after he left Richmond?"

* * * * * * * *

Two years after she'd bought Arnold out, Yetta sat at her desk posting her journals. She looked in her drawer for a sharp pencil and came across the "good-bye" letter from Arnold. *Why have I kept it?* She fingered the envelope flap. Maybe she kept it to remind herself of the pitfalls of love. She could recite the letter from memory. "You have lost your trust in me. I cannot continue in a relationship with no trust. So I am leaving Richmond. I wish you good luck in the future." Hah. Lost her trust in him. After she'd paid him off, he'd run away with another woman. Good luck in her future. Well, she wasn't depending on luck. She was working hard and using her good *yiddisha kuhp*, her good Jewish intelligence, and everything her father had taught her about how to run a business and make a profit. Thank goodness she'd found out who Arnold was before they got married. That would've been a real disaster.

If only she and Solomon Cohen had known he'd already helped himself to several thousands from the cash register. She didn't discover the pilfering until she started running everything herself and saw how much they actually took in each night. Thank God she'd never let him in her bed and the business had been open only six months. Just thinking about what he might have gotten away with made her break into a sweat.

"You *putz*." That had been a pretty lame thing to say when she'd been feeling such anger, disappointment, and hurt. She wished she'd been able to string together a few more curses. She knew if she'd had a gun, she would've shot him, or if she'd had a knife, she would've stabbed him. Thank heavens all she had was the champagne bottle. He wasn't worth going to jail for, but, at least, she'd had the satisfaction of making a mess. She could smile about it now.

Yetta looked at the two pictures on her desk. The 1908 family portrait and the one Arnold had taken of Randall and her outside the restaurant on opening day. She loved that picture of the two of them. She'd had no better luck with men than Randall'd had with women. She'd lost one scoundrel and a bunch of money, but Randall had suffered much more. He'd lost two loves—one worthy of him and one not. Although, she realized, her positive judgment of Linda might be flawed since she'd never met the girl. At least he'd landed on his feet financially. She footed the journals for the month. The December income had exceeded the expenses by a thousand dollars. The holiday season was finishing off a profitable year very nicely.

She was glad Randall was coming up for New Year's to help her out. It would be good to see him. She wondered what this latest girlfriend would be like. He seemed to have a new one every few months, some with more class than others. She guessed these short relationships were a kind of self-protection from being hurt again.

She put the ledgers back in the drawer and locked it, got out her New Year's Eve "things-to-do" list and made the calls to order the hats and noise makers. The Saturday night dance combo had been booked for the upstairs restaurant and the Friday night combo for the bar. The reservations were coming in. She was sure the whole place would be booked. She checked over the liquor order, initialed it, and put it in the bar manager's message slot so he could give the list to the wholesaler's delivery man.

Randall arrived two days before New Year's with Betty Anne Swaim who slept in Randall's old room while Randall slept on the sofa. Yetta did not allow carryings-on in her apartment. Betty Anne was nice enough, but she tried too hard to be Lauren Bacall. She wore her bleach-blond hair in a page boy and held her cigarette with a bent-wrist-sophisticated-look, resting her elbow on the arm of a chair or tight against her waist.

Lives in Exile

Betty Anne constantly touched Randall, on his shoulder, on his hand, on his cheek. Randall smiled at her every time. Soon after they arrived, Betty Anne took Randall's hand and looked up into his eyes making a big pout with her splendid lips and said, "Can we go shopping now? I can't wait to try on one of the long skirts I saw in Vogue."

Randall said, "Let's spend a few minutes with Aunt Yetta, have some lunch, and then we'll go."

Betty Anne batted her eyelashes and said, "Promise?"

Randall smiled and nodded. He obviously found her very appealing.

Next to the pseudo-sophisticated Betty Anne, Yetta felt like Ethel Merman.

Yetta had prepared a plate with tuna salad, salmon salad, deviled eggs, lettuce, tomato, spring onion and green olives. That morning, she'd driven across town to buy a loaf of fresh rye bread with seeds. While Betty Anne picked at her food, she chattered on and on about New York—what they wore in New York, what they ate in New York. She got all her information from fashion magazines. She actually quoted them verbatim to Yetta. But Betty Anne amused Randall. Yetta enjoyed seeing him happy but didn't anticipate much of a future for this relationship. It was obvious Betty Anne's goal was to get to New York and hoped Randall was her ticket. Yetta knew if Randall did take her, the girl would never go back to North Carolina. Randall appeared to understand too, by his vague promises.

On New Year's Eve, Yetta wore her "working cocktail dress," a black taffeta underdress with a chiffon overlay, cap sleeves and a simple round neck. She accessorized with a rhinestone necklace and matching earrings. It was appropriate for the evening—dressy yet something she could move around in easily.

Betty Anne put on one of the dresses Randall had bought her in Richmond. It was a strapless red taffeta number with a full skirt that swished with every movement of her hips. She wore a necklace of large black beads with matching earrings and bracelet. Yetta had to admit she looked quite swank.

Randall wore a pair of grey slacks with a white shirt and grey tie. When he got to the restaurant, he slipped on a red apron all the waiters wore.

That night, Randall worked as the manager/maitre d' of the downstairs bar and Yetta moved from place to place solving any problems that came up. When Yetta came downstairs, Betty Anne was perched on a stool—her right elbow propped on the bar with her cigarette drooping from between two fingers. A cloud of smoke enveloped her. With a toothpick, she speared the olive of her martini and swirled the liquid around the glass. She lounged back and looked down her nose at the man she was talking to with her eyelids at half-mast. Yetta marveled at the way men could be taken in by such a blatant performance. But they obviously were, because one was hanging over her shoulder and two were on the seats next to her. She wondered what Randall thought about his flirtatious girlfriend.

At 2:00 a.m. Yetta closed the upstairs restaurant and invited all the patrons to continue their parties at the bar. It was 3:00 a.m. when she noticed Betty Anne dancing the last dance, a slow one, with one of the regulars, a man named Stanley. There wasn't a quarter inch between them. The man's right hand was firmly planted on Betty Anne's bare back.

Yetta looked around for Randall. He sat at the bar with what looked like a scotch on the rocks, glaring at them. She wondered how many drinks he'd had. He swirled the ice around and tipped his tumbler to his lips for the last drop. Betty Anne gave Stanley a long and sexy kiss. Randall banged his glass down and stumbled to the dance floor. He seized Betty Anne's arm. "Don't you think you ought to save the last dance for the man who brought you?"

"You're drunk. Get away from me."

"Come on, Betty Anne," Randall said. "I've been real good to you."

Stanley gave Randall a shove and held his arm out to ward off any further lunges. Randall batted it away. Stanley positioned himself between Randall and Betty Anne with his chest puffed out.

Randall nudged Stanley aside and reached for Betty Anne's arm. "Is this the way you treat me after all I've bought you?"

Betty Anne held onto the top of her dress.

Stanley pushed Randall into the bar.

The Lauren Bacall look-alike had lost all her pseudo-class with her red lips pursed to scream, her eyes bulging in anger, and her arms flailing in outrage. "Yeah? Well, you're a real jerk loser. You're never going to take me to New York, are you?"

"You wanna go to New York?" Stanley said. "I'll take you to New York, baby."

"You will?"

"Sure." Stanley looked over his shoulder at Randall slumped against the bar. "Stay at my place tonight and we'll leave first thing in the morning."

Yetta was afraid Randall was going to slug him. She considered pointing out that it was already the first thing in the morning and maybe they should leave immediately but thought better of it.

To Yetta's relief, Betty Anne put her arm through Stanley's and said, "Let's go, honey. I'm with you."

"You can't treat me this way." Randall staggered toward the couple and ran headlong into a wall.

Betty Anne grabbed her coat. "You're pathetic."

They strutted out.

Randall bellowed, "Good riddance," then straggled up the stairs.

Yetta heard her office door slam. She turned around and gave the crowd the best smile she could muster. The party was over, so the last of the customers left and the work crew cleaned up.

When everything was done, Yetta went to Randall. He was sitting behind the desk with his head resting on his arms. At first she thought he was asleep or had passed out, but he looked up when she got to the desk. Yetta took the chair facing him.

He rubbed his scar. "I never learn, do I?"

"Learn what?"

"Never bring a woman to work with me on New Year's Eve. Remember what happened with Maggie? I got drunk that night, too. Maggie had to help me home. She thought I was attacking her. But I was just acting dumb because I was close to passing out and mad at my father."

"I remember now."

"I ended up having to tell her the truth about everything including Shining Star. It was the beginning of the end."

"I don't think this relationship with Betty Anne had much of a future."

"Probably not."

"I wish you'd find some nice girl and settle down. You should have children. You're only twenty-four."

"My mother died when she was only four years older than me." He looked over at the pictures on the desk. "Nice girls aren't interested in me. To Jewish girls, I'm not Jewish. To gentiles, I am Jewish. I'm living my life in exile."

"Why don't you go to a rabbi and the mohel and officially convert so there won't be any question?"

His face turned red. "I just can't."

Yetta leaned forward and put her hand over his. "There must be some nice girl out there who doesn't care."

"When you find her, give me a call." He pulled his hand out from under hers and stood. "No use talking. Let's go."

When they got back to the apartment, Randall gathered all of Betty Anne's belongings and dumped them in the hallway. "When she calls, tell her she can come get her things." He rubbed his eyes and strode into his bedroom.

Though exhausted, Yetta couldn't sleep. She ruminated over what Randall had said. "I'm living my life in exile." It was true. She was, too. Even though they'd both chosen their own paths, she certainly hadn't anticipated how she'd end up. The best solution for both of them was to find someone who loved them and get married. Obviously Randall was still too bruised and scarred to make a commitment, and she didn't want to get involved yet. The business with Arnold was still too painful. She didn't want to give up her business and her independence. She'd worked too hard for them. Moving back to Washington was out of the question.

The next morning Betty Anne called. Yetta told her she would find her things in the hall. She didn't tell her they were in a heap. A half-hour later, Yetta heard bumping and banging. She figured Betty Anne and Stanley had found her stuff.

When Randall woke up at one in the afternoon, Yetta made him a three-egg cheese omelette. He had a bagel, at least what passed for a bagel in Richmond, and two cups of coffee. They spent the rest of the afternoon reading the newspaper. When they spoke, it was about the weather and Randall's business.

Chapter Sixteen

Regina

1965

A phone rang somewhere in Randall's dream. He reached for the receiver. Sylvia nudged him. Slowly he realized the ringing was for real. He looked at the clock—1:15.

"She's gone."

Randall recognized his father's voice even though he hadn't talked to him in twenty-five years.

After Randall and Yetta left for Richmond, Jack wouldn't speak to either of them. He'd softened his attitude toward Yetta when he heard about her problems with Arnold. Jack knew what it was like to have your heart broken. But his heart never thawed toward Randall even when he heard Linda had been killed. His only contact with Randall was through Shining Star and Yetta.

"Pop? Is that you? How'd you get my number?"

"Yetta gave it to me a long time ago. Were you sleeping? I forgot about the time difference."

Randall wondered whether he was still asleep and this was a dream. "Are you all right?" Despite himself, concern infused his voice.

"Shining Star's gone."

His mind still wasn't working clearly. "Gone where?" It didn't sound like an emergency.

"Wherever *Métis* think you go when you die."

"Pop, what are you talking about? Start from the beginning." The more he awakened, the clearer it became. After all this time, his father was talking to him as if they had spoken only yesterday.

"I woke up this morning and there she was. Dead, next to me. Gone in the night. Didn't even know it. Called the doc. He came and said it was an aneurysm. I called her people. They came and got her."

"Would you like me to come?"

"That would be nice. It's been a long time."

Randall sighed. This was what he'd been waiting twenty-five years to hear. His father had forgiven him, but why did it have to come after Shining Star died?

"Who was that?" Sylvia said.

"My father. My step-mother died. I have to go home."

Sylvia sat up in bed. "So you're going to pack up and go, just like that?"

"Of course. My step-mother died."

"He's going to give you a lot of shit."

Randall turned his back to her. *What business of hers is this?* "I don't think so, not this time. He sounded very sad."

Sylvia shook his finger at him. "You mark my words."

Why's she being such a bitch? "This is my father you're screaming about."

Sylvia lay back in bed and turned away from him.

Two days later, the plane flew low as it approached the Regina airport. As they passed over the RCMP headquarters, Randall saw Mounties in their red dress uniforms performing dressage. The winter wheat fields were a dirty tan. Cattle and horses grazed in the barren pastures.

When he stepped off the airplane, Randall scanned the group standing at the gate. As he got closer to the crowd, he easily recognized his father. The skin on Jack's face was smooth, hardly any wrinkles, but his hair had gone completely white. When Jack started toward him, Randall was shocked at his stooped posture and his shuffling gait. He shook his father's hand.

"Glad you could come," Jack said.

"Always the best dressed man in your suit and tie."

"I'm fair to middling, but you've collected a few pounds around the middle."

"Sylvia's always after me to do something about it."

"You'll have to tell me all about Sylvia when we get home."

Home. Is this still home?

After they collected Randall's luggage, Jack said, "We could stop on the way for some dinner, if you're hungry."

"Thanks, Pop, but they fed us on the airplane."

As they drove through the city, Jack kept up a tour guide commentary on everything they passed. "You know I've been in Regina fifty years." He shook his head. "Hard to imagine. When I first got here, all the streets were dirt. Now everything's paved and you need a map to find your way around. All the buildings were one-story. Now look at 'em." He waved his arm around and pointed out the spot where the newspaper office used to be in 1911. Now it was a ten-story building. "I'm sure the Mounties never expected to find their headquarters in town. When I arrived, they were quite a ways out."

When they walked in the house, Jack said, "Your old room is waiting for you. How long has it been since you were here?"

"It was before the War—more than twenty-five years."

It wasn't his room anymore. The walls had been painted white and the drapes replaced by Venetian blinds. The twin beds were covered with pale blue bedspreads in a seersucker fabric. Bookcases lined two walls. A narrow dresser shared the wall with the door. This was obviously his father's library.

Randall found Jack sitting in his living room chair—a glass of scotch in one hand and his cigar in the other. Randall noticed something about Jack's eyes, a kind of vagueness. His skin was grey beneath the surface. Randall assumed it was old age.

Jack nodded toward the sofa and the drink on the end table. "You still like scotch?"

"Yes. And I'd love one of your cigars."

Jack gestured toward the humidor. "When did you start graying on the sides like that?"

"Just a few years ago. Sylvia says it makes me look distinguished."

"Have you seen your Aunt Yetta lately? How's she doing?"

"Sylvia and I went to Washington for Passover. We picked up Aunt Yetta on the way. She's doing fine."

"You like it in North Carolina?"

"Business is good. So's the weather. I love being near the ocean. You ever smell the ocean?"

"I've never even seen the ocean. I guess it's too late now."

"Something about that combination of sand and salt. Sylvia splashes around in the waves like a fish. Me, I'm all stiff. I guess it's the difference of having grown up near the beach."

"You have a picture of Sylvia?"

"Sorry. I never carry any."

"I'm glad you're here, son. Shining Star'd been after me for a long time to get you to come up. She told me what you wrote in your letters—about your sand and gravel business and about your lady friend. It's a shame Shining Star had to die to get me to see what a fool I've been." Jack covered his eyes.

"Do we have to make any arrangements for Shining Star?"

"She's already been cremated and her ashes scattered in the river during a *Métis* ceremony. That's what she wanted. They're a very stoic people. Her sister, Bright Moon, took care of everything." Jack pulled out his handkerchief and coughed into it. Then he wiped his mouth and nose. After a few moments he twisted the cigar in the ashtray.

"Pop, let's talk."

"I'm too tired now. I'm going to bed. We'll talk in the morning."

When Jack came into the kitchen the next morning, he found Randall reading the paper, smoking a cigarette. A plate with the remains of fried eggs and toast was pushed to the side and a half-cup of coffee sat in front of him.

"You're up early," Jack said.

"The time difference."

Jack poured himself a bowl of corn flakes and a cup of coffee. He sprinkled sugar over the cereal and poured cream straight from the bottle into the bowl. "When'd you start wearing glasses?"

"About ten years ago, but I only need them for reading."

"What's with you and Sylvia?"

"What do you mean?"

"Are you going to marry her?"

"I doubt it. Things are good the way they are." Randall shrugged. "I'm not the marrying type."

"Doesn't she want it—I mean the ring, children, and all?"

"I guess she would but she understands how things are with me." *What's this all about?*

"But have you taken care of her in your will and such?"

If Sylvia only knew how Pop worried about her, she'd have to say she was sorry about giving me such a hard time about coming. "Pop, we're not going to start about the money again, are we?"

"No, no. I need to talk to you about the future. That's all. But I've been thinking a lot about the might-have-beens. If your baby brother had lived, he would have been forty-one. Your mother and I would have been together forty-eight years. You know I turned seventy-two my last birthday." He coughed until he could catch his breath.

Randall snubbed out his cigarette and said, "Should I get you a glass of water?"

"I'm okay. Don't worry. Bob Harrison died last year. You remember him. He owned the lumber yard."

Randall nodded.

"I'd known him since I came to Regina," Jack said. "He was one of the first advertisers I signed up for the paper. We'd gotten to be very good friends. At the funeral his children, grandchildren, brothers, sisters, nieces and nephews pretty near filled the church, and they all loved him—really loved him. He was a great guy. I started thinking that at my funeral, I'd hardly have anybody at all." Jack shook his head. "I was down in the dumps for quite a few weeks. I'd focused on money most of my life instead of the important things."

Jack got the coffee pot off the stove and refilled his cup and Randall's. He sat and stared into the cup as if there might be answers hiding there. "About six weeks ago I got some bad news from the doc. I've got the big C. In my lungs. Nothing they can do." He looked up at Randall. "Shining Star'd been after me to get you to come up here and straighten things out. But I was afraid you'd say no. Then the day she died I was really afraid. I'd never been so afraid in my whole life. I always thought we'd be here for each other. I sat paralyzed the whole day. That's why I didn't call you till so late."

Randall felt numb, so much catastrophic news. "What can the doctors do about the cancer?"

"Not much. They say I've got about six months to a year."

Randall cringed.

"When I think of all the time I wasted . . ." Jack sighed. "I know it's too late to make up for everything, but, I hope it helps if I say I was wrong and you were right. I should have helped you do what you wanted instead of pushing you down the path I picked. When you left, I was just stubborn because my pride was hurt. I felt betrayed and wanted you to do what I wanted you to do. Shining Star told me and tried to make me see I was wrong. I have to admit I wanted you to fail and come crawling back to me, but I'm real proud of you now. No father could be prouder of a son, and I hope you can forgive me."

Randall wanted to shout in frustration and anger. He wanted to be angry at his father. How many times had he wished for such an admission? How many times had he imagined it? He had envisioned himself gloating and saying, "Too little, too late," and marching off. But, now in the moment of triumph he'd been waiting for half his life, all he could do was weep.

Jack handed Randall a paper napkin and put his hand on Randall's arm. They sat together in silence. Randall lit another cigarette.

Jack shook his head. "I never figured out what I was looking for in life. I thought in order to be content, other people had to tell me I was a good person. I didn't realize all I had to do was be happy with myself." He gazed out the window for a few minutes. "This whole idea came to me the day after Shining Star died. For some reason I don't understand, I needed to visit your mother's grave. I was standing there, in the church yard, when these thoughts came into my mind. Your mother was a very needy person. She needed *me*. That made me feel important and strong and good. But then she went inside herself and that made me feel weak and useless." He paused. "I know it's the first thing in the morning, but I need a drink."

Jack took a glass from the cabinet and headed into the dining room.

Randall could hear the sounds of pouring and then some more pouring. He put out his cigarette and followed his father. "Why don't we sit in the living room?"

"I wanted to marry your mother. But that was impossible in Canada. I wanted to marry Shining Star, too, but the law wouldn't allow that either because she was *Métis*. After I found out about the cancer, I tried to persuade her to get married, but she wouldn't have any part of that. She said it would change everything and it wasn't necessary."

"She was a strong person."

"I realized after she was gone how much I needed and depended on her. All along I thought it was she who needed and depended on me. She made me believe that so I would feel good about myself."

"I wish I could've seen her again."

Jack took a swallow of scotch. "I'm sorry. I wish I could make it up to you, but all I can do is try to make things right from now on. Even before Shining Star died I'd gone to see my lawyer about getting my will and everything in order. I wanted to take care of Shining Star and you, too. There are some legal things that need to be explained so I made an appointment with my lawyer for 11:30 today. I know all this is kind of sudden, but you're only here for a short time. The lawyer'll tell you all about it. Okay?"

Everything was happening so fast. "Sure, Pop, whatever you say." Randall fumbled. "Have you told Aunt Yetta about your illness?"

"I mailed her a letter yesterday about Shining Star. She'll probably get it today or tomorrow. I'm sure she'll call. That'll be time enough."

At the lawyer's office, Jack introduced Randall to Bill O'Brien. Mr. O'Brien motioned them into the chairs opposite his desk.

Randall looked around the office. It was like every other small city lawyer's office he had ever been in. In fact, it reminded him very much of his North Carolina lawyer's office. Both were in the center of town in stone buildings, on the second floor, over the bank. The lawyer's name was stenciled in black on the window facing Main Street. Since the window faced west, Randall could imagine the lettering casting a shadow which traveled around the office late in the afternoon as the sun was setting. The walls were covered with law books neatly lined up on bookshelves. Randall and Jack sat across from Mr. O'Brien at his highly polished wooden desk which was covered with neat stacks of manila folders.

Mr. O'Brien said, "Randall—I hope you don't mind if I call you Randall since there are two Mr. Marks here."

Bill O'Brien was about forty. He had a full head of wavy brown hair. His features were boyish, and Randall was sure he'd grown his mustache to appear older. Behind the black rimmed eyeglasses, Randall saw brown eyes that had a serious, intent focus.

"I don't mind," Randall said.

"And please call me Bill. Your father has asked me to speak to you about a very delicate matter . . . As you know, your parents were not married at your birth. Your mother didn't list your father's name, or anyone else's for that matter, on your birth certificate. As far as the community knows, your father is your father. You lived with him growing up and you have always used his last name. But so there can be no legal challenges to your inheritance and your legal standing, I strongly recommend that, through court proceedings, you take Marks as your legal last name."

"You mean Randall Marks isn't my legal name?"

"It is since it is the name you have always used, but the name on your birth certificate is Randall Swartz. This is just a legal formality to protect your interests in your father's estate."

Jack nodded.

"If this is what you advise," Randall said, "then that's what I'll do."

"Good," said Bill O'Brien. "I have all the papers prepared and ready for your signature. We just have to file them. You don't even have to appear. The whole process should take about three months."

Jack said, "I've already signed my will leaving fifty thousand dollars to Yetta, but everything else to you. Bill and I have accounted for the value of all my assets. This comes to about half a million dollars." Jack looked down at his hands. "I know your life is in North Carolina, and you will probably want to dispose of everything. I'd hoped we could spend the next few days looking everything over so we could discuss what I think would be best for you to do when I'm gone."

"I'm here to do whatever you want."

"I want you to promise me one thing," Jack said, "that you'll look after your Aunt Yetta."

"You don't have to ask."

Randall signed the papers and left them with Bill O'Brien. He and Jack strolled over to the newspaper office so they could have lunch with the editor, Paul McGowan. Jack introduced Randall to everyone in the office and explained their job to him. On the way back to the house, Jack said, "I forgot to tell you Shining Star's sister, Bright Moon, is going to be at the house this afternoon. I arranged for her to come to the house three afternoons a week. I'm going to pay her to cook and clean. I think she feels she's supposed to take care of me now that Shining Star is gone, but I insisted on paying her."

"I'm glad you have someone to look after you."

That night, before dinner, when Randall was in the bathroom, the telephone rang. Jack answered. Randall could hear the muffled sounds of a long conversation. At dinner, Jack told him it was Yetta who had called. That was all he said. Randall could tell from the look on his face he didn't want to say any more.

Over the next few days, they visited the potash pits and surveyed the cattle ranch and discussed their value and who might want to purchase them.

Lives in Exile

After dinner, the night before Randall was to leave, Jack brought out an old hat box that had a faded pink ribbon tied in a big bow around it. "Do you remember this box?"

"No."

"This is the box you and Yetta put all your mother's favorite possessions in. Then you tied it with this ribbon and put it in the attic. It's been there for about forty years." Jack laid the box on the kitchen table and wiped off the dust with a rag. He untied the ribbon and opened the lid. The first thing he pulled out was a picture frame. "This is your mother, her parents, and her four sisters. She kept it on her dresser."

Randall took the picture from him and examined it. "Not a happy looking group."

"In those days you had to stand still for a long time for the image to transfer to the film. The photographers always told you to look straight at the camera and not to smile."

Jack took out Bessie's comb, brush, and mirror set in silver and mother-of-pearl. "Your mother got these when she lived in Seattle, before I met her. They were very special to her."

Randall laid down the picture and examined the set. He looked for some strands of hair, but none were left.

Jack picked up a lavender-colored glass perfume bottle. "Your mother always wore a flowery perfume." He smiled. "I gave her this bottle on her last birthday." Jack handed it to Randall.

Randall squeezed the atomizer and sniffed at the nozzle, but there was no fragrance left.

"That's all that's in here."

Randall put everything back into the box.

"Yetta is going to come to see me in about six weeks," Jack said. "She wanted to come sooner but I asked her to wait. I need some time to rest. We've had a very busy time."

Jack took the ring off his pinkie finger. "I had this made after your mother died. I had given her a diamond pendant the day I bought the newspaper. After she was gone, I took the diamond out and had this ring made. I want you to have it."

"Pop, I can't. It's yours."

"It will give me great pleasure to know you have it."

"If you're sure."

Jack nodded and handed the ring to Randall.

Randall put it on his little finger. He wondered whom he would give it to when his time came.

"I have something else for you," Jack said. "I've had them since I was about thirteen or fourteen. I carried them to Montana and then here. There probably collectors' items now. They used to be considered naughty." He laughed. "I'd completely forgotten about them until I was rummaging in the attic looking for your mother's things."

He handed Randall the French postcards. Randall looked through them and chuckled. "These are pretty tame. You sure were a bold guy."

"I used to save my pennies to buy them. A few bookstores had them behind the counters. My friends and I used to trade them, too."

Sylvia picked Randall up at the airport when he came home. He showed her his mother's things and told her what his father had said about them. She got a good laugh out of the French postcards. Then he went to the office to check his mail and messages.

That night he was already in bed when she came out of the bathroom in her sheerest white negligee. He'd spent the last week surrounded by death, consumed by thoughts of dying and death. He was glad to feel life in his body again.

Afterwards, when they were lying naked next to each other, Sylvia said, "Can I try the ring on?"

He took it off his finger and handed it to her.

She placed it on the ring finger of her left hand and held it up in front of her face. "It's a beautiful diamond that sure would make a nice engagement ring."

Randall had been drifting off, but now his mind snapped to full alert.

Turning her hand so that the stone caught the dim light. "Yes, it's a very good quality stone."

He wondered how women knew such things when they seemed to have had no experience.

When Sylvia first came to work for Randall as his bookkeeper-secretary at Elizabeth City Sand and Gravel, Randall had a four-foot high divider between his section and her section of the trailer. But one day, after they'd become intimate, he came back from lunching with a customer and the divider was gone. Now they kept a folding screen in the corner and whenever Randall felt a customer or employee might want to have a private conversation, they put up the screen. Of course, it was only for show because Sylvia could hear every word that was said. Randall had no secrets.

It occurred to him that Sylvia had heard him call his attorney to make an appointment to rewrite his will. He put two and two together as he suspected she had and came up with five. He only wanted to go over his affairs with his lawyer now that his estate was soon to be doubled. He intended to leave some small bequests to his favorite cousins and Sylvia and everything else to Aunt Yetta. Aunt Yetta was the one who had loaned him the money to start his business and who had encouraged him all his life and he had promised his father to take care of her.

He decided he and Sylvia needed to talk, but not in bed. He would wait for the weekend. He held out his hand for the ring and said, "I hadn't thought about it."

She got up and went into the bathroom. Through the door, Randall heard her sniffling.

He didn't have to bring up the subject. Sylvia did. On Saturday morning, she brought him breakfast in bed, something she did as a special treat only on his birthday.

She said, in her slow southern way, "I've been thinking."

"That's something you want to be careful of."

She picked up his toast and started to spread the cherry jam. "Y'all so cute." She paused. "Why don't we get married? You've made up with your father. He's given you a beautiful diamond. It's almost like an omen. You know, something telling you the time might be just right."

"I don't think you should read too much into these things. Look, Sylvia, I'm forty-seven and you're forty-two. There aren't going to be any children. The last five years have been great. Why don't we leave well enough alone?"

"Don't you see? That's the issue. We're at the point in our lives when we should know who we're going to be with and who's going to take care of us when we get old. I love you and I want to take care of you, and I want to know you'll care for me."

"I decided a long time ago I wasn't ever going to get married. I always planned to take care of you, and I knew I could count on you. Anyway, if something really bad happens, you've got your daughter to look after you."

She waved her hand at him. "Pfft. She can hardly look after herself. How's she going to look after me? Don't waste time. I still get offers, you know ." She patted her hair.

He didn't know why but he found it very sexy when women patted their hair. He leaned over and kissed her. "Thanks for breakfast. It's wonderful."

Sylvia stood up and wrapped her robe around herself. "Welcome." She sailed out of the bedroom.

She went shopping on Saturday afternoon and spent Sunday with her daughter. Randall knew he was getting the cool treatment. He waited for her to get over it. But when she barely spoke to him on Monday, Tuesday, and Wednesday, he knew he was in trouble. On Thursday he called Yetta and arranged to drive up to Richmond to spend the weekend with her.

Their dinner on Friday night reminded him of Friday night at Bubbe's. Aunt Yetta made chicken soup with matzah balls, brisket and tsimmes. Over the main course Aunt Yetta said, "I'm glad to see you. But, from your long face I can see you have something on your mind. You want to talk about it?"

"That's why I came up here. You know me better than anyone else and I need some advice."

"'Dear Abby' is listening."

Randall smiled. "First of all, I'm going to be writing a new will and I want you to know where it and all my important papers are. I keep them in the safe in my office. I have the combination and so does the foreman of the company, Larry Wright. I've made a list of everything in the safe and I've written down Larry's name, address, and phone number on the same piece of paper. I'd trust him with my life. He's been with me from the beginning. I've also written down the name, address, and phone number of my lawyer."

"I'll put the paper in my metal box for safekeeping. What else is bothering you?"

"I'm worried about my father being up there in Regina all by himself. Bright Moon is taking care of him, but I hate the thought of him being alone toward the end."

"I understand. You've got a business to take care of. I've already written him that when the time comes that he needs me, he should call and I'll go. So don't worry. Together, you and me, we'll take care of everything. But that's not enough to bring you driving all the way from Elizabeth City. What is it?"

"The problem is Sylvia. She wants to get married."

"I see. And this is a problem?"

"I'm crazy about Sylvia, but I can't get excited about marrying her. I'm worried that if I marry her, I'll be marrying all her problems, like her daughter for instance. I keep saying to myself, 'who needs it?'"

"What's the problem with her daughter?"

"She's always taking up with losers. She's got two children by two different husbands. She's divorced again and most of the guys she hangs out with are drinkers and gamblers. She's always asking Sylvia to bail her out and buy stuff for the kids—including food and clothing."

"I can see why you're concerned."

With his fork, Randall moved the food around on his plate. "I'm sure Sylvia's figured out how much I make from the business and my other investments. She knows I'm going to be inheriting quite a bit. I'm afraid she's going to start wanting things like a bigger, fancier house and lots of clothes. You know."

"I'm no expert on these things, but I guess you'd have to weigh how unhappy you'd be without her against how happy you are with her."

"I'll have to think about that."

"If you have to think about it . . ." She shrugged.

On Sunday afternoon, when he arrived back home, all of Sylvia's things were gone. He found a letter on the dining room table.

> Dear Randall,
>
> I decided that it would be best if I moved out. I'll be staying with my daughter for the time being. So, if you want me, you know where to find me.
>
> Sylvia
>
> P.S. You should find a new bookkeeper, too.

He decided to wait a few days and then phone her. Call her bluff, so to speak. If she didn't come back, the next bookkeeper he hired would be some pretty, blond, young thing, but married. He'd have to find women somewhere else, not in the office. It was too disruptive when they left.

He did miss Sylvia. She'd taken such good care of him both in the office and at home. She made few demands and let him make most of the decisions about where they went and what they did. They had their best times together in Vegas gambling and going to the shows. The thrill she got from winning sparkled in her eyes. She loved to dress up and prance around in the mink stole he'd bought her. Above all, she was great in bed. But he didn't miss her the way he missed Maggie when she broke off their engagement or grieve for her the way he did for Linda when she died. He hoped he could convince Sylvia to come back on the old terms, but if not, he knew he could find someone else. Most important, he didn't want a binding commitment with anyone.

Randall called Sylvia on Wednesday, and she agreed to have dinner with him on Friday. In the meantime, he hired Larry Wright's cousin to keep the books temporarily. When he arrived at Sylvia's daughter's house, he brought a dozen red roses in a long florist box tied with a red ribbon. Sylvia blushed when he handed them to her.

Sylvia had squeezed herself into the tightest, shortest dress she could find. When she promenaded away from him with the box of roses, he watched her hips bump from side to side. She turned around and smiled as she cut the stems and put the roses in the vase one by one. Randall thought her breasts might fall out if she bent over. But, then, he realized that if she bent over her dress would split first. He chuckled to himself. After she was through, she patted her hair as she sauntered toward him. He thought he might jump her right then and take her on the sofa, in front of the daughter and the two-year-old in the high chair.

He took her to her favorite restaurant and then suggested they drive over to the ocean and up the coast. He amused her with all the funny stories and jokes he could think of, especially the off-color ones. He knew she liked being naughty. When they were about an hour from Elizabeth City, he spotted a motel with a "vacancy" and suggested they stop. Randall registered. When they got in the room, he put one hand around the back of her neck and drew her to him. He kissed her urgently.

When they parted, she said, "Oh, Randall, can I see the ring now?"

"The ring?" he said.

"Yes, the ring. You have it with you?" She started to put her hands in his jacket pockets.

He grabbed her wrists and said, "What are you talking about?"

"That's what this is all about, isn't it?"

He shook his head. "I was hoping we could have a good time and get back together, like it was before."

Sylvia sat on the bed. "You mean you aren't planning on asking me to marry you?"

"I thought you understood. I'm not the marrying type."

"Oh, God." Then the tears started.

He reached out to touch her.

She all but spit at him as she drew back from his hand. "Stay away. I knew going to see your father was going to change everything."

He sat on the only chair in the room and looked down at his hands. He knew their relationship was over and hoped he could get her back to her daughter's with the least amount of hysterics. He knew the best thing for him to do was to be as quiet as possible and wait for her to tell him what she wanted to do.

When she was able to pull herself together, she said, "Take me back to my daughter's, please."

The ride back was silent. Sylvia kept her head turned away from Randall, looking out the side window. On the radio came the song "Que sera, sera." To himself he sang, "What will be, will be." When he pulled to the curb, she said, "No need," and jumped out and ran to the door as fast as her tight skirt and high heels would allow.

Randall sighed and drove home. He didn't know what to do about Sylvia. He wanted her back, but he didn't want to get married. He was tangled in his dilemma, so he did nothing but hire a new bookkeeper—Susie. She was great to look at and smart, too. She met all his requirements except one—she was single. Larry Wright's cousin taught her all she knew, but Susie didn't need training. She picked up on things without being told. As time went by, he thought less and less about Sylvia.

After his trip, Randall telephoned Jack every week. They talked mostly about Randall's business and the newspaper. Jack didn't want to discuss his health. He always said he was fine. Whenever Randall suggested coming for a visit, Jack said he should wait until the summer because traveling in the winter was so difficult.

In June, Yetta called to tell him she was going up to Regina again. After talking to Bright Moon on the telephone, she decided it was time to make the trip. She promised to call him when she got there. By the time she got to Regina, Jack was in a coma. She called Randall immediately.

"I'll be on the first plane." Then he called Susie to tell her he was leaving so she could take care of things in the office. She insisted on driving him to the airport. Even though he told her it was okay, she sat with him until his plane took off.

He made it in time to hold his father's hand as he took his last breath. Yetta, Bright Moon, and he sat in the bedroom for quite a while afterwards. Randall couldn't accept that his father was gone. Even though he had known Jack was going to die, he was stunned.

They held a service at the funeral home and buried Jack in the Jewish section of the cemetery. The governor of Saskatchewan, many legislators, the mayor of Regina, members of the city council, the chief of the RCMP, and other prominent citizens came to hear the rabbi eulogize Jack as a valued member of the community who loved his city and who was loved by all the people there. Randall knew Jack would have been pleased to know how respected he was. About twenty people accompanied Jack to his burial—Yetta, Randall, Bright Moon, and people from the newspaper.

The rabbi had torn Randall's tie and the handkerchief that Yetta kept in her suit breast pocket. They decided to receive friends the afternoon of the funeral but not to sit *shiva* although they did wear their rent garments for the whole seven day period. Even though they had no friends in Regina who might help them grieve for Jack, Randall and Yetta stayed in Regina for two weeks.

Randall worked with Bill O'Brien on beginning the estate probating process. Yetta worked on sifting through Jack's belongings. She and Randall divided the photographs between them. Randall took the humidor and Jack's favorite ashtray.

Susie picked Randall up at the airport. She said, "I'm so sorry about your father's passing. How're you doing?"

"I'm still in a state of shock."

Chapter Seventeen

Loser

1966

How was he supposed to grieve for a father he hardly knew? That question had penetrated Randall's thoughts for a whole year. And here it was again, intruding, as he drove down Saskatchewan Highway One in his father's 1956 ruby-red Cadillac Seville. The father he had endured for forty-six years was not the man he came to know during the last six months of his life. During that period Jack had been philosophical and thoughtful.

Mr. O'Brien had said Randall didn't have to come all the way from North Carolina to Regina to finalize the estate. He could take care of everything and send Randall the papers to sign.

"So, why are you going?" Yetta said when he told her about the trip.

"I need to go, to see everything again. You know—the house, the grave, the town."

"You think going there is going to help solve your problems? He's dead, you know. He can't explain himself any more."

Randall was silent.

Yetta shook her head. "Your problem is you're just like your father . . . and me, too."

"What does that mean?"

"Look at the patterns of our lives. We choose to live among strangers, away from our family. We're loners."

"You have a close connection to everyone in Washington."

"Your only real commitment is to your business and you've been very successful. I'll grant you that. Your father left you half-a-million. But what else?"

His father had left him a lot to think about. Yetta reminded him of something his father said, that he'd focused on money most of his life instead of the genuinely important things. Randall liked to think of himself as a winner in life, but what his father said hit him hard. Maybe he was actually regretting the way he'd spent his own life. The thought frightened him.

This morning he'd gone to Mr. O'Brien's office and signed the final estate papers. Later he had lunch with the purchaser of his father's newspaper and met the real estate agent at the house. Then he was alone. *Am I mourning my own life?*

As he drove toward town, he spotted a young couple walking along the edge of the road. They stuck out their thumbs. Randall pulled the car up next to them. Even as he stopped, he wondered why. For a little diversion, for some company, he told himself. "Where're you headed?"

"Into town," the girl said.

"Me, too. Hop in."

The girl was young, barely out of her teens. She wore a short black skirt, black stockings, and a skimpy black top. She squeezed over next to Randall and turned toward him to give her companion space to get into the car. "Thank you," she said as she batted her eyelashes and ran her hand through her hair.

God, a counterfeit Marilyn Monroe. But he liked the view of her cleavage. When he raised his eyes and looked at her face, she smiled.

The young man was dressed in a brown polyester leisure suit and beige shirt, opened neck with no tie. His hair was long and unkempt with sideburns which reached almost to the edges of his square chin.

Randall glanced at the young woman's left hand. Her nails were carefully manicured with bright red polish and she had no wedding ring.

"Where y'all headed?"

"We're going to the Cue Ball to see the band they got playing tonight," the girl said.

"The Cue Ball? That place still around? Haven't been there in years." Randall swept the girl with his eyes. He wanted to tell her to get rid of the gum she was cracking every three seconds. Her face would be kind of pretty if it wasn't in constant motion. But then he would have sounded like her father.

"Thursday is locals' night," the girl said. "We know some of the guys who're playing."

"If you're not in too big a hurry," Randall said, "maybe you'd like to catch some dinner with me at the Holiday Inn? My treat."

The young man said, "We'd love to. I'm Jimmy Eagle and this is my girlfriend, Brenda."

"I'm Randall Marks." Randall pulled the car into a parking place in front of the motel. Brenda and Jimmy followed him to Mounty's Café.

"We'll sit at the bar," Randall said to the hostess as she approached them in the doorway. To Randall this place looked just like every other Holiday Inn he had ever been in. The usual easy-to-clean beige, textured, plastic-looking wallpaper covered the walls.

"Scotch. Make mine a double on the rocks," Randall said to the bartender as he leaned over the brass rail and ran his hand over the polished wood bar. He turned toward Brenda, "What would you like?"

"A sloe gin fizz," said Brenda. "If that's okay?"

"Make mine scotch, too, but hold the rocks," said Jimmy directly to the bartender.

Randall took out his cigarettes and offered one to Brenda and Jimmy. Brenda drew one out with her long red fingernails. Jimmy preferred one from his own pack and lit it with a match. Randall held his gold lighter to the tip of Brenda's cigarette, then lit his own. He ran his thumb over the engraved initials and smiled. The feel of RSM always gave him pleasure. The lighter had been a gift from Sylvia.

"What business are you in?" said Brenda. She took the gum from her mouth and wrapped it in a napkin.

Randall laid the lighter on top of the cigarette pack on the bar. "Concrete. Up here looking into potash suppliers."

"That's where Jimmy and I live—out near the potash pits. Where do you live?"

"In North Carolina."

"Where's that?"

"In the U.S. Near the Atlantic Ocean."

When Randall reached out for his drink, the light glittered in the facets of his diamond pinkie ring. "Feels good going down." Jimmy was sneaking looks at his ring. "Gift from my father."

Jimmy raised his drink in a toast to Randall.

Randall raised his glass in return. "Happy Fourth of July." He twisted his neck as he loosened his tie. "Hit me again," he said to the bartender. He looked over at Brenda. Her glass was only half empty.

"Me too," Jimmy said.

Randall pointed at the wall behind the bar. "Wouldn't you think they could find some real relics of the early pioneer days and the RCMP instead of these cheap imitations they've put up here?"

Brenda shrugged.

Randall liked the way Brenda's skirt ended about half way up her thighs. What was he doing, looking for some ass?

After several more drinks, he said, "How 'bout we get a table and order us some steaks?"

"Super," said Brenda. "I'm hungry."

Randall motioned for Brenda to lead the way. He picked up his cigarettes and lighter and put them in his jacket pocket. He watched from the rear as Brenda sauntered over to the table on her high heels. Her skirt barely covered her tight tush. He loved the way her hips swayed. She reminded him of Linda—the way she chewed her gum, the tight clothes, the way she flirted. He hadn't thought of Linda in a long time.

At the table he ordered salad, soup, and steaks for everyone and a bottle of red wine.

"Where're you from, Brenda?"

"Saskatoon."

"My mother was from Saskatoon. She died when I was six. Our housekeeper raised me. She was *Métis*."

"Jimmy's *Métis*," Brenda said.

Randall looked over at Jimmy. His hair was straight and jet black. His eyes were definitely Indian eyes. But the nose, cheek bones, and chin were all European. He noticed Jimmy's jagged, dirty fingernails as he lifted a forkful of salad to his mouth. Randall sighed. Shining Star never would have tolerated such grubbiness. Randall gulped down half the glass of wine. "You, people, aren't keeping up. Come on. Bottoms up."

"So, you're from here?" said Jimmy.

Randall sliced the steak the waitress had delivered and put a chunk in his mouth. "I've only been here three or four times in the last thirty years. Ever been to the ocean, Brenda?"

Brenda shook her head as she chewed on her steak.

"You should see the ocean sometime. You ought to hear the roar. First time, I couldn't believe it. This loud noise comes just from the rush of the water. Rroarrr." He imitated the sound. "My ex loved to splash and swim around, but I could never relax enough to do that. I grew up swimming in the river. Sometimes, though, on a clear night she and I'd drive over to the ocean and take off all our clothes and go in naked." He smiled. He remembered how sometimes they'd make love on the blanket. *How much have I had to drink? Sylvia used to say, "If you can't remember how much you've had, then you're plastered." Why am I thinking of Sylvia? Because the trip to see my father was the beginning of the end for us? Did I make a mistake not marrying her?*

After dinner Randall ordered a bottle of scotch from the bar. Brenda stuck with the wine. At ten o'clock the bartender told them it was closing time.

"Come on up to my room," Randall said. "We'll finish off this bottle. The night is still young." He felt good.

"We were heading for the Cue Ball," Jimmy said.

"Oh, come on, Jimmy," Brenda said. "This is going to be more fun. We've already heard Lester's band a dozen times."

Randall pulled out a wad of bills held together with a gold money clip and tried to count out the money to pay the bill, but he couldn't do it. Brenda had to help. She also had to help him with the key when they got to the room.

Inside, Randall took off his suit jacket and his already loosened tie and tossed them on the bed. Brenda pushed his jacket aside as she settled on the end of the double bed. Two glasses sat on the tray next to the ice bucket so Randall staggered into the bathroom and got another glass, in case Brenda wanted some scotch. Jimmy ambled over to the window and looked out over the parking lot.

After searching across the FM band, Randall found a station playing Nat King Cole. He motioned to Brenda to dance with him. That warm honey voice sang "The Very Thought of You." Randall held Brenda's hips to his body with his right hand and with his left gripped her back. She stood on her toes and wrapped her arms around his neck. *Is this what dancing with Susie would be like?* Jimmy's pulling on his arm intruded into his trance-like state.

"Hey, how 'bout a dance for me?" Jimmy said.

"You'll have to wait your turn," Randall said. "I got her now. Have another drink."

Randall smiled as Jimmy poured himself another glass of scotch and plopped into the one comfortable chair in the room. With his eyes closed,

Randall blocked everything from his mind except that soothing voice and the feel of Brenda's hips close to his and her breasts against his chest.

Randall heard Jimmy pound the table.

"Hey, Brenda, my turn."

Randall swayed over toward the bed and pulled his wad out of his jacket pocket. "Hey, what say I give you the cab fare home and a hundred dollars for your trouble."

Jimmy pushed away Randall's extended hand and took Brenda by the arm. "Come on. Let's get out of here. This old man's just a drunken lech."

"C'mon man," Randall said. "How much you want? I got another hundred I could add to the pot."

"C'mon, Jimmy," Brenda said. "What's the harm? Just sit down over there and drink your hooch." She gave him a little push toward the chair.

"No," Jimmy shouted. "You're coming with me."

"I think the little lady would like to stay."

Jimmy clutched the bottle of scotch. "She's coming with me." With his other hand, he snatched the money from Randall's hand and pushed Randall onto the bed, started toward the door.

Randall lunged at him. Jimmy swung around. The bottle struck Randall across the left side of his face.

Randall was spun around by the force of the blow. "Motherfucker." He lunged again at Jimmy as Jimmy pulled Brenda toward the door.

"Fuck you." Jimmy clobbered Randall across the left side of his head, and when Randall twirled around, he cracked the bottle across the back of Randall's head.

Randall slumped to the floor.

Brenda yelped. "Oh, God. Oh, God."

Randall wanted to lift his hands to feel his face. It hurt like hell. But he couldn't make his hands move. Moving his head was impossible. He felt a tingling sensation running down his spine like his back was falling asleep. Someone turned him over. He could barely make out Jimmy through the haze. He wondered why the room was so smoky. He felt Jimmy tugging on his pinky finger. Then he heard metal clicking like the sound a door latch makes when the door is opened.

"We've got to get out of here," Jimmy said.

Randall felt Brenda's hands on his chest and heard her say, "We can't leave him like this."

"What do you want me to do?"

"At least cover him over so he'll be warm there on the floor."

Randall heard things falling on the floor. Then he felt something being tucked around his sides. It looked like the bedspread through the mist.

"Now, are you satisfied?" Jimmy said. "Can we get out of here?"

Randall heard the sound of the door scraping across the carpet.

"Loser," Jimmy said.

Randall heard the door close.

Loser. I can't feel my feet, my legs, my fingers, my hands. Loser. I must be dying. Sorry. Sorry to whom? Aunt Yetta. That's all. Nobody else. Oh, God.

"The very thought of you," crooned Nat King Cole.

* * * * * * * *

After Yetta got the call she sat by the phone for several minutes not knowing what to do. She looked down at the piece of paper. She'd written down the telephone number the police officer had given her, but she didn't remember why. She couldn't believe Randall was dead. She'd tried to persuade him to let the lawyer handle everything but he just had to go. It was like he had an appointment with death. She called Dot in Washington. When Dot started to cry, Yetta realized she hadn't yet shed a tear. She supposed it was the shock. Dot volunteered to go with her to Canada, but Yetta was sure she could handle everything herself and Dot had young children.

First, she called the airline and arranged to fly to Regina the next day. Then she called the funeral home. She remembered the name from last year. She asked them to arrange for a grave site as close to Jack as possible. There was no reason to bring him back to Elizabeth City or even Washington. Let him rest near his father.

Last, she called Bill O'Brien. He'd already heard about Randall on the radio and called the police himself. In fact he'd been looking up her number in his files when she called. He offered to meet her at the airport and take her to a hotel. He said he'd make a reservation for her at a different hotel than the one where Randall had been. She hadn't thought of that but was glad he had.

He brought the articles from the *Leader Post* when he picked her up, but she couldn't read them just yet, so she put them in a drawer in her hotel room. He told her there had been coverage on the local TV news. Yetta didn't turn on the set.

Mr. O'Brien had gotten Randall's corpse released by the coroner and transferred to the funeral home. The funeral director asked if she wanted to view the body but she chose not to. "Better to remember him as he was," Mr. O'Brien had said. Yetta knew he was right, of course, but it was hard not to have had a chance to say good-bye.

Late the next afternoon Randall was buried in the Jewish section of the cemetery only a few graves away from his father. They held no funeral, just a graveside service. Who would've come besides Yetta, Bright Moon, and Bill O'Brien? They all met at the graveside with the rabbi who said the prayers. Yetta, as the only family mourner, had her handkerchief torn and said Kaddish. The cemetery workers lowered the box and filled in the hole. As Yetta stood by watching, she wondered what the rabbi would say if he knew Randall had never been circumcised and had a *shiksa* mother. She'd have to remember to be generous with the funeral director for his discretion.

What would Randall have said if he knew a rabbi had officiated at his funeral? He probably would've been bitter. But what else could she have done? Cremated the body, she guessed, but that would've gone against all of her upbringing and instincts. Funeral and burial rituals were really for the living. What the dead didn't know wouldn't hurt them, and Randall had been wounded his whole life.

After the cemetery Yetta and Mr. O'Brien went back to Yetta's hotel and had a drink. At six o'clock his wife joined them for dinner—so much for sitting *shiva*. She knew she'd be mourning Randall for a long time, by herself. After dinner Yetta excused herself and went to her room.

She had a date to meet the sergeant in charge of Randall's case the next morning. She pulled the articles out of the drawer and arranged them in chronological order. The article of July 5th read:

> City Police are investigating the beating death of a man believed to be from North Carolina, whose body was found in amotel room early today.
>
> The body was found in room 124 about 10:00 a.m. by a maidof the Regina Holiday Inn at 835 Victoria Avenue. The manager,who said he knew the dead man, could not recognize the man who police said had been bludgeoned with a whiskey bottle.
>
> Saskatchewan chief coroner, Dr. Steele McMartin examined the body at the scene but cause of death has not been determined.

The July 6th article read:

> Police have identified the body of the North Carolina man discovered beaten to death at the Regina Holiday Inn yesterday. He is Randall Marks, 48, a native of Regina and son of the former owner of the *Leader Post*, Jack Marks. Randall Marks resided in North Carolina for the last twenty-five years. According to sources he was in town to settle the estate of his father who died one year ago.
>
> Police are interviewing witnesses and searching for an unidentified suspect.

The July 7th article read:

> Jimmy Eagle, 21, of 1410 Alberta Street, was remanded in custody when he appeared in Provincial Court yesterday afternoon charged with murder in the bludgeoning death of a North Carolina man.
>
> Sergeant Patrick Woolsey of the City Police testified that items had been recovered at Mr. Eagle's home at the time of his arrest which implicated him in the murder.
>
> The body of Randall Marks, 48, a Regina native and son of the former owner of the *Leader Post*, and a resident of Elizabeth City, North Carolina, was found by a maid of the Regina Holiday Inn, 835 Victoria Street, in room 124 at 10:00 a.m. on July 5. Mr. Marks will be buried today in Regina Cemetery.
>
> This is the fifth time in the city this year a violent death has resulted in a murder charge.

The next morning Sergeant Patrick Woolsey greeted Yetta at the front desk of the Police Station. He was dressed in a blue suit—civilian clothes. "Sorry for your loss," he said. He was so tall Yetta had to tilt her head up to look at him. When he looked down, his dark brown handle-bar mustache seemed to hang right over her.

"I have my report upstairs," he said. "If you'll follow me . . ."

Yetta caught the scent of Mennen's Skin Bracer as he passed her and noticed his hair hung down to his collar. She doubted any police officer in Richmond had hair that long. He ushered Yetta through a large room filled with metal desks and people. The room reeked of sweat, tobacco, and coffee. The furniture was a mixture of gray and beige metal desks and file cabinets. File folders were strewn all over the tops of every surface. People sat every which way in all different types of desk chairs. The room practically sang with people talking, typewriter keys clattering, and telephones ringing. Across the room from Yetta was a blackboard with long lists of names. She spotted a column under the name Woolsey; toward the bottom was the name "Marks" with a line through it.

The Sergeant's private office was off the larger room with a glass wall. His name was painted in black letters on the paneled door. A large green blotter sat in the middle of an otherwise empty, battered, but well-polished wooden desk. It was obvious Patrick Woolsey took great pride in his old desk. The Sergeant offered Yetta a cup of coffee, and, when she refused, motioned her into one of the two chairs facing the desk and closed his office door before taking the seat behind the desk. The chatter from outside disappeared. One narrow end of the desk was pushed up against a wall with a bulletin board hanging on it. Attached to the board was a calendar, courtesy of "Beacon Auto Body," turned to June. Appropriately enough, a summer prairie scene decorated the flap. Several wanted posters and what appeared to be a duty schedule were thumb-tacked to the board. On the desk but angled so Yetta couldn't get a clear view of them were several family pictures.

The Sergeant pulled out a manila file folder from the desk drawer. He placed it on the desk, opened it, and slid it toward Yetta with hands that were smooth and thin. Now that she was seated eye-to-eye with him Yetta could see his clear blue eyes. He fixed her with an empathetic look. Yetta could imagine crime victims feeling comfortable and safe talking to him.

Yetta said, "I'd rather hear from you about what happened instead of reading it in a report, if you have the time."

"No trouble, ma'am. Just let me get out my notes." The Sergeant closed the folder and removed his pocket-size notebook from his inside jacket pocket and flipped through the pages. He smoothed both sides of his mustache. "The hotel maid found your nephew about 10:00 a.m. The manager called us immediately. We found your nephew fully clothed lying on the floor with the bedspread tucked around him."

She placed her hands on the desk, leaned forward, and fingered the folder. "A bedspread was tucked around him?"

"The perp, excuse me ma'am, the suspect says he tucked the bedspread around Mr. Marks 'cause he thought he was still alive and might be cold. He claims he thought Mr. Marks had been knocked unconscious and would eventually come to." His blue eyes turned cold.

"So this Jimmy Eagle confessed?" she said.

"Almost . . . he says it was an accident . . . I'll get to that. There was a large pool of blood under Mr. Marks' head, blood had clotted in his ear and at the corner of his mouth."

Yetta pulled a handkerchief from her purse and held it to her nose.

Sympathy returned to Woolsey's eyes. "Did you really want to hear all this, ma'am?"

She sat back. "Yes. It's just a little hard to listen to right now. We buried Randall yesterday."

Woolsey cleared his throat and purposefully wiped his mustache. "Next to your nephew, we found a broken bottle of scotch. Dr. McMartin has confirmed it as the murder weapon. The whole room reeked of whiskey. Your nephew's coat and tie were on the floor along with his empty money clip and card wallet which still contained all his identification and credit cards. The drapes were closed and the bed, while disturbed, did not appear to have been slept in. The air conditioner was on. The coroner determined Mr. Marks had been dead for eight to ten hours when we found him. That just about covers the crime scene."

"You didn't mention his pinkie ring. Didn't you find one? Randall wore it all the time."

"No, ma'am. The hotel manager noticed it was missing that first morning and mentioned it to us. We did look for it both at the crime scene and at the suspect's house. Right now we're canvassing the pawn shops."

Her hands compacted into fists. "I'd really like to get the ring back. It belonged to my brother before he gave it to my nephew."

"We'll do our best."

"How did you come to suspect Jimmy Eagle?"

"We developed him as a suspect from a description the bartender gave us of the people Mr. Marks had been seen with. Then the bartender was able to identify Jimmy Eagle from mug shots."

"He's been in trouble before?"

"Many times . . . he was pretty well known to us. His first arrest was at age sixteen and he's been convicted on twenty-four different charges, mostly petty stuff. After we developed him as a suspect, we arrested him at his home and obtained a search warrant for his premises. In a laundry basket we found a brown polyester suit and beige shirt like the bartender described. The suit had blood and dirt on the left knee, spots of blood and dirt on the pant cuffs, and blood on the edges of the sleeves of the jacket. The shirt had what appeared to be blood splatter spots across the front. All these items have been sent to the lab for processing. In Jimmy's wallet we found five hundred dollars in crisp new bills."

"You said my nephew was with 'people' . . . there were more than this Jimmy?"

"Jimmy was with a young woman named Brenda Wolf. She's left town . . . gone to Saskatoon to visit her mother. According to Jimmy's statement, she was just a witness."

"What did Jimmy say happened?"

"Jimmy says your nephew made an unwanted pass at Brenda."

Yetta made a clucking sound.

The Sergeant stroked his mustache. "I know this is going to be hard to listen to."

"That's all right. I know my nephew drank a lot and ran after women. We used to run a bar and restaurant together a long time ago."

"The three of them had been drinking together in the bar. All three were pretty drunk when the bar closed at ten, but they continued their party up in Mr. Marks' room. Jimmy took it personal when your nephew made this pass, and they got into a physical altercation. Jimmy ended up bashing the scotch bottle over your nephew's head and that's what killed him."

"He admitted to killing my nephew."

"He sure did. The prosecutor's hoping he can work something out with Jimmy's lawyer before we go to trial. Get it over quick and easy."

"How did he meet these people?"

"Picked them up hitchhiking . . . at least that's their story."

Yetta put her hand to her throat. "What does this Brenda have to say?"

"An officer in Saskatoon took her statement yesterday. She pretty much corroborates Jimmy's story."

"What did she say about my nephew's pinkie ring?"

"She remembers your nephew having it on. She claims she knows nothing about its disappearance. I'm sure the prosecutor will subpoena her for the trial if there is one."

"What do you think will happen?"

"I think the prosecutor will accept a plea of involuntary manslaughter and ask for the maximum jail time."

She slapped her hands on the desk. "Involuntary manslaughter?"

The Sergeant put his soft hand on Yetta's forearm. "I know it's hard to accept but that's what the facts support as we know them now."

Lives in Exile

When Yetta returned to her hotel room she sat on the bed and cried. The Sergeant had said the prosecutor, Frank Lewis, would be in touch with her before the trial to let her know what was going on. With nothing else to do, Yetta flew home to Richmond the next day.

Chapter Eighteen

Possibilities

1966 - 1967

Ike swallowed his last sip of port. "When did your mother die?"

Yetta put her glass down. "January 28, 1963."

"Didn't Jack and Randall see each other then?"

Yetta shook her head. "She died two days after one of Washington's huge snowstorms–eighteen inches. In Washington when it snows, even an inch, the whole city closes down. When it snows eighteen inches, forget about it." She chuckled. "The whole city was a mess for ten days. I'd gone to Washington the week before, when she'd been admitted to the hospital. Neither Jack nor Randall was able to get there in time. We just had a simple graveside service for the immediate family as soon as they could dig the grave."

"What did she die from?"

"A stroke. I spent several nights with her at the hospital because of the snowstorm. It was a good thing I was there, they were so short-staffed."

The maid asked if they were ready for dessert and coffee. Yetta worried that between Thanksgiving and all the sweets she'd been eating she'd put on a few pounds, but she didn't know how to politely refuse when the maid said she had made a chocolate layer cake just for tonight.

Ike spooned sugar into his coffee cup and stirred. "I know you planned to go home tomorrow. How about staying until Monday and spending the weekend with me?"

Yetta hesitated. What did "spending the weekend" mean? Did he think she was going to stay at his house? In his bedroom? He couldn't think that.

"Do you have plans?" she asked.

"About once a month I drive over to Greensboro to spend Saturday night and Sunday with my daughter's family. This Saturday is the date. I thought you could go with me. The kids can bunk in together. I'll take my grandson's room and you can have the guest room."

Yetta put a bite of the cake in her mouth. "Can I think it over and let you know tomorrow? I'll have to find out if I can have a room on Sunday night."

When Ike took Yetta back to the hotel, he accompanied her to the elevator, squeezed her hand, kissed her on the cheek, and said, "I'll pick you up at nine and we'll have breakfast."

Back in her room, Yetta changed into her pajamas, brushed out her hair, put on her hairnet, and creamed her face. She sat on her bed with her feet under the blanket and opened her book. She thought she'd be alone the rest of her life and now this. What was she going to do? He's a nice man—a thoughtful, considerate, happy person. Was he the man she'd been waiting for all her life? Was he the person she'd be willing to give up her independence for? This was too hard for her to decide right now. She thought she should go home to Richmond. She wasn't ready to meet his family.

The next morning she was in the lobby when Ike arrived. They continued on to the coffee shop. After their eggs and toast arrived, she said, "I'm going to go home today. I'm supposed to have dinner with a friend tomorrow night and I don't want to disappoint her."

"Have I scared you?"

Scared her? Terrified was more like it. "I think, until this case is over..."

"You're right. It might be better not to mix business with a personal relationship. But I'm warning you, when this case is over I'll be calling on you."

Yetta wondered if he was having second thoughts because he agreed so quickly before she even had a chance to finish her sentence.

On December 27th, 1966, Yetta was slicing onion at the kitchen counter when the phone rang. She ran her hands under cold water, wiped them on a paper towel, and picked up the receiver. It was Frank Lewis, the Regina prosecutor.

Lives in Exile

"We're agreeing to let Jimmy Eagle enter a plea of involuntary manslaughter," he said.

Yetta pulled out a chair and sat. "Involuntary manslaughter?"

"Exactly. He didn't have any intent to murder Mr. Marks," Lewis went on. "Jimmy planned to get your nephew drunk and rob him. That would fit his pattern. The argument over Brenda got out of control. Your nephew was a big man and Jimmy felt overwhelmed, so he used the bottle to even the fight."

Yetta, feeling desperate, said, "How about the money missing from my nephew's wallet and his pinkie ring?"

"Jimmy claims the cash was his and we can't prove otherwise. In fact, we have witnesses who said your nephew had much more cash than was recovered. We offered Jimmy the opportunity to turn the ring over for less jail time, but he refused. One of two things—either he doesn't have it or he has it hidden somewhere with the rest of the cash and thinks he'll be able to get to it after he's finished his jail term. We're going for the maximum five years but, of course, it's up to the judge."

Yetta had no faith in judges after her recent experiences in North Carolina. "If Jimmy doesn't have the ring, somebody does."

"Exactly, and if they do, they've committed, at a minimum, robbery. They're also open to charges of being an accessory after the fact. We've questioned Brenda and the maid. The police have canvassed pawn shops here in Regina and in Saskatoon. So far, it hasn't shown up."

Yetta thought he sounded like a man with a buzz cut. "It must be somewhere."

"There are two possibilities. One of the three of them could have the ring and be planning to hold it until things cool down, or an unknown person could have found Randall before the maid and took it without reporting the crime."

She rested her head in her hand. "What you're trying to tell me is there is little hope of getting the ring back."

"Exactly."

Frank Lewis and his "exactly's" were getting on her nerves. "When will Jimmy Eagle be sentenced?"

"On January 30th."

She wiped her eyes with the damp paper towel. "I guess that's pretty much it then."

"Exactly. Nothing else we can do, but the police will keep their eyes open for the ring. It'll remain in their files as an unrecovered stolen item. If, or when, it turns up they'll notify you."

Yetta sat at the table and thought. She called Ike Stein. "What can I do?"

"Nothing really," Ike said. "The prosecutor doesn't have to get you to agree to anything. He can do what he thinks is best."

Yetta could feel the tears start. "But he murdered Randall."

"Murder is a crime against the state, not the family."

She brushed away the tears with the towel. "Damn."

"I wish there were something I could say to make you feel better. You've been through so much."

At 10:00 p.m. on New Year's Eve the telephone rang in Yetta's apartment.

Ike Stein said, "I took a chance you'd be home. I wanted to wish you a Happy New Year." "Moon River" played in the background.

Yetta put a hand to her throat and smiled. "That's so nice. Since I closed the restaurant I haven't had any place to go on New Year's so I watch Guy Lombardo and the ball in Times Square and then go to sleep."

"That's what I'm doing too." He paused. "I've been thinking about you. I got the papers from the lawyer in Canada and I'm working on a draft of the motions and briefs. The judge set March 30th as the deadline for filings, and I think we should wait until then even though I doubt any more claims will be made. You should come down to Raleigh to look them over."

Yetta looked at her hand. She didn't like the way the veins bulged through her skin.

"So, when can you come down here? I'm looking forward to discussing all the novels you've been reading."

Yetta opened her calendar. "How about February 9th?"

"I guess I'll have to wait until then."

After she hung up, Yetta giggled. What the heck was she doing? What did she want with a relationship with this man? *Gottenyu, I'm sixty-five already. He's at least that. Forget about it. I'm on my own, always had been, always will be.* She'd have to find a way to tell him when she was there.

Just before Yetta left for North Carolina she received a copy of a newspaper article with a note from Bill O'Brien saying what a terrible mistake he thought the judge had made. The article was dated January 31, 1967.

> Judge Henry Adams sentenced a local man to two-and-a-half years in jail yesterday for involuntary manslaughter in the murder of Randall Marks, 48, of Elizabeth City, North Carolina. Mr. Marks was a native of Regina and son of Jack Marks, the former owner of the *Leader Post*.
>
> Jimmy Eagle, 22, confessed to bludgeoning Mr. Marks to death in a drunken brawl over the affections of Brenda Wolf. Frank Lewis, provincial prosecutor, had requested the maximum sentence because certain items missing from Mr. Marks' hotel room had not been recovered. Judge Adams agreed with the defense attorney that the prosecutor had not charged Mr. Eagle with robbery and had presented no evidence Mr. Eagle had stolen the missing items. In addition, he stated he was sentencing Mr. Eagle to the lesser time because Mr. Eagle had shown compassion for Mr. Marks by covering him with a bedspread before leaving the scene. With the time already served, Mr. Eagle will be eligible for parole in one year.
>
> In an exclusive interview, Mr. Lewis stated the judge had the right to sentence Jimmy Eagle as he felt appropriate, but Mr. Lewis still objected stating, "It was only at the behest of Ms. Wolf that Mr. Marks was covered with the bedspread. Mr. Eagle could have shown more compassion by calling the authorities instead of running away and leaving Mr. Marks to die alone on the floor of his hotel room." In fact he felt Mr. Eagle had shown almost no compassion and was more concerned with covering up the crime.

Yetta, who thought she had no more tears left, cried when she read the article. She decided not to share the article with Dot or anyone else in the family. Randall was gone, the murderer punished, and there was nothing anybody could do. She was more determined than ever not to let those Swartzes, those fortune hunters, get Jack and Randall's money. That would be one more injustice that would be too hard to abide in this *meshugene* world. She wanted to spit on them, those Swartzes.

Yetta took the train to Raleigh on February 9th determined to keep things friendly but businesslike. They'd had one more phone call before she left for Raleigh. Ike had been warm and friendly, but she had been cool and professional.

Ike picked her up and took her to the Brownestone Hotel and waited in the lobby while she washed up and unpacked.

He'd made a reservation for dinner at a restaurant five blocks away, so they walked. During dinner Ike leaned across the table as he talked to her and kept his hand on the table close to her. She thought if she put her hand on the table he might take it in his, so she kept it in her lap. She tried to keep the conversation focused on their business together. Finally while they were drinking coffee, Ike said, "Is everything okay? You seem distant tonight."

She took the copy of the article out of her purse. She'd planned to show it to him tomorrow anyway.

When he finished reading it, he looked up at her with such sorrow in his eyes it caused her to weep. She pulled her handkerchief from her purse. Ironically, it was her favorite. It had been her mother's and was embroidered with her mother's initials. Yetta kept her handkerchiefs in a drawer with a floral sachet which was the same as her mother's. As Yetta held the hankie to her face with both hands, she felt the embroidery and breathed in her mother's scent.

Ike reached over and held her forearm. His warm soft hand was strangely comforting. What was it about this man?

"I'm sorry, Yetta," he said. "I wish I could fix everything for you. You're a very caring person. You've taken care of everybody in your family. It's time to let somebody take care of you."

She looked at him. His look of concern touched her in a way she didn't remember anyone ever touching her before.

"It's one more reason those *gonifs*, those thieves, those Swartzes, mustn't win," she said.

"I'll do the best I can. We'll fight them together." He smiled at her, a smile of sympathy and understanding. "Let's get the check."

Ike's gentlemanly manners impressed Yetta. He always walked on the street side of the sidewalk and held her arm in a supportive way. When they got to the hotel, they sat on a sofa in the lobby.

"Why don't you come to my office tomorrow about one?" Ike said. "We'll have lunch, work on the papers, and then have dinner."

"I shouldn't be taking up so much of your time. You don't have to have dinner with me tomorrow night, too."

"Don't you get it, Yetta? I like having dinner with you. You always make me laugh with your witticisms and your take on the world. Not many people can make me laugh."

She didn't know what to say. It had been a long time since someone noticed and liked her.

Over lunch they discussed Ike's legal strategy for winning the case. Back at his office she sat alone in his conference room and read over the papers. Ike worked in his office on other matters. When she'd finished reading, she stuck her head in his door. They agreed to meet at 6:00 p.m. in the hotel lobby and discuss the case over dinner.

They decided to eat in the hotel dining room. As he helped her into her chair, she caught a whiff of his aftershave. She recognized it as Canoe. She smiled to herself when she remembered its slogan, "Canoe Canoe."

"You'll be our strongest witness when the case comes to trial," Ike said. "You'll have to testify about your time in Regina after Randall's mother died, about Jack's relationship with Randall, about everything the family and you did for Randall, Randall's will, and about opening the safe, and what happened in Elizabeth City."

Yetta kept her hands in her lap except when using her silverware. "I'll want to emphasize the total lack of relationship with the mother's family."

"Of course, but you'll have to stick to the facts, not your feelings about them. We probably should have your brother Sammy ready to testify, too. We might want to call one or two of your nieces and nephews to testify about their relationship with Randall. We'll see how the trial is going before we make a decision."

"Would you mind discussing all of this with my nephew, Art?"

"Of course not." A puzzled look came over Ike's face.

"Is there a problem?"

Ike looked at her with his intriguing hazel eyes. "I'm a lonely man, Yetta. I've been alone for five years and I've had many dinners with many widows, but I've never met a woman I've enjoyed being with as much as you. You're intelligent, compassionate, worldly, and an interesting storyteller, but you appear to be trying to keep a distance between us."

Yetta sighed and looked down at her lap.

"Life is short and getting shorter all the time," Ike went on. "I'm very fond of you and want to spend more time together so we can see if we have a future together."

"You're used to being married and having someone around. I'm used to being on my own. I don't know if I could adjust to sharing my life with someone. *Gottenyu*, I'm sixty-five already. Don't get me wrong . . . I like you. I like you a lot. It's me. I came close to getting married once and it was a disaster. I made up my mind then I was better off on my own. I think I made a wise decision."

A sympathetic look came over Ike's face. "He broke your heart." Ike put one of his hands on the table as if reaching for her. "I'm not him.

I would never betray you. I'm looking for companionship and a loving relationship. My life, as I knew it, ended when my wife died and I'm trying to rebuild it. I'd like to reconstruct it with you."

She longed to grasp his outstretched hand but gave him an anemic smile instead. "I know you're a good man and I hope you're able to find the right person to share your life. I'd like to continue to be friends."

"Every decision you make in life has a consequence. Once you choose which fork to take, certain things are decided. Some results can never be undone, some can never be made right. Look at the choices your brother and nephew made that led them into lives far from their families and loved ones, which left them virtually alone."

In exile. She exhaled.

Ike watched her for several seconds. "I'm going to be in Washington for Passover this year, at my son's. It might be a good opportunity to meet your family and select potential witnesses."

After the meal was over and Ike paid the check, he helped her from her chair and took her elbow as they strolled into the lobby. At the elevators she held out her hand to say good-bye. He took it and brought it to his lips.

Yetta smiled. *This could be in a movie.* The scent of Canoe lingered with her for a long time.

Over the next few months, whenever she saw that TV commercial, "Canoe Canoe," she thought of Ike. They communicated about the case on the telephone and by mail. A trial date had been set for June 10th. Passover was toward the end of April that year. Yetta was at Dot's when Ike called. She smiled to herself when she put the receiver back in the cradle.

Dot said, "So . . . what's going on?"

"Ike wants to meet with me and Uncle Sammy at Art's office. He has to figure out whom he's going to put on his witness list."

"I don't mean with the case. I mean with that smile when you hung up the phone."

Yetta blushed and turned to the kitchen cabinet so Dot wouldn't see. She took out a glass and stepped toward the sink. "He's a nice man."

"I see."

"That's it. He's a nice man. Okay?"

Dot smiled, a knowing look on her face. "Okay."

After the meeting in Art's office, Ike determined not to ask for a jury trial, to let the judge make the decision. Both Ike and Art thought it would be risky to let a North Carolina jury make the decision. There were too many people in North Carolina who wouldn't be sympathetic to a Jewish family when a "good" Christian family was claiming the money. All Jews are "money hungry," they might tell themselves to justify their decision. They hoped a judge would be more interested in the law.

Ike wanted to call Sammy to testify about how the family set Randall up in business in Washington. Yetta was to testify about Randall and Jack's relationship, the absence of any with the Swartz family, plus what Randall had told her about his will. He said they would probably have to come to North Carolina for depositions some time in May.

The Swartz family's lawyer didn't put any names on his witness list. They were only going to enter into the record legal documents to which Ike was going to stipulate. Yetta was very disappointed the Swartz family wasn't going to be there. She wanted a chance to confront them. She had a few things she wanted to say to them personally.

Ike planned to enter the blood type evidence, the Canadian documents changing Randall's last name, and Jack's will referring to Randall as his son. He wanted Sammy and Yetta to humanize their side of the story with their testimony.

Yetta and Sammy went to Raleigh in May to give depositions. Afterwards, the Swartz family lawyers made motions to limit Yetta's testimony at trial and ban Sammy all together. Even though Ike fought hard, the judge ruled in favor of the Swartzes.

Yetta was only able to tell the court about Randall's missing will and the safe. After the trial they had to wait a week for the judge's ruling which came on June 21st. Ike called her in Richmond with the news. "The judge gave everything but your fifty thousand dollar specific bequest to the Swartzes. He ruled they are Randall's only known relatives since no father had been listed by Bessie Swartz on Randall's birth certificate and Bessie and Jack never married. The fact they couldn't marry under Canadian law, yet lived together as husband and wife, and told people they were married, made no difference to the judge. The fact that Jack had supported Randall, raised him, and called Randall "his son" in his will doesn't meet North Carolina's peculiar and unique standards for claiming paternity."

Yetta was speechless. She'd been sitting in her recliner reading the City section of the newspaper, one of those annual articles about the Friday evening summer beach traffic. The paper slipped out of her hands and onto the floor.

"Yetta, are you there?"

"I . . . I . . . I . . . I don't know what to say. How could this have happened? This isn't fair. What about the truth?"

"That's a mistake a lot of people make. Trials are not a search for the truth but for the facts as presented under the law."

"I can't talk anymore. I have to hang up."

"We have to talk about an appeal."

"Later."

Later didn't take too long to come. Art phoned Yetta the next evening. "I've talked to everyone in the family and we're all agreed, we have to appeal. This ruling doesn't make any sense."

Yetta got up from her recliner and stretched the telephone cord to its limit so she could turn down the sound on Walter Cronkite. "If that's what everyone thinks then that's what we'll do, I guess."

"What's wrong?"

"I'm tired."

"Ike says he needs another ten thousand dollar retainer which would cover the appeal to the Appeals Court and the North Carolina Supreme Court, if necessary. When I talked to the family, they each agreed to pitch in another thousand bucks. Are you willing to put up four thousand dollars like before?"

Yetta put her hand to her throat. "I don't know. We might be just throwing good money after bad."

"That *shmuck* of an anti-Semitic judge didn't like giving the money to us. I could kick myself for insisting we go for a trial before a judge and not a jury."

"You don't know if a jury would have come down on our side, either. We all agreed. It isn't your fault. The appeals court judges could feel the same way."

"Yeah," Art said, "but two out of three would have to agree and then we can still go to the State Supreme Court."

"Let's take one step at a time."

"Then you agree to go ahead?"

She hesitated. "Let me think about it."

Yetta called Ike at his office the next morning. "The kids want to appeal. What do you think of our chances?"

"I think they're better than with the judge we had. He interpreted the state law very strictly. I don't think it's legal to require a resident of another jurisdiction, much less another country, to follow the laws of your state. We showed your brother had done all that was required of him in Canada. We showed why Randall's parents never married. I think the judge was dead wrong in his decision and violated the fourth amendment to the Constitution."

Yetta pictured him swivelled around in his desk chair looking up at the portrait of his father.

"I've been wracking my brain," Ike said, "trying to figure out if there was something else we could've presented which would have persuaded him, but I can't. He's just a strict constructionist."

"Art thinks he's an anti-semite."

"It's hard to tell. But he was within the law. Our appeal will be on the basis of two arguments. First, that a state can't require a resident of another jurisdiction, especially a foreign country, to comply with its laws when he's done everything required of him in his country, and, second, you were denied due process as the paternal relatives."

"So you think we should go ahead?"

"I think we've got a good shot."

Chapter Nineteen

Decisions

1968

To Yetta the appeal seemed to take forever. Ike called at least once a month to keep her informed of every stage. Their conversations often drifted to talk about their families and the state of the world. Turmoil was everywhere between the anti-war protests, the Six Day War in the Middle East, the Tet offensive in Vietnam, Martin Luther King's assassination, and the riots that followed, and in June 1968 Bobby Kennedy's shooting. Then there were the smaller tragedies like Jayne Mansfield's and Vivien Leigh's deaths and the excitement of the first heart transplant. They always had a lot to talk about.

He sent her a copy of the filing they made in September 1967 for the appeal. There were motions and replies to talk about until a hearing was finally scheduled for May 1968. He called her after the hearing and told her about the questions the judges asked each side. They had to wait three months for a ruling.

In late August, right after Soviet tanks invaded Prague, Ike called. "We lost the appeal two to one. They upheld the judge and his ridiculous ruling. How they can require a person from another country to come to North Carolina and appear in court to proclaim an illegitimate heir as his son, is beyond me."

Yetta put her hand to her neck. "You mean these Appeals Court judges couldn't see the lunacy of the law?"

"One did. I guess that leaves the U.S. Supreme Court. I think there's a good chance they'll take this case since the issue will be the constitutionality of North Carolina's law."

She twirled the telephone cord around her finger. "That's going to cost even more money." *Those damn people.*

"It won't be cheap because it'll be best if you hire someone with experience in constitutional law and the Supreme Court."

"All we're doing is using up the money in Jack and Randall's estates."

"It's up to you. Think it over for a few days."

Yetta massaged her forehead. "What if I decide not to appeal?"

"I'll tell the other side and have Elmer Smith draw up all the papers settling the estate. He'll issue the check for your inheritance. You'll have to sign all the papers and the checks as co-executor and everything will be over."

"I'm going to Washington on September 8th for the holidays. I always go a couple of weeks early for shopping and to help Dot with cooking. I'll call you before then."

Yetta sat on the sofa in the living room of Dot's home, resting after cooking all morning. She'd been reading when the mailman rang the door bell with the special delivery envelope. Dot was in the basement doing the laundry, so Yetta collected the envelope without her niece knowing. Ike had called the day before to tell her it was coming. As she held the envelope, she felt warm and a little dizzy. She knew her blood pressure was rising, so she tried to concentrate on something else. She fixed on the intense red of the Persian carpet. She absorbed the color, feeling her emotions burn inside her with the passion of that red. Her eyes roamed along a green line as it zigzagged in an intricate pattern of X's. She counted the number of purple flowers in each grouping—always the same.

Yetta puckered open the envelope. Inside she found the check for fifty thousand dollars. *"Oy."* She dropped the check in her lap. It tumbled to the floor. Before the tears started, she fumbled for the tissue tucked under her belt. She blotted her eyes and caught the droplets before they smudged her powder and rouge. Even though she knew the check was coming, when she held it, her skin tingled as though spiders were creeping up her legs and arms and neck. *Those damn people.*

She imagined herself in far away Persia standing outside a square adobe building with mere openings for doors and windows. She felt the searing sun. She envisioned women inside the bare, beige room, sitting at looms, chatting as they wove the carpet one strand at a time. She wondered who designed the patterns. Did the women make the same pattern over and over again or was each carpet a new adventure?

Yetta clasped and unclasped her hands. She realized that, like a Persian carpet, you wove your life one strand at a time, one day at a time. She took several deep breaths. Calmer now, she removed the sheaf of papers from the large brown envelope and set them on the sofa without a glance.

She flinched at the sound of the automatic garage door opener whirring into action. It surprised her as it did every evening. The call went out, "Daddy's home." She crammed the papers and the check back in the envelope and stuck it under the sofa cushion, hoping to eventually hide it in her room. She needed time to get her emotions under control. She preferred to keep her decision to herself until after Rosh Hashanah which began that night. It would be hard because she sensed the topic of conversation at tonight's dinner would be whether to continue the appeal or not. She didn't want to tell them she'd already discontinued it.

Dot shooed the children upstairs to get ready for the holiday dinner at the community center. Yetta retrieved the envelope and climbed the steps to the guest room. She stuffed the envelope in the top drawer, under her lingerie. She picked up her comb and lightly brushed her pin curls. She didn't pull too hard because her hairdo had to last a couple of days. She stared in the mirror at the lines that flowed from the corner of her eyes.

Would she ever see or talk to Ike Stein again? When he'd said, "That's it, I guess. Good-bye, Yetta," it had seemed so final. She couldn't imagine not seeing or talking to him again. After the last two years, he seemed like a permanent part of her life. What was she doing? She was the one who had insisted on a business relationship, and now that was over.

She twisted her body this way and that to see in the mirror how her white hair lay in the back and how her dress fit her matronly figure. She was going to miss Ike. She'd come to think of him as a special person in her life. Someone she could share her concerns and feelings with. She wondered if Ike was in Washington for Rosh Hashanah. He hadn't mentioned coming to Washington. If he was, maybe she'd get a chance to see him at Temple tomorrow.

Yetta heard the knock on her door and the sweet voice of her eight-year-old great-nephew. "Aunt Yetta?"

"Yes, *boychik*?"

"Mom says it's time to go."

"I'll be right there."

Evelyn Auerbach

Yetta found her niece in the kitchen pulling the large jars of chicken soup and the container of Yetta's famous matzah balls from the refrigerator. The large soup pot already sat on the counter. During the whole evening the topic of the appeal did not come up because Sammy's oldest granddaughter announced her engagement to the law student she'd been dating for a year. Yetta was greatly relieved.

The next morning, Yetta dressed in the ensemble she'd just bought. As a child, her new Rosh Hashanah outfit had always been a winter one, made of wool, but Washington weather almost always turned warm and sometimes even hot in time for the holidays. The weathermen call it Indian Summer. So, as an adult, Yetta favored dresses with short sleeves and a jacket, like the red dress she had just put on. It had a round neckline with a slit down the middle and strings to tie into a bow at the neck. The matching jacket had black piping around the edges. She wore large round black earrings made of crystals and a matching pin. The dress ended below her knees.

The family drove to Temple and walked in together. They split up in the enormous marble lobby. It was an elegant foyer but rather cold. She remembered the vestibule of the old shul in southwest which had served as the lobby for her parents place of worship as a warm and welcoming place filled with the noise of prayer and chatter. This lobby didn't invite that kind of intimacy.

While the children attended the young people's service in the small chapel, the adults went into the main sanctuary, shaped like a slice of pie—the point was the altar with the stage in front. The maroon upholstered seats fanned out from the stage. The plush carpet in matching maroon muffled the sounds of feet and voices. The ceiling was two stories above, and the far wall, all stained glass biblical scenes. As they walked down the center aisle, Yetta scanned the crowd looking for Ike. She didn't see him, but maybe he was seated in a section she couldn't see. She caught the scents of many perfumes and aftershaves. Dot and Howard attended Columbia Hebrew Congregation where men and women sat together and participated equally in the service. Many men didn't even wear yarmulkes. No Yiddish was spoken and very little Hebrew was used. This was very different from the orthodox shul where she and her mother sat in the women's section which was the balcony while her brothers and father sat downstairs. In those old shuls, everything was wood—floors and chairs, even the extra folding chairs added for the holidays. All the prayers were in Hebrew and everything else was spoken in Yiddish including the rabbi's sermon.

During services Yetta tried to concentrate on the chanting of the cantor and the sermon of the rabbi but her mind kept wandering. She would've liked to have been able to see outdoors, get a glimpse of the changing leaves as she could in the old place. She thought it odd the Jewish New Year was in the fall. The spring seemed a more appropriate time to celebrate a new beginning. But as she mused about it, she realized Rosh Hashanah wasn't only about new beginnings. It was about assessing your life and trying to make amends for the wrongs you had done toward other human beings and toward God. Maybe the fall was the appropriate season for that kind of introspection and assessment when the weather was cooler and people prepared themselves for shorter, colder days and when leaves turned colors and then faded away. Of course, the ancestors who first celebrated these holidays were desert nomads. What did they know about tall trees and leaves that turned crimson and purple and brown when the air was crisp? But that, of course, is the beauty of belief. You can make it into anything you want. Too bad Jack's "in-laws" didn't believe in making assessments and amends.

The blare of the shofar interrupted her thoughts. The moaning sound followed by the staccato notes and then the long wail somehow brought to mind the weeping and shrieking of a parent crying for her child. Yetta realized in the context of the story told every Rosh Hashanah, of Abraham's near sacrifice of Isaac, the shofar call could be Abraham wailing for his son. But it could also be the sound of God wailing for his children who have sinned and need to repent.

Let Randall's mother's family have the money. They had nothing else. No memories of shared jokes and laughter. No memories of shared sorrows. No memories of shared struggle and triumph. Those were the important things, not the money. She didn't need the money anyway. She had scrimped, saved, and invested well. Her brother Sammy was doing fine. She'd tell them at dinner it was all over, she'd already gotten her inheritance.

But what about her? What was she going to do with the rest of her life? She'd spent the last two years burying her family, mourning them, and fighting for their estates. Now that was all over. She pictured Ike's hazel eyes and warm smile. She could even smell his Canoe. She would miss him. She was an old maid, too old to change her ways, and yet . . .

All of a sudden she realized people all around her were gathering their things and standing up. Services were over. They spent a few minutes mingling out front wishing everyone a *shanah tovah*, a happy new year.

Dot and Howard kissed and hugged their closest friends. They walked the few blocks to the car and drove back to the house. After quick trips to the bathroom and a change of clothes for the children, they gathered up the honey cake and baked apples and drove over to Art's house in Bethesda.

When dessert was over, the children went outside to play. Yetta said, "Before we clear the table I should tell you the North Carolina Supreme Court ruled all the money besides the specific bequest to me was to go to Randall's mother's family. I've decided not to appeal any further and end the fighting at this point."

Art said, "What was the vote?"

"Two to one."

Marty, the negligence lawyer, banged his hand on the table and said, "That's absurd. The Supreme Court'll never uphold their narrow interpretation of the law. Hell, the law is probably unconstitutional anyway."

Yetta placed her hands palms down on the table. "That may all be true, but I've had enough. I invested eight thousand dollars. You've each put up two thousand dollars which I'm going to reimburse you."

They all protested.

"I've gotten the fifty thousand from Jack's will," she said, "so it's only fair I pay you back and I don't want to spend the rest on more legal fees. Hiring a lawyer who practices before the Supreme Court is very expensive. That's enough. Let them have it all and let them *gei gezoonter heit* and let it be on their conscience."

"I agree with Aunt Yetta," Dot said. "The strain on her has been enormous. Let Uncle Jack and Randall rest in peace and let's put an end to this mess. Let's remember them as the fun-loving, storytellers they were."

Yetta could always count on Dot to take her side. Yetta gave her a hug. She'd said what Yetta had in mind.

"But they wanted us to have their money," Marty said. "Not these strangers who didn't even know them and refused to have anything to do with them."

"We all know that and I'm sure those damn people do, too," Yetta said. "But we can't prove it with the will being destroyed. So let it go. *Que sera, sera,* or as your grandmother used to say, "*Bubele, vuhs vet zain, vet zain.*"

Art said, "If we appeal to the Supreme Court they'll have to hire a lawyer, too. They'll be using up more of the estate paying for their own attorney and that isn't such a bad thing if they're going to get everything in the end."

"It's too late. I already told Ike my decision and received my fifty thousand dollar check."

There was silence around the table.

"Have you told Uncle Sammy yet?" Art said.

"No, but I'm sure it'll be all right with him."

"You know it will," Dot said. "He always goes along with whatever you say."

Yetta rose. "So that's that. Let's clear the table and clean up from this wonderful meal."

Marty said, "*Rachmones* on them."

Marty's wife washed the pots and pans. Dot and Yetta dried. Art's wife, the hostess, put everything away. When they were close to finishing, Rachel, whose Bat Mitzvah would take place in six months, approached Yetta with a family scrapbook.

"The back of this picture says 'The Marks Family, 1908,'" Rachel said. "It's the oldest picture I could find."

Yetta took the scrapbook. A smile spread across her face. "This picture was taken before your great-uncle Jack left for Montana. Your great-grandmother Esther insisted we get all dressed up and make this memento. She made a copy for Jack to take with him and a copy for her sister, Golda, in Helena."

"That's what I need to write about for Hebrew school. We're supposed to write about where our families came from and why they came to the United States."

"We better go sit in the living room because that's going to be a long story."

After she finished the tale, Yetta smiled at Rachel and gave her shoulders a squeeze. "I was a lucky child. I had a wonderful family." She sighed. "I guess you could call Uncle Jack the 'black sheep' of the family because he couldn't wait to escape."

That night as she lay in bed in Dot's guest room, she thought about the stories she'd told Rachel. Was she so different from Jack? Or from Randall, as far as that goes? *What do I have to show for my life—a pile of money people will fight over? I want someone to care I've been here. All my nieces and nephews care about me, especially Dot. But they have their own families—parents, husbands, and children. Who's there to care about me as the main person in their life? Randall, but he's gone. May he rest in peace.*

The next morning after the children had gone to school and Howard to work, Yetta and Dot sat at the kitchen table finishing their coffee.

Dot said, "You look down this morning."

"I guess I am, a little. Everything I've been thinking about and working on for the last two years is over and I don't know what to do next. I signed the papers Ike sent me as co-executor of Randall's estate. Howard's mailing them for me this morning." Yetta looked in her coffee cup. "I've been thinking about Ike a lot recently." She smiled. "What a nice man he is—how kind and considerate. In the beginning he wanted to . . . have more than a lawyer/client relationship."

Dot looked at her in amazement. "I thought you were just friends."

"I know he's interested in me."

"You sure you want to take a chance? You have your life, a routine, your friends. He's in Raleigh. You're in Richmond. How could this work out?"

Yetta was shocked. She thought Dot, the romantic, would be in favor. "I realize I'd have to make some compromises."

"Compromises? You don't know the half of it. You're so used to being on your own and doing things when you want and how you want. I don't know if you fully appreciate all the concessions necessary in a marriage, if that's what you're talking about."

Yetta didn't answer. She wondered if Dot and Howard had a disagreement that morning. What was the point anyway? She didn't know if Ike was still available.

Before she left Washington, she called Art to say good-bye. He said, "Dot tells me you're interested in Ike Stein. I think that's a mistake."

"Why?"

"You're sixty-six years old and you've always been alone. He's about the same age. You could end up spending you're the rest of your life caring for a sick old man. What would you want that for?"

Another county heard from. What makes them think they have a right to express their opinions?

When Yetta got back to Richmond, she moped around the apartment for a couple of days. The next big event in her life was Thanksgiving and that was months away. She wanted to call Ike . . . but what was she going to say to him? "Are you still available?" Maybe Dot was right. What if he'd found someone else? She'd be humiliated. Maybe Art was right and she was too old. She didn't feel too old. If she didn't give him a call, she'd never know for sure. What would be worse—taking a chance and getting hurt, or not trying?

She phoned him Monday morning. "Wanted to wish you a *shanah tovah*."

"Happy new year to you. Glad you called."

She twirled the telephone cord around her finger. "The weather was beautiful this year."

"Wish I'd been there. I spent the holiday in Greensboro with my daughter."

After she hung up, Yetta was annoyed with herself. She should have planned the conversation. He'd spent the holidays with his daughter which meant he couldn't have too serious a relationship going. So she learned that. And, she established she wanted their friendship to continue, maybe that was enough.

She wondered what he was thinking. Did he get the subtle message? Maybe she shouldn't have been so subtle. She'd have to call him again. How long should she wait? Would a week be enough . . . should she wait two weeks . . . or even longer? No. She didn't want to wait more than two weeks.

"Aha," she said out loud. She'd thought of a good excuse . . . to ask him if he got the papers she'd sent back to him and if she had to sign any more papers as the co-executor of the estate. She wouldn't have to wait even a week. She could call him in a day or two. She smiled.

That night as she lay in bed, she figured she better make a plan. She was calling him for a business reason—that was the excuse, so she'd have to turn the conversation to more personal things after the business excuse was settled. Should she ask what he was doing for Thanksgiving? Should she ask about his children? What could she say that would give him the idea she wanted to continue their relationship? She fell asleep considering what to do next.

When she woke up on Tuesday morning, she realized she couldn't call Ike until Thursday since Wednesday was Yom Kippur. If she didn't want to appear too anxious, she probably should wait to call until Friday. *Oy*. She was going to have several days to think about her next move. She got dressed and went to the bank to deposit her fifty thousand dollar check. Then she went to the beauty shop to get her hair and nails done and finally to the grocery store.

On Thursday afternoon while she was writing her checks to pay her bills, the telephone rang. She was surprised to hear Ike's voice. "I wanted you to know the papers arrived in the mail. I forgot to tell you the last time you called."

She was flustered. Which of her topics should she bring up? "Will there be more papers for me to sign?"

"Yes, there will be final accountings and final tax returns. But that won't be until sometime next year. I've told Elmer Smith to send everything directly to you, but if you have any questions you can certainly contact me."

How could she turn this to a more personal tenor? "I've been thinking of going on a vacation but I can't decide where to go. I was thinking about Miami Beach. Do you have any plans?" This was one of the ideas she cooked up during the night to test out whether he had any "lady friends."

"As a matter of fact, I'm planning a Caribbean cruise for early December. Several of my old friends are going and asked me to join them . . ."

He seemed to be mulling something over. Was he going to tell her about his new woman? "That sounds lovely."

"Would you like to join us? I could give you the name of the travel agent who's making all our arrangements."

This was more than she could've hoped for, but she didn't want to appear too anxious. "That sounds like an interesting idea." Now she was in it—up to her neck.

"I know it's pretty late, but this cruise is before the high season so maybe there's something still available, maybe a cabin near mine."

"Are you sure this wouldn't be an imposition on your friends? Maybe you should talk to them first."

He paused as if considering what he should say. "I'm sure it will be fine with them. It's up to you. You have to figure out what you want."

She understood. She got his message. "Give me the name of the travel agent and I'll think about it. I'll let you know." *I'm waffling.*

"I'll be waiting to hear."

What to do? She hadn't felt like this in thirty years, since Arnold. What made her think of him? She tried to finish writing the checks but thoughts of Ike intruded. Finally she put all her papers away for another day.

Maybe I should wait until Monday to decide what to do. Oy vei ihz mihr, *I'll be* meshuge *by then. Maybe I'm making too much of this—it's just a cruise. I'm not making a lifetime commitment. Who am I kidding? What would I tell the family?* "I'm going on a cruise with Ike Stein and I hope he *asks me to marry him." Marry him? But how can we have a relationship if he lives in Raleigh and I live in Richmond. I'd end up having to move to Raleigh. Moving? Give up everything I have in Richmond. But what do I have? Some money? A few friends? What if Randall had agreed to the circumcision and married Maggie? What would his life have been like? Would he have lived a life in exile? Would I?*

She picked up the phone.

GLOSSARY

The following is an alphabetic listing of Yiddish terms that appear in this book and their English equivalents.

a guten nacht	good night
alte	old
awch un vei	alas and alack!
boychik	young boy
bracha	a blessing
bubele	a term of endearment
gei gezoonter heit (kumn gezoonter heit)	go in good health (return in good health)
glezele tei	a small glass of tea
gonif(s)	thief, swindler, burglar
gottenyu	Oh God!, Dear God!
goyim	non-Jewish people
ihn mihtn derihnen	in the midst of, suddenly
kinder	children
kuhp	head, brains, intelligence

landsman	a person from the same village
landsleit	people from the same village
macher	one who makes things happen, a wheeler-dealer
maidel	a girl, a young unmarried female
maivin	expert, authority, connoisseur
mamzer	bastard!
mein	my
meiseh	a story
mensch	a man, a person of worth and dignity
meshugene	crazy
meshugene velt	a crazy world
mohel	a person trained to perform circumcisions according to Jewish law
mutshe	to nag or pester, to annoy, to torment
nacht	night
nechtihger tawg	nothing of the kind!, forget it!, nonsense!, it never happened!
nu	well?, so what?, what about it?
oy vei ihz mihr	oh!, woe is me!
potchki	to play around
putz	a fool, a stupid person, penis (slang)
rachmones	pity, compassion
rebbetzen	rabbi's wife
saichel	brains, common sense, intelligence, good judgment, shrewdness

shiksa	a non-Jewish woman
shiva	The seven-day period of mourning for an immediate relative, beginning upon the return from internment
shmate(s)	a rag
shmuck	a contemptible person, a foolish person, penis (slang)
sheine	pretty, beautiful
shochet	a person certified to slaughter cattle and fowl in accordance with Jewish law
shuhkl	shake, sway
shvester	sister
tate	father
trayf	non-kosher food
vershtate	understand?
vuhs macht deer	how do you feel?
vuhs vet zain, vet zain	what will happen, will happen
yahrtzeit	the anniversary of a death, observed by the lighting of a memorial lamp for twenty-four hours
yawren	years
yiddisha	Jewish-like
zeen	son